MW01489411

Fourteen Tales of

Thirteen Covens

Bloodlines

Part One

Audrey Brice

FOURTEEN TALES OF

THIRTEEN COVENS

BLOODLINES

PART ONE

AUDREY BRICE

Darkerwood Publishing Group
Colorado, U.S.A.

Darkerwood Publishing Group
Colorado, U.S.A.
First Paperback Printing, September 2017 - U.S.A.

ISBN: 978-1-938839-09-2

This is the first compilation book of [Fourteen Tales of] **Thirteen Covens** series of novellas: A Rising Damp (1), Temple Apophis (2), Lucifer's Haven (3), Shadow Marbas (4), The Watch (5), Ba'al Collective (6), Order of Eurynome (7)

Thank you to the entire editorial staff and all the beta readers for your help in making the first seven stories a success!

For the members of OFS, ToA, TTS, OTH, and all the other covens out there. You know who you are.

http://www.the-quadrant.com

Sign up for the Audrey Brice Newsletter to receive **free fiction** and updates on Thirteen Covens, the OTS Series, and other releases!

TABLE OF CONTENTS

A Rising Damp - 1

Temple Apophis - 16

Lucifer's Haven - 57

Shadow Marbas - 109

The Watch - 168

Ba'al Collective - 220

Order of Eurynome - 283

Incident Report Directory - 361

A RISING DAMP

From the Memoirs of Evelyn Winters

Eldon Jenkins was found dead on a cold, soggy day in September. I sat on the porch shelling peas with Grandma Ann Louis when the sheriff came by.

After a short greeting, the balding Sheriff Jackson, who was probably the town's oldest bachelor, got to business. "You hear anything from the direction of the Jenkins residence, Ann Louis?"

Grandma shook her head. "I ain't heard anything. Somethin' happen?"

He nodded. "George Kirby found Eldon Jenkins dead in front of his place just this morning. Was sittin' face down in the mud. Looked like an animal got him," the sheriff said, scratching his neck.

My eyes went from the sheriff to Grandma and back again.

"Wasn't no animal that killed Eldon Jenkins, Sheriff," Grandma said, matter-of-fact.

The sheriff lifted an eyebrow. "No?"

I knew what Grandma was going to say before she said it. She'd told me someone was in trouble the night before. Someone whose *stink* was around our cabin.

"It was a devil." Her tone remained cold and stoic.

"Now Ann Louis..." he started, "Why do you say things like that?"

Knowing why, I looked down at my bowl of peas. While I believed Grandma, that didn't mean anyone else would. After all, I was here when the devil sniffed around the cabin. Just thinking about it sent a shiver up my spine. It had a growl like a rabid dog and it scraped at the windows with sharp claws. If it weren't for Grandma's incantations while we stood inside the circle of salt, it may have gotten us, too. Looking at the window next to me, I noticed just below the windowsill what appeared to be a claw mark. I shuddered.

"It came by here last night. Circled the cabin six times. Jenkins put in my new windows just last week. They got his stink all over 'em. Somethin' musta scared it off." Her expression didn't change.

The sheriff snorted, but seemed nervous. "You know I don't believe in that witch stuff."

"Just because you don't believe don't make it any less true, sheriff," she told him. "I know what I heard. Evelyn heard it, too." She nodded toward me, her aging hands working deftly, scooping the peas from their shells.

"Did you see a devil last night, Evelyn?"

I shook my head. "No sir. I didn't see it, but I heard it plain as I hear your voice right now. It tried to get into the cabin but we had protection. I bet Eldon Jenkins had none of that," I said.

"Of course he didn't," Grandma said. "You say George Kirby found him?"

Sheriff Jackson narrowed his eyes. "Yes, ma'am."

"Interesting," Grandma quipped. Her hands stopped suddenly and her steel blue eyes looked through the sheriff.

"How so?" the sheriff prodded.

"Interesting how the one to have the curse put on him was the one to find him." She shook her head. "Dark magick, that. Probably the work of Isabelle LaPierre."

"You mean to tell me you think Eldon Jenkins was murdered?"

"No, sir. I mean to tell you Eldon Jenkins was cursed by Isabelle LaPierre because George Kirby paid her to do it." Grandma stopped short then.

The hair on my neck rose up. I felt it, too. The moon would still be full tonight and the daemon would be out again. It would likely come out tomorrow night, too, before finally going back to hell. Grandma told me that's how spells like that worked.

Grandma began gathering up the peas. "Get inside, Eve," she told me.

She handed me her bowl of peas and I carried both bowls into the house, leaving her to put the shells on the offering altar by the woods.

I heard the sheriff say, "Ann Louis, why you have to go an' tell them kinds of stories?"

"They're not stories, sheriff. If you were wise you'd walk away. Write this one off as Eldon Jenkins getting drunk, passin' out in a puddle, and being scavenged on by hungry animals."

I watched her through the kitchen window as she carried the shells across the dirt roadway to the edge of the forest where she left them on the small stone altar. The sheriff watched her. He didn't say anything until she returned and started up the porch steps.

"Well I was pretty sure he just died of a heart attack, but I gotta check everything you understand. Now I gotta ask why it is you think George Kirby had something to do with it." The sheriff seemed genuinely interested.

"George Kirby's mama has the witch blood. Lots of people 'round these parts do. You do, too, sheriff. I suppose Eldon done found out something about George Kirby that George didn't want him knowin'. George ain't no stranger to the devil, you understand." Grandma tipped her head to one side, waiting for a response.

George Kirby owned the local hardware store and was on the town council. He was one of the few wealthy people inside Graham County. Being outed as a devil worshiper was the last thing he'd want.

"If George is so in league with Satan, why did he need to hire Isabelle to send a daemon after Eldon?" The sheriff laughed. "I've heard everything now."

"Not daemons. Daemons is a different kind of spirit. No, I'm talkin' devils. It's the devils you gotta watch out for. They're pure evil intention. Raisin' devils takes a powerful witch and very dark magick, sheriff. That's more than George Kirby can handle. Isabelle, on the other hand..." her voice trailed off. "I've said too much. It's getting dark. Ward your house sheriff. The devil hasn't run its course and will be loose for another twelve days at least. Those who had contact with Eldon still have his stink on them."

Sheriff Jackson blinked at her.

"Eldon put in my new windows last week," Grandma said, stepping into the house. "I should lock up now. It'll be dark soon."

Shaking his head, the sheriff said nothing, just got in the car and sat for a moment as Grandma came inside and locked the door. I couldn't shake the feeling that something was watching us from the forest.

"Eve," Grandma said.

I jumped.

"You feel it to. The witch blood is strong with you. You'll always feel them when they're near. Get away from the window," she said. She closed the drape.

"Grandma, if the devil killed its intended target, why is it still coming around?" I asked. It didn't make a whole lot of sense for the devil to keep up its nightly wandering if the person it was summoned to go after was gone.

"'Cause chances are it was summoned to go after more than one person," she said, focused on her task.

Going around to each window she made sure it was locked and closed the drapes. Again, she checked the doors, not that locks could hold a devil. Then she placed salt on every sill and in front of the doors. We'd set up the couch with blankets and a table in the middle of the room earlier that day. Grandma busied herself getting our dinner, drinks and snacks together, along with the bucket we'd go in until first light hit. Grandma said when devils came 'round, there was no going to the bathroom because chances are it would smell you and come through the window to get you. So we used the bucket at night. I hurried and made one last pit stop while Grandma assembled all we would need for the night inside the area in the living room that would become our consecrated circle.

Once we'd both taken care to use the facilities and bring together knitting, books and cards, and closed the doors to the bedrooms and bathroom of the small cabin, we sat in the living room and lit a couple of candles.

A strange noise came from the forest across the way. I admit it was tempting to go to the window just to see what was making such a strange sound. Grandma grabbed one of five large boxes of salt. Pouring it directly onto the wood floors, she walked in a circle, clockwise, intoning her incantation leaving a trail of salt in her wake.

I sat on the couch; my knees pulled to my chest, watching Grandma and hearing the thing get closer to the cabin. It audibly sniffed at the front door, but since it was already dark and there wasn't electricity and no porch light, I couldn't see anything. Not even a shadow. The only light glowed from the candles sitting on the dining room table.

The thing growled, low and menacing. I wanted to ask Grandma why it was still there. Did it smell the stink on us? Did it think Jenkins was still alive? Or did it think we were kin? Then I remembered that I'd handed Eldon more than one glass of lemonade the days he'd come to put the windows in. I wondered then if Eldon's stink was still with me.

We sat quiet that night, listening as the thing moved around the cabin a handful of times, left, and came back to do it all over again. When it wasn't there, looking in at us through cracks in the drapes, growling or pacing around, or scratching at the windows, we played a few hands of gin rummy and I finally fell asleep by candlelight. I woke the next morning when the sun shone through the window so bright that it blinded my eyes. Grandma must have opened the drapes. I looked around. All the drapes were open. The salt on the floor had been cleaned up, and brand new candles had been placed in the holders.

With a stretch I got up and looked around. "Grandma?"

Then I saw the note on the kitchen counter. I went to it, glancing out the open windows to the bright day outside. I picked up the note and read it.

Went into town for some things. Tend the garden. Pick tomatoes and cucumbers for lunch.

Aside from the devil, this vacation had been like previous ones. Long, lazy days from August to the beginning of September spent toiling in the garden, and taking meandering walks through the forest. This was the last week I was here because school started next week. I grabbed a basket, gardening sheers, unlocked the front door and stepped outside, making my way around the veranda to the garden out back. The sunlight felt good against my skin. Grandma always had a beautiful garden brimming with witching herbs and plump vegetables. The cucumber vines climbed the back fence along with pumpkins and other squashes. I found two good sized cucumbers and snipped them from the vine then made my way to the tomatoes in the middle of the garden. Choosing four large ripe tomatoes, I slipped them in my basket and looked around to see if anything else looked like it needed to be harvested and eaten soon. I checked around the plants, pulling the large weeds as I saw them. Once I was satisfied I'd done the weeding to my grandmother's satisfaction, I decided to grab a bell pepper to add to lunch along with some lemon balm to add to the sun tea I planned to make before heading back into the house.

The day wore on. I finished a novel I was reading, washed the vegetables, made myself lunch, made the sun tea, and spent a short while sitting on the porch. Grandma still wasn't back. So when five o'clock came and went I started to get a little nervous. It wouldn't be dark for a few hours, but deciding to err on the side of caution, I went back inside, locking the door behind me. Going straight to the phone, I dialed the sheriff's office.

A woman whose voice was laden with boredom answered the phone. "Graham County Sheriff's Department. Is this an emergency?"

"No. I'm just calling to report my missing grandmother, Ann Louis Parker," I said, feeling incredibly stupid.

"How long has she been missing?" The woman on the other end of the line seemed annoyed now.

"Well, she left this morning to go into town for groceries, and she's not back yet. I'm worried she may have hurt herself walking into town. I was wondering if maybe you could have someone drive the road from town to the cabin to make sure she's not hurt?" It seemed a huge imposition to ask.

Evidently the operator thought so, too. "Honey, you're her granddaughter, right? How old are you?"

"Seventeen, Ma'am."

"Well you could of walked that road yourself in an hour, why didn't you?"

I could scarcely believe my ears. "Well, if I did find her, it could take me even more time to get to a phone to call for help. I don't have a cell phone."

What I wanted to say was is was almost dark and I didn't want myself, or my grandmother, outside when the devil came back. I shuddered, on the verge of tears. Ashamed of my own fear to walk the road myself, and feeling stupid for behaving like a child and not walking the road earlier in the day when it became evident that something was wrong.

"Well, all right. I'll send Deputy Dave out that way to see if he can find her," the woman said. "What's your name, honey?"

"Eve Winters," I said.

"Don't worry, honey. I'm sure she'll turn up. Ann Louis is a tough cookie. She may have stopped for a drink before heading home."

As I hung up, I gulped. That sensation that something was watching me was back. My mind raced to the protection spell Grandma always used. Why was it that the things you didn't want were always the things you ended up needing? That's how I felt about witchcraft. It never particularly interested me, but now that I was facing the possibility of confronting the devil alone, I wished I'd paid attention. I immediately went to Grandma's room and found the family grimoire she kept hidden under the blankets in the old wooden chest at the end of her bed. Pulling it out, I unwrapped the silken cloth covering it, revealing a thick tome hand bound in leather. On the cover was stamped the serpent within a triangle. It was a family seal of sorts. I ran my hand over the indentations and ran out into the living room where there was more light. Outside, the daylight was fading fast. My hands were shaking so hard I could barely open the book. I didn't even know what I was looking for. So many things, and symbols, and practically none of it in English, let alone readable. Strange writing covered most of the pages. It was no use. I closed the book and pushed it away from me.

"Calm down, Eve," I told myself. "What has Grandma been doing every night?"

A cold chill slid straight down my back. I went to the kitchen and looked out the window, hoping to see Grandma coming up the road. That's not what I saw. No, what I saw was a dark figure lurking, watching me from the forest. Whatever it was – it had red glowing eyes.

With tears streaming down my cheeks I focused on making sure all the doors and windows were locked and that the drapes were pulled. If Grandma did show up she had a key, but what if the devil got her before she was able to get in? There was no way I could leave the door unlocked. The thing would get in. It would kill me like it had killed Eldon Jenkins.

When I'd finished the task of locking up, I took up a box of salt and began pouring it on each window sill and in front of the door. I never really paid attention to the incantations Grandma used, so I made up my own.

"Oh please gods, keep the devil out. He can't cross the salt," I kept saying over and over again.

By the time I was done, the light outside was gone and it was dark.

The devil in the forest let out an angry yowl that chilled me to the bone.

I began making the circle of salt around the couch. "Please gods, keep the devil out! He can't cross the salt." I was sobbing now.

I stopped short when I heard it. The beast hobbled up the steps, growling the entire time. "Evelyn," it said, its voice cold and dead.

My hands instinctively shot to my mouth to cover the cry of terror that emerged.

"Let me in," it said. It sounded like nothing I'd ever heard before.

The doorknob in the kitchen began to jiggle.

I stifled another scream.

The door knob stopped moving just as suddenly as it had started. Then I heard the thing move across the porch and saw its shadow move by the window. Silence.

Where did it go? Maybe it was gone? Still terrified, I couldn't move. I was safe inside my circle of salt.

Sweat poured from my skin and suddenly, it felt strangely humid in the house. Dank. Like a rising damp. That's when I smelled it. The scent of rotting flesh seemed to come out of nowhere, permeating the room, causing me to gag.

I heard a creak behind me, turning just in time to see the devil, replete with gray horns, step out of Grandma's bedroom into the main living room of the small cabin.

With a scream, I grabbed the spell book and clutched it to my chest, making sure to stay within the circle of salt. That's when I realized that I'd put salt on the sill in Grandma's room, too. Obviously it hadn't worked. Not without the incantation.

The devil, gray skinned and slick looking, grimaced at me, displaying a row of razor sharp teeth. It lifted a clawed finger to its mouth as if to tell me to be quiet. Those red eyes, with black slits for pupils, sized me up. Its mouth contorted, "Evelyn, come to me. Join me."

Still clutching the book, I backed away. "Go back to hell!"

It cackled, amused at my feeble attempt to banish it, then it took a step forward.

Gods damn it, where was the deputy? He had to have driven the road already. My eyes glanced over to the phone. As if I had time to call for help. What would I say? *Hi, there's a devil in the cabin, send the sheriff?*

The devil grimaced at me again, taking another step toward me.

The grimoire felt like a safety net and I clutched it for all it was worth, hoping it contained some sort of power to help me. "What do you want from me? You killed Eldon Jenkins, your job is done!"

"I didn't come for Jenkins," it said. "I came for you."

I felt my eyes go wide. Who would want to kill me? I was a kid who never hurt anyone. Not George Kirby and certainly not Isabelle LaPierre.

"Why?" I finally managed after a brief moment of shock.

This time it took two steps and I found myself at a crossroads. It had me pinned against the back wall. There were two rooms - the guest room, where I was staying, and the bathroom. The only way out of either was through a window, out in the darkness of swampy forests.

It took another step closer. I had to make a choice.

The devil was a hunter; an animal built to kill and destroy; to rend its prey limb from limb. And it was after me. I was too young to die.

"Why?!" I shouted this time, hoping the thing would answer. Maybe I could reason with it.

When it didn't answer again, I hurled the grimoire at it, but the devil was fast. He caught the grimoire in mid-air and looked down at what he held. That evil, tooth filled grin covered its face again. It paused and opened the book.

That's when I realized that I'd gotten used to the stench and the walls of the cabin were sweating. Water was dripping down the walls and off the ceiling. The rising damp became more palpable.

"You can't have me," I whispered, gauging whether or not I could make it past the devil, to the door. No, I decided quickly, there was no way. My only way out was through the guest bedroom, out the window. Of course if the devil was smart, which it appeared was the case, it would know what I was doing. The short of it was this: Either way, I was fucked with a capital F.

Meanwhile, the devil seemed to keep one eye trained on me while he flipped through the pages of the grimoire until he seemed to find what it was looking for. When he found it, he flipped the book around, pointing to an open page.

"You are mine," it hissed. "Come to me. I'll get you either way."

I gulped again, the rising damp making it harder and harder to breathe. It took another step toward me, dropping the grimoire on the ground.

The sound and light from the car coming down the road caused the beast to stop and turn, just for a second, but that second was all I needed. I ran for the door, expertly unlocked the deadbolt and threw the door open. The fresh air smacked me in the face like manna from heaven. I sprinted outside and down the stairs. All I could hear were my own screams.

The sheriff's car jerked to a stop and the sheriff himself jumped out of the driver's seat. "Evelyn, girl, what's wrong?"

I couldn't speak, just pointed to the house.

The sheriff pulled his gun and started into the house. A deputy got out of the passenger side of the car and helped me into the back of the car.

"Calm down, stay here." He drew his own gun, shut the car door, and started toward the house.

I was a sitting duck.

One shot. That's all I heard. One shot and something darted out the front door of the cabin and past the headlights of the car. It was the devil. I know it was because when it passed I heard, in my mind, in the devil's growling voice the words, "Maybe not now, Evelyn, but eventually. Eventually you will be mine."

When the sheriff and his deputy got back to the car, the sheriff turned to me. "What the hell was that?"

"The devil," I said quietly. "Did you find my grandmother?"

The men looked at each other then back at me. The sheriff said, "We can't find her anywhere. We'll take you back into town and call your parents. You can stay at Meryl's Bed and Breakfast tonight and collect your things tomorrow. We'll keep looking for your grandmother."

The sheriff was visibly shaken.

Neither of them said anything the entire drive into town.

That night I didn't sleep. The bed at the B&B was sterile and I could feel eyes from the forest watching the window. I could feel the cold of the rising damp. It knew where I was. It always did. It always would.

***

"What is that weird writing?" my little brother, Trent, asked.

"It's called Theban Script," I said, watching the snow fall outside our upstate New York home.

"That's a cool book, where'd you get it?" he asked.

"It was Grandma Ann Louis' book. She gave it to me," I lied. Actually, I'd taken it the day my parents picked me up, when we went back to the cabin to get my things. They still hadn't found Grandma. I was pretty sure the devil had something to do with it.

Now, four months later, I found myself much closer to finding out what the devil meant when it pointed to the page. I'd learned the book was written in a type of witches' alphabet called Theban Script.

"Can I look at it?" Trent was only eight, and always wanting to be involved in everything I did.

"Trent, I'll let you look at it later, but could I have an hour to myself? I have to do some stuff." I pointed at my bedroom door.

"Aw! Why can't I look at it?" He stomped his foot.

"You can, later. I'm translating it. If I can learn how to read it, I'll teach you, okay?" Bribery was the easiest way to deal with little brothers.

His green eyes lit up. "Okay. Promise?"

I nodded. "Cross my heart, swear to die, stick a booger in my eye!"

He laughed and happily left my room, even closing the door behind him.

I went back to translating the page. It appeared to be some sort of water spell. A chill washed over me as I read the last few lines back to myself, suddenly remembering Grandma Ann Louis' incantation:

A rising damp.
The turning wheel.
The witch's heir.
Come the devil.

TEMPLE APOPHIS

1

They all said it behind her back. "Belinda Applegate is so sweet. I wonder how she fell in with a crowd like Temple of Apophis."

She'd overheard the shop owner Evelyn Winters saying this to Esther Branson, Karen Lamm, and Sandy Foreth at the coffee shop only this afternoon. They hadn't seen her sitting in the corner booth with her nose in the latest Stephen King novel, nursing a latte and pretending to be engrossed in the book. She didn't draw attention to herself, though she easily could have. Instead, she quietly sat back, pressed her back into the stiff, cold orange vinyl of the booth, and listened to the women gossip. This town, Haileyville, was rife with gossip.

All afternoon and through dinner she mulled it over. Didn't they understand love? Belinda loved Warren and Warren loved her back. Certainly that wasn't the only reason she became a member of the temple, but she had to admit it was a factor. Besides, Temple of Apophis wasn't as bad as some of the other covens thought. They weren't on the inside like she was. They didn't see how kind and compassionate Brady, Tara, Warren, Gayle, and Lawrence could be behind closed doors. So what if they occasionally killed rodents and chickens during carefully planned rituals? At least they weren't killing household pets and babies. Yes, admittedly Brady and Lawrence could get rowdy, and once – for shock value – the pair had killed a chicken and ate its raw heart during a public Walpurgisnacht Rite that all thirteen covens attended. Shadow Marbas, The Watch, Temple of the Magi and the Ashtaroth Briarwood covens had all laughed about it afterward. But the other eight covens weren't amused. There were children there, for Daemon's sake. The communal ritual had been canceled ever since because one-third of thirteen covens refused to sign the code-of-conduct agreement proposed after the incident.

She grabbed a frying pan and plunked it into the warm soapy water in the sink.

Those pansies in Tiamat-Leviathan and Lucifer's Haven were the worst, closely followed by the Cult of Lucifuge and the Ba'al Collective. Self-righteous assholes. The solitaries, while they seemed to take the side of the softer covens most of the time, tried not to choose sides. After all, Eve and Esther made their living off of all thirteen covens. They were like stray dogs, their loyalty only extended to those who were paying customers. For Eve, she owned the largest occult shop in the area and kept all thirteen covens in supplies. Esther, on the other hand, was a powerful seer. She made her living reading for everyone in the area, and for an extra fee, she'd perform as the seer in any Goetic or Enochian operation, provided nothing else besides seeing was required of her. The covens kept her busy because it was hard to find a seer with the kind of talent she possessed.

If both of them weren't under the protection of the other covens though, Belinda was pretty sure members of the Shadow Marbas, or more importantly, Ellie Ayer, the formidable leader of that group, would have cursed them both by now. That was Shadow Marbas' claim to notoriety – a high priestess with bi-polar disorder, sex addiction, and anger issues. The point being, she thought, was that none of the covens labeled *shady* by some of the others, were any different than those who judged them. They were all human and flawed, and Belinda knew that someday they'd all see that.

"Babe, what's out there?" Warren came up behind her and followed her gaze out the window into the backyard. Their small house wasn't much, but it was theirs. Well, Warren's, but technically hers too. Since she moved in, she'd redone every room and turned it from a metal-head bachelor pad into a welcoming home that she wasn't embarrassed for her parents to visit. Warren didn't seem to mind the takeover. He was the last male in the group to enter a long-term relationship, and he didn't seem upset to see the remaining vestiges of his bachelor life come down. She looked into the window at his reflection and the reflection of the large framed print of an inverse pentagram hanging over the kitchen table behind them.

"Nothing, I was just thinking. I should be done in a few minutes." She started scrubbing the pan again. They'd had fried pork chops for dinner. Despite having spent a few years in jail for possession of marijuana, Warren made enough working on computers that she was able to stay home and keep the house. Cooking and cleaning wasn't a bad gig. She liked it as it gave her time to read and work on her divination skills, which had grown stronger in the past two years. Warren had even suggested she ask Esther Branson for lessons, hoping that with the elder seer's help, Belinda would access something untapped so the tri-county area would have another talented seer. Esther was, after all, fast approaching her twilight years with no one to take her place once she passed.

He smacked her ass playfully. "Well hurry it up, Bel. I want to do the ritual by eleven."

18

"Hour of Saturn," she said with a smile. Every Friday night she and Warren did some necromantic work at eleven. That was Warren's area of interest. More than anything, he wanted to be a Sem-Priest. Sure, one would think he would have joined the Order of Eurynome instead of Temple of Apophis, but the Order of Eurynome was friendly to the Apophis group, and Brian Price, one of the leaders of that coven, and Warren had become fast friends. They often talked about Sem-Priest things. Binding souls to energy and releasing souls from lifeless bodies. Sometimes they'd talk for hours. While Belinda enjoyed the sessions where he acted as the operator with her acting as the medium for the dead, she found his fascination with the dead a mystery. She wondered if she and Warren would eventually change covens, but she knew Brady and Lawrence had been Warren's best friends since high school. Their fathers before them had been Temple Apophis and their grandfathers before that, too. It was doubtful he'd ever jump ship. There was no rule saying Warren couldn't be a Sem-Priest and a member of Temple of Apophis. Brady and Lawrence knew of Warren's interest and didn't seem to mind it one bit.

The doorbell rang, causing her heart to catch in her chest. Who could it be at this hour? She knew before Warren opened the door. Brady and Lawrence stood there dressed in black pants and shirts, Brady with a heavy chain, like a dog choker, around his neck. Even if they weren't hoodlums, they certainly dressed the part. Of all of them, Warren looked most like a rough ex-con because he'd kept his long hair and he only shaved every three days or so. Though she didn't think marijuana possession qualified him as a convict. Everyone else did, certainly. Even people who didn't know the details filled them in, and inevitably rumors would surface saying he'd killed a guy, or raped someone. Other rumors pegged him as a thief or a counterfeiter. She'd heard it all.

Yes, she could have overhauled him like she had his house. Asked him to cut his hair and wear khakis and button down shirts, but the truth was she liked his rough and tumbled look. And she liked his rough looking friends, who were no more criminal than Warren. They all smoked their dope; it's just that Warren got caught. But that was years ago.

"We need Belinda," Brady announced, skipping any formal greeting.

Lawrence held up a stapled bit of paper. "We got it."

Warren lifted a scruffy dark eyebrow. "The true conjuration of Apep?"

"Gayle's brother returned from Egypt yesterday. He even translated it for us, but was hesitant to give it up at first," Lawrence explained. "Guess he was worried Apep might throw down some old-school biblical chaos if conjured."

Belinda didn't bother correcting him. Apep, aka Apophis, was far more ancient than Judeo-Christian Bible stories.

"We'll do the conjuration and Belinda can channel him." Brady's excitement was contagious, so much so that Warren didn't protest about missing their usual Friday night necromantic work in favor of this one thing. The one thing Brady wanted more than anything was to speak to their coven patron, directly. Sure, they'd tried it before. Long drawn-out rituals laden with ceremonious décor and dress wherein Brady recited tedious orations that sounded hollow and insincere. The rituals usually looked and felt like an amateur theater performance. There was always that one person, usually Lawrence, who sounded like a ten-year-old schoolboy, asked to read aloud to the class. Belinda hid her distaste and forced a smile instead. She had no choice but to indulge them. If Apep showed up, that would be fine. It would be like all the other times the Daemonic presented itself in the mirror. She could see, hear, and feel them. Confined to the obsidian scrying mirror in the center of the triangle of art, the only power the Daemons had were in their words. There was a lot of power in words if one chose to listen and act accordingly.

Then it occurred to her that Brady had said he wanted her to *channel* Apophis. She noticed the three men looking at her, waiting for her answer. "Channel? Why don't we just use the mirror? It's easier."

While she could see the appeal of channeling an ancient Daemon for them, the idea didn't appeal to her at all. The mere idea of channeling made her feel queasy in her stomach.

"I want to be able to have a direct conversation with him," Brady said in earnest.

She fought rolling her eyes and gave him a kind smile. It wasn't that she disliked Brady, not at all. But it was just like him to not consider the toll channeling a Daemon would have on her. Warren gave her a wary look as if he knew exactly what she was thinking.

"Go down to the ritual room and we'll be right behind you," he told them. The guys moved through the living room, through the kitchen, and down the stairs leading to the basement. Warren waited for the sound of their footfalls to reach the bottom step before saying anything. "You don't have to do this if you don't want to."

She shrugged. "I don't mind scrying, but channeling? You know how tired that makes me. I don't want to sleep my weekend away."

The stronger the Daemon, the more it was like being plugged into an electrical socket. Sometimes she wished people who thought it was easy could have her gift for just a day, so they would know it wasn't a walk in the park. It was because of this that anytime someone said they channeled or spoke to certain types of spirits with little effort and no consequence, she knew they were lying. Those same people often found that

Angels, Daemons, or spirits, agreed with them on everything, too. Nothing was ever a revelation, just a confirmation of their own worldview.

But Belinda knew better. Real connection was jarring, and often it tipped your worldview on its head and challenged what you thought you knew. One time she'd connected with Amducious and found herself terrified by her own understanding when he revealed to her that killing another living thing wasn't murder. It simply was. It was humans who deemed good and evil and put everything in neat and tidy boxes so they could wrap their small minds around their emotional responses and socially conditioned thoughts. What was most disconcerting was that for a brief moment, she imagined she could kill, and then she regained her faculties and her intuitive human responses to right and wrong. *It is always wrong to hurt someone else*, she'd thought, as if the point required the reminder.

With a deep breath, she gave Warren a weak smile. "It's okay. We should do it. I know Brady has been looking forward to this moment most of his life."

Warren chuckled. "He has."

Together, they made their way back through the kitchen and down the back stairs into the basement to find Brady and Lawrence already setting everything up. At least they hadn't just called and insisted Warren and Belinda go to Brady's, or to the storefront they rented off of Oak Drive for official temple functions.

No, what Brady wanted required privacy and for that Belinda was grateful. After it was done, she could go straight to bed, not having to worry about whether or not the men wanted to stay up and discuss what they saw, or run out for a late night bite to eat at the Crossway Diner off of County Road 11.

Lawrence lit the candles while Brady sat facing the south wall in meditative silence. Warren said nothing, merely looking on from the corner of the room. He sat down in a chair there and pressed the tips of this fingers together. He often sat off to the side during group ritual because he didn't want to get in the way. Or at least that's what he always said.

Belinda waited patiently until finally, Brady turned to face them.

Then Brady, enunciating each word, said, "All right, I am prepared."

Whatever that meant.

She grabbed her meditation cushion from a shelf and set it in the center of the circle on the floor, and then she sat down with a deep sigh. Channeling a Daemon, especially such a powerful and ancient Daemonic force as Apophis, meant being comfortable doing it.

Lawrence turned off the light and Warren stayed where he was. No one had asked him to do anything, and so he didn't. As the resident onlooker during group ritual, the only time he took an active or dominant operator role was when it was just Belinda and him. He seemed to prefer working magickal and worship ritual with her and no one else. That was okay, she told herself, because if anyone in the coven died, those would be the rituals Brady might allow Warren to preside over.

She closed her eyes and took another deep breath, and then centered herself and relaxed into that mental state that made channeling easy.

Brady began intoning words. Foreign vocalizations in a language she didn't recognize. Perhaps it was Egyptian or something equally obscure. Belinda wasn't sure. Because of this she was able to focus on the vibration each word made and in that vibration she felt the energy in the room rise, pulsating. Each new vocalization added to the last, raising the vibration even more. Higher and higher until her entire body vibrated with such intensity that her hair stood on end, and her flesh became electric. Every pore trembled, and her hands became unsteady in her lap.

She took another deep breath to steady herself and opened up, knowing the spirit of Apophis was with them. Apophis gladly obliged.

Her own consciousness drew inside itself, into a dark place in some obscure corner of her mind as Apophis took over her tongue and sight. She felt her mouth open and heard the words falling from her lips, but the voice sounded hollow and deep, it wasn't hers. She wasn't even sure what it was saying at first. So lost in the sensation of being cast aside in her own body, she lost focus on what was going on outside herself. Thank goodness she could still hear. She just couldn't see or speak. Focusing on the sound of voices, they finally became clear.

"Is there life for us after this world?" Brady asked.

"Yes," Apophis said.

"Can you make us successful in all our endeavors?"

"We can reach an agreement on that," the Daemon said.

"Is there anything you want us to do differently?"

"No."

"Which of the covens will be difficult for us in the next year?"

"Human infighting bores me."

Brady tried again. "But will our enemies harm us?"

"Only if you allow it. Be watchful always." Apophis was starting to sound bored. Belinda could feel his annoyance growing. Sharing the same finite mental space with a spirit as strong as Apophis had that effect.

"Does our sect please you, Lord Apophis?" Brady asked.

Inwardly she laughed. He'd just summoned an ancient Daemonic force, and *these* were the questions he chose to ask? Brady had never been one for thinking things through. Warren would have drawn up a list and labored over it for weeks before the channeling to make sure he missed nothing. Brady was far too impatient for something like that.

"This body pleases me greatly. I can use it to make manifest my will on this plane," Apophis said.

She heard Warren stir in the chair to her right. "Wait," he said. "What do you mean you want to use her body?"

"I am the patron of your coven, am I not?" the spirit asked.

"You are. If it is a body you need, I'm sure Belinda would give it willingly," Brady said.

Oh sure, she thought, *he'd hand me over in a second*. Then she wondered if Brady had been asked to give his own body if he would. It was such a bizarre feeling being displaced in darkness.

"You can't just give over her body, isn't that dangerous?" Warren sounded upset.

"It's Apophis, and it is our obligation to do his will." Brady's voice was stern. "Belinda knows this."

The only one who hadn't weighed in was Lawrence, but he never did. He was Brady's sidekick, and the two never went anywhere without the other. The only time Lawrence ever objected was when something negative affected him directly. Otherwise, he appeared to have a policy of not getting involved.

"I will come again within the month to do what must be done," Apophis said. Then, in a flash in Belinda's consciousness, a set of red eyes with black slits, showed themselves to her and she heard the words, "You will be my hands and eyes," hissed at her through razor sharp teeth.

Catapulted back into her own consciousness, she gasped for breath and found the dim candlelight of the basement blinding. The light hurt her eyes. She felt the Daemon separate from her body, as if someone had given her a charge and wrapped her in latex, then pulled it off all at once. When it had finally gone, her body felt cold and violated.

Once she was able to open her eyes without pain, she realized she was breathing somewhat heavily.

"That's it?" Lawrence frowned, disappointed.

He wouldn't have been disappointed had Warren been in charge of the questions, she thought. Her eyes traveled from Brady to Lawrence then to Warren, who wore a worried expression.

"I have to agree with Lawrence. There was so much more we could have asked," she said. The prospect of Apophis coming back to borrow her body, while disconcerting, didn't bother her nearly as much as it seemed to bother Warren.

"Did he seem nefarious or malevolent toward you in any way?" Warren asked.

He hadn't, and Belinda shook her head. "No. It felt like he had something he needed to do."

Then she had an image flash in her mind's eye. It often happened like that. "Something about the State Capitol building," she told him.

A flash of horror washed over Warren's face.

Belinda yawned. Connecting with Daemons sucked the life out of her. She got up. "Anything else gentlemen?"

Brady appeared lost in thought, but he shook his head. Lawrence followed suit, but Warren took her by the arm and pulled her to him.

"Get some sleep, okay?" Then he kissed her forehead.

Thank the gods *he* knew how much channeling cost her. With a weak smile, she bade them goodnight and went upstairs alone and lay on the bed still fully clothed, listening to see if she could hear what was being said.

She could hear the low murmur of men's voices, but she couldn't make it out, and it was that low murmur that finally lulled her to sleep.

Awaking at five in the morning wasn't strange at all, it was what woke her that was strange. Opening her eyes, Belinda could feel it. He needed to talk to her because he needed her body. They'd discussed it in her dream, but she found herself hard pressed to remember the conversation fully. In the dream, the Daemon stood shrouded in a dark colored cowl hooded robe and sat across from her at an outdoor café. She had coffee and a croissant in front of her, he had nothing. In the distance, the Eiffel Tower loomed on the skyline.

A Paris coffee shop? What a bizarre dream, she remembered thinking. But Apophis had something to do. Something to tell someone – at the Capitol. "Can't we just send them a letter?" she asked.

"I can't influence him indirectly," the Daemon said.

"But my body isn't strong enough to accommodate you," she told him. "Not long enough for a trip to Albany."

Even the thought of hosting a Daemon for the almost two-hour drive through rush hour traffic, let alone through parking and delivery of the message. It was too much. There was no way she'd make it home. The Daemon insisted on other bizarre things, too, but she couldn't remember them.

Of course, he was Apophis and as Brady pointed out, serving him as the coven patron was not something that any of them could ignore. One couldn't claim to serve in the temple of a god only to deny that god the only thing it had asked of their coven in at least several decades.

She looked over at Warren, who slept soundly beside her; then she got up. Not bothering to shower or change yet, she went straight through the house to the basement and descended the stairs, feeling the presence of the Daemon more strongly by the time she reached the bottom of the stairs.

Apophis was a mass of darkness in the far corner, shifting and moving like a cloud of insects. There was even a buzz that accompanied his presence, but it wasn't one of locusts or flies. Instead, it was the low hum of energy, like current through wires. The Daemon stayed still, and she approached him.

"Lord Apophis," she greeted, simultaneously in awe of him, and terrified.

"I am the order in chaos and the chaos in order," it told her.

She wanted to say, "Yes, yes, I know," but thought better of it. Instead, she said, "I can drive there myself without you needing to possess me. Then, once we get there you can use my body and mouth to deliver the message."

Apophis said nothing at first, just hovered there, buzzing with a billion black molecules, drawing on the house's electricity to manifest. She could tell because the light flickered and she was sure that before the morning was out, she'd have to wake Warren to replace a fuse, or throw a breaker. Whatever. She didn't know anything about electricity; she was just guessing.

Finally, Apophis moved toward her, and her stomach turned. Too much energy on an empty stomach was a bad idea; it made her feel nauseated.

Apophis didn't care. "I will agree to that, but you will need me to guide you first to the cemetery to take the picture, then to the man you need to see."

"Just tell me the name of the cemetery. I'll map it on my phone, and then when we get there, you can lead me. But I think Warren needs to come," she said. Someone was going to have to drive because, by the time she finished in Albany, after having channeled the likes of Apophis twice, she certainly wouldn't be able to drive. She would sleep.

Apophis didn't seem happy about the prospect of involving Warren. She could tell by the way the Daemon withdrew as if considering the notion. In her mind's eye, she felt him breathe a sigh of contempt.

"Don't you like Warren?"

"I neither like nor dislike humans. That one, however, is not mine. He belongs to the path of Eurynome and Anubis." It wasn't an accusation, but rather a statement of fact and she couldn't argue the point.

"But he's mine," she said just as plainly.

The Daemon seemed to consider this for a moment, then gave her a mental nod. "If you require him, then let it be so."

Then, much to her disappointment, the Daemon dissipated without having answered even a small fraction of her questions. There were things needing to be done, plans to be made.

With a frown, she started back upstairs and by the time she reached the kitchen, she felt like she would pass out. What little energy she had left helped her back into the bedroom and into bed. There, next to Warren, she fell back asleep and didn't wake for another six hours.

2

The Daemon lied, of course. It had no intention of allowing anyone else in on its plan, whatever the plan was. A mysterious cemetery visit, and a message to deliver... Belinda was tired of waiting to hear from Apophis and Warren couldn't stay home waiting for Apophis to show up either. The bills still had to be paid. That afternoon she went into the small downtown section of Haileyville to Esther's, only to discover the medium wasn't in her shop. The closed sign hung firm on the door. There were only two other places Esther could be. The first was The Black Raven, Evelyn Winter's shop, and the second was the café across the street from The Black Raven.

There was no such thing as confidentiality in this town. You couldn't go anywhere without someone in a rival group raising an eyebrow, or perhaps it was just her. It was easy to get paranoid.

She went to the café first, hoping she'd find Esther there, but as her luck, or lack thereof would have it as she exited the café she saw Esther having a conversation with Evelyn inside The Black Raven, along with members of Tiamat Leviathan and Lucifer's Haven. Two groups that would only be too happy to learn that Apophis was asking shady things of his followers and that young whipper-snappers like Belinda Applegate didn't know what they were doing and were putting themselves in danger with their ignorance and reckless practice of magick.

Oh, the rumors this would start. But she didn't have a choice. She'd been wanting to talk to Esther about lessons in divination and seeing for some time now and had never gotten around to it. Who was she kidding? She was afraid of anyone outside her own coven, the exception maybe The Shadow Marbas, but Ellie Ayers couldn't be trusted. Ellie was manipulative and conniving, which is why she'd never gone to anyone in Marbas with a problem. This was a situation where, pride be damned, Belinda needed someone more experienced to guide her because Brady and Lawrence were no help, and all Warren could do was listen to her and offer to be there for her. Who could truly understand the fears and needs of a medium other than another medium?

Taking a deep breath, she looked both ways for oncoming traffic, then crossed the street directly toward the door of The Black Raven. With two more steps and with another deep breath she went inside the shop, breathing in the strong scent of frankincense and sandalwood. She needed to get Warren more mandrake root anyhow. He notoriously depleted the stores of Saturn herbs on a regular basis, and while she hadn't intended to go to Black Raven until the coming weekend, an early trip couldn't hurt.

She forced a smile at the people gathered around the counter in conversation when their attention turned to her, then went directly to the shelf where she knew the mandrake to be. They were out.

If she turned around, she knew she'd find them all watching her. She was right. No one had a snide look or anything as malevolent on their faces, but she did get a sense she had interrupted a conversation they didn't want her to overhear.

Here went nothing. "You don't happen to have any more mandrake root, do you?"

Evelyn gave her an apologetic look. "Oh, I'm out at least until tomorrow. Jim over at Herbal Alliance said he'd bring me more by the weekend. But could you let Brady know several of his books are in? I've had a few people eyeing them, and I can't shove them any further under the counter." Eve gave her a genuine smile.

THIRTEEN COVENS: BLOODLINES

There may have even been some pity in there; she wasn't sure.

"Yeah, if I see him I'll let him know," she said, then turned to leave. Her mind screamed at her to grow-up, and so she turned on her heal back toward Esther. "Esther, is it possible you might be in your shop later today? I need to talk to you about…" The lie slipped out easily. "My grandmother. She hasn't been well."

Esther's eyes showed a flash of surprise, but then the older woman gave her a kind smile. "If you give me just a few seconds dear I'll be done here."

The elder seer nodded to Eve, took up her bag, and said her goodbyes to the members of the other covens. Then she came up behind Belinda and ushered her from the shop almost protectively.

They hadn't made it halfway up the block when Esther said, "Dear, both of your grandmothers have been dead at least five years now."

"I know," Belinda said. "But I have a unique issue, and I don't need it blabbed all over town. I know that people already think I'm under some kind of spell and that everyone in Temple Apophis are a bunch of young, uneducated, derelicts who are dabbling with things they don't understand."

She didn't bother hiding the hint of malice in her voice. "I've also wanted to talk to you for some time about one thing, but this other thing, it's very… delicate."

"Well, you know I have no allegiance to any of the covens. While I do think you and Warren could *both* do better for yourselves in the company you keep, I suspect even Brady and Lawrence will eventually grow up." They'd reached the door of her shop, and Esther slipped the key in the lock and opened the door.

Her storefront, too, had that same faint scent of frankincense and sandalwood with a hint of patchouli. It was likely Eve's scent of the month. Esther slipped off her jacket and sat down at a table, motioning Belinda to sit across from her.

There was nothing Belinda could say about Esther's assessment of Temple Apophis because she'd occasionally thought the same thing, but they were her friends. She decided to shake off the criticism; there were more important things to discuss. Of course, one of those things was Apophis himself.

Esther waited patiently while Belinda put her thoughts together.

"The first thing I've wanted to talk to you about for a while is, I want to hone my talents, but I've hit a wall, and I think I need the guidance of someone more experienced to help me over that hurdle," she started.

Esther nodded. "I've been expecting you to come to me about that. It could be wise to have more than one seer in this town. I'm certainly not getting any younger." The seeress nodded, her gray hair appearing more silver on the left side where the light streaming in from the window touched it. "But it seems you are rather accomplished in your own right. Especially considering the bigger, more immediate problem you'd like advice about."

How did she do that? Belinda marveled in awe at the talents of the seeress and let out a deep, defeated sigh. "Brady and Lawrence finally found a way to effectively summon Apophis. When they did, they asked me to channel him."

"I see," Esther said, and Belinda had no doubt the old woman did.

"I'm uncomfortable with the situation. I mean, the Daemon hasn't been up front with me, and he hasn't been back since this past weekend so I have no idea when he'll show up and ask me to uphold what I said I would do."

"Which you agreed to because you felt it was your duty as a self-proclaimed member of a coven dedicated to him, and that you questioned because you haven't truly given Apophis your true allegiance. Your allegiance is with Warren." The elder nodded and took the scarf from around her neck and draped it on the back of her chair. "Love makes us do many things we wouldn't otherwise do."

"Well, I can't back out. That would be rude." Belinda frowned and pretended to push back a cuticle.

"And what does Warren think about this?"

"You know he's not some violent ex-con like people think, right?" For some reason, Belinda needed to state that up front.

"My dear, what you think people in this town think and what they *actually* think, is clouded by your own insecurities. Perhaps that will be our first lesson. Not allowing our fears to color our vision."

"Well, I don't think my vision is clouded on the Apophis issue. Apophis wants me to get in my car, let him drive, and he plans on stopping at a graveyard before heading to Albany to give someone a message at the Capitol. And he intends to use *my* body to do it." A deep feeling of melancholy overcame her.

Esther let out a forlorn sigh of her own. "I'm afraid you're correct there. Your vision is not clouded. That much contact with a Daemon for that duration has made some magi insane. Others, their bodies will start to shut down."

Belinda opened her purse and grabbed her wallet. "I need you to look into the future and see what you can tell me. If Warren and I will be okay and if Temple Apophis will be okay."

Esther reached across the table and shook her head. "Put your money away my dear." She let out another sigh. "You and I are kindred, and so I am going to tell you this for free. Chaos has existed long before mankind. Even in chaos there is order, and that means if Apophis has a plan, even if that plan is destructive, then he would find a way with or without you. You are simply a *willing* vessel and a Daemon will use a *willing* vessel long before wasting energy on one that isn't. The problem being that the human body does not support channeling infinite energy in a finite space. Strong Daemonic forces like chaos can be damaging to a human body with long periods of connection. You, being a willing servant of Apophis, give your body and soul to him and so if he knows it can destroy you, you are still a willing sacrifice and a much better choice than someone who has not given themselves over to him in free will. Do you see what I'm saying?"

"That I'm to blame if this kills me and need to accept responsibility for it."

"I can tell you that it won't kill you because I am prepared to offer you seer lessons for one-hundred dollars a month. However, I can also tell you that this will forever change you, and I'm going to tell you what you need to do to make this work in your favor." Esther leaned across the table, holding Belinda's gaze in her own. "Don't wait for the Daemon to come to you. Have Warren summon him. Leave Brady and Lawrence out of it. Then strike a deal with the Daemon."

Belinda felt herself blink in disbelief. "A deal?"

"What?" Esther looked surprised. "You think that just because you've dedicated yourself in service of Apophis that he owes you nothing, and you're just a groveling servant to do his bidding? The Daemon could forcibly use you against your will, but it is far easier for him if he has your full cooperation. Ask him for whatever it is you wish. Wealth, enhanced sight…"

A sly smile appeared on the old woman's lips.

Belinda's mind raced and wavered between fear and excitement. "But only Brady and Lawrence have a copy of the invocation. And the other times Apophis approached me, it was on *his* terms."

"Then find a way to get the ritual from Brady or Lawrence. If you have to go over there and *borrow* it, so be it. Perhaps Warren could pretend he wanted to study the vocalizations." Esther was proving to be far more interesting than Belinda ever imagined she could be.

"Brady would only allow that under his *own* watchful eye," Belinda said aloud, absently. "But maybe during the football game this weekend I can slip into Brady's study and find it."

She knew it was probably somewhere on his desk, unless it was in the ritual chamber.

"You'll see what you need to see when the time comes," Esther said. Then her face went from serious to kind again. "And we'll start your lessons next Tuesday. Once a week on Tuesday."

Belinda took her wallet back out. "Can I pay the first two months in advance?"

Esther smiled. "Of course."

3

Perhaps it was luck or perhaps it was fate, but Apophis didn't show up to collect on their bargain the remainder of the week, and Belinda kept her plan to sneak into Brady's office, or study as he called it, to borrow the invocation from him. She felt bad keeping her plan from Warren, but she knew that Warren would object to her taking it. It didn't belong to her, after all. Well, technically it belonged to Lawrence. If Brady wasn't around, she knew that just asking Lawrence would procure the invocation for her, but Lawrence deferred to Brady every single time. That's what friendship and desperation to be liked by the leader did. The truth of Lawrence's insecurities made her uncomfortable because she wanted to believe everyone in Temple Apophis was there of their own free will and making their own decisions, but that wasn't necessarily the case at all, if it ever had been. The men were all members because they were born into it and had been friends since childhood. The main group rites included parents and grandparents – those still living anyway. It seemed the paternal lines of the Apophis group were a bit thin due to early death.

But Lawrence was as active and involved due to Brady, just like she was involved due to Warren. Whether or not any of them had any true allegiance to Apophis except out of fear or honor remained to be seen. Even Brady and Lawrence's wives weren't nearly as involved in ritual as the men and Belinda were. They attended the yearly celebrations with the entire coven, yes, but the quiet magick circles and divination sessions – no. Never had anyone in the group, young or old, actually done a true invocation of Apophis – one that caused him to physically manifest. Not until last weekend. Other Deamons yes, Apophis, nada.

Because of this distinction, practicing vs. non-practicing, Belinda felt like an outsider among the coven wives. It didn't help that they all had kids or jobs, and that's mostly what they talked about. Belinda rarely had anything to interject in the conversation, and the other women never missed her. She left the living room at Brady's under the guise she was going into the kitchen, but instead, she slipped into Brady's office. The guys were wrapped up in the football game, and she heard the yammering of women's voices from the kitchen. They were talking about kids and schools from the sound of it, neither topic of any interest to Belinda. Of course, if she and Warren ever had kids one day, maybe then she could join the conversation. But until then, she was stuck in the world of men and football, and her quiet, home-making life in Haileyville, New York. A smile covered her lips. Her life was anything but boring. She and a Daemon had a deal to make.

Brady's desk looked like a cyclone hit it. Made of oak veneered pressboard, the paperwork on top was, at least, four layers thick. But right on the corner sat Brady's hand bound grimoire, its cover black, soft virgin goat skin, and the book corners pure brushed silver with an ornate pattern that resembled waves. She pulled out her phone and opened the scan application. Because she knew how much Warren would hate that she took something from Brady and put him in an awkward position if anyone found out, he couldn't be angry if she'd just scanned it. Then, she hadn't really *taken* anything at all. Just made sure the invocation had proper distribution to the members who required it. She'd already decided she would tell him that if Brady expected her to be Apophis's body, eyes, and mouth, then she had every right to a copy of the invocation.

Warren couldn't argue that.

She found it as the final journal entry. Meticulously copied from Lawrence's brother's notes. She scanned

Lawrence's note first, then Brady's grimoire page, and once she was sure she had both safely on her phone, she closed the grimoire and started toward the door just as the door opened and Brady walked in.

"Bel, what's up?" He looked around suspiciously, then looked at her hands. She only had her phone.

"Sorry, I ducked in here to take a call from my mom," she lied, giving him an apologetic smile. "I hope you don't mind."

His eyes went back to the grimoire, closed and still in the same place on his desk. "Oh, yeah, no problem. I was just coming in here to grab something for Warren. Anything new on the Apophis front?"

She shook her head, wanting nothing more than to be sitting on the couch next to Warren, watching the clock so they could leave. "Nothing so far. I'm still waiting and, to be honest, it's making me a bit nervous."

"Maybe we'll get together later this week and call him up again, see what's going on," Brady offered. His suspicious behavior subsided now and she could tell he felt confident or had somehow convinced himself, that she was not doing anything underhanded in his office.

"Oh," he paused, stopping her before they left the room. "I heard you got the old bat to work with you on your divination and communication skills. How did you manage that?" He grinned and chuckled.

His attitude stirred annoyance inside her. "She's a nice woman. She was very willing and said she'd been looking at me as a student." She shrugged as if it was no big thing.

Brady turned suddenly serious then, and his dark eyes clouded a bit. "It's a good thing. You can use this as an opportunity to find out what all the other covens are doing. Be our eyes and ears and keep us informed of what might be coming. You know what I mean?"

Fighting to maintain a cool and collected expression over the shock and disgust she felt, she forced a smile and nodded. "That's always been at least part of the plan. Once I learn to tap my abilities for foresight better, I'll know everything going on with everyone, without needing help." The comment came out sounding more threatening than she'd meant for it to, and it appeared to give Brady pause.

He clearly hadn't considered that Belinda, armed with stronger powers, would know what even he was doing behind closed doors. Brady seemed uncomfortable the rest of the afternoon. She even caught him glancing at her with uncertainty once or twice. Her power scared him, but why? Unless he had something to hide.

It should scare him, she thought. Perhaps Warren would step up to take over Apophis sooner than she'd imagined.

4

Warren seemed overly preoccupied on the way home. "Brady is worried maybe you shouldn't train with Esther," he finally said.

She felt her jaw set. "Let me guess, he said that right before we left when I was in the bathroom?"

The bathroom had provided a safe and quiet place for her to email the scans of the invocation to herself, just in case something bad happened to her phone. Not that it would, but she didn't want to be too careless, just in case. Having a backup never hurt.

"Yeah, why do you ask?"

"Well, when I stepped into his office to take a call from my mom, he came in behind me and asked about my lessons with Esther," she said, still sticking to the lie just in case. "Then he told me to keep my ear to the ground to see what I could find out about the other covens. I told him that with lessons I should be able to get to a point where I can do that on my own and know what everyone is doing and saying without help. That's when he started acting strangely. Why do you think that is?" She gave Warren a knowing smile.

"What do you mean?"

Warren knew damn good and well what she meant, but she would have to spell it out for him. Then he might get pissed and go down to the basement to listen to music and mull it over, and by the time seven or eight rolled around they'd be made up, and he'd come around to her way of thinking. That's usually how that worked. If Belinda was good at nothing else, she knew how to pick and choose her battles when it came to Warren's friends, and this was one battle she wasn't backing down from. She needed Esther, and she needed that gift of foresight that Apophis was going to give her. She *was* willing to risk her life for that. Especially if it meant finding out what Brady was up to behind everyone's backs.

"I mean, why is Brady so afraid of my potential all of a sudden? He knows my training with Esther will make me stronger and increase my skills. When I talked to Esther, she made a suggestion." Belinda gave him a mysterious smile.

Warren was still thinking about what she'd said about Brady. She could tell by the way he furrowed his brow. It took him a few moments to respond, and then he surprised her with, "It might be useful to find out what Brady is up to."

She cocked her head to one side. "So, you've felt it, too, then? That feeling that he's not upfront with everyone in the coven?"

Warren nodded. "I think he and Lawrence have been doing a lot of spell work together, and they've kept it hush-hush. They've even been leaving me out of it, making me wonder if it's something I would morally reject on principle."

"Like curses or something?"

"That, or bids for power." Warren frowned, and that far-away look covered his face.

Maybe convincing him she'd done the right thing in scanning the invocation wouldn't be so hard after all, she thought. Finally, she said, "Don't you want to know what Esther suggested?"

"Yeah." This time, he smiled at her, nodding. "I want you to improve your skills, so if you really think Esther can help, then what Brady thinks doesn't matter."

"Good. Because Esther suggested we get Apophis to help me out. That instead of giving Apophis my body, eyes, and tongue for free for an afternoon, that he give me something in return. The gifts of knowing and foresight." All she could do to keep from cringing was smile. She wanted to cringe because she was still worried how Warren would take it. She was right.

"How? You've already agreed to it." He frowned. "You might just piss him off next time he shows up if you start making demands."

"Don't be mad," she said, drawing in a deep breath. Pulling out her phone, she opened the scanning application and pulled up the picture of the invocation and handed her phone to him. "But I need you to invoke Apophis. Esther seems to think I can strike a bargain with him, that he won't mind a tit for tat exchange."

The look of disbelief on Warren's face was almost comical. "You snuck into Brady's office to get a picture of it?"

Belinda looked down. "Well... I need it and in all fairness – it was *Brady* who agreed to hand my body over to Apophis. Not me. Technically."

Warren handed the phone back to her and blinked. "When he finds out he's going to be pissed."

"He's not going to find out unless you decide to tell him. He just thinks I was in there talking to my mom. Besides, you're just as good an operator as he is, if not better. He should let you preside over ritual more often. Of course, I'm biased." The truth was out. When it came to ritual with Brady at the helm, the energy was never as active as it was with Warren.

Warren stared off into the distance, deep in thought.

"So? Will you help me do it? Esther said to invoke Apophis and just tell him my terms for use of my body. In turn, I get what I want, the Daemon gets what he wants, and everyone is happy. Except for Brady because I'll find out what he's up to."

With a resigned sigh, Warren's eyes fell on her. "All right. Let's do it, but I'll tell you right now I wasn't too keen on Brady offering your body up for Apophis' use the first time, and I'm not too excited about you making a deal with him. It sounds dangerous."

"Of course, it's dangerous," she said. "We're working with pure chaos."

5

Warren liked it when it was just him and Belinda. He seemed to enjoy ritual more. She could tell by the way he carried himself. It was this enthusiasm that he brought to summoning Apophis. Unlike when Brady did it, Apophis showed up with energy unfurled, and manifested in shadows just beyond the light of the candles in the far corner of the room. They both heard the Daemon clear as day.

"Why have you summoned me?"

Warren turned to Belinda and stood aside, knowing this deal was between her and Apophis and no one else.

Fighting back her fear and the chill air the Daemon brought with it, Belinda summoned her courage. "I want to amend Brady's agreement that allows you to use me as your earthly vessel. I was never the one who initially agreed to the terms. I only gave into them after I was offered up by someone else."

Apophis was quiet at first but then said, "Very well. What did you have in mind?"

It always surprised her how easily Daemons slipped into the common, modern vernacular of human speech. But their words weren't just auditory. They projected emotion and feeling to those they communicated with, causing the room to vibrate at frequencies uncomfortable to most earthly beings. Belinda was no exception, and his voice sent her body shaking with cold. "I wish to have clear sight and foresight. That my gifts will be strong and never steer me astray. This in exchange for you using my body to deliver your message."

The Daemon didn't take long to make his decision. "All right," he said.

Surprised, she almost asked him if he was sure, but she knew he was. Even Warren appeared shocked at the quick agreement.

"I'd also like to know when you plan to use my body. I need to schedule my time." Now maybe she was pushing it, but she really did want to know. The worst the Daemon could do at this point was ignore the question. Well, that and perhaps kill her, rending her limb from limb.

"Thursday," the Daemon said plainly, then vanished in a sweep of whooshing air.

Warren let out a held breath. "Thursday?" was all he could get out.

"Apparently." Belinda shrugged. She didn't know why Daemons did what they did, but evidently Apophis had things to do, and he'd penned in Thursday as the day they'd take a jaunt to the graveyard, then off to Albany. It was inevitable that once he took over her body and they shared consciousness in such proximity, that she would understand the Daemon's motivation more clearly. While she wasn't looking forward to it, knowing what the Daemon found so important, a task worth possession for, definitely piqued her interest.

Warren closed the ritual with only the words meant to honor the Daemon upon its departure. Once the final candle gave up its flame to a wisp of smoke, and the lights were on again, only then did Warren finally speak. "I don't know that I like this."

Belinda frowned. "I'm not sure I like it either, but, at least, this way I'm getting something out of it." She paused for a moment. "We both are."

He nodded and didn't mention it the rest of the night.

Fitful sleep found her tossing and turning to images of people and places, and noise. The overwhelming noise blinded her, caused her heart to pound with ferocity, and turned her mind numb.

"This is what it is to see. I show you this prelude now if you wish to recant..." a masculine voice rumbled over it all.

"No!" Her voice rose about the noise and visions, higher and higher until she shot straight from the cacophonous dream into the real world, stumbling from her bed in a cold sweat, still screaming until Warren calmed her.

"Just a bad dream," she said, sipping the glass of water he brought her.

"Maybe it was the cup of coffee you had at six." By the edge to his voice, she knew he knew that wasn't it.

She agreed. It was obvious neither of them wanted to discuss it. There was nothing to discuss. After calming down, she tried to go back to sleep.

6

Her cell had a full charge, and her car had a full tank of gas when Thursday arrived. Warren didn't want to go to work, but Belinda had since reconsidered bringing him for the comfort of the Daemon, and insisted his job was more important. After fifteen minutes, Warren begrudgingly left, insisting she contact him once an hour on the hour.

So she did, until that afternoon. Sometime between noon and one, she came to and found herself driving on an unfamiliar road. The Daemon, realizing she'd pulled herself to the forefront of her consciousness, pushed her back, and the world faded black around her. In a panic she realized she couldn't regain control even though she could hear the sounds around her. She couldn't speak, and she couldn't see. She could feel the Daemon, and she now knew then what he intended to do.

Knowing all too well that staying connected to his consciousness too long would cause her to pass out, she disassociated herself and stayed in that dark place the Daemon had made for her when he entered her body.

"Do not be afraid, priestess of Apophis, for you will come to no harm." It was her voice, but it wasn't, and it was distant, almost outside of her consciousness. The disconnected feeling caused another swell of panic somewhere deep in a primal part of her brain.

She focused on calming herself by listening to the sounds around her. The Daemon had turned on the turn signal. Laughing inwardly, she wondered where Apophis had learned to drive. Was there a Daemon driving school?

"I draw from your skillset," the Daemon answered.

It was easy to forget that when you allowed a Daemon into your body, you gave it full access to your mind. Not only did Apophis know what she was thinking, but he knew everything she did. It was the most intimate of connections, a violation if one didn't consent to it.

The sound of the car engine stopped, and then the car door opened. She heard the car keys jingle in the Daemon's hand. Her hand, she corrected herself.

Perhaps one of the strangest parts of being so disembodied wasn't lack of sight as much as it was a lack of physical feeling. She couldn't feel her body move; couldn't feel her body at all. *That's creepy as fuck*, she imagined Brady would say. He was that kind of guy. If he only knew that she had amended his deal with the Daemon.

She wondered what he would have said if he knew. Would he tell her she had no right? Would he admonish her as the high priest of the coven? She laughed inwardly again. "He is an impotent lackey," she said, surprised when she heard her own voice say it.

Apophis laughed along with her. "When you and Warren take over they will bow before you."

"They'll fight it first," she said.

A bright flash of light blinded her eyes, and she squinted, moving away. That floating feeling vanished, and the heaviness of her body returned in a flash, causing her to stumble and land knees first on the soft grassy earth. Pausing for a few minutes, she slowly opened her eyes as a wave of nausea ran through her gut.

"Sorry," Apophis said. "Your body is not as strong as I hoped. You will need to follow my instructions for now."

The early afternoon sunlight flooded her eyes and then it all came into focus. They were in the cemetery. She was lucky she hadn't fallen and hit her head on a gravestone, but she had fallen on a grave. Directly in front of her stood a tall headstone. It read: *Emily Branson, Born May 2, 1999, Died July 8,*

2015. Beloved Daughter. That was it. She was sixteen when she died.

"And that's what we want him to remember," Apophis said. Then he ordered, "Take a photograph of this headstone on your phone."

She nodded, still feeling out of sorts, and took the photograph, making sure it was sharp and clear. Drawing in a ragged, deep breath, she didn't get up for another minute. Apophis didn't push. The Daemon knew she needed a few minutes to regain her faculties.

Once she was stable, she stood and looked around, finding the narrow roadway where she parked the car. She started back toward it.

"Where to next? Albany?" she asked.

"Yes," Apophis said.

"What will we do there?"

"We need to see a senator," the Daemon said.

Two hours later she parked in front of a meter and began searching her purse for quarters.

"It's time for me to take over again," he said. Just like that – her consciousness was shoved aside in favor of his own, and she was left floating in darkness.

"Make sure you put coins in the meter," she told him. The last thing she needed was a ticket, or worse, to have her car booted or towed and impounded.

"You humans worry far too much about insignificant things," Apophis said in her voice. "Perhaps you should sleep now."

Before Belinda could protest, she felt herself falling deeper and deeper into darkness, the sounds of the world around her fading into a surreal dream world. She knew the Daemon was only trying to protect her sanity. Her body would already be badly exhausted and traumatized from the takeover.

A large gray cat with black stripes and a brown chest walked up to her. "If we don't remind the senator that his daughter died, and it was up to him to make sure no more children die, he won't sign the bill that will allow a terrorist faction to blow up a plane carrying over a hundred high school students to their death," she said. The cat then began to lick her paw.

"Who are you?" Belinda sat down on the grass next to the clever feline.

"I am Dim, minion of Bastet. You are Belinda, priestess of Apophis," the cat said.

It took a few minutes for all of this to sink in. "Wait, so Apophis is trying to avert people dying?"

"Much chaos is unavoidable," Dim said. "This is chaos that should not be. Apophis did not sanction it. Humanity did, and Apophis does not like humans acting as gods."

In the distance, she heard the ringtone she used for Warren. From a grassy knoll, he appeared dressed as a Musketeer, complete with high boots and a feathered hat. His dark hair drawn into a ponytail, he had a goatee and mustache. "My lady," the dream Warren greeted.

"You must remember her and not allow what will happen. If you do, you allow chaos and Apophis will punish you for it," her voice said aloud, booming through the pink clouds in this orange-skied world. "You have been duly warned, Jacob."

Dim jumped up on a tree stump with grace and sighed. "The message is delivered. Now we wait to see if the human listens."

Dream Warren drew his rapier. "I banish you!"

Looking over at dream Warren, Dim shook her head. "You corporeal beings are a strange bunch."

"Well, he's certainly no d'Artagnan," Belinda said, also shaking her head at the overly theatric Warren. "We do worry about such insignificant things."

She smiled then, realizing that having her car impounded would have been a small price to pay if a plane full of teenagers survived because of it.

"Bel!" Dream Warren shouted, fading into a haze.

Then around her the entire dreamscape shifted, fading slowly. Dim was taken with it until the blackness remained. A pinpoint of light stood in front of her.

"I banish you, in the name of Ra! I banish Apophis from this body." This time, it was Warren's voice, and it was right in her left ear.

She felt a light smack on her cheek.

"Bel?" his voice came again.

"Maybe we should have brought Brady." It was Lawrence. Lawrence and Warren.

Her eyes fluttered, assaulted by the bright afternoon light. She was in her parked car. The passenger side. Warren to her left, Lawrence to her right. Both car doors were open. Her body felt like she'd strained every muscle. Her skin felt tight, and her tongue felt swollen with thirst.

"I need water," she managed, feeling like she would pass out.

"I'll get some. There's a Starbucks over there," Lawrence said, motioning to the other side of the street. He hurried off leaving her with Warren.

"You make a terrible d'Artagnan," she told him. "Dim was right. Humans are so weird."

"Bel? You're not making any sense. Are you okay?"

For the first time, she saw the fear in his eyes. She didn't answer him.

"I should have never let you do this. When I see Brady, I'm going to tell him where he can fucking go…"

"Warren, I'm okay," she said, a yawn escaping her lips. "I'm just really tired, and really sore."

Warren's eyes followed Lawrence as he bounded back across the street with a bottle of water in hand. "I'll drive you home and have Lawrence drive my car back."

"How'd you know where I was?"

"Phone GPS," he said.

Lawrence opened the water and handed it to her.

She took a long drink, almost spitting it back up.

"Take sips," Lawrence warned. "You're dehydrated."

After half the bottle was gone, she handed the bottle back to Lawrence, who immediately capped it and reached over her to set the bottle in the cup holder.

Warren handed his keys to Lawrence. "You take my car."

Lawrence nodded wordlessly.

"And don't you dare call Brady," the usually docile Warren said, anger seething in his voice. "I will deal with him later."

She didn't see Lawrence's reaction to that since she'd already closed her eyes. More than anything she wanted to rest. No dreams, no Daemons, and no talking cats named Dim.

Apophis obliged.

7

"That's mutiny," came Lawrence's voice from the living room. He sounded scared, upset even.

"I don't give a shit if it's mutiny. I've had enough of Brady using the rest of us for his gain. Do you know he told Bel that he didn't want her taking classes from Esther? Because he knows if her talents grow, she'll be able to see everything Brady is up to, too." Warren still sounded pissed.

Another voice that she couldn't quite place said, "I've never thought Brady was ever a leader. He excludes most of us in whatever he's doing. It's only you two he works with outside the coven."

"Or just Lawrence," Warren said. "Admit it, man, he almost got Bel killed, and he treats you like his trained lap dog. When was the last time Warren ever took one of your suggestions or let you have an opinion opposite his own without getting pissy? Ever?"

Belinda had a flash of insight then. This was it; the vision she had of a change in leadership. Brady had finally done it. Pissed off the last two people in the coven keeping him in power.

"So, let's take a vote," yet another voice said. This time, she recognized it as Mark, their coven scribe. "All for revoking Brady's title as high priest?"

"Come on Lawrence. Seriously?" It was Warren again.

Another flash of insight, clear as day, rushed through Belinda's head. She saw Brady having sex with Lawrence's wife.

Climbing out of bed, she made sure she was properly clothed, then made her way through the dark hallway toward the living room, still having to work to regain her equilibrium.

Finally, when she stood in the hallway, her eyes bloodshot and her hair a mess, the entire coven went silent and looked at her.

"Bel," you should be in bed. Warren started toward her.

Putting up her hand in protest, Belinda shook her head. "Brady has been sleeping with your wife, Lawrence."

Whispers moved through the room in a wave of shock.

She pointed to her head. "See, after you and Brady left last time, I got that invocation and Warren and I made a deal with Apophis. I now have the sight. For good or bad, it's strong, and I see things."

Her eyes searched the sea of coven members until she found Ellen. "It's not cancer," she told her, noting the rush of relief wash over the young woman's face.

Then she found Roy Martin. "Your brother will be going to jail for a few years so you might need to help your sister-in-law."

The information came to her almost instantly, rushing in waves that came faster and faster. Her knees buckled, and she slid down the wall, holding on for support.

"Take your vote again, Mark," she said, feeling Warren's hands catch her and help her back up.

This time, everyone raised their hands.

"Who replaces him," Mark asked.

Ellen chimed in. "How about Belinda?"

The entire coven looked around as if seeking approval from one another.

"Why not?" Warren said, holding Belinda steady on her feet. "She's the only one who's communicated directly with Apophis. Channeled him even."

"With you as my operator," Belinda said in a voice barely above a whisper.

"Fine, all for Belinda and Warren taking over as priest and priestess of the coven, raise your hand," Mark said.

All hands went up except for Lawrence. He paused with uncertainty and then slowly put his hand up. He was going to take more convincing, but Belinda was up for the challenge.

She had another flash of insight into how pissed off Brady was going to be knowing there was a secret meeting that removed him from power. He would yell and scream profanity at them, and it was possible he'd leave the coven for good, especially after the divorce. Perhaps go down South for a few years to cool off, or stew while plotting his revenge. She wasn't sure which, her sight didn't extend that far. Yet.

Though there was no doubt, her sight was more powerful than it had ever been. She wouldn't complain because she'd asked for this, and Apophis obliged.

LUCIFER'S HAVEN

1

They weren't your typical coven leaders. Connie Hudson sat across from the three slender, professionally dressed siblings at a diner, two miles outside the small town of Haileyville, New York. Finding and getting a potential membership interview with one of the thirteen covens had been surprisingly easy. Evelyn Winters, owner of *The Black Raven* simply asked her who her patron was and what kind of group she was looking for, and produced the phone number of Carl Devlin. It seemed surprising that the mayor of the small upstate town and his sisters were openly witches, but allegedly their family had been heading the coven, Lucifer's Haven, for at least sixty years.

"Do I need to redo a dedication?" she asked, thinking that maybe this was almost too easy. Her father had warned her it wouldn't be. He'd said they would be suspicious of her. Despite this, she'd agreed to infiltrate the group because it needed to be done. The non-believers had to be purged.

Carl looked at the younger sister, prematurely gray, who sat between him and the quiet but pleasant woman at the end of the table. She shook her head and her eyes flashed with knowing. Their sister Lacy was a genuine empath.

Sure, Connie had met empaths before, or people who claimed to be. But nothing like this. Lacy appeared slightly uneasy at first, but she seemed to warm up when she sensed Connie's deep devotion to her cause. Not surprisingly, she didn't flinch when Connie told them where she grew up, which covens she'd been involved with, and about her dedication rite to Lucifer at seventeen. Connie practiced the story for months, to where she almost believed it herself. She'd even run it by her father who said it sounded more convincing than some true stories he'd heard.

The three siblings had a welcoming warmth about them despite their formal attire, and Connie felt immediately at home. It was enough to convince her that maybe these people were the real deal, and that Lucifer's Haven would be easy to clean out.

"We do insist everyone participate in our quarterly rituals to remain a member of our coven, but I can't imagine you would contest that," said Linda, the older of the sisters. She dyed her hair a stark black, but it didn't wash her out. Her complexion handled it well.

"And we meet once a month just to socialize - nothing formal. Being that you're new to the area, I'm sure one of our other members would love to show you around. Corrina perhaps?" Carl said, lifting an eyebrow at Linda.

"I was thinking Jason," Linda said. Then she turned to Connie. "Corrina is fine if you're more comfortable with a woman, but Jason, well, you're both about the same age and probably have more in common."

Connie gave them a kind smile. It didn't matter to her who showed her around. The more coven members she had access to, the better. "How about whoever is available and willing?"

Carl chuckled. "You're right, of course. We should probably see if Corrina or Jason have time."

"Of course, you'll want to come to our communication rite," Linda said, then explained to Connie, "We bring in the town seer, Esther Branson, every so often to communicate with Lucifer for us."

"Did you hear Belinda Applegate is training with her?" Lacy quickly asked her siblings, appearing to forget Connie was even there. "It appears she's vying for the new job of town seer once Esther retires."

Carl gave a doubtful sigh. "I don't see how that will work, with Warren being the new head of Apophis."

Linda chuckled. "Belinda is the one running that coven. Warren is a Sem Priest. Sem Priests are loners and don't tend toward leadership roles, unless there's a funeral." She gave Connie and apologetic smile. "You'll find living in the tri-county area with the thirteen covens somewhat gossipy, and for that we should probably apologize."

"Coven rivalries?" Connie asked, feigning ignorance, then realizing after the fact that Lacy saw right through her lie. "I mean, I've heard stories about rivalries between the thirteen, but... never mind. It was rude of me to ask."

"Oh, you'll hear it all eventually. Of course it's true," Linda said in a rather dismissive way. "Ever since the incident that broke up the initial coven over sixty years ago, we can live in the same vicinity without too much difficulty, but we still have minor issues with problems between covens. There's a reason the mother coven split. One of the wonderful things about Esther is she's neutral. A solitary. She won't take sides or gossip about everyone's private rituals. She prides herself on being discreet and keeping her work for each coven confidential. We need another seer like her, and I'm afraid Belinda may not be it."

"Belinda is such a nice girl, though," Lacy said absently. "I can't imagine she would be any different, unless something that happened during a session directly affected Apophis."

"Regardless," Carl interrupted, giving his sisters a warning look, then turning his attention back to Connie, "You are invited to work with us and socialize with our group for a few months, and then you can decide if you seek initiation. Some rituals will be closed to you, of course, and you won't be able to directly participate until initiation happens..."

She nodded quickly. "I completely understand."

With any luck she wouldn't need to be with them longer than a month to do what needed doing.

Carl gave her a nod back. "Good. Then we have your information and we'll have one of the younger members get in contact with you."

He stood and his sisters followed suit. Then he reached out his hand.

She took it in a most practiced way. "Thank you," she said.

"It was good to meet you and we look forward to seeing you," Carl said. Lacy and Linda shook her hand, too, also with promises to see her again. After that, they left, and Connie was left sitting alone in a diner planning her next move.

2

Jason looked at his watch again. The new girl was late. He hated being the welcome wagon for every new coven member under the age of thirty, but his mother insisted and it only happened once or twice a year. As an extra bonus, the coven viewed it as his contribution and didn't bother asking him to help much during rituals or social gatherings unless a box needed lifting or a table had to be set up. It was a nice trade-off.

"Hi, are you Jason?"

He jumped a little, startled. "Where did you come from?"

"Hell."

His eyebrow lifted in response.

The slender blond with soft blue eyes laughed at his reaction, and then smiled and pointed back toward the bakery. "From Grayson Road, back there."

Not amused in the least, he forced a smile. "You're Connie then."

"In the flesh," she said with devilish grin. "Lighten up and have a sense of humor."

His stomach did a little dance, but not in a good way. There was something off about Connie, and while he wasn't sure what it was, he guessed it was probably because she was one of those high maintenance types. She looked it. Her fine boned features, pointed chin, high cheekbones and thin, pointed nose gave her a frail appearance.

He gave her a wary look. "Then yeah, I'm Jason."

"Do you want to do the whole shaking hands thing?" She stuck out equally thin, well-manicured hand just in case. Gold bracelets adorned her wrists and she wore rings on all but her thumb and pinky.

He laughed. "Nah, I think we can skip it. So you're obviously new to the area and I'm supposed to show you around. What do you think so far?"

Shrugging, she pivoted on one leather sandal clad heel and looked around. Then, with a thoughtful look on her face she said, "It's a lot quieter than what I'm used to."

"Where are you from?"

"Boston. Suburbs," she said as if it required clarification. "I went to Emerson College."

"What did you study?"

"Business," she said offhandedly.

His internal alarms lit up. Everyone knew that was a liberal arts college. The only business majors available had a creative bend.

"What's your creative passion?"

"I don't do creative. I'm more the practical type," she said in an almost mechanical way.

Now he knew she was holding something back. Jason didn't consider himself a master magician, or special to Lucifer, or even gifted, but if he had one esoteric gift he trusted, it was his intuition.

"Do you waste your time with creative nonsense?" she asked him pointedly.

"I like music," he said. In his opinion, uncreative people made the worst magicians and witches, let alone friends. Usually the only things they talked about were exercise, their children, or fixing the plumbing in their house. An uncreative person was about as interesting as watching cement dry. Whether he liked her or not, he had to be kind to her. *You don't have to like everyone you go to church with*, he thought to himself.

"How was Boston?" All the small talk was beginning to annoy him.

"Noisy," she said, as if that explained everything.

Forcing a smile, he said, "I went to school in Buffalo, but came back afterward. I prefer it here. There's nothing like country air."

"And what is, as they say, your profession?" She didn't really seem interested in an answer. Instead, she watched a garbage truck pull up to a dumpster at the gas station a block away, fascinated when it lifted the dumpster and emptied it.

Jason raised an eyebrow. What kind of response was that? Who were *they*? "I work in insurance actually," he said.

Turning back to him she wore a puzzled expression as if she never heard the word before. "Insurance?"

"Life, home, automotive," he said. Sure, his job wasn't interesting and it didn't get the girls, but never before had he ever had anyone give him a quizzical look because of it. Besides, at least he had creative hobbies.

"Fascinating," she said, now bored. "I want to try fried ice cream."

Then, as if he wasn't there at all, she started toward one of the café's further down where a sidewalk sign advertised the dessert.

With an audible groan, he followed. Great, she was high maintenance, boring, and just plain weird. Usually the Devlin elders were good judges of character when they brought in new people, but maybe they'd had an off day, or maybe Connie was having an off day. Or maybe it was him.

They went into the café, ordered the fried ice cream, and found a table in the back to sit at. He couldn't help but stare while she devoured the ice cream in five big bites. Her table manners could have used some refinement.

Finally, she stopped and wiped her face, then lifted an eyebrow. "Why are you staring at me like that?"

Jason had two choices. He could lie and tell her nothing was wrong, or he could be honest, so he weighed both options before finally deciding that an emissary of The Haven, and of Lucifer, would have to be honest. There was no other way. Lucifer represented knowledge and enlightenment. Not lies and deception. Finally, he said, "There's something off about you. You're weird."

A panicked look washed over her face, but she quickly banished it. "Why do you say that?"

"You have the table manners of a mountain man, you ask weird questions, and you're shifty. I'm pretty sure you lied about where you went to college," he said. He half expected her to lose her cool and storm from the café, but she didn't.

Instead, she regarded him with cool detachment. "You're a dedicant of Lucifer?"

He felt his eyes go wide with disbelief. Wasn't she even going to address the lie? "Why are you changing the subject?"

"I didn't lie," she said simply. "I graduated with honors. Look it up. Now, are you a dedicant of Lucifer?"

He felt his cheeks flush with anger. "Of course. Are you?"

"I am bound to him by blood," she said, matter-of-fact, almost seeming offended he'd even asked.

"As am I. I took the same blood oaths and initiation as you did, sister." Jason got up and started toward the door, surprised when she followed.

She waited until they were on the sidewalk before she asked, "What has the light bringer brought you?"

"Apparently only enough patience to deal with you in small doses. I'll have to pray on that. Perhaps leave twenty sticks of incense in offering, and increase my nightly meditation to forty minutes." Sarcasm dripped from every word.

The blond laughed, or rather cackled.

That made him dislike her even more. "Look, I promised the elders I'd show you around, so let me give you the highlights."

"You're trying to get rid of me." Her eyes grew dark and she frowned.

Ignoring her comment, he walked her back to main street and pointed up. "To the right is Black Raven, Eve Winters' occult shop, the biggest one in the tri-county area. She has everything you could possibly need for magick or spiritual practice. All the way up at the top of the hill on the left is the seer's shop. That would be Esther Branson. Nice lady. That's really all you need to know. That, and you should stay out of coven politics if you don't want to become a target."

Wordlessly, she looked at him, then took in main street as if she'd never seen a street before.

Then she said, "So let's talk about that."

"What?"

"Coven politics." A strange smile appeared on her lips.

"No. The less you say about the other covens, the less you have to worry about becoming a target. You can talk about Lucifer's Haven to Lucifer's Haven members all you want. But you don't talk to members of other covens about the inner workings of Lucifer's Haven, and you don't talk about other covens with anyone. Unless you're a shit stirrer and like creating drama…" He felt his jaw stiffen.

She gave a slight shrug. "Fair enough."

He fought back another groan and looked at his watch. "Wow, look at the time. I have things to do. I'll leave you to it then and I suppose I'll see you at this weekend's group social meeting at the Devlin house. You know where that is?"

She nodded in that strange mechanical way she had about her. "What about the younger people. Don't you all meet on Fridays?"

"Yeah, but I think you need to meet the others first on more neutral ground before we start inviting you into our private group."

"Your clique," she corrected.

"Fine. Our clique."

"So, what you're saying is you don't think I'll fit in? Or perhaps *you* don't want me there."

Both of those things were true, but he kept that to himself. "I can't make that decision. I just don't think you'll fit in. But if I'm wrong, then you'll be asked to the next one."

She nodded as if she understood. "Very well. It was nice to meet you Jason Tate."

A chill went up his spine. He hadn't given her his last name. Besides, it was the normal social convention in Haileyville that most people went by first name and coven, unless there were two people with the same first name in the same coven. Even then the only people referred to with last names in this town were often notable. That included the solitaries, the sheriff, and the coven leaders.

With a sly grin, she passed him on the sidewalk and started toward The Black Raven. She didn't look back.

That's one creepy, weird chick, he thought.

3

Eve Winters' shop was definitely well-stocked and appeared to contain everything Connie needed for the exorcism. The air was thick with the scent of sandalwood and cinnamon and the shop itself seemed open, airy, and bright. She began collecting items as she saw them and when she arrived at the checkout to pay for it all, her thin hands were so full that two boxes of Frankincense dropped onto the counter next to the register. Then she saw it. A Lucifer amulet with a sapphire in it.

Connie frowned down at the pendant. The color of the stone was wrong. She preferred amethyst. "My grandmother always wore amethysts," she lied, letting out a big, sad sigh.

Eve Winters, a tall, mature woman with graying hair, gave her a sympathetic smile. "My grandmother was partial to them, too."

She looked up, catching the woman smiling at her. "Were you close to your grandmother?"

"Yes, I thought so." The older woman's eyes went distant.

In that moment, she felt bad for the woman. Despite her mission to purge non-believers, that didn't make her cold or callous to the feelings of others. Besides, it seemed the shop keeper wanted to talk, and if Connie possessed any single gift, it was getting people to talk. To tell her things they usually only shared with close friends, or to get them to open up and be honest. It was part of the reason she'd been chosen for this task. "How did she die?"

Eve shrugged and shook her head, letting out a sigh of her own. "One day she simply disappeared, left everything behind, and we never heard from her again."

Connie narrowed her eyes. "Well, didn't someone look for her?"

"We did. The police figured she probably got drunk and went out into the swamp and drowned. There was no evidence of foul play, but no evidence she picked up and left either. There weren't any witnesses. I was staying with her that summer. I was away from the cabin, in town, and when I got back, she was gone." Eve's lips were a straight line, her eyes distant with memory.

"What do you think happened?"

With another shrug the shop keeper pulled out two amethyst necklaces from the display case and set them in front of Connie. One was an alchemical symbol of air. "Well, she wasn't a drinker, not when I was around. But after what I saw that night, I think she battled the devil and lost."

Connie gulped, hard. Devils were a tricky lot. She'd had to banish a few herself. "So you know a lot about the devil?"

"I know my fair share about devils. The ones we call Daemons aren't necessarily always malevolent, but sometimes people call up something negative and it's not divine intelligence," the woman said as if Connie was young and naive, and then she motioned toward the necklaces. "What about one of these?"

The young blond woman reached out and took the air pendant with an antique looking chain and held it up to her neck. Then she looked at the price tag, only thirty-five. Reasonable. "I'll take this one."

Pausing long enough to hand the necklace back to Eve, she said, "So what if you find the devil wants you to do something you're not quite sure you should do?"

Surprisingly, Eve laughed. "Devils are conjured to kill and destroy. So unless it's asking you to kill or maim someone, it's not a devil. It's more likely a Daemon."

"But what if what it's asking is still ethically..." She paused, thinking for just the right word. "...unsound in your opinion? Is it a devil then?"

"Hypothetically," the wise shop keeper said, lifting an eyebrow, "what type of ethical quandary would it be?"

"One involving destroying non-believers. I mean - if the Daemon is right, then we've purged and cleansed. But if the Daemon is wrong..." Connie stopped talking all at once. Maybe she'd said too much. Then she narrowed her eyes again. "You won't say anything?"

"I try not to spread rumors," Eve said, giving her a measured look.

Unconcerned by the woman's new found suspicion, Connie took her purchases and left with lightness in her step. Perhaps she wouldn't just purge *The Haven*. Perhaps before she was done, she'd purge this whole damn town.

The furnished apartment she stayed in consisted of three rooms. The living area and kitchen were one room, the bedroom was the second room, and the smallest was the bathroom. It didn't need to be fancy. She'd only be here for a few weeks at most.

Dumping the contents of the bag on the table, she quickly turned the marred and discolored coffee table into a makeshift altar. Two pillars sat on either side and in the center she placed an old ashtray she'd found in the night stand drawer. She lit the charcoal, waited until a line of spark raced across its surface, then dropped it into the ashtray and placed a small mound of Frankincense onto its surface. Tendrils of smoke rose thick into the air and the sweet scent of frankincense permeated the room.

She began the ritual of exorcism. It was time to begin; to drive out the non-believers as she'd been tasked to do. As she chanted the ancient angelic incantations, a swift rush of wind raced through the room and his presence filled the small space. His wings stood flat against his back. Unfurled, they were a sight to behold, even for her. The Angel of Light stood before her.

"I will have the entire town cleansed in two weeks," she said with her head bowed out of reverence.

"Just *The Haven*," the angel said.

"But…"

He raised a hand to silence her. "Only *The Haven*, and it will most certainly take you more than several weeks."

She opened her mouth to protest, but then he was gone in a bright flash of light. He certainly seemed determined to keep her here. *Whatever*, she thought, and set about raising more spirits to destroy those who didn't revere Him. If those spirits got out of control and took out people aside from those within Lucifer's Haven, it wasn't her fault.

4

The Devlin siblings had a monthly barbeque in the warmer months of the year. Sometimes in the autumn and even early spring as long as it wasn't snowing. Small clusters of coven members dressed in casual summer attire, stood or sat scattered across the large stately lawn behind the Devlin mansion. It was a big coven. Much bigger than some of the others. Of course not everyone attended every single gathering, but it was a warm early summer day and it appeared the entire coven was here.

Jason saw Brian and a few of the other guys over by the large smokers and barbeques with beers in hand. Most of them clad in jeans and t-shirts. He was just about to join them when Linda Devlin in a blue summer dress stepped in front of him.

"Jason, I've been meaning to ask how things went with Connie." She smiled broadly and gave him an inquiring look. Her smile seemed to pull at the corners of her eyes revealing the fine lines of a woman entering her fifties.

Honesty is the best policy, he told himself. With the most apologetic look he could manage he said, "She and I didn't really get on. Maybe she'd do better with some of the women."

"I see," Linda said. She seemed disappointed.

"I think we just clash energy-wise," he said in a most diplomatic way. "She's more fire than air."

That seemed to appease the high priestess outright. "Oh, I see. Perhaps we were right to suggest Corrina to begin with."

He nodded emphatically. "You know; I could see them getting along rather well."

Linda's eyes traveled over his shoulder and she smiled. "I think I see our new pre-initiate now. Thank you for helping out Jason. I appreciate all you do for the new members."

He tipped his head politely. "Yes. Ma'am. You're always welcome."

With a gentle squeeze of his arm, she passed by him and glided across the lawn toward the uncertain looking newcomer.

With a head shake, Jason approached his friends and was immediately handed a beer by the thin, dark haired Brian, who stood at least six foot three. "What was that about?"

"Welcome wagon," Jason said bitterly, opening the beer. His eyes traveled to Linda and Connie as they walked toward a gaggle of women at a table under an umbrella near the pool patio. Corrina was there along with several coven matriarchs. He shook his head again.

"Who's the new hottie?" Vic asked.

"Connie," Jason said absently. "Pre-initiate from Boston."

"She single?" Vic lifted an eyebrow, craning his neck to see her better.

"I didn't get the far. She is an arrogant, high maintenance…" His voice trailed off.

Vic smiled. "None of that is relevant, man."

Brian laughed. "Yeah, none of that matters if you just want to fuck her and move on."

"Tact," Jason said, sounding far more scolding than he meant to.

With a small nod of deferment, Brian relented and dropped it.

Vic, on the other hand, didn't. "She's got a nice rack. I need to get a better look."

"Man, seriously? Could you be any more of a man-whore?" Jason wasn't one to chase after women just to get them into bed. Perhaps he was old-fashioned, but he believed there was something to be said for long-term-relationships.

"Okay Mr. Rogers," Vic said, sarcasm dripped from his voice.

Chuckles erupted from the group.

"Fuck you, Vic," Jason said.

"So what did she do, turn you down?" Vic really wasn't going to let it go.

With a resigned sigh, Jason shrugged. "We just clashed. I tried to be nice, she insulted me, and I found her arrogant and annoying. It's that simple."

"Could I impose upon you all to gather more chairs from the barn?" Carl Devlin asked, breaking into their banter. The Mayor of Haileyville and High Priest of Lucifer's Haven, who usually dressed in suits and silk ties, was decked out in khaki shorts and a white polo shirt, along with a white baseball cap. On his feet were Nike sneakers, a far cry from his standard black leather dress shoes.

The group of twenty-something males, including Jason, all mumbled agreement, set their beers down, and started toward the barn. Thirty minutes and forty chairs later, they all found themselves sitting under an oak tree in the mid-day heat, eating burgers and hot dogs and quietly watching the rest of the coven around them. The entire scene resembled a family reunion picnic rather than a coven meeting.

"So who do you think is next in line?" Brian asked.

It was a well-known conundrum that no one knew who was next in line for the Priesthood once the Devlin siblings retired. Sure, Carl had a son, but he'd moved to Missouri and joined some Baptist church, and found his family practices abhorrent. Linda had one son and one daughter, but her son, Frank, was autistic and didn't speak, and her daughter, Karla, had already made it clear that she didn't want to run the coven alone. Since she would never marry a man, she was gay like her aunt Lacy, that left the position of High Priest wide open if anything happened to Carl Devlin. It was a common topic of conversation among the younger males because they figured it would likely be left to one of them to take up that mantel of responsibility.

"When that time comes the elders of the coven will choose someone responsible to help Karla manage things," Jason said. It was at least fifteen years before that would happen anyway.

Vic shrugged. "I don't see why Jennifer and Karla can't run it. Do we really need a high priest?"

"I don't think anyone thinks that two women can't run the coven. I imagine Jennifer will be very involved with managing events and rituals right alongside Karla. I think the reason we need both a High Priest and High Priestess is for the balance of male and female energy during construction of the ritual space. Especially during the solar plays and the gate openings," Jason said. Unlike some of them who were members of the coven because their family had always been members of the coven, Jason had truly committed himself to the practice of magick and his dedication to Lucifer. Though he often kept it to himself and didn't have deeply spiritual discussions with his coven brothers. They were far more interested in drinking, parties, cars, and women – all traits he hoped they would outgrow by the time they hit thirty or so. One day he hoped they would take their membership in the coven as seriously as he took it.

"Well," Vic said, trying to sound reasonable. "In lesbian relationships one is more masculine than the other."

"Dominant," Brian said. "I think you mean one is more dominant. Not masculine."

"But dominance is a masculine trait. Same difference."

"It's not the same thing," Brian said.

Jason came to Brian's defense. "He's right. It's not the same thing. A female can be dominant but she's still wired female, even if she likes females. So she still possesses potent female energy."

"So are we talking energy, or hormones?" Vic held up his hands making quotes in the air when he said *energy*.

"Hormones give rise to energy," Brian said as if he truly knew what he was talking about.

Jason laughed. "This is a stupid conversation."

"What's stupid is that Karla would need to have a high priest. I mean, if she and Jen get married, then they're both Delvin's and they run the coven like it's been ran for all these years," Vic said with a hint of finality to his voice. Despite his sexism toward the women he wanted to bed, he was fiercely protective of Karla and consequently, gay rights. They'd been friends since they were young. Jason presumed that Victor thought of her as an older sister since he was an only child and Karla was, by far, the closest thing he had to a sibling.

"Well," Jason said. "Maybe she'll choose you to preside alongside her. You are one of her closest male friends."

"I'm the closest male friend. I'm more like a brother," Vic said matter-of-fact.

"Well, there you are then. Why are we even worried about it then? Vic will likely be Karla's left hand man, and Jennifer will be her right hand woman." This time it was Jason's voice that held a tone of finality. It was a ridiculous conversation, and yet they kept having it. He just hoped Vic would straighten up and start taking the coven more seriously before he was thrust into its overall operations. *Fifteen years*, he reminded himself again.

With a deep sigh, his eyes traveled back to where Connie Hudson sat laughing with some of the women. They all seemed to find her charming. Maybe he was the odd man out, or perhaps both of them were just having a bad day, and that's why the clash happened.

Brian started talking again, this time about something going on at the racetrack in Saratoga, and Jason tuned him out. Thinking that maybe he should rework the wards around his family home. Embarrassing as it was, he still lived with his parents, albeit he lived in the small house on the back of the property, but he paid rent and he helped his parents out by mowing the lawn, trimming trees, and helping with maintenance on the house as needed.

It was Connie's voice that pulled him out of his own thoughts.

"It's good to see you again, Jason," she said as if he was the noob and she were the one born into The Haven.

"Oh, Connie, have you been introduced?" He pointed to his group of friends, none of whom offered any introduction on their own. "That over there is Vic, then Shawn, Brian, Gary, and Scott."

Each of the men nodded as Jason introduced him and Connie smiled politely. Then she asked a very personal question – one that Jason found himself annoyed by. "So if each of you could extend an offering to Lucifer in exchange for something, what would you offer for what?"

"Oh, that's easy," Vic said. "A glass of beer for a date with you."

Jason let out an audible groan and shook his head.

Brian chimed in next. "I'd give him a cigar for a million bucks."

The males laughed and Jason continued to shake his head.

"You don't approve?" the blond newcomer asked.

"Offerings and requests to Lucifer are a very personal, spiritual thing," he said. "And it's rude to walk up to a group of strangers and ask that type of question."

She seemed oblivious to the accusation that she was being rude. "So I take it you won't answer my question then?"

"No. My offerings to Lucifer and the dialogue between us, stays between us. It's no one else's business." This being honest felt good.

Surprisingly, she seemed mollified by his answer, accepting it completely. Then her attention turned to Brian. "Money?"

"Why not?" He shrugged.

Jason knew Brian was just showing off in front of the guys. Were he having a heart-to-heart with Jason, he likely would have answered differently. The one thing Brian wanted more than anything was companionship. Ever since his grandmother passed, he'd been the coven orphan. Both of his parents had died in a car accident when he was three, and he'd been raised by his grandmother. For five years now he'd been alone with no close family except for The Haven. It must have been hard on him, Jason surmised.

"Hey, what about me?" Vic asked, pulling Connie's cold steal gaze from Brian.

She lifted an eyebrow, hands on her hips, and said, "A date with me will cost you more than a beer."

"Blood pact?" he offered.

"That's more like it, but I have work to do first and if you make the cut, I'll consider it." Her attention turned back to Brian, who seemed to somehow have stoked her ire. Or it seemed so with how clipped and threatening her tone was. "I'll start with you."

Brian's eyes went wide. He was awkward with women as it was and couldn't hide his surprise that one was even speaking to him of her own accord. "Start with me?"

"Yes, let's go out." Her expression softened and she smiled at him.

It screamed fake.

Jason opened his mouth to say something, but thought better of it and clamped his jaw shut, his eyes moving from Connie to Brian and back again.

"Next Friday night. Seven," she said. Then she turned to leave, only pausing long enough to call over her shoulder, "Later boys."

He shook his head and looked at his friends. "You see what I mean, right? She's weird, and arrogant."

"Jace, man," Vic said, then nodded toward Brian. "Apparently she goes for the tall, skinny ones. We're not her type."

"Why does she want to go out with me?" A genuine puzzled look adorned Brian's face. His skin turned pale.

It was Gary who finally agreed with Jason. "She is a strange one for sure, and not because she asked Brian out. The way she did it. All dominatrix-like."

Brian's eyes went wide and he gulped. "Do you think she's a dominatrix?"

Vic began laughing. "Oh man, that would be classic. If she is, you have to give us details man!"

"Fuck you, Vic," Jason said for the second time that day. Now that he thought of it, not a day passed where he didn't tell Vic to go fuck himself.

"Yeah, fuck you, Vic," Brian parroted, giving Jason a helpless look.

"It will be fine," Jason assured him. "If you change your mind, you don't have to go out with her. There's no law saying you have to."

"But dude, you have to!" Vic said, cracking another beer. It was his fourth. "That's one hot slice…"

Drinking. *Another bad habit that Vic would need to overcome or set aside if he was entrusted with the responsibility of the coven*, Jason thought.

"She's not a piece of pizza, Vic," Jason said.

Gary, Shawn and Scott laughed. Brian was too terrified to laugh, and Jason could only manage a weak smile.

Vic just shrugged and said back. "Yeah, but she sure has a nice ass."

Jason groaned again, but didn't say anything. There was no changing Vic. At some point, Vic would have to change himself.

That night he went home feeling an uncomfortable sense of foreboding. In the back of his mind, something nagged at Jason about Connie. She wasn't right. Some of her reactions and questions seemed almost…alien. Like she didn't belong to this world. She had no social skills and seemed genuinely mystified by social convention and interaction. Sure, he'd met socially awkward people before, but this went beyond that. Someone who allegedly studied business at one of Boston's premier liberal arts colleges, still a lie he was certain for obvious reasons, would have much better social skills.

As he got ready for bed he tried to shove his suspicions about Connie to the back of his mind, so he focused on the supplies he'd need to re-establish all the wards over the houses and property. He and his mom redid them every six months. It was time again. After jotting a few notes on a pad of paper next to his bed, he went to his altar, lit an incense and prayed to Lucifer on the matter, asking for wisdom in a dream. Then he went to bed and fell into a fitful sleep.

He woke the following morning unrested and cranky. After calling Shawn, The Haven's resident computer guru and security expert, and convincing him to run a background check on Connie Hudson, along with doing some research into her time at Emerson College, he headed to The Black Raven for warding supplies before heading into work.

On weekdays, Eve opened earlier than most stores selling similar wares. Haileyville wasn't your typical town and The Black Raven wasn't your typical occult store. Due to the sheer number of practitioners, it was better for her business that she opened at eight in the morning and didn't close until six. Today the shop was quiet. A lone man stood looking at sigil charms, debating between amulets of Gamigin and Vapula, and after looking at his watch, decided to grab both. *Nothing like needing to get to work to help you make a decision*, Jason thought with a smile.

He grabbed a new bottle of sage oil and a smudge stick. It was always prudent to cleanse the entire area before re-establishing the wards. Then he grabbed an oak branch from a barrel and a stick of black Daemons chalk. He already had the Lucifer oil and powder at home ready to go. His mother had made a fresh batch only this past weekend, before the barbeque.

When Eve saw what he carried up to the register she smiled. "Time to re-establish those wards?"

With a nod, he set everything on the counter. "Every six months."

"You know, you're one of the few practitioners who does that. I honestly don't know why more people don't." She began scanning the items.

"My grandmother, when she was alive, insisted upon it. I guess it just became habit after she left us."

"I was talking to someone else about their grandmother just last week. A young woman in your coven. The new girl," Eve said. She paused and lifted a finger, then reached to a bookshelf behind her and pulled a book from it, handing it to him. "The Book of Lucifer, did you want a copy? They just came in this morning."

He thumbed through the book, quickly noticing some interesting recipes and knowing he'd eventually be sent here, by one of his parents, to get a copy. Maybe he'd read it first. Nodding, he handed it back to her. "Thanks, yes. The new woman in our coven, Connie."

Eve nodded and gave him a strange look, then, in a voice laden with caution, said, "She was buying exorcism supplies."

He felt his brow furrow in response. "Exorcism?"

"Like old school angel exorcism."

"Huh. Interesting."

"That's what I thought. I don't mean to meddle, but did the Devlin's check her out?" Eve, who tried to stay out of coven politics and inner workings as much as possible since it wasn't good for business, appeared to have a genuine concern.

"I don't think so, but I think I'll have to rectify that. I agree that there's something not quite right about her." He frowned and watched Eve slip his purchases into a bag. He handed her his credit card.

"There's something about the way she looks and speaks."

He nodded. It wasn't just him. "Almost like she's…"

"Not human," Eve finished.

A chill raced down his back. "If she's not human, what is she?"

"Well if she's not human and buying supplies for ancient exorcism magick, my guess would be an avenging angel, or even something like a spirit of the dead? I honestly don't know." She gave him a helpless shrug and forced a smile. "But if you want, I could talk to Esther and ask if she senses anything."

"Would you?"

"I'm just as curious as you, and to be honest, I planned to ask Esther anyway because I found the encounter unsettling," she said, handing him the bag.

"Thanks, Eve. Would you call me when you find out?"

She nodded. Eve had everyone's phone numbers.

"I'll see you then. Thanks again."

"Jason," she called after him.

He paused.

"Be careful."

He nodded and left, feeling even more unsure and more desperate to get those wards re-established than he had in some time.

That night, upon returning home from work, Jason received two phone messages. One from Eve saying that Esther sensed nothing but Daemons and conjured spirits in the immediate area, and one from Shawn confirming that Emerson University had no records for a Connie Hudson.

Eve's words, Avenging Angel, came back to him. Maybe that was it. Connie was something someone had conjured. Now he had to decide who he would tell, and what they would do about it. He didn't wait to begin re-establishing the wards. There wasn't time. If there was an avenging angel on the loose, he wasn't taking any chances.

5

Brian Blake was found dead, face first in the river, on Saturday morning.

Jason blinked a few times just to see if he'd heard Carl Devlin right.

"Son, you okay?" Carl asked.

"I just saw him yesterday. For lunch," Jason said, still stunned. It wasn't every day you were told one of your best friends was dead. Carl had called all of them to the house to give them the news. Now, he, Vic, and Scott, the three of them who had been closest to Brian, sat around the Devlin dining room table with Carl, Lacy, and the sheriff, who was a tall thick man from the Blackrose coven, Steve Watson.

"He went out with Connie last night," Vic said absently.

The sheriff cleared his throat. "Connie Hudson, yes. She said he brought her home at around ten and he was alive and well when he left. A few neighbors confirmed that they saw him leave. We think he decided to walk the path by the river to his apartment, slipped, and hit his head."

"Walked?"

"They both live so close to town it makes no sense to drive those few blocks," Lacy interjected looking weary and thoughtful. Wise even.

"The weather was nice," the sheriff said, as if to agree. "Unfortunately the park had watered the lawns late last night, and some of the stones in the path got wet, slippery, and in the dark, poor kid just lost his footing. It's tragic an accident like that could happen."

I bet, Jason thought. If Connie was an avenging angel, then someone had sent her into The Haven for a reason. She'd honed in on Brian almost immediately. Was he her target? How had Brian, one of the world's nicest guys, have pissed off someone so much that they sent a spirit to kill him?

"Jason?" Lacy said, a concerned look adorning her face. "Maybe I should take you home. Someone can bring you by later to get your car."

"No, I'll be fine. I'm just in shock." In silent agreement, no one else spoke, heads just nodded.

After thanking Sheriff Steve, Carl and Lacy led him out. Some of the covens didn't trust Steve Watson. The Blackrose coven was known for having its share of trouble makers, including Gerald Greer, local businessman and bully. But Steve and his wife Allison seemed nice enough, and Steve, having to deal with all thirteen covens, appeared to stay pretty neutral since he was charged with policing everyone in the county, including other coven members. Jason never took issue with the man, but this time, he knew Steve was wrong. This wasn't an accident.

Vic was the first to speak after the elders left. "Man, this is so fucked up."

"This wasn't an accident," Jason blurted.

Both Scott and Vic shot him wide-eyed looks.

"It's a long story but I think Connie Hudson had something to do with it," he said in a whisper, leaning in to them. "Let's go back to my place where we can talk. I'll tell you the whole story."

Both of his friends looked doubtful, but got up anyway and pushed in their chairs.

Lacy breezed in, that exhausted, wise look still on her face. "Are you all leaving?"

Jason nodded. "We probably should go. There's nothing we can do here. We can be upset at home."

She knew something was up. The empath wasn't an idiot. Narrowing her eyes, she said, "All right, but if any of you recall anything that might be important, you'll let someone know?"

"What's there to know?" Vic jumped in. "One of our best friends just died in a stupid, pointless accident."

She gave Vic an apologetic look. Instead of trying to counsel them through their anger and grief, she led them to the door and bade them goodbye, and for that, the men were grateful.

They arrived at Jason's fifteen minutes later. In his small house, situated on the back of his parents' property, Jason told them everything that had happened. No sign of Connie, made up lies, and how she'd been to Black Raven to buy exorcism supplies.

"So wait, you think the bitch is trying to exorcise us?" Vic took any opportunity to get angry about things. His mouth and misogyny aside, he was a tolerable sort of fellow. Ignorant mostly.

"Or one of us."

Scott, the quietest of the three, gave them a puzzle look. "Brian?"

"I know," Jason said. "I find it hard to believe too, but here we are."

"Are we sure that Sheriff Steve isn't right? Maybe it was just a freak accident and maybe Connie is ashamed of where she comes from so lied, and maybe all those supplies were to clear out her new apartment of nasty juju," Scott said, turning into the voice of reason. "It seems far-fetched man."

"But she acts like an alien," Jason countered.

To this, Vic vigorously nodded his head in agreement. "She really is weird. Normal chicks don't act like that."

"To you they do," Scott said, a half grin appearing on his lips. He shook his head. "You are the worst with women. You're a pig."

"At least I've gotten laid in the past six months," Vic started. It was their equivalent of *your momma* and it happened any time Vic and Scott were left alone. Or when they were alone with Jason.

"Okay, stop it you two. We need to figure out how to catch her." He looked at each of his friends, trying to gauge a reaction.

"What do you propose we do? Exorcise her?" Scott asked with sarcasm.

"Well, I've been thinking about it. We get a few of the other younger members. Maybe Karla and Jen, and we trap Connie in a spirit trap." He leaned back and crossed his arms over his chest.

"That's old school," Vic said. An appreciative, smug look crossed his face.

Scott drew in a deep breath. "Fine. Spirit trap it is. And when she walks right out of it, you're going to feel like a huge paranoid asshole, bro."

"I am willing to take that chance."

His coven-mates nodded and then Vic lifted his beer. "To Brian."

Scott and Jason followed suit in a chorus of, "To Brian."

That's how the plan to capture Connie Hudson in her own game came to be.

Jason drew the spirit trap on the cement floor of the garage with magically formulated chalk. Then he threw a rug over it. The rug looked out of place, admittedly, but Karla brought a meditation cushion and threw it right in the middle of the rug.

"This is where everyone will kneel to be anointed. When it's her turn, she kneels, and if she is a spirit, she can't get out." Karla wore a self-satisfied grin. Initially Jason was worried she would be skeptical like Scott was, but she wasn't. Instead, she and Jen had both been eager to help. Both of them agreed there was something off about Connie. Something neither of them could quite put their fingers on.

With the ritual space prepared in the thousand square foot garage that usually housed Jason's father's Mustang and Corvette unless they were hosting a ritual, it was time to invite Connie over. Karla and Jen came up with the story to tell her it was her official *welcome into the coven* ritual. They agreed to warn her ahead of time there might be light hazing involved. Usually there was, when someone was actually accepted. This was no hazing party, however.

Unless it was, Scott pointed out. Because if the spirit trap didn't work, then Connie Hudson was just a supremely weird chick, who didn't have to work, because she had no job. This also meant there was a reason she didn't want to talk about her past. If she wasn't a spirit, the entire faction of Haven members under thirty would laugh at Jason.

It wouldn't be the first time. They all laughed at him when he decided to go into insurance, despite having a degree in graphic arts. But there weren't a lot of graphic arts jobs here, and insurance paid the bills. Besides, he didn't need tons of money anyway. He was fine living in the small house on his parents' property and they only charged him eight-hundred a month, which included electric and water. The rest of his income was his to do whatever he wanted. He was making forty-thousand a year because he was good at selling policies. That meant that after rent, and after the other six hundred a month he spent on necessary bills and the two hundred he threw into his savings every month, he still had around six hundred in disposable income. Not bad for someone his age.

Connie Hudson, if she wasn't a spirit, could be a trust-fund baby, he thought.

"Earth to Jason," Karla said, pulling him out of his thoughts. "So, do you want me to call her and invite her over? Or do you want to do it?"

He nodded. "You should do it. She might think it was strange if I did it."

Jennifer had the number ready to go, which seemed to impress all of the male members present. Yes, Jennifer and Karla would make a good team and could run the coven alone. Even if Vic was chosen to preside as high priest for the balance of masculine energy, it would definitely be those two women who ran things. He let out a relieved smile, knowing the coven was in good hands.

Karla stepped outside with her cell phone and made the call, and two minutes later she came inside. "She says she'll be here in a bit. She didn't think we'd want to get together so soon after Brian's death. She sounded concerned about how we were doing."

Jason raised an eyebrow. "Well, maybe she's a good actress."

Scott shook his head, still obviously convinced that Jason had lost his damn mind.

6

Connie Hudson showed up twenty-nine minutes later wearing all black and the new alchemical symbol of air pendant she'd purchased.

Jennifer commented on how pretty it was.

Forcing a smile, Connie said, "Thanks." Then she quickly manufactured some concern. "How are you all doing after Brian..."

"We can't stop living. Brian wouldn't have wanted that," Jason said. His tone wasn't friendly at all, and it gave Connie pause.

"Don't be a dick, man," Vic said with a smile. "You want a beer or something before the ritual?"

"Ritual?"

"What? Karla didn't tell you?" He didn't wait for her to answer. "This is your official welcome into the coven initiation, girl."

The smiling faces of Lucifer's Haven's younger members all beamed back at her. This wasn't quite what she expected, but then they still didn't know she'd been sent here to cleanse The Haven of non-believers.

A slow smile made its way across her face. "All right." She'd play their game.

"Good," Karla said, sounding pleased. Then she explained the ritual to Connie in some detail, even describing how each of them knelt before the acting priest and priestess, she and Vic, to be anointed in the name of Lucifer.

It sounded harmless enough, though Connie wasn't stupid. She was sure there would be some stupid hazing involved. This wasn't her first rodeo. One coven she'd cleansed down in Cleveland had made her swear allegiance to a rubber devil duck. Another made her recite the Lord's Prayer backwards. It depended on the coven and how seriously they took themselves. The Lucifer's Haven crowd, the younger crowd anyway, was full of partiers. She had her bets on something like the devil duck incident.

Pretending to act nervous in anticipation was probably the hardest part, but at least she'd get to see the younger members in action. Assess their belief through their ritual construction and the seriousness with which it was, or was not, conducted.

Karla and Jennifer seemed the most serious of the bunch. Surprisingly, Jason, who Connie didn't like at all, he just rubbed her the wrong way, was also rather serious, followed by Scott. Vic, on the other hand, was a jackass. He would be the next one on the list to be purged.

She went through the motions along with them and when it was her turn to be anointed she knelt on the cushion and allowed Karla to carefully place a smear of Lucifer oleum on her third eye. It tingled. Someone had obviously made it properly.

When she was asked to rise and return to stand with the others, she was somewhat surprised. This was usually the part where someone brought in the goat, or the weird hat, or other ridiculous thing used in hazing the new member. Instead, she got up and moved toward the rest of the group, only to hit an invisible wall nose first. She backed off, startled and held out her hand, hitting the wall again. It was made of pure energy and appeared to be solid, even though transparent. With these human eyes she couldn't see into the astral.

Try as she did, she couldn't get past the barrier and felt a rush of panic swell in her chest.

The rest of the coven stared at her wide-eyed, shocked at the captured spirit, held fast by the spirit trap.

Connie looked up, unable to find the source of her captivity.

"Looking for something?" Jason asked, pulling back a bit of carpet over the concrete, upon which the trap had been drawn in special chalk.

"Let me out now!" She felt heat rising in her cheeks.

"You really thought we were stupid enough we didn't know you weren't human? We also know you had something to do with Brian's death." Jason gave his coven-mates a satisfied smug look as if to say, told you so.

She was convinced then and there if it wasn't for him, none of them would have ever known. "Let me out now. If you don't, my father…"

"What are you?" Karla asked. It was the serious ones you had to be careful of. They were strong enough in their faith that they couldn't be purged. They were the ones her father wanted to keep anyway. "An avenging angel?"

Connie shook her head in disbelief. They seemed to think she was working for someone else's side. "I am the daughter of the light-bringer, sent to purge your Haven of non-believers. There is no room in my father's kingdom for anyone less than those dedicated to Him…"

In the dark corner of a room, a small light went on and the theme song to the Exorcist began to play. It was someone's phone.

Jason broke the circle to answer it.

"Hello?" he said into the receiver, not caring that he sounded annoyed.

"Jason Tate?"

"Yes, speaking."

"It's Esther Branson," the woman on the other end said. "We need to talk. I've just gotten a message for you from Lucifer."

The room went cold and all the air went out of his chest. He was vaguely aware of his coven-mates staring at him, curious what was so important that he hadn't just hung up already. "Okay."

"He wants you to let his daughter go, and he will have her explain everything." Esther sounded quite calm about all of this. Then again, the woman had been communing with Daemons and other spirits for the better part of sixty years or more.

"Can I put you on speaker?" He turned to look and his coven and slowly shook his head.

"Of course, dear," Esther said, almost mother-like.

He tapped speaker and set the phone down on the altar. "Would you repeat what you just told me?

"Yes, Lucifer has just contacted me. Interrupted my dinner no less, with a message to you to let his daughter go and she would explain everything." Esther's voice echoed through the garage in an odd way.

"I'm not explaining myself to humans," the captured Daemon said. She put her arms across her chest in defiance.

"Your father says you will, Cresil. There is a reason he sent you here," the seeress said.

"Yes, to remove the lazy and impure from his legions on earth!"

"While that is your usual purpose, he's afraid he's not been straight with you," Esther said. "This time he needed to hide you from the Daemonic plane because he is worried his enemies would destroy you. Until he has that worked out, he was hoping Lucifer's Haven could be your home and that they could be your protectorates until he calls you back. He thinks it may be some time before you could come back…"

"You lie!" she spat.

"I wish it wasn't the case, but he knew you wouldn't have come willingly. He honestly never expected you would find Brian, of all people, impure. And you will need to rectify that mistake." The old seeress sounded matter-of-fact, as if this sort of conversation happened often in her world. For all Jason and the others knew – it did.

Connie sat silently, shocked for a few minutes, and sat down on the cushion. "I need to hear this from him, himself."

"Of course you do. That's why he contacted me to have Jason and his friends let you out of the spirit trap. So you could go have a talk with him about it." Esther's voice rang through the garage, tinny sounding.

Jason stepped next to the trap and folded back the rug, wiping away six inches of the circle, effectively releasing the Daemon they'd captured in the trap.

Connie stood and strode out of the trap with a frown on her face. "This isn't over yet."

Esther sighed the way a parent sighed when confronted with an errant teenager. "No, it isn't. There is the matter of raising Brian from the dead."

"Are you kidding?" This time it was Karla who spoke.

"He was an innocent victim in a ruse meant to keep Cresil, or Connie, here, so she'd be safe from harm," the seeress explained.

"So wait," Jason said. "You mean we're supposed to be protecting her?"

"Yes."

"And she can bring Brian back from the dead?"

"Of course, but she'll need the help of a sem priest," Esther said. "The sem priest will have a stronger bond with the death Daemonic than any of you, or her."

"But what if they've already embalmed him," Karla said, horrified.

"I called the coroner and the sheriff first. He's merely been on ice, so the wrong can still be righted." Esther's calm was beginning to make Jason feel queasy.

Scott took a step toward the phone as if that would make him heard better. "No one in the Order of Eurynome will do this."

"No, you're right," Esther said. "But as luck would have it, the person you want is Warren Leonard from Temple Apophis."

Jason swallowed, hard. Temple Apophis was one of the seedier, rowdy covens, and they weren't above practicing darker magick. *Like raising people from the dead*, he thought.

Even though he hadn't said anything aloud, Esther said, "Precisely. That's why you need Warren. He will do it. He and Belinda have no issues with Lucifer's Haven."

Jason looked over the coven, realizing that Connie was still there, glaring at him and the voice on the phone. "Then I guess we need to conjure Lucifer so Connie, or rather Cresil, can have a chat with her dad. Then I'll get in contact with Warren."

"Fine," Connie said, and then motioned to the spirit trap. "But get rid of that first."

With a shrug, Vic removed the cushion and the rug, and Scott grabbed some water from the hose and a stiff broom to wash away the magickal holding cell.

Meanwhile, Jason and Karla bid Esther goodbye.

Jason turned to Karla then. "How about you deal with the communication session with Cresil and Lucifer, and I call Warren."

Karla nodded gratefully. Calling Warren didn't sound fun to either of them, but Jason figured he'd get further with an acolyte of Apophis than she would. Then again, the balance of power in Temple Apophis had recently changed and it was now Belinda Applegate in charge.

"Whatever," he whispered to himself, leaving the garage and the coven behind him, and heading to his house with his cell phone in hand. He wondered briefly if they'd all be safe in the presence of the Daemon Cresil, but decided quickly that they could handle themselves and if they wanted to bring Brian back from the dead, time was of the essence.

7

She allowed the coven to re-construct the circle and invoke her father from the Daemonic plane. Her father answered the call almost immediately. He appeared in the thick, tangled tendrils of smoke rising off of the burners on the altar.

His physical manifestation, though not as solid and formed as her own, seemed to impress the young dedicants. *Hopefully serving to make them more serious and dedicated*, she thought.

They couldn't hear him, but she could. To them, Lucifer's voice sounded like howling wind, but to her, he sounded like he always did.

"Why the ruse?" she asked. "I know what the seer said…"

"Exactly as I told the seer," he answered. "You are too stubborn, Cresil. Would you have stayed on earth under protection of those who serve me there?"

She felt the physical flesh of her face contort into a frown and she realized he was right. She would have fought him tooth and nail, metaphorically of course, rather than come to earth and put herself willfully under the protection of humans. They were weak, and…

Her father seemed to know exactly what she was thinking. "They are not as weak as you think, Cresil. They would lay down their life for you if I asked them. I honestly did not expect you to find a lazy, impure one among them."

Frowning more deeply, she swallowed.

"He wasn't, was he?" The smoke figure of Lucifer loomed before her, leaning into her.

She couldn't lie to her own father. He'd see through it. "No."

"All the more reason you need to make things right. Now, deal with that and let me see if one of them can be easily possessed so I can speak directly to the priestess." The figure weighed his options carefully, then bolted forward in a stream of incense smoke, right up Vic's nose.

Vic leaned forward and coughed, wheezed, then straightened upright in a strange way. His eyes traveled over the coven members. He addressed Karla directly. "My Haven will protect my daughter, Cresil, and take her in among you for safety."

Karla visibly gulped and nodded before speaking. "Yes sir."

"Good. And Cresil, you will be kind and helpful to those who protect you, not using your powers or servant spirits to harm any of them. Is that clear?"

Cresil fought the urge to roll her eyes. "Yes. I promise."

"Very well. Then I will take my leave. Please take care to give this young man some water once I've gone." With that, Vic's mouth opened and dark smoke raced out of it, vanishing into the air.

Vic coughed a few times, and Scott grabbed him a beer since there weren't any glasses to bring him water. Vic dry heaved a few times and took the beer gratefully from Scott, downing half the bottle in one swig.

"Are you okay?" Jennifer asked.

Vic nodded. "It was really weird. Like I was in my body but so was he. I felt like I was being electrocuted."

Cresil groaned. "This is going to be hell."

She could tell the coven members were biting their tongues. "Look, I'm sorry I sent my servitors after Brian. I'll bring him back from the dead."

None of them said anything until finally, Karla spoke. "Well, what's done is done, it will be corrected, and we'll do as we've been asked."

"Wait," Vic said. "Does that mean we can't tell anyone she's Lucifer's daughter?"

"Duh," Jennifer said.

Karla laughed. "No. The fewer people who know she's Lucifer's daughter, the better. She's just Connie Hudson, new member. That goes for the elders, too."

"We're not telling the elders?" Scott asked.

"No."

"I don't think we should…" Scott was shaking his head.

"Scott," Karla said, "We can't tell anyone. Not even my mother, aunt, or uncle. The fewer people who know, the better," she repeated.

He nodded with reluctance.

"No one, Scott," Karla said with a warning tone.

Cresil gave him a hopeful look, then with a deep breath, went over to the fridge and helped herself to one of the beers. The coven just watched. Finally, she turned to them. "Well, now that I know why I'm actually here, I won't be any trouble."

Jennifer said, "You shouldn't be alone either. Maybe you should move in with Karla and I. We have an extra room."

Karla shot her a surprised look.

Jennifer shrugged. "It makes sense. We need to keep her close. If something happens to her while she's too far from us, how would we know?"

"How are we supposed to protect her from Daemons?"

Cresil groaned again. "That's the thing. When I'm among humans, Daemons can't detect me unless they know where I am. So as long as I'm here, hiding among The Haven as one of you, they won't find me."

"All the same, I'd feel better if you were close," Jennifer said.

"You can come stay with me," Vic said, bouncing his eyebrows.

"Oh, unholy Christ Vic!" Karla shook her head. "Really?"

Cresil smirked.

8

Warren Leonard answered his phone on the first ring. "Hello."

For some reason, Jason half expected him to answer differently, with something wittier. "Hi, uh, Warren?"

"Yeah."

"This is Jason from Lucifer's Haven. We have a problem and you're the only one who can help us." He waited for a sarcastic remark or a snort. Neither came.

"I heard about Brian," was all he said. "Sorry to hear about your loss."

"Thank you, but actually that's what I need to talk to you about. You're going to think I'm crazy…"

"Try me."

There was a brief moment of silence.

Finally, Jason came out with it. "Brian was accidentally killed by a Daemon whose job it is to rid Lucifer's covens of the lazy and impure. Cresil is her name. She didn't mean to kill Brian, but she did. She can reverse it, but she needs the help of a Sem Priest with a good rapport with the death Daemonic."

He felt like an ass saying it.

"I see why you called me."

"Order of Eurynome would never…"

"I know," Warren said, then decidedly added, "I'll do it. Where and when?"

Immediate panic washed over Jason. He hadn't really worked that part out. "Um, the morgue in half an hour?"

"Okay. I'll be there. Belinda might want to come."

"That's fine," Jason said, not knowing if it was or not. After all, he doubted Esther had shared with the Coroner and sheriff, Connie's true nature, and he hadn't really told Warren that Connie was merely Cresil in the flesh. But he would have to know she was the Daemon.

"I'll see you then," Warren said.

"Thanks man."

They hung up and Jason took a deep breath. He had to go back out there and while he wanted to take his time, he knew he needed to hurry.

Entering the garage, he found the entire coven, along with Connie, sitting around drinking beer. "I take it everything went well?"

"We were just talking about who Connie will stay with," Vic said.

"We can talk about that later. She and I have to meet Warren at the morgue." Jason looked at Connie. "He's going to have to know who you are. Which means Belinda will know, too."

"Oh great! That means the whole fucking town is going to know! I thought we couldn't tell anyone?" Scott glared at them. "How are we going to keep this from everyone?"

"I'll ask Warren to keep it between him and Belinda."

"Will it be that easy?" Karla asked.

Connie rolled her eyes. "I could just erase their memories."

"No," Jason said. "We're not erasing anyone's memories. I have a feeling we can trust Warren and Belinda. Besides, isn't Belinda the one in line to replace Esther? Discretion kind of comes along with the territory."

Mumbles of agreement ran through the garage.

"Let's go then." Connie tossed her empty beer bottle in the recycling bucket and she followed Jason out to his car.

"So what do we do now?" he asked her as they drove toward the morgue. It was a good twenty-minute drive and there was no reason to go in silence.

Cresil stared at the road straight ahead. "Your necromancer will invoke his death Daemonic and together, we will resurrect Brian."

"That's rather unspecific."

She turned to him, annoyed. "It will draw his spirit back to his body. The death Daemonic will put the soul back inside, I will send energy to his brain and restore his memory, and we will heal his body."

"So he won't be some freaky zombie then?"

"What is a zombie?" The look on her face was almost comical.

Jason smiled. "The undead."

"Like vampires?"

"Yeah, except they don't drink blood, they eat brains."

Much to his surprise, the Daemon laughed with genuine amusement. "I think we will settle with him being human as he was before. All he'll remember was walking home."

A few minutes of silence passed between them.

Jason couldn't stand the silence. "So the group decided you need to live with someone in the coven?"

She snorted. "Apparently I need to be protected and they think me living with a coven member would keep me safer."

"I suppose it makes sense. If we're responsible for you…"

"Won't it raise suspicion though?"

He nodded. "You have a point. I think you should be able to stay where you are. In the meantime, you should get a cell phone and if anything bad happens, call us."

"Will that help?"

He gave her a curious look. "What do you mean?"

"If I'm being attacked will it really help if I call someone?"

"Good point. Maybe you should be staying with one of our coven-mates."

"Do you really think you humans could protect me from other Daemons?" She yawned then, a confused look on her face.

"It's been a long day. After we're done, I'll take you home so you can get some rest." He paused, considering her question. "And yes, I think Karla and Jennifer could probably offer some protection. Not to mention, you could really use some lessons in being a human female."

She lifted an eyebrow. "You don't think I'm human enough?"

"Haven't you wondered how I suspected you weren't human to begin with?"

"Hmm. I guess I hadn't considered it. You think I need lessons?"

Jason laughed, realizing how it all fell into place now. "Yes, you even made Eve Winters raise an eyebrow."

"I see."

"Don't take it to mean I'm insulting you. It's just an observation." He pulled into the morgue parking lot, noticing the black Subaru with the Apophis symbol in the back window. "Looks like Warren is here."

Jason pulled into a parking space right next to Warren. They got out of the car and Warren and Belinda got out of their car. There in the parking lot the members of two covens met.

Jason held out his hand. "I'm Jason and this is Connie. She's our coven healer, currently imbued with the power of Lucifer to bring Brian back once your death Daemonic is invoked."

Connie gave Jason an impressed look, then nodded politely at the Temple Apophis leaders.

"Did you say the Daemon's name was Cresil?" Belinda asked.

Both Jason and Connie nodded.

"The Daemonic Dictionary says she was a Christian creation. A Daemon of sloth and impurity." Belinda smiled.

Connie lifted an eyebrow. "Actually, a Daemon who seeks out and destroys sloth and impurity. Usually for the Daemon she serves under, who happens to be Lucifer. She's his daughter actually."

"I see." Belinda narrowed her eyes at Connie.

Jason felt slightly sick. Apophis' seeress knew. "Well, regardless, it was a mistake. Cresil didn't mean to hurt Brian, and that's why Lucifer wanted the wrong righted and we're here to do just that. And we'd be really thankful if maybe this didn't get out…."

Warren and Belinda exchanged glances and then Warren nodded. "We won't say anything. It's no one's business. Besides, I'd just as soon it not get out that I'm helping to raise the dead. That's not a practice looked kindly upon."

"Everyone already knows Brian is dead," Belinda said. "Don't you think they might wonder what happened?"

"They must have been mistaken. Or perhaps it was just a nasty rumor," Connie suggested.

"I bet everyone would buy nasty rumor," Belinda agreed.

For whatever reason, Belinda and Connie seemed to get on rather well, and it was starting to make Jason wary.

"Let's go in," Warren said.

Inside, the security guard on duty happened to be a friend of the Coroners, and they'd already been cleared to go "*into the freezer*" on Esther Branson's recommendation.

"I was told no one was to know about this and I saw nothing." The guard went back to his magazine. The new issue of *Fly Fishing*.

"Thanks for that," Jason said, giving the man a grateful smile.

He didn't return it, just pointed them toward *the freezer* and went back to reading.

The room they entered was cold, and on the table was a covered body. The toe tag said *Blake* on it. Jason felt his chest tighten. He hadn't wanted to see his friend like this. His feet were already gray looking.

"Not a zombie right?" he whispered to Connie.

Belinda and Warren gave him a weird look.

"Not a zombie," Connie assured him. "Come on. Now which death Daemonic will we be working with?"

"Anubis," Warren said, as if it should have been obvious.

"Oh, of course," Connie said.

"All right," Warren said. "Everyone stay calm and focused."

With that, he pulled the sheet off of Brian. Jason turned away. There was no reason he needed to look. This was Connie and Warren's area of expertise. The only reason he was there was as a mediator between Connie and Warren. The only reason Belinda was there was as moral support for Warren.

So it surprised Jason when Belinda gently took him by the arm and led him to the door. They stepped into the hallway, closing the door behind them, leaving Connie and Warren to deal with Brian's resurrection.

"I could tell that was not a good place for you to be," Belinda said, smiling. "I never expected a Daemon to take one of our forms."

"You…"

"She's obviously Cresil." Belinda shrugged. "Though I'm not sure she's actually here for the reason you think she is."

"I can't talk about that. I hope you understand."

She nodded. "I understand. They don't need our help in there. Maybe we should find a blanket or some clothes for Brian. He's going to need them."

"Oh shit." He hadn't even thought of that.

"I have a suspicion that our security guard friend might be able to help." She started back toward the front desk.

Thankful to be doing something, anything but waiting, Jason followed the seeress, whose hair was currently dyed black with blonde tips.

Sure enough, the security guard begrudgingly found them a pair of sweat pants and a t-shirt and handed them over with, "I don't want to know."

They went back to the freezer and stayed in the hall. No sound emerged from behind the closed door and that made Jason nervous.

"Necromancy isn't a loud art," she told him, sensing his worry. "Also, the security guard is a member of The Blackrose Coven. He knows what we're up to, but he will keep it to himself."

"Thank Lucifer for that." Jason let out a big sigh.

Belinda followed suit, taking her own deep breath as if to ease the tension.

The door cracked open drawing both their attention to Connie, who poked her head out. "Clothes?"

Belinda handed them over with a smile, and Connie took them, wearing an equally broad smile.

"She seems nice enough," Belinda said after the door closed.

Jason snorted. "She's terribly inhuman once you get to know her. She's still working out how to behave socially."

"I can see how that would be an issue."

The door opened again, and Warren came out first, looking a little pale. Belinda rushed to him, checking him over to make sure he was okay. He was, of course, but she had to fuss being that she was his fiancé and all that.

It was Connie who helped Brian, barefoot and swimming in the too short sweats and an oversized t-shirt into the hall. Brian was no longer gray. He looked pink and healthy, just disoriented.

"Hey bro," Jason said, almost afraid to touch him. But he slipped an arm under his arm anyway, and helped him along, taking the weight off of Connie.

Luckily Brian's skin was warm.

"Where am I," Brian asked.

"I think you had too much to drink, bro. Hit your head. We're going home, okay?" Then Jason realized he didn't have Brian's key to his apartment and he wasn't even sure if Brian still had an apartment to head back to. "Actually, how about I take you to my place. You can sleep it off."

Brian seemed placated by this and limped along, still bleary-eyed and exhausted. The security guard didn't even glance up as they passed and they left through the front doors.

When they reached the parking lot, Jason overheard the women as Belinda turned to Connie, "Such an elaborate ruse to keep a close Daemonic eye on The Thirteen Covens."

"It's not the Covens we're worried about. It's what they conjure from beyond into the physical world. Things they can't control."

"Things you can control?"

"Would it be so strange if I could?"

"I suppose not."

With that, Belinda and Warren said goodbye and got into their own car, and Connie helped Jason put Brian in the backseat of his car. Then they got in and headed back into town. Brian fell immediately to sleep, which Connie assured Jason was fine.

"So is it us protecting you or you protecting us?" he finally asked her.

"Would it matter either way?" she asked, then smiled at him. "Besides, you heard what my father said, do you have reason to doubt him?"

"No, I just overheard the seeress…"

"She means well," Connie said, that small smile still playing on her lips.

That's how the Daemon Cresil, Lucifer's daughter, became a member of Lucifer's Haven.

SHADOW MARBAS

1

Ellie looked into the crystal ball on the coffee table next to her. The swirling smoke cleared and there in the orb she saw Jacob talking to a young blonde woman. All she ever wanted was a little alone time with him. When he'd fended off her advances she found another way to get him into her bed. It was under the guise of sex magick, but that hadn't worked either, and it really pissed her off. She pouted, running her manicured nails through the length of her long black tresses. Her husband Marcus didn't mind. They had an open relationship, and he had other women all the time. The only thing she'd insisted on was not allowing emotional affairs. Physical, fine, emotional no. Truth was she had no emotional attachment to Jacob outside of friendship. She just wanted to have him. He was physically attractive and she wanted him to want her as much as she wanted him. No man had ever refused her before now. She seethed at the thought.

The front door slammed as Marcus came in from clearing the gutters. The sound shattered her thoughts and caused the crystal to go clear. Martin 'Six' was with him. Six had been Marcus' right hand guy for a few years now. "El, what are you doing? Where's lunch?"

She pulled away from the crystal ball and jumped up. The beef stew she'd made was still simmering on the stove.

"Come on," she said. The men followed. She rolled her eyes wondering that if she died tomorrow if Marcus and his buddies would even be able to feed themselves. She had to lead them to it and dish it out. *Lazy bastards.*

She'd even left the damn bowls on the counter for them, for Satan's sake. Annoyed, she filled the bowls. They sat down at the kitchen table. *Good Gods!* By Marbas and Lilith, they weren't even going to take the bowls from her. She'd have to bring it to them, too. She shook her head, took the two filled, steaming bowls of stew and set one bowl in front of each of them. Then she got spoons, napkins, butter, a knife, and a few slices of bread. "You'll have to butter the bread yourselves."

"Yeah, okay." Marcus mumbled, then went on talking about restoring the Mustang. Something about mufflers. He and Six were Mustang guys.

Six just nodded, his attention completely on Marcus, oblivious to Ellie's presence.

That was all she got. No thank you, fuck you, or anything else for that matter. "If you want more it's on the stove. Help yourselves," she said, going back into the living room. Men.

That's when Six's girlfriend, Nicole, showed up. Just walked right in the front door. The entire coven came and went as they pleased. "Hey El, Six here?"

"Kitchen," Ellie said, waving her hand absently toward the kitchen. "There's beef stew on the stove and a bowl in the cupboard if you want some. Help yourself."

"Nah, thanks," Nicole said, heading toward the kitchen.

"Suit yourself," she whispered under her breath. If you asked her, Nicole could stand to eat a thing or two. No one who ate real food was that skinny. Sure, Ellie wasn't scrawny, she was about average size, perhaps ten pounds over where she should be. But she was comfortable with herself and unlike Nicole, she wasn't afraid to eat something now and again.

"That fucking asshole, Ellie!" came Marcus from the kitchen.

She groaned. "What?"

"Come here, you have to hear this."

Reluctantly she headed back to the kitchen.

He didn't even wait for her to get there. "So get this, evidently Jacob cursed us."

She didn't believe it. It sounded too far-fetched. "And you know this because?"

Nicole's eyes went wide. "I saw him buy Valefor and Focalor oil, red candles, and a black cord from Black Raven."

Ellie blinked a few times. "And this proves he cursed us how?"

"What do you mean?" Nicole asked, looking positively baffled. "Of course he cursed us."

"No it just means he was stocking up. Red candles are used for more than cursing and Valefor is his Patron. Not to mention Focalor can be used for protection. Even if he did curse us, do you see anything bad happening? When you guys were cleaning the gutters, tons of opportunities to fall and break your necks, but you didn't." Ellie rolled her eyes.

"Yeah, maybe, but I'm not taking any chances," Marcus said. "I'll go throw a curse right back at him." With that, Marcus and Six stood up and with Nicole at their heels, filed out of the back door and headed toward the barn turned temple on the far side of the property.

"Suit yourselves," she called after them. "I'm not wasting my energy on something so stupid and petty."

Besides, she liked Jacob. He was a nice guy. Too nice. He refused to perform theophany rituals, which she didn't really understand, and he wasn't into group sex magick, which in a way she did understand. Some people were like that. A few other members had politely bowed out of that ritual, too. But for Jacob, it was the last straw. He'd told Marcus and Ellie that if this was the direction the group was headed in, he needed to move on. Yes, it did piss her off, but mostly because he didn't reciprocate her desires. She was a big girl; she'd get over it. Besides, if he wasn't into theophany then maybe he didn't need to be a member of the group. She was actually glad he was gone. A pang of jealous anger ran through her then.

She looked down toward the temple, grabbed her jacket and followed. "Hey, wait for me!"

Maybe she did want to curse Jacob after all. Maybe a little.

2

They were after him. Just like in the old days when a witch betrayed his coven, they went after him. Now, he was left looking over his shoulder just because he'd disagreed with Marcus and Ellie and Shadow Marbas. No one disagreed with the high priest or priestess without paying a price. It hadn't helped that he'd thrown a curse straight at them. He regretted that now. Adam's coven offered some protection, but with existing tensions between the Cult of Lucifuge and Temple Apophis it was doubtful the Cult of Lucifuge would be able to offer him much protection.

Okay, so Jacob hadn't *really* cursed them. Just sent back all the negativity they'd given him. That's usually what he did in situations like that. It wasn't in his nature to practice execration magick unless it was something major, like bitch-slapping a politician, and helping murderers and rapists get what they deserved a little quicker. Not that he'd known any murderers or rapists but there were times Ellie and a few of the other women of Shadow Marbas would get an idea and decide to curse serial rapists and killers based on nothing more than newspaper articles. It never failed that the criminals were always caught within a few days of the curse. One was even found dead after one of the women he kidnapped got hold of his gun and used it on him. Jacob never felt bad about cursing people like that. He never felt bad cursing the likes of beady-eyed politicians who made policies that hurt the little guy either. Political based magick was a favorite among Shadow Marbas members. They always got the politicians they wanted elected to office and took down the ones they agreed weren't fit to lead anything or speak for anyone. Together, if they agreed on something, they were a force to be reckoned with. Which is why he was afraid they were cursing him. Not all victims they cursed died. Some just had a really hard time finding work. Others were stricken down with wasting diseases that would kill them slowly. Others still would find themselves alone or crippled or whatever. In Jacob's case, the jobs had started drying up. The construction company he usually worked for didn't need him right now.

So the curse he threw was really just a deflection. He was convinced the saying that the negativity you send out will come back to you three-fold was a phrase coined by someone who'd been cursed and who'd sent it back with delightfully good results. So yes, it was paranoid on his part for sending their negativity back to them, but even more paranoid of them for cursing him to begin with.

He pulled up to his house and looked around before putting the car in park, turning off the engine, getting out, and finally locking it. Now it was time for a perimeter check. He looked over his lawn for cursing jars or freshly turned dirt. Sadly, the rain from earlier would have washed away any sign of tinctures, powders or oils that may have been poured onto his property. He investigated the flower beds next to the porch. Next door, old lady Branson, the seer, was locking the door. She didn't live in the house anymore. Nowadays she rented it out, and the most recent tenants, an older couple, had just moved out.

"Hey, Esther," he said with a brief smile. "How are you this fine, soggy day?"

She smiled back at him. "Just fine Jacob. What are you doing?"

"Checking for signs of disease in the lawn and flower beds," he lied. He knew she probably knew he was lying, but he didn't care. It was easier than trying to explain his coven woes to her.

She raised an eyebrow but didn't question him. Instead she said, "I've taken out an ad to rent the house again."

A cold chill washed over him. Sure, it was paranoid to think anyone from Shadow Marbas would move in next door just to torment him or keep an eye on him, but he wouldn't put it past them. "Oh yeah? Can you rent it to a nice single woman this time?"

She let out a light note of laughter that seemed to brighten the gray autumn day. "I will do what I can. You're too nice a young man to be single at your age."

"Well..." It was all he could think of to say. "Well I hope you're able to rent it out quickly."

She looked warily up at the sky, pulled her tan, knee length coat around her, and ventured down the front steps and sidewalk to her waiting car. "If you'd keep an eye on it for me I'd really appreciate it."

Jacob nodded. "You got it, Esther. Thanks for letting me know. I'll see you around."

The old woman nodded politely, got into her tan BMW, and drove away with a wave and a smile. Jacob went back to looking for any signs of a curse. He checked the front porch, the sides of the house, and gave the backyard the same consideration he'd given the front. So far nothing looked amiss. With that, he went inside and locked the door behind him, disarming and rearming the security alarm. He took a deep breath and looked around. It all felt right. With a sigh he relaxed, noticing the answering machine light was blinking. He walked past the phone table, clicking play as he went.

The machine let out a beep. "You have two new messages. First Message..." The voice of his mother blared back at him. "Jacob, you need to call me. I want to know if you're coming out for your father's birthday. Don't ignore me, I'm your mother. Call me back, love you. Bye."

He cringed. He hadn't planned on going home to Iowa for a mere birthday, but he hadn't been home in four years. However, if he was going to go he knew he'd rather go out for

Thanksgiving or Yule even though he didn't like the idea of a long drive in snow and ice.

The machine beeped again "Next message." Eve Winter's voice toned, tinny on the machine. "This message is for Jacob Mallory. This is Eve over at Black Raven. I finally got in that specialty sleeping balm you ordered. Have a good day and I look forward to seeing you soon."

The machine finished and clicked off.

While to an outsider the fight between Jacob and his coven may have seemed stupid, it wasn't really. Jacob had morals and ethics and there were certain lines he wouldn't cross. Ellie and Marcus knew this about him, and yet they pushed him toward crossing the line anyway. Why did they want to perform a theophany operation anyway? Not to mention the whole sex magick aspect to the rite. Jacob wasn't against sex magick in general if it was one-on-one. One person with someone he cared about. Yes, that was probably a prudish or Judeo-Christian way of thinking, but it was honestly how he felt. Group sex and being free with oneself like that had never been his cup of tea. And again, why did they want to raise a Daemon into the corporeal world anyway? But that was Ellie and Marcus and quite frankly he wasn't sure how much of it was Ellie and how much was Marcus. He sometimes thought Ellie was the one running the show and Marcus was just another whipped guy who would do whatever his wife wanted. Yet Marcus seemed excited about the prospect. Probably because Ellie was letting him have sex with other women. All in the name of sex magick, of course. Condoned infidelity. No, Jacob was a one-woman kind of man.

One woman, hold the Daemonic manifestation.

Certainly, it was true he hadn't been with anyone in two years. Not since Kelly Rayes, and she'd dumped him for some trucker passing through and moved to Wyoming of all gods-awful places. Even that relationship hadn't been serious. Come to think of it, none of his relationships had ever been serious. He seemed to attract or be attracted to women who were emotionally unavailable and who were only looking for a man to give them what they wanted in the bedroom, take them out once in a while, and perform chores as needed. He let out a deep sigh and looked out the dining room window. That's when he saw it. The six-inch poppet sat wedged in the window frame just outside, its sewn on eyes staring at him through the glass. Around its tiny neck, a noose made of narrow frayed rope. How had he missed it? Then he realized it was likely hidden behind the snowberry bush that he allowed to grow feral the past few years. He liked how it looked right there on the side of the house, but it did hide that part of the window frame. Clever bastards.

The poppet was likely Ellie's handiwork. With a groan, he went to the window, unlocked it, and opened the sash, carefully pulling the poppet into the house and closing the window again. He looked over the poppet and quickly decided he'd have to burn it.

The doorbell rang and he jumped, tossing the poppet onto the dining room table. He looked out the peephole to find Corrina, the woman who lived across the street, standing there. She was a member of Lucifer's Haven and kept to herself. But she was always kind and never had a bad word to say about anyone. She seemed to get along with everyone too, regardless their coven affiliation. At least twice a month she would stop by to bring him pastries or bread she'd made, which he always accepted graciously. First because he was a bachelor and rarely got homemade goodies, and second because Corrina was a damn fine cook. Recently he'd seen a young blonde woman going in and out of Corrina's house. Perhaps a niece or friend was staying with her. He opened the door, immediately realizing she didn't have baked goods with her this time.

"Hi Jake," she said, preferring his shortened name to the more formal *Jacob*.

He didn't mind. "Hi Corrina, how are you?"

"I'm good. I actually stopped by because my friend who's staying with me, Connie, you've probably seen her?" She didn't wait for an answer. "She saw someone with a ladder over by your window this morning after you left for work. Two women. We thought you should know," she said, a marked look of concern on her face.

"Yeah, I found it," he said, then realized he'd now have to explain. "I'm sure you heard that I pissed off Ellie and Marcus?"

A look of surprise washed over Corrina's smooth face. For a woman in her thirties, Corrina didn't look a day over twenty-five. "Oh. No, I hadn't heard that. Is there anything I can do to help?"

That was Corrina. Always helpful. She'd even offered to take in his mail and water his plants when he went away with friends for a week last summer. He'd let her do it and had no complaints. Marcus had gotten pissed at him for it. Not because anyone expected that Corrina was the type searching for gossip, but because when you lived in the tri-county area you were naturally suspicious of most of the other covens even though the postal workers, police, grocers, and so on, all seemed to have their own coven affiliations.

"No. But thanks. Right now, I'm under protection of Lucifuge for all the good it seems to be doing. I think they're too embroiled in their issue with Apophis to be of any help." He shook his head because he hadn't even bothered to call any of the Lucifuge elders. The last time he called, he'd gotten the brush off with, *just deflect anything negative they throw at you with a deflection spell.* So that's what he'd done.

"I've heard a few other covens are pissed at Apophis at the moment, too. And Esther," Corrina said with a sad sigh.

"Personally, I think Belinda will be fine as a seer to replace Esther when the time comes. She's never been nasty or vindictive to anyone, but people are still discussing the possibility of recruiting an outsider to take Esther's place. They're all *so* worried about Apophis knowing their business. As if any of it is *that* secret to begin with."

"Well, it's not like Apophis did anything. I sometimes wish all this stupid infighting would stop. I mean, does anyone even remember, or care, why the original coven split to begin with?" He really didn't know. He hadn't grown up in any of the covens like so many around here had. Instead, he joined it when he was twenty-two, because when you moved here as an outsider, it was only a matter of time before you had to pick a side. He had become fast friends with Marcus and Six. So when the time came where he felt forced to choose, the decision to initiate into Shadow Marbas had been easy. Little did he know then how fickle they could be.

"It's a long story. If you want to hear it, you can come have dinner with Connie and I in about a half an hour. I have beer," she offered with a warm smile. Again, she didn't wait for an answer. "Come over. I've got a roast in the crock pot and a loaf of bread in the oven. You can meet Connie. She's new in town, so it's good for her to meet people."

He considered it for a moment. Every time he'd asked Marcus and Six about the original coven's demise they'd say something stupid like, "Well, one guy took too much power and that was that, you know?" He'd learned early on that it wasn't a question you asked if you wanted a straight answer, so the lure of someone freely offering to tell the story was strong. "Okay."

"Good. It should be ready in thirty minutes," she said, obviously delighted in his acceptance of the invitation. She started toward her own house but stopped and turned back, "Oh, and Connie said to bring it and we'll destroy it."

"What?"

"Whatever the women put up by your window. If you bring it over, Connie will eliminate it. That's her *super power* as *they* say. Destroying bad juju." She beamed a bright smile up and him and then turned back toward her house.

He found himself staring after her, but then closed the door. The doll wasn't going anywhere for now. He at least had time to change and clean himself up a little before heading across the street.

Once he felt respectable and cleaned up and before he left the house, he grabbed two things: A bottle of wine, because his mother taught him it was impolite to accept an invitation and then show up at someone's house empty-handed, and the poppet. Hopefully it hadn't been in place long enough to do any damage.

3

Connie was quiet, mid-twenties and blonde, and the way she looked at him unsettled him a little. Corrina did most of the talking between random bites of her dinner. Mostly the topic stayed on the weather, cooking, and great places to eat around town and in the surrounding areas.

Finally, he decided he'd have to direct the conversation to what she'd promised. Not that he didn't appreciate the home cooked meal and the company because he did. But also because he'd really been looking forward to finally hearing a story he'd been deprived of for the better part of eight years. "So Connie, I'm kind of an outsider too. I moved here in my early twenties for a good paying job with a construction firm and the promise of a house. What brought you here?"

"Lucifer," she said matter-of-fact. "I was in a coven down in Massachusetts, wanted to move to upstate New York, and I called ahead and got an interview with the Lucifer's Haven elders."

"Oh, nice." A pang of disappointment tugged at him. Everyone who moved here seemed to already know about the covens and came here with the intent to join one. He was one of the few who had entered the tri-county area blind to anything about witches or magick. The downside being he always felt like the uneducated noob around the table, and some people were more than happy to treat him that way.

But Corrina and Connie weren't like that.

"Connie wanted to live with a coven-mate and I was tired of living alone in this house, so she decided to move in with me. I love having a roommate, and someone to cook for," Corrina said, then motioned to his empty plate. "Let me get you some more."

Without waiting for him to decline or accept, she already had his plate in hand and crossed the kitchen to the crock pot to dish him more. She continued, "I promised to tell you the story of how the thirteen covens came to be. I don't think Connie's heard it either, have you?"

"Vague bits and pieces," the young woman next to him said with a shrug.

"Well you should both know the story because it's kind of like a rite of passage to hear it. Or it was in my family." Corrina had been born into Lucifer's Haven, and her mother was still a member even though she was retired and lived most of the year in a house overlooking Saratoga Lake. She would drive her over for major rites, like the big spring and autumn festivals Lucifer's Haven always held.

Jacob had met Corrina's mother once, two years ago in the autumn, and she was every bit as pleasant as Corrina herself.

Corrina returned to the table with another plate of food and set it in front of Jacob, then looked at Connie's plate, noticing it was still half full. "Is it bad?"

"Oh, no," Connie said. "It's fantastic. I'm just full from the two meatloaf sandwiches you left me for lunch."

This seemed to placate Corrina's need to feed people to stuffed, and she took a long drink from her wine glass. Only then did she begin the story. "Okay, so the thing you need to know about the original coven was it was ran by a man named Myron Therion Blackwood. His descendent is the Magister Thaddeus Blackwood of The Magi. Myron Blackwood's right hand guy was a man named James Watts, whose descendent is, of course, Neal Watts of The Watch. Anyway, there were thirteen core members of the coven and everyone else was in the outer circle. In nineteen-fifty-two, Myron and James had a falling out. Apparently, Myron's magickal tastes veered toward darker pursuits like curses, using corpses for necromancy and that type of thing, whereas James wanted to hold everyone, including Myron, to rigorous social behavioral standards. James was also big on titles, ranks, and the whole chain-of-command. "

She paused and took another drink, draining her wine glass. Once she was sure Jacob was eating, she went on. "Myron looked down his nose at anyone who didn't practice magick, and those who practiced magick but who had ethical quandaries with digging up corpses and the like. A rift began to develop between them until Myron couldn't stand James and James couldn't stand Myron. So initially, when the coven split, it split into two groups. Those who followed Myron and those who followed James. Those with a more religious bend to their practice followed James and those who were into magick tended toward Myron's side."

She stopped long enough to pour Connie and herself more wine. She glanced at Jacob's beer, which was half full still.

Jacob said nothing, just ate and listened. It sounded like the typical wars that went on in the esoteric community. So much so, in fact, that it was almost laughable.

Corrina continued. "Myron and James both became power hungry, each trying to rule over his half of the original coven with an iron fist. The story goes, how I've heard all my life anyway, that both were tyrannical in their behavior. Anyone who spoke up against either man was ostracized and left to fend for him or herself. The remaining eleven members of the inner circle eventually fell out with James and Myron and picked up their own groups of sympathizers along the way. Then, back in nineteen fifty four, in October that year, something terrible happened. Myron and James, and five of the other original thirteen were found murdered within two days of each other."

Her eyes darted from Connie and Jacob as if to make sure she had their attention completely. "Everyone involved with the original coven believed that someone had evoked an ancient devil to exact vengeance on the original thirteen. Or so they all thought. Naturally everyone began blaming the remaining six members of the original inner-circle. People started taking sides and several non-inner circle members died before the devil that had been conjured went back to hell."

Jacob could feel the look of disbelief on his face. "So wait. Who did it?"

Corrina shrugged. "To this day no one knows. Some of the Lucifer's Haven elders insist that Myron was the one who raised a devil to kill James, and then that same devil turned on him. The other victims were allegedly just people who *got in the way*. But who knows. I do know that it's the reason everyone is always so suspicious of those outside their own coven, and yet we all have to live and work together and trust that members of other covens will show up to help when there's a fire, or someone needs an ambulance, or when someone goes to the hospital. You never know who will accuse you of something nefarious. We still haven't grown past that in all these years."

"Over sixty years ago…" Jacob said thoughtfully.

Neither of the women replied.

They finished dinner in somber silence as if speaking of the dead had conjured them forth from the other side. When they were done, the women cleared the table while Jacob finished his beer.

Finally, with her hands on her hips, and in a rather decidedly fashion, Connie said, "So let's get down to business."

Jacob followed her gaze to the poppet sitting on the old oak sideboard next to the dining room table.

Corrina grabbed the thing and turned it over in her hands. "Hand-made poppet."

She started toward the door leading to the backyard. Jacob and Connie followed.

Once they were outside, Corrina handed the doll to Connie and then crossed her arms over her chest as if to ward away the cold, even though the air felt humid and comfortable.

Connie addressed them both. "Well, I don't feel an actual curse emanating from it. It appears to be just a general sense of anger toward Jacob. It probably made them feel better to do the curse. Had they wanted to hurt you, they could have." She looked directly at Jacob then. "The whole intent behind this effigy is to let you know they're angry with you. I also suspect they want you back. They want you to apologize, of course, but they want you to return to them with a change in your opinions and attitude."

"I already knew that," Jacob mumbled, leaning against the railing of the deck. "So there's no *actual* curse attached?"

The blond shook her head. "No."

Then Connie did the most extraordinary thing. She held the doll in her left hand, and the thing burst into blue flame, disintegrating into ash almost instantly. A gust of wind from nowhere grabbed the gray ash and it vanished into the air completely.

Jacob jumped, wide-eyed. "Whoa!"

Corrina didn't seem surprised at all. "That's it?"

With a shrug, Connie nodded. "That's it."

He realized his jaw was hanging open and made a conscious effort to close it. "Damn."

"I like you, Jacob," Connie said.

His eyebrows lifted.

"As a human being, I mean." Connie gave him a strange smile. She was definitely odd. There was something off about her that Jacob could sense, but couldn't quite put his finger on. It was her demeanor. It seemed practiced, even forced.

She doesn't have good social skills, he thought.

"I think what Connie is saying is that you should come over more often. We're having a barbeque Friday night. You should come. Some other friends from Lucifer's Haven will be here. Jason and Seth from The Haven, along with Mike and Sharon from Tiamat-Leviathan. Do you know them?"

Corrina was trying to feed him again. He smiled. "Maybe I will. I'll play it by ear, see how I feel Friday after work." *If I have a job by then*, he added silently.

"Do you want another beer?"

Glancing at his watch he noticed it was only quarter to eight. "Sure, why not?"

With a happy smile, Corrina disappeared inside to grab them more drinks. Connie seemed to be studying him in a practiced way.

"So is Haileyville everything you expected so far?" he asked her. It was small talk, yes, but at least it was light considering the dark subjects they'd been discussing.

"I haven't quite decided yet. I'm still meeting people and gaining my bearings."

"Where are you working?"

She frowned. "I haven't decided if I am going to work or not. I have, what you call, a *trust fund*?"

Just the wording. So. Weird. He shook off the feeling. "Well, I know the dentist, Doctor Frank, is looking for a new receptionist. It might be a good way to help you get to know more people."

"Ah," she said as if the idea had never occurred to her. Then she said the strangest thing ever. "So the dentist. That's a human who looks at your teeth, right?"

A chill washed over him and he nodded.

She forced a laugh.

Just then, Corrina reappeared with three beers and handed one to Connie and one to him. He took it, fighting the urge to cross his arms over his chest and hug his shoulders just

126

as Corrina had done before the poppet had ignited in Connie's hand.

"Don't worry about Marcus and Ellie," Corrina said, dragging his thoughts away from Connie's oddities. "They'll come around."

She always seemed to see the best in people.

"It's not them who would have to come around. It's me," he corrected her. "Since that's not going to happen, I suppose I need to either consider selling my house and moving away, or joining one of the other twelve covens."

He took a swig of beer. It was going to get worse before it got better and he couldn't help but feel a sense of dread. Ellie Ayers would not be refused. She didn't give up easily.

4

The curse wasn't working. All reports back from various coven members told her that Jacob was fine, and that he'd been seen, just last night, at a barbecue attended by people across four or five covens. Maybe the situation required a different approach.

She sat across from Nicole whose entire focus was on her new manicure. The red and black lacquer on her acrylic nails had been done in a spider web pattern. Black nail, red webbing.

"You know, I'm angry with Jacob but I don't want to hurt him," Ellie started.

Nicole merely glanced up. "You just want to fuck him."

"You would, too, if Six said yes." Ellie sighed.

Finally, Nicole stopped looking at her nails. "That's why the curse didn't work you know. None of us really wants to hurt Jake. He's our brother and we all like him. Even Six said last night that he wished Jake would pull his head out of his ass. He's just being unreasonable."

Nicole really was more than just a pretty face. Her outward looks and frequent primping often hid what an emotionally intelligent woman she was.

"Perhaps we've gone about it the wrong way." The idea in Ellie's brain grew, and a sly grin slid across her lips.

Crossing her arms over her chest, Nicole gave her *that* look. The one that said, *what are you planning now?*

"What? I was just thinking a little lust and friendship spell. Increase his need to have his friends back since the guys have been moping since he left, and a lust spell for me so he'll give me exactly what I want when I want it." The sly grin stayed firmly put.

A slow smile spread over Nicole's lips. "You are absolutely devious El. Yeah, I think even Marcus and Six would agree to that."

Ellie stood up. "Let's go tell them."

With a new resolute plan, they went to tell Marcus and Six what they'd come up with.

Six was far more enamored with the idea than Marcus was, at first. Marcus was still pissed off that his friend of eight years had betrayed them.

Ellie knew how he felt. "He is just having a bad couple of weeks. He really does want to remain in Marbas, he just doesn't know it yet."

"What if you're wrong?" Marcus asked.

"Then we let him go and that will be the end of that." She cocked her head thoughtfully to one side. "But if we're right, and he's just throwing a temper tantrum, he'll stay once the spell wears off."

"You just want to fuck him," Six said, echoing Nicole's earlier sentiment.

"Just once. If you were a woman you'd want him too. Nikki would fuck him." Ellie gave Six a bratty smirk.

Six snorted. Marcus chuckled.

Finally, Marcus looked at Six. "What do you think, man?"

Shrugging, Six took a drink of his beer and said, "I think the ladies are right. Jake is having a hissy fit because he's afraid of Daemons and he's scared shitless of Ellie and what she might do to him if they were naked in the same room."

Everyone but Ellie broke into laughter and Ellie blushed. "I'm not that bad."

Marcus reached out and smacked her ass. Hard. "You're a succubus, babe, and you own that shit."

Six stood up. "Let's go do it."

With murmurs of approval, the four got up and left the house, making their way to the barn. Inside, the entire floor had been done in concrete. With great care, with glow in the dark paint, Marcus, Six, and Jacob had painted a circle with the seal of Marbas in each quarter. Atop each seal stood an altar and a tall pillar candle. One for water, one for air, one for earth, and one for fire.

Nicole ran to the center altar and grabbed a piece of chalk from the drawer inside it. "I'll write the summoning for Sitri and Asmodeus in the circle."

No one stopped her. Nicole had the prettiest handwriting of all of them, and constructing the ritual was always something she helped with.

Marcus pulled out the coven grimoire, bound in goatskin, with Six looking over Marcus' shoulder as he flipped through the pages until he found the right spells. Ellie disrobed.

When they were ready, Six turned off the main light and rejoined them in the center of the circle. He turned to Nicole. "Aren't you going to get naked?"

"Fuck you, Martin," she said.

Ellie snickered.

"Shut up people. This is serious," said Marcus, always the killjoy. "We need to focus on Jacob and bringing him back into the fold."

"And into Ellie's pussy," Six deadpanned.

Marcus chuckled at that one. Ellie just shook her head. Nicole slapped Six's arm.

"What? It's true," he said in a mere whisper.

"Focus, okay?" Drawing in a deep breath, Marcus began the incantation, intoning it loudly so that it echoed through the entire barn. This space could house fifty coven members, though most of the time they had thirty or less.

Ellie listened to the foreign words, Daemonic invocations. They sounded harsh and beautiful and Marcus enunciated them perfectly. His vibration of them changed the feel of the entire space and she felt her body warming and tingling between her thighs. She loved it when Marcus summoned various Daemons and gave her to them. She could always feel them inside her, pulsating, warm energy. And she would always orgasm, gasping, writhing in their glory. It was about to happen now, in front of Six and Nicole and she wanted it to. Ellie loved being the exhibit and focus of attention, it excited her. In her mind's eye, she could see the Daemon, feel it, and she projected the image of Jacob onto it. *Bring him to me*, she thought. The Daemon smiled.

The others began intoning the spell along with Marcus and she heard her own voice, so distant, chiming in. The Daemon moved toward her and through her. When it was finished, she dropped to her knees, exhausted, but instinctively she knew that, unlike the curse, this one had worked.

Now they just had to wait.

5

Jacob couldn't sleep. No matter how many people he surrounded himself with, he missed Six and his stupid jokes and Marcus' deadpan humor. Even Ellie's bright smile and Nicole always slapping Six on the arm, followed by, "Martin!" in that high-pitched way she said it. Maybe he was being too hard on them. These thoughts went on for hours until he drifted into a nightmare.

He was standing in quicksand and his former coven-mates stood just outside it.

"Why should we help you?" dream Ellie asked.

"You betrayed the coven. We trusted you, took you in, and this is how you let us down," dream Marcus said with a frown.

"We should save him," dream Six said. No matter what, Six was probably the nicest guy out there, but he gave in to Marcus on everything. Dream Nicole clutched at his arm and nodded as if to agree.

"Just give me a damn rope!" Jacob shouted into the dream. His legs struggled to break free, but struggling only pulled him down further.

Just as the panic rose in his chest and he was about to go under, he felt a hand take his and then he was rising from the thick sludge that embraced him.

"Come back to us, brother," Marcus said.

Jacob woke in a fitful sweat, his hair matted to the back of his neck. He felt exhausted and his stomach was in knots. "Fuck," he croaked, sitting up.

He took a few deep breaths to try to slow the pounding of his heart. Then he got up and went down to the kitchen to get some water. There was no way he'd be able to sleep now. An eerie feeling, like he was being watched, permeated the house. Grabbing a bat from the corner in the living room, he went to the windows and peered out each one to see if anyone was there. It was just past two in the morning. No one was out there. The entire town was like a morgue, content in its somber slumber.

Then why did he feel he'd just been violated? As if he were being watched?

With a sigh, he sat on the couch and turned on the television. Like usual, there was nothing on. A lot of infomercials and some old television re-runs from the fifties. He settled on *I Love Lucy* and drifted off to sleep on the couch. This time, the dreams came but they were muted behind a heavy fog of sleep born of exhaustion.

He awoke to a knock at the door. A quick glance at the clock on the wall told him he'd overslept. Not that he had anything to do today except take care of the yard next door. Odd handyman jobs kept him busy when he wasn't working with the general contracting firm. In the meantime, neighbors including Esther and an older couple up the block depended on him to help them out with their landscaping and the other to-do's that home ownership demanded, and old age wouldn't allow.

The knock came again, louder this time. It definitely wasn't a woman knocking at his door. Too hard. He got up and went to the door, still in sweatpants and a t-shirt, and opened it. A man wearing a suit stood there. His Mercedes was parked out front. The man's gaze appraised Jacob for a moment and then he cocked his head to one side.

"Jacob Mallory?"

Jacob had a sick feeling in his gut. Good gods, he was being sued, he just knew it. "Yeah?"

"I'm Thaddeus Blackwood. I was told that if I needed someone to put in a paver patio that you would be the one to contact." His gray eyes surveyed the surrounding neighborhood as if he felt out of place. As if someone was going to jump him and steal his wallet. It was almost comical. "I was in the neighborhood and thought I would stop by directly."

Well that was creepy. Temple of the Magi members, much like members of The Watch, kept a low profile and usually sent their *paid help* to gather supplies and hire contractors. It was rare to see one of them outside the country club or big estate parties in Bedford Falls or Oakland Heights, two of the wealthier enclaves where the rich hid themselves from the working middle-class. Jacob immediately felt the urge to hide any weaknesses. "Okay."

The man produced a card and gave him an expectant look.

Jacob opened the screen door a little and took the card from him. He also got a better look. Italian leather shoes, an expensive suit, and a manicure. *So that's how the other half lived.*

"I have all of the building materials, but the initial crew I had scheduled to work on it could not meet my time frame. I was told you were currently not busy except for Esther's yard. I will pay ten-thousand for the labor if you can have it done by this coming weekend." Thaddeus forced a smile.

Jacob, still groggy, narrowed his eyes. It had been Esther who told Thaddeus to come see him. That much was obvious. Even the wealthier covens had regular meetings with the Seer. "I would have to put together a crew. How big is *the patio?*"

"Ah, details. Of course. It's two-thousand square feet and I have a particular design in mind. It's already planned out on paper, and the area has already been prepared, dug out, tamped down. Really, it's just a matter of laying the pavers in the proper order." He seemed to be getting fidgety now. "If you can come over this afternoon and get started, it would be appreciated."

His mind raced. This was usually something he would call Marcus and Six in on. The three of them could knock out a paver patio that size in a few days if they worked from seven in the morning until seven at night. Plus, he didn't want to go over to Blackwood's alone. Temple of the Magi had real power, and it was rumored they had done everything from necromancy to ritual sacrifice to maintain power, prestige, and affluence. Judging by the looks of this guy, he had no doubt.

But then why would Blackwood want him? He obviously could pay for a professional installer. Most would jump at the chance to do a prestigious project like this.

As if Blackwood had read his mind, he raised a manicured eyebrow and said, "Fine. The real deal is that this project is best suited to be kept within the thirteen, within a coven that isn't opposed to *darker* pursuits."

Then it dawned on Jacob what he meant. The patio was likely some kind of outdoor ritual space meant for something nefarious. Like cursing or necromancy, or opening a gate to hell. "You know that I'm at odds with my coven right now?"

Thaddeus snorted. "That's not my problem. Getting this patio done by this weekend is. Find a crew within the thirteen who aren't opposed to dark magick and I'll be happy. Just call me before one this afternoon if you don't think you can do it."

"I expect to collect some of the money up front," Jacob said as Thaddeus turned to leave. He noticed Connie sitting on the porch across the street, watching Thaddeus. Undoubtedly other neighbors were watching, too. It was so rare to see someone like Blackwood in a humble neighborhood like this. Sure, Esther drove a Mercedes, too, but it was nothing like Blackwood's.

"Fine. One fourth up front, today, cash, if you and a crew show up this afternoon." Thaddeus started down the walkway back to his car then turned and said, "And be assured if you back out after you start…"

Then the magus gave him a look. One that said if Jacob jilted him, he was a dead man. Jacob forced a smile. *Don't show any weakness* he told himself inwardly. "I don't back out of a job once I take it, Mr. Blackwood."

"Good. Try Temple Apophis if you need crew. I hear there are a few there who are currently unemployed." Then with a graceful, almost arrogant stride, Thaddeus Blackwood got into his black Mercedes and drove away.

Jacob gave Connie a quick wave and a brief smile, and slipped back into the house, turning the black calling card with embossed silver lettering over in his hand. That was Blackwood's home address and personal cell phone printed there. He started the coffee maker and then picked up the phone. It was ten in the morning now. He had two hours to put together a crew, collect them, and make the half hour drive up to Bedford Falls. The grass at Esther's rental could hold another day. He'd mow it tomorrow night, when he got home.

An hour later, he was crewless and mowing Esther's lawn seemed like a good plan after all. All of the people he'd called, guys he'd worked with in the past who weren't part of Shadow Marbas, were either working already, or they were out and not answering their phones. With a sigh, he went out and grabbed the mower from the shed, made sure there was enough gas in it, and mowed both the front and back of Esther's rental. Doing physical labor helped him think and there was still time for him to back out. Maybe he could just call Six and Six could grab a buddy or two. After all, Six couldn't be pissed at him and Six, much like Jacob, made his living doing odd jobs when there wasn't a big construction project going on. No, Six couldn't be mad, not really. It was Ellie who was being a spoil sport. Marcus was upset because Ellie was upset, but there was no other reason, was there?

But then he knew that since a curse was thrown out, Six had likely been there. He mowed his own lawns next, and thirty minutes later there was nothing left to mow. After looking across the street at Corrina's perfectly manicured lawn and realizing he couldn't go over and offer to mow hers, too, he put the mower away. He had a half hour to clean himself up and decide if he was going to call Thaddeus Blackwood and turn down the job. *Do his friends call him Thad?* He wondered.

He wondered then if he and Six could do a job that size alone. That would amount to five thousand each if they could. There was no way Six would turn that down. Even if it was a full week of work with just the two of them. Feeling upset and quite alone, he went inside, picked up the phone, and dialed Six's cell number.

Six answered on the third ring. "You're the last person I thought I would hear from," he said into the phone.

Jacob didn't respond to that. Instead he said, "I've got a big job over at the Blackwood estate. A patio. It pays ten grand if we can get it done before this coming weekend. I couldn't find anyone who was home and I know you wouldn't mind the extra paycheck."

There was a long pause on the other end of the line, then finally, "How big is the patio?"

"Two-thousand square feet. Apparently, all the materials are there, the space is already prepped. We just have to lay the pavers in a precise pattern. But if we're going to do it, we have to be there by one." Jacob wanted to ask him questions, to thank him for even answering the phone, but he didn't. Much like with Blackwood, he didn't want to show any weakness.

"All right, I'm in. You picking me up?" Six almost sounded like Six before Jacob's altercation with the coven.

"Yeah, give me twenty minutes."

"Okay. I'm at Ellie and Marcus'."

Jacob's stomach lurched. "That's fine."

As long as they won't be there, he added silently. But then he knew they would be. Probably just to give him the stink eye.

After hanging up with Six, he ran upstairs and changed into a pair of work jeans and a white t-shirt. Then he grabbed some gloves and knee pads and got in his truck. The block was quiet now.

When he arrived at Ellie and Marcus' farmhouse off of Greyson Road, he saw Six standing at the end of the driveway, waiting. With him was Marcus.

Son-of-a-bitch. Thank gods Ellie was nowhere to be seen. He pulled the truck over and Six jumped in. Marcus climbed in alongside him.

Jacob, having been brought up to be polite, didn't say anything. He just checked to make sure they were dressed appropriately.

"I figured you wouldn't mind if Marcus came. We could use the extra hands and just split the payoff three ways," Six said, as if there hadn't been an argument between them at all.

Job-wise, Jacob couldn't argue with that logic. "That's fine. I would have invited Marcus personally, but, you know…"

Marcus grunted something inaudible then said, "Man, you're like a fuckin' chick sometimes. You overthink shit."

Jacob pulled away from the house and started toward Bedford Falls. An uncomfortable silence filled the cab of the truck.

"So why did Thaddeus come to you about this again?" Six asked once they were on the highway.

"Esther," Jacob said, painfully aware that they were both looking at him, perhaps with anger. "At first, he told me some bullshit story about the original crew not being able to meet the time frame, but then he came out and admitted he wanted people not opposed to the *dark arts* to put the damn thing in."

"Huh," Marcus said. "Sounds like Blackwood is having some kind of *dark mage* party this weekend. I can't wait to see his digs."

"It might be more fun to crash the party," Six said with a laugh.

"Until they cut off your balls and keep you locked up in the wine cellar like their eunuch bitch," Marcus deadpanned.

Jacob couldn't help but laugh. It was almost like old times. Almost, except that a dark discomfort stood like an unmoving cloud inside the cab of the truck.

"You know, Jake," Marcus said, "We were kind of hoping you would have called before this."

The phone works two ways, asshole, Jacob thought. Instead he cowered. "I know, but I needed time to think."

"Well, I hope this means you're getting over it, because we're having a party this weekend and you should come," Six said, matter-of-fact.

"Yeah, man. We have a couple of new girls coming in for initiation. We need to hook you up," Marcus said, as if the offer of a potential hook-up would get him there.

Dread rose in Jacob's gut. A party where they kick his ass? Get him drunk and use him in some ritual? His mind ran wild with possibilities how they could punish him for leaving the coven. Then his logical mind stepped in and reminded him that beyond curses here and there, Shadow Marbas had never done anything like that before, and he knew that Six and Marcus weren't violent like that.

"Next exit," Marcus said, pointing at a sign as they whizzed past. Here, the roads had seen more upkeep and the exit looked like it had just been repaved. Even the sign announcing Bedford Falls looked brand new. Daemons forbid a nasty old sign announce a hoity-toity town full of wealthy witches.

Jacob turned down the nice clean, perfectly manicured street that led right into the heart of Bedford Falls. Reaching up on the dash, he grabbed the card Blackwood had given him and handed it to Six. "That's the address we need."

Six immediately pulled out his phone and plugged the address into the map. "Keep going straight until you get to Lily Lane, and take a left."

"Tell me when we're getting close to Lily Lane," Jacob said. Now, all focus was spent finding the Blackwood estate. It didn't take long.

Lily Lane was a narrow two-lane road that wound through a heavily wooded area. Finally, the trees cleared and a huge mansion rose before them. Gates and brick walls stood sentry at the outer perimeter, but the house was grand enough that it was enough to make Six say, "Fuck me!"

"We are doing shit wrong, people," Marcus said in agreement. "I wonder if they'd give us some pointers on getting rich."

Six snorted. "Man, we're peons to these fucks. Shit under their shoes."

Jacob shrugged as he pulled up to the gate with a guard house next to it. "They need us more than we need them."

"Damn straight," Six said.

The man inside the guardhouse wore a suit. "Can I help you?"

"I'm Jacob Mallory. We're here to do some brick work on a patio for Mr. Blackwood."

The guard looked into the truck then back at Jacob. "And who are they?"

"Martin Randall and Marcus Ayers," Jacob said, annoyance teetering on the edge of his voice. Blackwood never said whoever he brought would be scrutinized by security.

"Which covens?"

"Shadow Marbas, and you knew that before you asked. You're just being a dick," Marcus said.

The security guard put on a shit eating grin, and opened the gate. "Park up by the garden building on the left."

"Who's that asshole?" Six asked Marcus after they'd driven past the open gate and began the drive toward the house.

"I think he's Ashtaroth-Briarwood. No, actually I'm sure of it," Marcus said as if he'd just taken a bite of something nasty.

Ashtaroth-Briarwood was the coven that wanted to be The Watch or Temple of the Magi, but didn't quite make the cut. Many of the members were consummate professionals with the random security guard or doctor thrown in. They were the fair-weather sort. At least the *lower* covens weren't nearly as backbiting. At that moment, Jacob realized that maybe Shadow Marbas was where he belonged after all because he couldn't think of any other coven he would fit in with. Except maybe Lucifer's Haven. Then again, they seemed so nice that Jacob felt out of place, even around Corrina and Connie.

He found the garden building off to the left, and parked. He was sure Blackwood would appreciate that Jacob's green Ford F150 wasn't old and shitty. While it wasn't brand new, Jacob took care of it and it looked like it might have belonged there, next to the garden building at least. Not a shed, a building. It almost looked like its own house.

Together, the three got out and stood by the truck, unsure where to go, when a glamorous woman with long black hair drawn into a pony tail came toward them on a walkway that led from the back of the house. She wore a black bikini top and a sarong that cut off just above the knee. Undoubtedly there were black bikini bottoms under that.

"Are you guys the workers for the *patio*?" The way she said patio suggested there was something mysterious about it.

"Yes Ma'am," Jacob said. It never hurt to be polite, especially on the job.

She narrowed her eyes and approached them, looking them up and down. "Which coven?"

"They're Shadow Marbas, dear. All of them," came Thaddeus Blackwood's voice from the right. He had just come from the house and with him he carried several pieces of paper. He looked at Jacob. "I take this to mean Shadow Marbas has settled its differences?"

Marcus and Six gave Jacob a look.

"Lead us to the patio Mr. Blackwood," Jacob said, all business. *It was a dick-move on Blackwood's part to even mention that*, he thought.

With a knowing look, Thaddeus, still clad in black slacks and a light blue button-down dress shirt, and still wearing the Italian leather dress shoes, motioned them to follow.

The scantily clad woman led the way, her hips swaying with each step. The path to the backyard was lined with plants and creeping vines that trailed over trellises that they walked under. They passed through an iron gate and around a pool that looked more like a forest oasis. Then another cast iron gate and down several steps to a walled in enclave surrounded by trees. To the left were stacked hundreds, if not thousands of pavers in five different colors. The entire center of the area, and it was huge, had been cleared and tamped down. To be fair, it was a perfect outdoor ritual space and Jacob surmised that there was nothing like it back in Haileyville. Not so secluded and forested like this and certainly not so big. An entire house, two houses even, could have fit there. At the far end, there was another gate leading through an iron archway, and a stone path leading to the right.

"Here we are," Thaddeus said, holding out his arms as if to say, *behold*.

"You mentioned you had a specific pattern you wanted us to adhere to?" He looked at the papers in Thaddeus' hands, expecting him to hand them over.

"Do you really think three men can finish this in a week, Thad?" the woman asked Thaddeus as if the three men weren't even there.

Jacob stifled a grin. *Thad* it was.

"I have every confidence these three gentlemen will work sun-up to sun-down to make sure it's finished in time," he told her, smiling at the Shadow Marbas members. "Why don't you go inside and have a drink. I'll be with you shortly."

Dismissed, the woman shook her head and retreated back to the pool and presumably back into the house as instructed.

Thaddeus handed the papers to Jacob, who took them eagerly. The faster this was done, the faster they could all get back to their own lives. Shadow Marbas to Marcus and Ellie's old farmhouse and Thaddeus to his pool parties and beautiful girlfriend or wife. Never again would they meet, unless, of course, Temple of the Magi needed more work done.

His eyes moved over the design, then to the pavers, and back again. Marcus and Six looked over his shoulder.

"A gate opening sigil," Marcus said. He was always blunt.

"Yes," Thaddeus said plainly. "It must be perfect."

Six looked like he was about to ask something, but then he shut his mouth and a look of understanding washed over his face.

"Precisely," said Thaddeus, now smiling. "How long do you think?"

Jacob started to feel a little nervous. He wasn't as well versed as Marcus and Six in certain types of magick, but he'd read enough that he understood the application of what they were about to build. "Four days, maybe five if we work seven to seven," he finally said.

Marcus and Six both nodded in agreement.

"Good." Thaddeus' smile grew broader and he shoved his hands in his pockets. "Esther told me I could count on you Jacob. While she wasn't too keen on my little project, rest assured Shadow Marbas has the favor of The Temple, if you do it right."

"So when we're done here for the day, around seven, I expect you'll come out to pay the initial down payment?" If he was going to build a pave-stone gate to the realm of the Death Daemonic and potentially incur the wrath of Ocat and Marbas, he at least wanted to be sure they'd get paid for their trouble. Perhaps that's why Thaddeus was willing to pay so well.

"Of course," he said, then added, "I like you, Jacob. You're all business. Have you ever thought to go into business for yourself?"

Jacob gave him a dark look.

Thaddeus laughed and patted him rough on the shoulder. "You should consider it. If you find you need an investor, I could probably hook you up."

Once he was gone, Jacob, Six, and Marcus looked at each other and back at the design on the paper.

Finally, Six said, "I don't know what we've just gotten into, but I think we just made friends with Temple of the Magi."

Marcus scoffed, "With friends like that, we won't need enemies."

"It's ten-grand," Jacob said, knowing the thirty-three hundred each of them would make was enough to pay each of their household bills for at least a month or two. Six could probably stretch his for three months. "For four or five days' work."

Both Six and Marcus nodded and they got to work.

Five hours later they'd completed the outer ring and part of the northern quadrant. They were admiring their progress when Thaddeus joined them at the bottom of the steps.

"Brava! It looks stunning. I can see it as I live and breathe." He clapped his hands together.

The woman, now dressed in a short white cocktail dress stood at the top of the stairs. "The sigil looks off."

Marcus was about to explain how it wouldn't look right until it was done due to perspective, but Thaddeus got there first.

"It's fine Marla. Trust me on this. Robert and I designed it perfectly." He took the pages out of Jacob's hands and looked at it, then went over and counted the bricks. "It's dead on, darling. You have nothing to worry about."

"Except a portal to hell in my backyard," she mumbled loud enough for Jacob, Six, and Marcus to hear.

Jacob turned to her.

"I was only kidding," she said in a sweet voice, then said as if she had to explain, "This is an outdoor temple."

Apparently, she thought they were idiots.

Thaddeus returned with the papers and handed them back to Jacob. "Don't lose these, and I want them back when you've finished."

Then he reached into the back pocket of his dress pants and drew a leather wallet from which he took out a wad of crisp hundreds. He counted out exactly twenty-three and handed them to Jacob. "I'm afraid I don't have anything smaller than hundreds today. I'll pay you more tomorrow when I've seen more progress. Depending how it goes I'll adjust the amount and pay the balance when you've finished."

With that, he personally saw them back to their truck and even gave them a wave as they drove off.

"Anything about that seem creepy to you guys?" Six asked.

Marcus just shook his head. "I'll be glad when we're done with this one. Now the question is, how do we split twenty-three hundred bucks?"

In an act of trust, Jacob pulled his black nylon wallet from his front pants pocket and handed it to Six. The twenty-three hundred was the only money in there aside from his debit card and the one credit card he kept. "That's roughly seven hundred sixty bucks each. Split it up as seven hundred each and let's take the rest and get some dinner and change, and when we're done we'll split the rest."

He was pleased when he heard mumbles of agreement.

Six took his job of counting out seven bills for each of them seriously. He even counted each stack twice just to be sure. He handed Marcus his first, then took seven for himself, then put seven hundred back in Jacob's wallet, leaving two hundred in his hand for their dinner. "Let's do Hades!"

"Should we call Ellie and Nicole?" Marcus seemed torn.

Six shook his head. "No women tonight. I don't need to listen to Nicole yammer on about her cousin's wedding while I'm trying to relax, eat, and drink my beer."

Jacob breathed a sigh of relief.

"Besides," Six said, "Nikki and Ellie can have a girl's night that way."

With a nod, Marcus called Ellie on his cell. "Hey babe. You're on your own for dinner tonight. Me and the guys are going to stop somewhere and eat on the way home."

146

A pause.

"Yes, Jacob is here. No. What? I made five hundred bucks today." He only lied because Ellie liked to shop. Hiding money from her was his standard MO.

Another long pause. They could hear Ellie's voice through the phone, but not what she was saying.

Finally, he said, "Yeah, I don't know where we're stopping to eat. You and Nikki do whatever you want. I'll be home like ten or eleven. Love you. Bye."

Then he put the phone away and shook his head. "Jake, I can totally see why Ellie drives you nuts. I'm married to her and she drives me nuts."

"Nikki makes me crazy, too," Six said, as if both of them admitting their women drove them mad would somehow reinforce Jacob's want to come back.

After today, after seeing what Temple of the Magi had them building in their backyard, going back seemed the right thing to do. He didn't want to fight and the truth was, he missed Marcus and Six.

"Well," Jacob said. "Sucks to be you guys."

Six laughed. "So are you back?"

Jacob got off the highway and headed toward Hades Bar and Grill. "Yeah," he said, making the decision resolute in his brain. "I'm back."

"Good man!" Marcus said. "Now let's go eat and talk about this crazy shit we're building in Blackwood's backyard."

Just like that, their fight was over, though he still didn't want to practice sex magick with Ellie, and theophany still made him nervous.

Hades Bar and Grill was a different kind of place. People passing through often expected it to be at least a little bit country. It was nothing like that. There wasn't a single cowboy boot in the whole place. Instead it was modern and upbeat. On the walls were silhouette murals of demons with pitchforks and there were statues of horned gods everywhere, including goat head wall reliefs inside pentagrams. The host carried a plastic pitchfork as he showed them to a table in the back. All the wait staff wore plastic horns on their heads with black t-shirts that said, *Hellfire & Damnation Torture Staff* in white, the word Staff bigger than the rest. They played trendy rock softly in the background, currently a song by *Paramore*.

Once they were left with their menus Jacob leaned forward. "What are you guys getting?"

"Hades Burger," Marcus said.

"Let's get Cheese Styx and Sixth Circle of Hell Hot Wings for the table. But I'm gonna have a Hades Burger, too, with some Hellfire Fries!" Six rubbed his hands together like a little kid.

It wasn't like they never ate here. On the contrary, they ate at Hades Bar and Grill at least twice a month.

"What about you Jake?" Six asked.

"Same."

After the waitress came and got their order, Marcus' look turned thoughtful and he turned his attention to Jacob. "You do realize we're creating them a portal so they can practice theophany, right?"

Jacob sighed. "Yeah, but it's not like we're going to be there when they do it."

"Oh! We could do something like that out back behind your barn!" Six said it loud enough to attract attention from several tables. Then he lowered his voice. "We could make something similar."

"I'll help you build it, but that's one ritual I'm sitting out," Jacob said, reasserting his stance on the matter.

"That's fine, man. You're right, we were being stupid. If there are rituals we do that you're uncomfortable with, you don't have to join us. I just think we bond more as a coven when we all participate. But I totally understand. You weren't born into this. You should have the option to bow out," Marcus said.

"Thank you," Jacob said. "That's all I ever wanted. A choice."

"Ellie won't like it," Six said.

"Ellie will get over it," Marcus said decidedly.

Apparently they had missed him, too, and didn't want to fight over something so stupid, for which Jacob was thankful.

Their food came and they ate, all the while debating what Temple of the Magi were up to.

"We could crash their ritual," Six suggested again for the second time that day.

"Fuck that," Marcus said. "You don't fuck with Temple of the Magi and you don't fuck with The Watch."

"Look, we know what they're up to, but why?" Jacob liked knowing what motivated people.

He must have been frowning because Marcus shook his head and said, "That look, man."

His friends always said when he was sullen and brooding he looked like a pissed off serial killer.

"I guess the real question is, is it really any of our business?" Marcus shrugged. "We do the work and make the money, they open a pit to the abyss to conjure Daemons."

A sick feeling sunk in Jacob's gut. There was no backing out now, of course, because Marcus was right. They were only paid to do the work, not ask questions. And Blackwood had made it pretty clear what would happen if they backed out of the job once it was started. Again, he really didn't like the idea of theophany. Doing rituals was one thing, but for some reason the idea of conjuring a spirit to physical manifestation was more than he could handle. After all, conjuring a spirit, whether one called it a God, Angel, or Daemon, made it all too real, and Jacob liked his occult hidden, just like the word suggested. It was the reason he was too afraid to involve himself in rituals that thinned the veils so completely that the non-corporeal became corporeal.

Six snorted and gave Jacob a rueful look. "Dude, there are thirteen fucking covens and a lot of solitaries in the area. Like this hasn't happened before? Shit – we conjure Marbas all the time. And Lilith, and Asmoday."

"This is theophany though," he said, as if that explained everything.

"You gotta get over your fear of that shit, man. It holds you back. Six is right – for all we know several of the covens out there have something similar and use it on a regular basis. I bet if we went and asked Esther right now, she would confirm it." He motioned to across the restaurant and Six and Jacob turned to see Esther sitting there reading a book with a plate of Hellfire Fries and Cheese Styx.

Jacob got up. He had to know. Had to make sure he wasn't doing something he would feel guilty about later – even though there was no getting out of it. Not if he wanted to live. In the last two weeks he'd seriously considered moving back home, back to Iowa. Living in Haileyville was proving dangerous. If you screwed over your own coven, you were in danger. If you screwed over another coven, you were in danger. If you didn't have a coven, you were in danger. He wondered how the solitaries managed. Truth was, he liked his life enough to play the game, if he hadn't, he would have moved back to Iowa years ago.

He approached Esther's table cautiously, barely aware that Six and Marcus watched after him with wide eyes. "Hey Esther. I wanted to thank you for recommending me and the guys for the Blackwood job."

"Oh, Jacob." She gave him a broad grin and set down her book. "I saw you managed the lawn at the rental today, too. Well, Blackwood asked who he could trust to do some work and I told him you were one of the best men in town for the job."

Her eyes went past him to Six and Marcus.

While he wasn't the psychic one, he knew what she was thinking. "Yes, we're back together again. On the agreement that I don't have to participate in Ellie's shenanigans."

"Mm. Well, I knew that would happen. Now it's just a matter of getting Ellie used to the idea," she said with an understanding nod.

"You know what Blackwood is having us make, right?"

"Of course." She didn't seem upset or surprised. "Jacob, you worry yourself right into your own problems. What others do, they'd do with or without you. You can't control others any more than they can control you. You either involve yourself or you don't. In the case of Blackwood, I thought you could use the money. If you refused to build it, someone else would have. Blackwood wants his *patio* and he'd get it no matter what. What he does with it is between him and his own conscience."

She didn't seem so sure about that last part.

Jacob narrowed his eyes. "What aren't you saying?"

A forced smile quickly covered her lips. "It's nothing. I've just seen it coming for some time. When it happens, it will happen regardless who started the chain of events." She sighed then said, "Seeing you and Shadow Marbas back together gives me great joy. You were so miserable. Now go, back to your meal. You have four more days of hard work ahead."

"Do you think it's the right thing? Me going back?"

She gave him a kind nod. "I think you know it's the right thing."

THIRTEEN COVENS: BLOODLINES

With a resigned sigh, he turned to leave. "Thanks Esther."

She just continued to smile and went back to her book, and he went back to his table where Six and Marcus were waiting.

"She told me it wasn't my problem and if we didn't build it, someone else would have. She just thought I could use the money, which is why she recommended Blackwood talk to me." He frowned again.

"See?" Marcus polished off the last fries in his basket and leaned back in his chair, content.

"She told you more than that. What did she say?" Six prodded. Of the three of them, Six was probably the most superstitious. He wouldn't even step on cracks just in case they did, in fact, break his mother's back.

"I think she knows it's a bad idea, and she eluded to something bad happening." He gave them an offhanded shrug even though he felt uneasy. It was likely he'd feel this way until Blackwood's outdoor ritual space was finished. Esther was right – the only person he could control was himself, and how he reacted to what others did.

"Maaaan!" Six gave a dramatic shake of his head. "I heard from Nicki who heard from Allison, that Belinda said something like that, too. That there was an ancient evil rising or some shit."

Marcus began laughing. "Yeah, ancient evil my ass. Goddamn seers are all alike. There's always a dark energy or black cloud or some shit. It's how they keep their business running."

Jacob looked at the time. It was past ten. By the time he dropped Six and Marcus off, then drove home, it would be closer to eleven. He was right. When he finally got home, he tried to shove the day out of his mind, and sleep found him in no time.

It did take four more days for them to finish the ritual space patio, and when they were done, it was a perfect match to the design specs Blackwood had given them. Each brick hand lain, even and straight. The center brick had to be removable for some reason, but that wasn't an issue. It was a tight fit, but it came out with gentle prying. The various colors morphed into sigils and markers. All three Shadow Marbas members stood back and admired their handiwork. The patio was impressive. Blackwood had been watching from an upstairs window and he came down immediately, all smiles, with Marla, today dressed in a blue mini-dress and matching three-inch blue heels, close behind him.

"Ah, gentlemen! This is a sight to behold." Blackwood put his arm around Jacob. "I had my doubts, but you have exceeded my expectations. And on time!"

Jacob tried hard not to pull away or openly cringe. "This is exactly what you wanted, right?"

The affluent magician nodded and pulled out his wallet. More hundreds. He must have had a safe full of them somewhere in that beast of a house that towered over them. "Very good! You guys have done me proud and I'll be sure to contact you again if I need similar assistance in the future."

Marla cleared her throat and gave Blackwood one of those looks that suggested he better do something.

Blackwood noticed her scolding glare and relented to it. "We are planning to break it in tomorrow night, and we'd like to extend an invitation to the *three of you* to join us."

Marla stepped forward then. "Nonsense. Anyone from Shadow Marbas who would like to attend is welcome."

Blackwood's jaw tightened.

"Oh, thanks for the offer, but we have some plans tomorrow night," Jacob said. His response was met with a thankful look from Marcus, and a disappointed look from Six.

"Suit yourself," Blackwood said, his happiness at their refusal evident. Only Marla looked disappointed.

"Well then we'll have to have a mixer some night with your coven and ours." It was obvious now that Marla was more than just Blackwood's bound concubine or some bimbo he kept around for fun. She was, in the very least, in charge of coven hospitality, which was a much bigger role than most people realized.

"Yes, perhaps some other time." Blackwood seemed to like this idea better.

"Absolutely," Marcus said, forcing a smile.

Then, like he did at seven every night, Thaddeus Blackwood walked them back to the truck and watched them go.

Probably worried we'll stick around and snoop. Wants to make sure we're gone, Jacob thought. Then he said aloud to Six and Marcus – a captive audience, "Why is Temple of the Magi so keen on getting buddy-buddy with Shadow Marbas all-of-a-sudden?"

Marcus snorted. "They probably think if they suck up, we'll come over and help them with projects like that for free." Marcus' cynicism was welcomed by Jacob.

They drove in silence for a while until finally Marcus said, "Let's go back to my place for dinner tonight. Ellie put a roast in the crock pot."

Jacob's stomach did a flip. He hadn't seen Ellie since he'd stormed out of the farmhouse after she made an unwelcome advance. But he was going to have to face her at some point. So he nodded in agreement. "That sounds like a plan."

Six said nothing.

6

Martin "Six" Randall parked his black Mustang next to the line of Mercedes' and limousines in the front parking area of the Blackwood mansion, just where Marla Blackwood had told him to park. She'd seemed happy to hear from him and glad that a member of Shadow Marbas would be there to represent the coven. He hadn't told Marcus or Ellie, or even Nicole where he was going. Only that he had something to do so he would be late to the Saturday night gathering of Shadow Marbas. He had noticed something that Jake and Marcus hadn't. The bits of copper in each brick. It was so slight one could barely tell it was there. He needed to see why because he was curious like that.

He got out of the car feeling terribly out of place. Of course once he donned his black ritual robe he would undoubtedly blend with members of Temple of the Magi and no one would be any wiser to his presence. Pulling his robes from the back seat, he pulled them over his head. A tight ponytail kept his long hair back. It was a last-minute decision to come and so he hadn't bothered shaving. Just a phone call to Marla, a quick shower, and then he'd driven up, a swell of excitement running through him the entire time.

There were others milling around the parking lot. Some of them drivers for the extremely wealthy members of the coven, and a few obvious members of the temple who wore black robes themselves. One of them was Frank Wood, an investment banker at the firm where Martin kept his poor excuse of an IRA. Not poor because of how they managed it. On the contrary, it wouldn't have been worth what it was had the investors at *Phillis and Wood* not managed it, but poor because he only put one hundred a month into the damn thing. It was all he could afford on a laborer's salary.

Frank recognized him immediately and started toward him, smiling, hand outstretched. "Martin! I had no idea you would be here tonight."

Neither did I, Martin thought. He reached out and took the man's hand, and forced his own smile. "Mr. Wood."

"Please, call me Frank. I had heard Shadow Marbas was invited." Then he looked around, as if expecting to see Marcus or Ellie close behind. "The rest of the coven couldn't make it?"

"We had a gathering already planned tonight, but thought at least one of us should come. It would have been impolite to ignore the invitation," Martin said, trying to adopt Frank's almost regal manner.

"Well we're glad you're here. I saw the work you guys did. It should be a good night. By the way, I've been looking over your portfolio. You should really put more in there every month," Frank said, all business.

"Now Frank," said a woman's voice from behind a cowl hood. The woman pulled down the hood. She was about fifty, with bottle blond hair and blue eyes. "Welcome, I'm Laura Marple. Don't mind Frank, he scolds us all about putting more into our investment accounts every month. So, you're from Shadow Marbas?"

The woman took him by the arm and started leading him around the back of the house, but not to the left by the pool, which was the only way Six, Jacob and Marcus had ever gone into the back when they were working on the patio. No, this time she led him to the right, alongside the huge structure of the house, and toward the back. Frank and another man followed, discussing stocks and bonds in low voices.

"Marla told me your coven was sending at least one person, and we want you to feel welcome," she said as they went.

"Well I appreciate that. It's easy to feel out of place…"
That nervous excitement he felt grew as they rounded the back
of the house to a great lawn set up with tents and string lights.
More than fifty people were back there, talking and drinking
champagne.

"Oh, it's not so bad when you do as much public
speaking as I do," she said, giving him an encouraging smile.

"Oh? What do you do?" Martin asked, trying to be
polite. He expected her to say sales or marketing.

Instead she said, "I write business books. Most of them
about public speaking."

He laughed and she laughed right along with him. For
a second, he almost felt like he belonged to their clique.
Almost.

She led him right up to Marla and Thaddeus
Blackwood.

Marla looked relieved. "Six is it?"

"Well, Martin actually, but my friends call me Six," he
said, uncomfortable in Thaddeus's piercing gaze.

"And why is that?" the high priest, Thaddeus, asked.
"How did you get that nickname?"

"Yes, do tell," Laura said. She appeared to be genuinely
interested.

The reality was the he'd gotten the nickname because
of his superstitions. Martin, ever since he was a young man,
liked things in sixes. A six pack of beer, never a four pack,
which he felt was a rip off. When they did ritual, he insisted
they chant all incantations six times. He checked all the locks
on the doors before he went to bed six times. He bought shirts,
socks, and pants, in sixes. He'd decided six was his lucky
number. As a result, the nickname Six. But instead of telling
them that, he simply said, "I once won a five-thousand-dollar
lottery with the number six."

It was partly true, he had.

Marla clapped her hands together with delight. "That's fabulous! It's your lucky number!"

Thaddeus smirked and shook his head. "You should embellish that story a little. Make it to where you had six women in one night."

Marla gave him a playful slap. "Thad, that's terrible!"

The crowd around them chuckled in appreciation of Thaddeus' suggestion.

Then Thaddeus let out a sigh and said, "Well, it's time. Let's assemble."

Slowly, people began setting down their glasses, many empty now, on the provided tables. They pulled up their hoods and began making their way around to the back entrance of the newly constructed patio enclave.

Six followed feeling much better with his hood up. Less out of place. Here, hidden behind the folds of fabric, made by Ellie and Nicole, his emotions were his own. No one could see his expressions or reactions to the ritual.

Now, they all stood in a semi-circle on the perimeter of the new patio, a three-foot span near the southern back gate open so that Thaddeus and his assisting priests could enter the circle. Six stood on the east side next to people he didn't know, but it was no matter, it wasn't like they were talking. Everyone focused on Thaddeus, who entered now wearing a black robe with red trim, the hood down. He carried a staff that looked like something out of *The Lord of the Rings* movie, with a large crystal ball on one end, and a metal cap on the other. Behind him, three cowled figures followed, one holding what appeared to be another brick on a maroon pillow and two carrying highly decorative jars. One of the jars appeared to be filled with liquid.

He stifled a laugh. It looked so odd, almost like they were going to Christen the patio. Perhaps that's what they were doing, he had no idea. He stood quietly, watching, amused at how the black robes seemed to remove all social status and barriers. In this moment, they were all magi, wizards, and witches in the eyes of the spirit world.

Thaddeus snapped his fingers and pointed to the center brick, the one they were supposed to leave free floating so it could be removed. Two men came forward from the West quadrant and one of them removed the loose paver. The second man took the ritual brick from the cushion and kneeled down, placing it in the other's place. He had to give it a few shoves to get it in there.

That's when Six felt the ground rumble slightly beneath him. He swallowed. Hard. Then one of the men produced a ritual dagger from the side-belt he wore and began working his way around the ritual space invoking spirits. Focalor. Marbas. Azazel. Murmur. Lucifuge. And finally – Abaddon.

Thaddeus raised his arms wide, still holding the staff. He began invoking the supreme gate keeper of the dead – Ocat.

What the fuck are they doing, Martin wondered. Opening a gate, yes, that much was obvious. He could feel the air around him turn electric. The fine hair on his arms and the back of his neck stood. His feet felt a thrum of electricity beneath him. The pavers. The copper.

Then Thaddeus shouted one last invocation and thrust the end of the staff into a hole in that ritual paver, activating the entire thing. Fine lines of blue energy pulsated forth, the entire patio looking like a circuit board. It lit up with blue light. The crystal orb at the top of the staff began to glow. It was so bright that everything outside the circle seemed to fade into darkness.

The coven began to chant an incantation. One that Six didn't know, so he didn't join in. He merely listened to the voices synchronize, further charging the space with something.

Thaddeus took the bottle of liquid and poured it in a circle around the now glowing staff. "By blood we bind you, great Sorath! Come forth!"

A brilliant gold light pulsated from the staff.

It had to be smoke and mirrors. It had to be. But what happened next was certainly a feat of magick if there ever was one. Six's jaw went slack as a black figure made of smoke rose up from the staff, large and bulking, over seven feet tall. The damn thing had horns on top of its head. He could almost feel the onlookers gasp inwardly as it rose full height with glowing golden eyes.

Thaddeus, completely unmoved by the manifestation, took the second bottle from his final ritual assistant, and opened it, setting it on the ground before the manifested Daemon. Then he took a ritual blade from somewhere under his own robes and said, "Bring the sacrifice."

Six held his breath. *Sacrifice? Oh hell no,* his mind screamed. His heart pounded in his chest, thumping so hard he could hear nothing but.

Then came the sound of wheels as a box was rolled in to the center of the space, right in front of the thing that now hovered over all of them, its eyes blazing with electricity. Sorath. Six looked down at the box, no, it wasn't a box. It was a coffin, and it didn't have a top. Inside lay a corpse of a man who looked to be about forty at the time of his death. Six's stomach shuddered, but he didn't dare react.

Thaddeus shoved his dagger into the corpse's chest, then poured more of the liquid over it from the first bottle. "Rise!" he commanded.

There was a surge of energy, a whoosh as the air seemed to leave the space, and the lifeless body in the box sat up. One of the assistant's used some type of tool to pry open the dead man's mouth. Then there was a mighty wind, a loud noise that sounded like one of those howling firecrackers, and the manifested Daemon shot straight into the now sitting corpse. Someone to Six's right turned to the high walls of the enclosure and threw up. No one seemed to notice or care.

Six held it together even though he wanted to do the same.

The skin of the corpse began to glow that same golden light and the corpse got out of the box with the help of two kneeling assisting priests. The coffin was wheeled away, leaving on the Daemonic possessed corpse, a bottle, two kneeling priests, and Thaddeus himself.

Thaddeus walked around the Daemon three times counter clockwise, chanting incantations as he went.

The thing howled, its eyes still blazing, but this time in rage. It seemed unable to move, trapped by the glowing paver patio beneath it.

Finally, Thaddeus picked up the bottle, uncorked it, and shouted one last command at the Daemon. Had Six not seen it with his own eyes, he would have never believed it. The Daemon infested corpse turned into a sharp sliver of pulsating light, and as if sucked by a vacuum, the Daemon and its corporeal corpse body went straight into the bottle.

High Priest Blackwood put the cork back in and began chanting what Six recognized as a binding spell. The bottle glowed an eerie gold. Six could see something moving inside it and he fought the urge to bring his hand up to his mouth.

The assisting priests closed the circle, then finally Thaddeus addressed the coven – all smiles. "We have succeeded where my grandfather and great grandfather failed before him! Behold the death aspect of Sorath. With him under our control, no one will defy The Magi ever again. We have the power to bring fame and destroy fortune! If we can raise Daemons, we could easily raise a devil!"

"Hear, hear!" said a voice on the far end of the enclosure. With that, the ritual ended and everyone, still subdued, filed out of the enclosure, back onto the pristine lawns of the Blackwood Manor.

The next hour, filled with champagne and soft-spoken conversation, was a blur. Six didn't know what they did with the Daemon in the bottle since it was taken away, presumably into the house. Six had managed to bid Frank and Laura goodnight and thank Marla and Thaddeus for inviting him. When Thaddeus asked him how he *found* the ritual, Six said, "Very impressive. You have skill sir, and if I wore hats I'd tip mine to you."

Sure, it sounded ridiculous, but Thaddeus ate it right up and seemed incredibly pleased with himself, and thankful for an audience outside his coven.

Six didn't remember much of the drive back to Ellie and Marcus' place. The image of the manifested Daemon diving into the corpse, then the subsequent bottling of the thing had chilled him to the bone. That was something a person couldn't un-see. Now he understood Jacob's aversion to theophany rituals. In theory it was fine. To see it first hand was terrifying.

7

While dinner with Ellie the night before had been awkward, they both had gone out to the back porch afterward and settled their differences. Ellie apologized for coming on so strong to Jacob, and he apologized for reacting so harshly. It was a heartfelt apology at that. Marcus seemed happy to see them getting along, too, which helped. Jacob could only imagine how hard it would be to remain friends with him if Ellie insisted on being unreasonable.

"I want to do a channeling," Ellie announced Saturday at dinner. It was just a few people. Marcus, Ellie, Nicole, Jacob and a few other coven members. Six had some errands to run for his mother. Gods only knew how long that would take.

So, with a shrug and with beer, the coven members present all went out to the old barn. Marcus and Jacob stood back and let the women deal with it this time, choosing to be passive observers to Ellie's whim. The only other man present was Vince, and he sat down in a lawn chair in the corner to take a nap. The four remaining women went to work constructing the ritual space, invoking Lilith, and assisting Ellie as she went into a trance, her eyes rolling into the back of her head.

Jacob wasn't sure exactly how it worked except when Ellie opened her eyes and spoke, it was Ellie but it wasn't. The spirits inside her always seemed calmer than her, more eloquent in their speech, and far less stubborn. Whether she hypnotized herself or there was actually a spirit in her was anyone's guess. Most of the coven believed she was actually channeling.

They sat for a long time, drinking and watching. The women chanting and Ellie's body moving back and forth in a seductive dance that was highly hypnotic.

"You should go ask the Daemon questions," Marcus whispered in Jacob's ear.

Jacob's focus was on Ellie though, and everything around them, the entire barn, seemed to shift right out of existence. There was something there, inside Ellie, luring him, beckoning. He felt himself getting hard, not at the thought of Ellie, but at whatever she was becoming. In a slightly drunken stupor he stood, left his finished beer, his fifth one, behind and approached her, putting his hands on her hips to stop them from moving. Moving. Swaying. Enticing. Soft, supple skin.

He reached out his hand and hooked her around the ass, drawing it up under her short skirt. She wasn't wearing panties. Damn everything, he wanted her. In this trance like state where time seemed to slip by more quickly, he took her, bending her over a table they sometimes used as an extra altar. In a few swift motions, he entered her from behind. She didn't struggle. Instead, she threw back her head and moaned, shoving against him with every thrust. She wanted him. Bad. Her deft fingers worked her clitoris while he fucked her. She came with a shattering scream, falling forward, and he quickened his pace.

It wasn't until he climaxed, buried deep inside her, that he came to, fully realizing what just happened. He pulled out with an immediate swell of panic. Beneath him, Ellie gave a contented sigh, stood up and faced him. On tip toes, she gave him a quick peck on the cheek. "Now that wasn't so bad, was it? That's all I ever wanted, Jake."

Nervous as hell, he put his dick back in his pants, terrified to turn around because his face flushed deep crimson and he knew the coven was behind him. Marcus included.

A rough hand settled on his shoulder. "Welcome back into the fold, brother," Marcus said.

Jacob stiffened, then relaxed when he realized no retaliation would ensue.

Those present left the barn and headed back up to the house, leaving Jacob to his own thoughts. He didn't stay alone long though, because Ellie came back out to ask him if he wanted apple pie or cherry, as if them fucking was an everyday occurrence. Was that what he was avoiding? Marcus didn't take issue with it. Even Six had fucked Ellie, though he'd stopped once he and Nicole hooked up, at Nicole's request. The only person who seemed to have a problem with it was him.

Esther's words rang back at him. His own thoughts really did help him create problems that were entirely his own.

"Cherry," he said, and followed Ellie, who was happy as a lark, back up to the house. He didn't know if she'd been taken over by a Daemon or not, but who was he to argue? It was probably the most interesting sex he'd had in the past few years.

They were eating pie and debating the merits of the television show *Supernatural*, when Six walked in. He looked pale and frightened. His eyes were sunken in a little. Both Marcus and Jacob set their plates on the table.

"Nicki, get Six a beer," Marcus ordered.

Nicki ran to the kitchen and Ellie pulled Six to the sofa and set him down next to her. "Are you okay? What happened."

A current of fear ran through the room and the knot returned to Jacob's stomach. He already knew, or he thought he did. "You went to The Magi ritual."

Six, his gaze still downward and in shock, nodded absently. "They stole a corpse," he croaked.

"What the fuck?" Marcus grabbed his phone. "I'm calling Sheriff Steve."

Marcus never called him Sheriff Watson, it was always Sheriff Steve. In Marcus' younger years, he'd had enough run ins with the cops to see a few nights in detox here and there. Shadow Marbas had been a wild bunch back then.

"It's gone now." Finally, Six looked up. "You'll never believed what we just built."

"A portal," Marcus said, ignoring the mouth drops of the surrounding coven members who weren't there.

"A portal that's a spirit trap, man. They put it in a corpse and bottled it up like apple butter." He took the beer from Nicole and drank it down.

Jacob felt a chill creep up his neck. Esther was right. "We can't control what other people do, Six. Only how we react to it."

Nods of agreement made their way around the room as if Jacob had said the wisest thing anyone had ever said. He didn't bother telling them those were the words of Esther, not him.

"And what if what someone else is doing is raising Daemons to take out their enemies and bring their friends success? What if they raise a devil?" Six's gaze pierced Jacob in a way that terrified him.

Six had seen something that scared the shit out of him. While raising Daemons, as in divine intelligences, was one thing, devils were altogether different. Daemons didn't exist to harm physical beings. While they could be dangerous to work with, they often worked toward the betterment of the magicians who conjured them. Devils, on the other hand, existed only to bring death, chaos, and destruction and one could not conjure them to any other end.

Suddenly Jacob thought of Connie and Corrina. Connie especially. For some strange reason he wanted to tell her this. To bring Six to her so he could spill his guts and relive whatever it was that had him so spooked.

"What if they raise a devil?" Six asked again, this time in a much smaller voice. His face had gone blank and his gaze distant again.

No one in the room said anything.

Jacob took a deep breath. "Then, when the time comes, we rise together and do what we have to do to stop it."

THE WATCH

1

Neal put a small piece of quartz on the map spread out on the oak dining room table. The quartz marked the Blackwood estate. He leaned back and gave Aaron a dark look. "So, what do you think?"

Aaron frowned, unsure how to put it in a way that wouldn't piss Neal off. He looked over the map, his mind racing. Thaddeus and Marla Blackwood's home was a fortress. The easiest way in was through the acres of woodland property that bordered the massive estate. Even then, the place had high walls, iron fences, and guards brandishing guns who patrolled the property. They were often accompanied by mean-looking German Shepherds.

Aaron loosened his tie, gave Neal a wary look, and shook his head. "This is impossible. First, who would we hire to attempt a break in? And second, they're going to know it was one of the other covens. That gives them twelve suspects and I'm certain we'd be at the top of that list."

"Don't be an idiot," Neal growled. He shoved aside a wisp of long black hair and let out a deep breath. "We hire a few thugs from out of town. Money talks with people like that. Right?   Or better yet, we could hire a couple of solitary practitioners cheap. We'll promise to share some ancient magickal secret with them as part of the payment. We don't tell them what they're stealing. That way if they get caught, it wasn't us, and the solitaries don't know who we are. If they don't get caught, we get that damn bottle and the Temple of the Magi coven grimoire. Then we'll figure out how he did it."

"A stranger might hold it all for ransom and a solitary would steal the grimoire once he realized what it was. We can't trust anyone except a person we have some control over. Besides, last I heard, the spell requires a corpse, and that is out of the question." Aaron leaned back into the chair, waiting for Neal to shoot down this commentary, too. For better or worse, Aaron didn't want to steal anything, and now, he only threw out suggestions as a show of support for Neal's frustration at not knowing the secrets of the Temple of the Magi.

But Neal didn't shoot the idea down. Instead, he bit his lower lip and narrowed his eyes. "We're not actually going to do the ritual. We just want to look at it. We get a few of the kids to steal the book and the bottle. Thaddeus won't prosecute kids if they're caught. They could say it was a prank and we'll all agree it wasn't funny."

Aaron still didn't like it. Sure, he or Neal could have approached Thaddeus on behalf of The Watch, but Thaddeus was far too arrogant to share his secrets. Though the rumor that Thaddeus could raise Daemons and even devils to physical manifestation was too intriguing not to be curious. The first utterances of Thaddeus' successful theophany operations came from Shadow Marbas. Some low-level members had claimed, to those outside the coven, that at least one member of the inner circle of Shadow Marbas had been made privy to the operation, and what he saw scared him.

"Maybe we should just use magick to get it."

"Because magick works like that." Neal's sarcasm wasn't lost on Aaron.

"No," Aaron said, annoyed now. "I mean, why can't we just approach the spirits for the answer? That alleviates our need to steal anything."

"Because Thaddeus already has the formula, and whatever is in the bottle is proof." Neal stood. "Besides, that means either going to Esther or Temple Apophis' new queen. I don't trust either of them."

"I don't know…" Aaron started.

"We're called The Watch for a reason, Aaron. We are the watchers in the dark. The guardians of the tower. It is we who will foretell the coming of the witches' savior. The One. We will be the one to crown him, and bring about order to the thirteen covens. We're the metaphorical monarchy among them, and they need our guidance." Neal wore a smug look on his face and he crossed his arms over his chest. He looked sharp in his Giorgio Armani shirt and black slacks, the same thing he wore every day even though he didn't have a job to go to. He had no need to work. His family had more money than they knew what to do with. Old money that brought with it the kind of affluence that even the nouveau rich didn't have.

Aaron fought the urge to roll his eyes. Neal could be downright histrionic at times. While Neal was his oldest, dearest friend turned lover, they did differ in ethics - in that most of the time - Neal had none. They balanced out nicely as a couple though. In that respect, Aaron was Neal's conscience and Neal would often defer to him, which had probably saved Neal's ass a time or two.

Aaron's family had money, too, but he still had to work for it. To that end, he headed his father's financial firm during the day, working as a financial consultant to their wealthy clientele base. When he showed up to coven meetings wearing a suit and tie it was because it was necessary to his job, not because he wanted to look important. He would have been perfectly happy in jeans and a t-shirt. Most of the members of The Watch showed up to coven meetings dressed in suits. It's just how they were. Now, he ran his long fingers through his blond hair and looked at Neal thoughtfully.

Being a member of The Watch was a privilege afforded few. It was rare they brought in anyone from the outside. Watch members were exclusively generational, unlike some of the other covens who were open to outsiders whether they had ties to the original coven or not.

But perhaps one of the starkest differences between The Watch and the other covens, was that members didn't bring their wives or female lovers to meetings. Females had no place in The Watch. Their coven, comprised of ceremonial magicians, still subscribed to the old beliefs - that women were unclean and forbidden to practice magick. Though many of the members had wives and girlfriends who were practicing witches of one flavor or another. The Watch did operate in coven territory, after all. But who the women practiced with, or if they were solitary, was a mystery that Neal, nor Aaron cared to examine. As long as their feminine essence wasn't openly defiling The Watch's Angelic or Daemonic temples, that's all that mattered.

While Aaron went to the couch and sat down, Neal moved across the great room of their large house to pour himself a scotch. "You want one?"

"Sure." Aaron waited until Neal had poured both glasses, then moved the heap of blanket from the place next to him on the black leather couch so Aaron could sit with him. If one wanted Neal to listen to him, one had to play his cards carefully. "Let's sleep on it and decide what to do tomorrow."

Neal sat, handing over a scotch, and then he put his arm around Aaron. "Do you really think there will be another solution that will crop up by morning?"

Aaron took a sip of the scotch and cringed a little. It burned. "Yeah. I think by morning you'll have come to your senses and realized that a book and a bottle are no reason to entertain a visit from Sheriff Watson."

"You worry too damn much." Then he leaned over and kissed Aaron on the lips and smiled at him. "But I don't know what I'd do without you, love."

Aaron wasn't sure what else he could say. Instead, he leaned back into the couch while Neal turned on the television and kicked his feet up on the coffee table.

"The Late Show is on."

Neal mumbled, "Oh yeah," and changed the channel.

While they sat there, content in watching Stephen Colbert and nursing their drinks, an idea grew in Aaron's mind. On his way to the office in the morning, he'd swing by the Blackwood estate. It wasn't a betrayal, it was common sense. It was possible Thaddeus was so arrogant he was bound to at least confirm if the stories were true, maybe even share part of the secret of how he did it. Perhaps he'd even show Aaron the bottle. He almost laughed at his own optimism. No, the person who was more likely to spill was Marla, and Marla liked Aaron. When it came to The Watch, most of the other coven leaders preferred to deal with Aaron anyway. He was wholly likeable and pretty sure that if he had any enemies, they were only enemies because he was Neal's significant other. He took another drink of the throat-burning scotch and relaxed. It was all going to work itself out.

The Blackwood estate rivaled the size of Neal and Aaron's grand house. Aaron was pretty sure it had at least fifty rooms, if not more, and rumor had it that Marla Blackwood had hired interior decorators to furnish it top to bottom for a hefty price tag. Despite the Blackwood's wealth, Marla had managed to remain approachable and down to earth while still maintaining impeccable taste and fashionista sensibilities. It was probably due to Marla's amiable personality that Aaron was allowed through the gate and up to the house to begin with. When he got there, he found Thaddeus and Marla, both dressed to the nines as usual, standing on the front patio waiting for him.

"Aaron!" Marla greeted with a wide smile. Her black hair was pulled up in a loose bun, with a few strands left out on the sides, softening the look. She went up to Aaron and kissed each cheek. "You look well. We missed you at our last gala."

Thaddeus' expression remained placid and his voice was firm. "To what do we owe this early morning visit?"

Aaron smiled at Thaddeus, but addressed Marla instead. "I've been so busy at work, and I was in Jersey that weekend. I'm sad I missed it."

"Neal would have been miserable," Thad said. There was a tone of finality in his voice.

"You and Neal are far too much alike, that's why he annoys you, and you him," Marla said in such a sweet way that it tempered any reaction from Thad. "So, how are you?"

"Forever vigilant," Aaron replied. "But I am here on business. Coven business I mean."

"Told you," Thad said to Marla, not quite under his breath.

"There are rumors…"

A slow smile spread over Thaddeus' face, and his expression turned smug. Marla was right. Thad and Neal were two peas in a pod. Marla gave Aaron an apologetic look.

But Aaron felt a spark of anticipation, because this was exactly what he'd hoped for.

"So, what does *The Illustrious Watch* want to know? That I actually did conjure a Djinn to physical manifestation and put

THIRTEEN COVENS: BLOODLINES

it in a bottle?" Thad radiated self-importance and leaned back against the cast iron railing that encircled the porch.

He clearly wanted everyone to know he'd done it. Whether he enjoyed seeing others' fear, or the power it afforded him as the other covens looked on in awe, Aaron wasn't sure.

"Yes. And we want to know how you did it," he said. There was no point beating around the bush.

Thad's grin widened to Cheshire Cat proportions. "Of that I have no doubt."

Marla shook her head, but said nothing.

"I take it Neal sent you over."

"No, I'm here of my own accord. We are The Watch."

"Yes, the Watchers who oversee the covens, the judges of our actions. Blah, blah, blah." Thad straightened a cuff link, then wiped a bit of imaginary dust from his lapel. "It took me a long time to figure out how it was done. I won't give you the ritual itself, but I'll show you…"

Aaron felt the pang of disappointment then. What had he expected? That Thaddeus would actually hand over the rite? But at the promise of seeing the bottle, he kept a collected smile on his face. "I'd like that."

"Come by tonight around six. Bring Neal. We'll have dinner." Thaddeus' eyes narrowed.

Marla nodded with enthusiasm. "We look forward to seeing you *both*." Her eyes went to the expensive two-tone watch, set with diamonds, on her wrist. "Oh, I have a meeting with Brenda for the charity event in a half hour. I should go."

Then she went inside and Thaddeus walked Aaron to the car. "Be sure to keep Neal on a leash."

Aaron forced a laugh. "I'll do what I can, but you know how he is. Plus, he doesn't know I came to see you, so he might be pissed at me anyway."

"You could do better," Thad said.

Aaron wasn't sure what to say to that, so he said nothing, just gave Thad a polite nod and got back in his car.

Thad stood there in the drive, watching him go, and only turned back toward the house when Aaron's car reached the gate. An uneasy feeling gripped Aaron's stomach. Thaddeus had always been a braggart, but why was he so keen on showing the djinn to Aaron and Neal?

2

"Gods dammit! Why did you tell them that we knew about it? Now if it goes missing, they'll know it was us!" To say Neal was pissed would have been an understatement.

But Aaron kept his voice calm and collected. "Because maybe, just maybe, we'll get more information by asking. At least now it's not illegal. Besides – I think he wants people to know about it, and we wouldn't be The Watch if we didn't know, would we?"

"You and your fucking moral compass." Neal frowned.

"Jail would have been better?" Aaron lifted a stern eyebrow. He'd picked this battle and he was going to see it through.

"I hadn't intended on being caught. Now, not only does Thaddeus know we know, but I have to spend my evening with him." Neal undid his tie in a huff and threw it onto the king-size bed that graced their master bedroom. "I can't tie that god-damned thing!"

Aaron picked it up and went over to Neal, putting the tie back around his neck to help him tie it. "It won't kill us to go. Just focus on Marla. She's always liked us."

"Marla is an airhead. She likes everyone." He frowned like a stubborn toddler.

With a sigh, Aaron finished Neal's tie, then bent over to grab his shoes. "It will be over before you know it."

"You realize at the next coven meeting I'll have to tell our membership it's because of you we don't have any chance in hell of getting the ritual?"

"That's fine," Aaron said, unaffected. He didn't care what the members of The Watch thought, if Neal had really planned on telling them anything. At least this way, Neal wouldn't get himself arrested, and the coven's integrity remained intact.

Neal let out an exasperated sigh. Even through all the complaining and biting comments, he went willingly, which told Aaron that secretly, Neal was probably relieved that at least one of them had a conscience. No ritual, whether it raised djinn or devil, was worth the potential backlash – legal or other.

Not a word was said as they drove to the Blackwood estate except the stray comment here or there about the trees changing, road work, how warm it had been for early autumn, and how light traffic was. When they arrived at the gate at three minutes after six, they were flagged straight through. Neal didn't bother parking in one of the parking spaces, instead, he drove right up to the front door, put the Mercedes in park, and turned off the ignition.

He looked over at Aaron, then at the patio that led to the grand entryway leading into the Blackwood house. "I guess here goes nothing."

Aaron shook his head, unclasped his seatbelt, and exited the car, pausing long enough for Neal to make it around the car to his side. They went up the steps to the door together. Aaron didn't bother to reach out and ring the doorbell. He kept his hands in his jacket pockets. With another headshake, Neal did the honors. They could hear the doorbell chime lightly from beyond the closed door.

It was Marla who greeted them, all beaming and smiles. "You two are so prompt!" She didn't wait for a response, but instead said, "Dinner should be ready shortly. You both can join Thad in the drawing room."

Neal waited until Marla turned her back then rolled his eyes. Aaron bit back a grin, then wiped a white piece of fuzz, likely from the towels or socks in the laundry, off his green shirt. They followed as Marla led them to the drawing room where Thad stood nursing a tumbler of scotch.

Thad looked at them, then his watch, then back at them. Imperiously he said, "Thank you for not making me wait."

Aaron could almost feel Neal bristling at the comment. He decided to step in and smooth things over. A task he had grown good at over the years. "Well, how could we be late when you've promised such an entertaining evening?"

Neal bit his lip, a sure sign he was fighting with every ounce of his being a cutting quip, or smartass remark.

Thad's expression turned to amusement. Much like Neal, he too wore an expensive shirt and tie ensemble, along with black slacks and black dress shoes as well. Two peas in a pod. If one didn't know better, they could have easily been mistaken as brothers. Both had similar hairstyles and facial expressions. And they were both, utterly, pains in the ass.

In the absence of Thad offering anything else up for conversation, Aaron decided to take the lead. "So, I hear you had Shadow Marbas' construction crew over here doing some landscaping."

"Why am I not surprised that at least everyone in four counties knows *exactly* what's going on, on *my* private property?" This time it was Thad's turn to roll his eyes. Then, as if remembering his well-bred manners, he set down his scotch, and walked across the room toward the minibar. "Can I get you gentlemen something to drink?"

Neal's eyes traveled over the walls of the room as he pretended to be engrossed by the rooms decor. "I'll have scotch on the rocks."

"Same, *please*." Aaron emphasized the please while shooting Neal a look that warned him to be polite.

"Two scotch on the rocks coming up," Thad said, watching as Neal scrutinized a painting over the fireplace. He motioned toward it with ice tongs in his left hand. "My great-grandfather."

Aaron wasn't sure what to say so he said the first thing that came to mind. "Striking eyes."

"He was an intense man." Thad dropped exactly three ice cubes in each tumbler then pulled out a bottle of very expensive scotch from the cabinet behind him. He was generous with both pours, then recapped the bottle and set it aside.

Aaron thought it was only polite to at least meet Thad halfway to retrieve his scotch, instead of making him walk all the way across the room to hand it to him. "Thank you," he said, taking the tumbler.

Neal, on the other hand, moved further away, this time admiring a dagger on display on the wall. "Ritual blade?"

Thad appeared as though he was holding back a scowl, and approached Neal's side practically thrusting the tumbler into his hand. "Yes."

It was almost comical to watch. Neither man seemed to want to open the conversation enough for it to flow freely. Instead they exchanged brief terse questions and answers that left little room for extraneous discussion.

Aaron tried again. "Have you heard that Esther Branson is training Apophis' new high priestess, Belinda Applegate, as the new seer?"

But it was no use. Thad replied, "Yes."

No additional commentary, nothing. At least earlier that day he and Aaron were able to have a dialog that wasn't quite as clipped. Obviously, the problem was Neal. Aaron breathed a sigh of relief when Marla returned, bringing with her an infectious air of sociability.

"I hope you two have managed to be polite to one another in my absence." She was certainly direct.

"They haven't killed each other yet," Aaron said with a smile. Then he took a drink of scotch, welcoming the slow burn in the back of his throat.

"So, Neal, how is The Watch these days?" Marla smiled sweetly at Neal, making it impossible for him to be rude to her.

Thad seemed interested in Neal's answer. It was the first time since they'd arrived that he leaned forward and looked at him, receptive to anything Neal might have to say.

"Always watching," he said, eyeing his scotch and then taking a drink. Then he smirked.

"We're planning on petitioning the Haileyville Council to reinstate regular full moon rituals," Aaron offered. He ignored Neal's disapproving look. "They are good for the kids, and the older people tend to like them as well."

Thad moved over to one of the red upholstered high backed chairs and sat down, crossing his legs. "Marla bring me my scotch. It seems to me that we tried this once before. And some of the unrulier covens ruined the entire thing with animal sacrifice."

Marla, having retrieved Thad's scotch, handed it to him. "Oh Thad. You know those young men of Temple Apophis were only attempting to rile everyone up. Besides, it was only a chicken."

"Yeah, but regardless, it was a disaster. The fact is that *the thirteen* cannot get along at a single event."

"I disagree," Aaron said. "I think heavily moderated events will be well attended and have little in the way of disruption. Those attending merely have to sign an agreement for their code of conduct."

"I agree," said Marla. "Besides, that was five years ago, and hopefully the covens have matured since then."

Thad snorted. "Well, for Sheriff Watson's sake, I hope so."

"What about Temple of the Magi? Anything new with all of you?" Neal asked with a raised eyebrow.

"We have our annual polo game next weekend," Marla volunteered. The heightened pitch in her voice and the sparkle in her eyes told them that she was really excited about the event. These were the things members of the wealthier covens had to look forward to. Polo, along with a luncheon that included wine and cocktails no doubt. The covens whose members were in lower income brackets, well, they looked forward to beer on the back porch on Friday night.

"Maybe we should just cut the bullshit and move this conversation along to the real reason you both are here," Thad said. "You both know that I have unlocked the secret to conjuring and capturing spirits."

A heavy silence fell over the room.

"Maybe we should just have dinner," Marla said, forcing a smile. When she did this, the crow's feet beginning in the corners of her eyes became more evident. "We should save magick talk for afterward."

Marla was far more interested in entertaining, or so it seemed. Undoubtedly, she organized all the temple's events. As social as she was it was no surprise. Aaron appraised her outfit. It was a simple blue frock that hit just above the knee. It probably cost several hundred dollars, but it was tasteful and classic. Much like Marla herself. Aaron wondered then how Thad and Marla had met. They seemed an unlikely pair. He didn't dare ask though. That might have been a conversation he could have with Marla away from Thad, but both Thad and Neal would likely find it annoying.

"Should we go through to the dining room?" Marla asked. She held out a hand to Thad who took it and stood. Neal and Eric hung back a few paces behind their hosts and followed.

Just as Aaron suspected, every inch of the Blackwood mansion had been considered by the decorator. Interesting artwork ranging from alchemical woodcarvings, to Qabalistic prints, and everything in between, graced every single room. They passed through the library on their way to the dining room and Aaron fought the urge to pause and admire the wood carved Enochian tablets he saw sitting on a shelf. The overstuffed bookshelves were also tempting. He managed to catch a few titles as they went by. One being a rare copy of *Decium Daemonia*, or *Ten Daemons*; a book of dark conjuration of ten of the most formidable infernal spirits. He made a mental note to stop back in this room at some point before the evening was over.

The long mahogany dining room table had already been set with four places at the far end next to the French doors leading out to the balcony on the back of the house. The room was filled with various species of houseplants, including two large ferns with variegated leaves. Naturally, Thad took the head of the table. Marla sat to his right. Aaron thought it best to sit at Thad's left, just so he and Neal had someone between them. Marla lifted a small bell from next to her plate and shook it. The soft tinkle of the clapper against the silver sound bow filled the room and made Aaron bite his lower lip to keep from grinning like an idiot. It was so stereotypical; a privileged woman summoning her servant with a bell.

An older, nondescript woman about fifty, emerged from the kitchen with a large covered platter. Thad stood and took the platter from her, setting it down in the middle of the table and removing the lid. A complete meal of grilled fish, asparagus, and butter sauce sat inside.

"I hope you both like fish. Thad and I try to eat light in the evening," she said in an almost apologetic voice.

The cook, or perhaps it was a maid, had disappeared back into the kitchen.

"Oh, that's fine. You shouldn't have gone through the trouble. It looks wonderful," Aaron said. He gave their hostess a reassuring smile.

Neal said nothing and didn't argue when Aaron took up his plate so Thad could place a piece of fish onto it along with several of the asparagus spears. Once everyone was served, Thad sat back down and they began eating in silence. Marla, calm and collected, watched them with pensive green eyes while nursing a glass of white wine.

It was probably the most uncomfortable dinner Aaron had ever experienced. The tension was so thick it would have required a chainsaw to cut through. Of course, he knew it was worse for Neal, and probably just as bad for Thad. He would've much rather had dinner with just Marla. He had no doubt that they would have plenty of things to talk about. Especially regarding the quirkiness of their husbands.

A light meal didn't take too long to eat and they were finished within fifteen minutes. When they were done, Marla poured Aaron a large glass of white wine and they all went to the back porch that looked out over the back of the estate. Thad motioned them to follow down the steps, around the pool, through a gate, and down more stone steps into what appeared to be a large walled-in clearing.

Both men followed obediently.

"This is what I had the Shadow Marbas crew put in for me." He motioned toward the space with his outstretched hand like a salesman presenting a luxury car. "What do you think?"

Neither Neal nor Aaron said anything. They were too busy studying the symbols inlayed into the stone pavers.

"Is that copper?" Neal finally asked, leaning down to inspect one of the center stones more closely.

"It's a complete energy grid," Thaddeus said, as if that explained everything. When he realized they didn't understand, he sighed and further explained, "You conjure the spirit to physical manifestation, the grid catches it, and you draw it into the vessel you wish to keep it in. Depending on the spirit, the vessel would contain the spirit's metal, or seals meant to keep it. As with a brass vessel or an iron pot like a Nganga. Of course, you can amend the operation by opening certain gates or drawing the spirit through…"

"Corpses?" Aaron offered.

Thaddeus narrowed his eyes and that sly smile slid over his lips again. "Yes. Exactly."

Neal's jaw dropped, then he cocked his head to one side, narrowed his eyes and said, "You're screwing with us."

"There are two things I never lie about. The first is magick. I am *Magister* of the Temple of the Magi, after all. The second, my experience in said magick." Thad wore a smug smile. "Now, do you want to see the spirit?"

Aaron had a bad feeling about this, but he gulped it back and looked at Neal for a clue on how they would proceed.

Neal, of course, wanted Thaddeus Blackwood to prove it, and wore his look of disbelief proudly. "I want to see it."

With a pleased look and another sly grin, Thaddeus beckoned them to follow.

The basement of the Blackwood mansion was not basement-like at all. It was completely finished, impeccably decorated with Romanesque god-form statuary and expensive tapestries, and boasted eight-foot ceilings and recessed lighting. Even the large temple, that could easily fit seventy-five people comfortably, didn't have that basement-feel.

"This is nice and private." Aaron said, stretching his neck to see how the ceiling vaulted upward, through the main floor, the second floor, and to a windowed tower in the roof, bringing the last rays of soft evening sunlight into the basement. That's when he noticed there was a stair case leading from the main floor to the second floor that wrapped around the conical rise of the room. The temple actually opened to the rest of the house. It wasn't just private – it was genius and awe inspiring. Now he knew why the mansion appeared to have so many rooms from the outside.

Most of the covens had private temples, save for the few who had found old churches and converted them. The public temples were always in danger of being graffitied. Not by members of the thirteen covens, but rather ex-coven members, usually converts to outside religions. But it was rare that it happened. Those covens who didn't want to be bothered with excess security, or the expense of cleaning graffiti off the sides of their buildings once every five years or so, maintained private temples like this one.

It was truly a sight to behold. Beautiful altars stood at each elemental quadrant, draped with black and red silken altar cloths, and covered in glass to keep wax and whatever else from destroying the fabric. Upon each altar sat matching pillar candles, and gilded tools befitting each element. Much like a Christian church, there were two rows of richly polished mahogany pews with padded kneelers that took up at least half of the temple area. A crimson carpet led the way between the two rows of pews from the vestibule, into the nave, and up to the main altar. The main altar, and the lectern, also made of mahogany, stood before the pews for public address and ritual. But behind the altar there was a large empty space where a nine by nine black slate circle had been carefully inlaid into the gray marble floor, so that invocations and sigils could be written down in chalk, and later changed or erased to fit the ritual. Now, the circle was black, with no chalk traces of a recent ritual. Undoubtedly, Marla Blackwood had it scrubbed clean by the maid after each ritual. To the left, there was a door, likely leading to a vestry. Tall stands for pillar candles lined the back wall next to the large gold pentagram that hung as a dominant focal point in this holy church.

Thad watched their reactions with an appreciative look. He was every bit the show-off. "Come," he said, leading them to the back of the temple to a locked door on their right. Instead of a key, he punched in a code on the keypad. The door's inner workings made a mechanical whir, and with a click it unlocked.

Marla followed behind them, hanging back a few paces. Inside was a cozy alcove of alchemical delights. Aaron wondered why he felt so apprehensive. There was a vibration in the room that made him want to leave. It filled him with dread, as if any minute, something bad was going to happen.

Various apparatus had been set up on two long counters in the middle of the room, but none of it looked as though it had been recently used. Books on herbs and alchemy lined the shelves. This also appeared to be where Thad and Marla stored supplies for the temple. Three shelves were filled with candles of every color, two with oils and elixirs, and five shelves almost eight feet long sat filled with herbs and incenses. The far wall housed a long window that looked out into the clear blue water of the deep end of the swimming pool. It was strange looking out into water. In the winter, with the tarp over the pool, Neal imagined it looked rather dreary. Abyssal even.

Neal and Aaron didn't even notice it until Thaddeus reached toward it. The bottle, entwined with silver and copper, was a foot tall and about eight inches in circumference. It might have been mistaken for a fancy wine bottle if the damn thing weren't glowing with an eerie golden light.

Taking it into his hands, Thad lifted it. "Here it is."

Neal cocked his head to one side. "The spirit you put in a bottle? Djinn?"

Thaddeus laughed. "To some people a Djinn. That's the official story anyhow." Then he uttered a single name that made Neal and Aaron both recoil with fear. "Sorath. Death aspect."

Neal gulped hard enough that it was noticeable. "You can't be serious."

"Don't get testy, Neal," Thad said, gently setting the bottle back on the shelf amid other bottles, none of which glowed. "It's just a major solar Daemon."

Aaron stepped up to Neal and took his hand into his own. He wasn't sure what to say. Just when the silence grew uncomfortable he let go of Neal's hand and said, "What are you going to do with it?"

Neal shot him a perplexed look, as if it was the dumbest question ever asked.

"I haven't decided yet." Thaddeus said with a smug shrug. "I initially just wanted to see if it could be done."

"And you chose fucking *Sorath*?" Neal hissed, as if the Daemon would hear him and become enraged. "This is the most irresponsible…"

Thaddeus held up a hand to silence him. "I don't need lectures from *The Watch* about the magick I perform. I assure you it was carefully thought out."

"Apparently not well enough if you had no good reason to do it to begin with…" Neal started.

Marla stood in the doorway, quiet as a mouse.

"My reason was to see if it could be done." Thad ushered them toward the door and back into the temple, closing the door behind him. It locked automatically.

"This is a disaster," Neal said, eyes locked on Thad. "You have to let it go, and try not to kill yourself, or anyone else, when you do it. You know – it's this kind of arrogance and ignorance that destroyed the original coven to begin with. This is the reason our grandfathers grew to hate each other. Your family has always been reckless, Thaddeus. The apple doesn't fall far from that tree."

Thaddeus took Neal's lecture in stride, his expression not deviating from smug superiority. "Your objection is duly noted. I thought for sure you would be more interested in learning the technique instead of admonishing me for my success."

Neal let out an exasperated sigh. "I do want to know..."

"Very well. Let's go to the library and take our coffee there, and I'll explain the procedure."

Despite the revelation that Thaddeus was willing to talk about the operation openly, and that Neal was mortified, a reaction Aaron hadn't expected based on Neal's original plan to steal the bottle and the ritual, Aaron couldn't help but be happy to be going back to the library. The comfort of theory and armchair magick was exactly what he needed right now.

But when they got there, Aaron couldn't find comfort in the books, despite the shelves filled with old volumes, some of them extremely rare. He ambled along the bookshelves, reading titles and touching hand-bound leather spines, his lips pursed, his jaw set. He couldn't just ignore what they'd just seen and start pulling books from shelves to flip through them. He realized then that Thad and Neal weren't talking. Instead, their eyes followed him.

It was Thad who finally spoke up. "It wasn't what you expected."

"No," Aaron admitted. He turned on his heel and faced Thad and Neal. "I hadn't expected it to be so..."

"Disturbing," Thad finished.

"Yeah." Aaron brought his hands up to his eyes and rubbed them, then his temples. Thank Daemons they hadn't gone with Neal's original plan. Having the black sun, Sorath, in a bottle, would have been a nightmare. Then he corrected himself – it *was* a nightmare.

Thad motioned to an empty chair next to Neal. "Sit. I'll show you what I did."

There was a hint of compassion in Thad's voice, and his arrogance vanished. He reached behind him and pulled a book from one of the shelves. It looked like a plain hardbound journal. Nothing nearly as fancy as a coven grimoire, which were generally bound in leather. This appeared to be an experimental journal, and when Thad opened it, that's exactly what it was. "I tried a lot of different methods before I found the right one," he said, thumbing through to the back. When he found what he was looking for, he opened the page and placed the now open book on the coffee table between them. "Here."

He sat back then and didn't even flinch when Neal leaned forward and grabbed the open book and began reading. Aaron read over his shoulder, his stomach twisting with knots the entire time.

The ritual was quite simple really. It worked by drawing the spirit to the ritual with invocation, then luring them into the spirit trap, through the corpse, and straight into the vessel, which contained elements pleasing to the spirit. The vibration of the invocations and the energy conduits were crucial elements.

When both men had finished reading, Neal offered the book to Aaron, who shook his head. Neal set it back on the table.

"Why did you want to share this with us?" Neal asked in a resigned voice. "It wasn't just to brag."

"Everyone knows about it, right? It only seemed fair I at least share it with The Watch. Just in case anything happens to me." Thad looked at the closed door as if he expected Marla to barge in at any second. She could have, but she didn't. "Look, I already intended to let the energy of Sorath go. But I need people I can trust to deal with it if something goes wrong. That's The Watch's job, right?"

Much to Aaron's surprise, Neal didn't make any sarcastic comments, and instead said, "I understand."

"Good," he said, retrieving a folder from the same shelf he'd stowed the book on. He handed the folder to Aaron, not Neal. "But don't you tell a damned soul you have this. This is for your information only just in case there comes a need for you to have it. The only other person who has a copy is my temple Scribe. He can be trusted. It contains all of the specifics and dimensions down to the millimeter."

Aaron thumbed through the folder and saw copies of what they'd just read. However, there were additional pages. One that included precise dimensions for the spirit trap and how each paver was to be put together and placed.

"You think something bad is going to happen," Aaron said.

Thad shrugged. "Well, since word is out, I could be murdered for it, or Marla kidnapped. Or my home broken into. It doesn't seem safe to keep it to myself. But I trust you, Aaron."

Neal scoffed. "You realize we're a package deal, right?"

A sly grin covered Thad's lips. "Unfortunately, yes."

With another beaming smile, Marla entered the room with a tray of coffee and Danish. "Time for dessert!"

The raspberry Danish was warm and flakey and the coffee was dark and smooth, unlike the bitter, cheap coffee most people served.

"I picked the raspberries myself," Marla told them proudly. As they ate, Aaron mused how her pride in her raspberry Danish matched Thaddeus' pride at sealing a spirit in a bottle.

They left after that. Neal drove home, too, since Aaron had drank not only the scotch, but also several glasses of wine.

"Did that seem sudden and odd to you?" Neal asked. His eyes did not avert from the road ahead of him.

"Yes. I'm not sure what to think. I can't believe he gave us the folder." Aaron clutched the folder in his hands, realizing it felt damp. Then he noticed his hands were tense and sweaty, and rubbed them on his knees.

"I feel like we've just been played for idiots. Or we're part of some larger plot. There's something going on here and we need to get to the bottom of it." Neal sounded a little worried.

Aaron didn't blame him, he felt worried too. It was possible that Thad was being honest, and sincere. But it seemed so out of character for him to start the evening out so arrogantly, and then change to become responsible and forward thinking. True, it was possible that Thad could become a target. After all, Neal and Aaron had been talking about stealing the bottle and ritual from him just the night before. How many other covens were having that same conversation right now? And what would Sorath do if unleashed? There were so many variables and scenarios, few of them ending with a positive outcome.

Neal seemed to know what he was thinking. "We need to do a divination," he said. "There's something going on here and I feel like we haven't been told the whole story."

"The temple was amazing." It was the only thing Aaron could say because he had nothing else to say about Sorath, or the ritual in the folder on his lap.

When they arrived home, Aaron felt grateful to be in familiar surroundings. Safe surroundings. He and Neal went through once a month and checked the fence line for curse sigils, and made sure the protective witch bottles they'd buried at all four quadrants of the property were still intact. Undetectable markers had been painted on the fence were each one was buried. If the dirt was undisturbed, the bottle was fine. Though there had been times that Aaron had wanted to dig them up, so he could see the tops - just to make sure they were still there. Only he and Neal knew they were there, but one could never be to certain with the number of seers and mediums in the tri-county area.

Now inside the comfort of the house and the openness of the great room that contained their large kitchen, the dining room, and the living room, Neal pulled out his Thoth tarot deck from the black box on the main bookshelf in the living room. While their house was big it didn't have a drawing room, or as many rooms in general, but it did have a dedicated office and a library. The Watch, too, had an impressive collection of books, but it lacked some of the rarer titles. Aaron mused how if they ever did break into Thaddeus Blackwood's house, forget stealing rituals and Daemons in bottles. He would steal a few of those rare volumes he saw sitting on Thaddeus Blackwood's bookshelves.

While Neal sat down on the couch and began shuffling the tarot deck, Aaron felt the need for another drink. If for no other reason than to remove his care for that strange buzzing feeling that still hummed through his body after seeing the bottle with Sorath encased in it. "You want a drink?"

Neal set the cards on the table in front of him and cut them three times sideways. Then he brought them back together. His eyes were set on his task and he didn't look up. "Just some water."

With that, he took the cards aloft in one hand and begin drawing one card at a time and placing the cards drawn in a Celtic cross spread. Aaron waited until Neal was finished and leaned back on the couch, eyeing the cards intently. Then Neal leaned forward again and studied them more closely.

Getting up and moving to the bar, Aaron made a black Russian for himself, and an ice water for Neal, then went back to the couch to sit beside Neal and look at the cards.

Neal took a sip of water, set it down, and said, "Distant past foundation shows Thad's arrogance and determination. Recent past foundation shows recklessness and lack of

restraint. Current position, a problem that must be solved."
Neal gave Aaron a sidelong look that said *did you expect anything
else?* Then he continued, "In his head deception, planning, and
work. Directly ahead, things not going as planned. Imagine
that. Paths to the final outcome, struggle and strife. The final
outcome - harmony. I think that's pretty damn clear."

Aaron took a long drink, his eyes never averting from
the cards, not even for a second. After another minute studying
the cards himself he said, "And here I thought maybe
Thaddeus had grown a little."

Neal laughed. "The ritual he gave us is probably
something banal. A self-curse perhaps."

"He probably began hatching the plan after I left this
morning. I just wish I knew what that plan was." Aaron
finished his drink.

"We'll figure it out," Neal said, matter-of-fact.

3

Esther Branson, Haileyville's solitary Seer, not bound to any coven, woke with a pain in her chest. It felt like someone had stabbed her. She sat up and swung her legs over the side of the bed then grabbed the phone. But the receiver fell from her grasp and she fell forward, her vision blurring into thick gray smoke. She heard a strange whirring noise, then she saw flames, and from those flames deep piercing yellow eyes looked back at her. They belonged to something not of this world. Of fire. Something from the Daemonic plane. She heard a single word then, hissed by the flames. *Death.* The message was clear. Someone in one of the thirteen covens was going to die. Maybe not today, but soon.

4

It was Aaron who picked up the phone at six thirty in the morning. On the other end of the line was one of their members with the news that Esther Branson had a heart attack the night before. It was her protégé, Belinda Applegate, now priestess of Temple Apophis, who made the call to 9-1-1, and sent them over to Esther's. Apparently, Belinda had gotten a vision in her sleep, woke, called Esther and when no one answered, she had known something was wrong. It was information like this that The Watch collected on all the covens and solitaries day-to-day.

Like it always had been done, Aaron made an entry into the logbook, a large black and red hardbound ledger, with the date and incident. The Watch had hundreds of these logbooks stored in a fireproof vault, chronicling the history of thirteen covens over the past fifty years or more.

It was less than an hour later when the phone rang again. Aaron answered.

"Aaron, something terrible has happened," she said.

It took him a few seconds to realize he was talking to Marla Blackwood. "Marla, what's wrong?"

Whether it was the alarm in his voice, or something else, it drew Neal from the other room. He stood there waiting for Aaron to give him some indication of who he was speaking to.

Aaron put the phone on speaker.

"Thaddeus had to go to New York and left early this morning. But when I woke up, the back-patio doors were open, the library was a mess, and the bottle was missing from the basement. Sheriff Watson is on his way, but when I told Thaddeus - he told me I needed to call you right away."

Aaron wasn't sure what to say. This could have been part of Thaddeus's plan. For all they knew Thaddeus had done it himself, and staged a break in before leaving for New York. Or perhaps it was all a ruse and the bottle wasn't missing it all. "Do you want me to come over?"

What she said next furthered Aaron suspicions. "No I should be fine. Sheriff Watson just pulled up. I must go. Thaddeus just wanted me to let you know that it happened."

The line went dead. Aaron couldn't help but feel like he and Neal were being pulled into some sinister and dramatic play where they were unwilling actors. He set the phone back on the charger on the kitchen counter and shook his head, looking at Neal. "Do you believe this crap? He has his wife call to tell us his *bottled Sorath* has gone missing."

In that moment, Aaron changed his mind about Marla Blackwood. She drew people to her with her charm and charisma, and yet it was all a manipulative act. Even though it was likely through Thad's prodding, the fact that she complied made her complicit.

Neal nodded. "How convenient."

"We do log entry on this?" But he already knew the answer. They always made a log entry, even if it was bullshit drama.

Neal nodded. "We may need to write up a full report on the entire incident."

Aaron groaned. Major incidents required they write up an entire report and put it in a filing cabinet in the vault. There were two filing cabinets down there now. If things kept going like they were, by the time Neal and Aaron were old men, there would be a third and perhaps a fourth. Life was never dull in the tri-county area. "Blessed are The Watchers."

"Is that what we are? Blessed?" Neal laughed and went back to the other room to listen to the news.

Aaron made the log entry, then grabbed his laptop and started a file he saved as *The Blackwood Incident* and then the date. When he was done with the file, it would be uploaded to a remote server and a copy would be printed for a plain Manila file folder that would go down to the vault. Aaron and Neal didn't have a large temple in their basement - just a game room with the bar, storage, the furnace room, and that damn vault. Their temples were located on Neal's parent's estate, five miles away.

When he was finished, he joined Neal in the living room. He felt slightly queasy and tired, and maybe even a little hung over. He had six drinks the night before, which was well over his usual limit. Being a lightweight was never good when it came to alcohol. Sitting down next to Neal, he put his feet up on the coffee table. "I'm so glad I don't have to work today. I have a feeling we're in for dramatic weekend."

Neal took Aaron's hand into his. "Maybe we should get out for a while. Go into Haileyville and visit Black Raven. Maybe take in a movie, or go visit Tiamat-Leviathan for their afternoon public mass. It will be good to get out of the house."

Aaron nodded. It was good for Neal to get out especially. Not working, he spent more time at home than he probably should have. They weren't close to town anyway. It was a good twenty-five-minute drive. "I'd like that," he said. Then he got up and went to the bedroom to take off his pajama bottoms and put on some actual clothes.

Convincing Neal not to wear a suit took some doing, but Aaron managed it and they left the house with Aaron in jeans and a T-shirt, and Neal wearing khakis and a polo shirt. Instead of driving the Mercedes, they took their black convertible Mustang, and drove it with the top down into Haileyville. It was a bright, clear beautiful day. Blue Oyster Cult's *Don't Fear the Reaper* played on the radio. And at least for the drive, Aaron forgot all about the thirteen covens.

All of that changed the second they pulled onto Main Street in Haileyville. The small town bustled with activity. It was a warm Saturday morning, and it seemed everyone was out shopping and socializing. As they went, Aaron realized just how many people they saw that they knew. Two members of Shadow Marbas sat at a table sipping coffee on the café patio. A group of members from Lucifer's Haven were having lunch at one of the picnic tables in the park.

"Should we do lunch?" Neal broke Aaron's thoughts with the suggestion. "We could go to Hades."

It'd been over a year since they'd been to *Hades Bar and Grill*. The upbeat burger joint was an oasis for the blue-collar covens. It didn't often see the likes of Aaron and Neal. A burger sounded good, and Aaron felt his stomach growl in response to the suggestion. He hadn't had a burger since the last time they gone to Hades. "Yeah, that sounds good."

Aaron also knew that Neal wanted to go to Hades to listen to the gossip. Haileyville was like a Mecca to the covens. And when one visited Mecca, one could tell who was hanging out with who, who had had a falling out with who, and without even trying you could learn what was going on. It was the perfect playground for members of The Watch. Of course, usually when members of the other covens spotted members of The Watch, their conversations turned to whispers. But try as they might they could never fully keep their secrets because, as the saying went, *the watchers were always watching*.

Hades, being one of the few coven-only establishment within a twenty-five-mile radius, on a Saturday afternoon, was busy as, well, Hades. The minute they walked in the door they realized they'd be waiting at least ten minutes to get a table. Neal didn't seem annoyed by this at all. But Aaron knew it was because it gave Neal time to sit and eavesdrop. Or people watch as he sometimes liked to call it.

The young twentysomething hostess behind the podium at the front door regarded them with a quick cheerful smile. She wore a red headband with two red fake horns and carried a plastic pitchfork. "Welcome to Hades Bar and Grill, how many?"

Neal gave her a smile as if to say, *how quaint.* Instead he said, "Two."

"It's going to be a fifteen-minute wait," she said with that same perky tone. "Your name?"

"Neal," he said, looking past her into the busy dining area of the restaurant.

Aaron looked, too. Inside, they saw their coven mates Ken Franklin and Alex Sinclair having lunch with their wives Jen and Anna. Neal nodded in acknowledgement when Ken and Alex noticed them. Dave and Rachel Tidwell from Circle of the Black Moon, were trying to wrestle their toddler into a booth. Three members of the Temple Dagon sat conspiring in the far back. It seemed that at least one member of each of the thirteen covens was present. Aaron looked over at Neal and saw the small smile on his lips. It was nice to see Neal enjoying himself.

They moved back against the wall so that more incoming could leave their names with the petite hostess. For the most part, the people waiting with them made an effort not to look at Aaron and Neal, but a few times, out of the corner of his eye, Aaron caught one or two of them looking. The waiting area was strangely silent.

From the look on his face Aaron knew that Neal was enjoying this far too much. He really needed to get out more.

It wasn't long before Neal got tired of the silence and said, addressing the entire group of waiting patrons, "Has anyone heard how Esther is doing?"

The wild haired redhead with striking green eyes, Chelsea DeLint of Ashtaroth Briarwood, was the only one to offer an answer. "I hear she's going to be fine. She was lucky that Belinda called the ambulance when she did."

The woman next to her tapped her elbow, as if hinting that she should shut up. It looked to be her sister, though Aaron couldn't be sure. There were some coven members who were very active and well known in the community and others who lurked in the shadows of their more extroverted coven mates.

"Oh good. We were distressed to hear what happened. Is she at Tri-County General?" Neal asked.

"Yes," Chelsea said, enduring another tap on her elbow from her sister.

Neal turned to Aaron and said, "We'll have to send flowers and a get-well note."

"Agreed," Aaron said absently. He was busy watching two whispering, black-haired teenagers on the far side of the waiting area. The girls wore black lipstick. It was anyone's guess whose spawn they were. But they were obviously whispering about Neal and Aaron, and looking at them.

Neal smiled at them. "You have a question, ladies?"

"No," one of them said.

She looked like she was about to say more when the hostess interrupted and said, "Neal, your table's ready. Is a booth okay?"

They were led through the maze of filled tables to the back, right next to the table of Temple Dagon members. Which, of course, immediately went silent upon their approach. They sat and took their menus, and the hostess left.

Jeff Meyers, a folksy man in his late thirties who ran a small farm just outside of town, regarded them coolly. "Well now, if it ain't the heads of *The Watch*. We don't see you two out here that often. To what do we owe the pleasure?"

One of the women with them, Danette Lyons, tittered.

"Is it okay if we decide to come into town and have lunch on a Saturday afternoon?" Neal asked, not looking up from his menu. Neither of them needed to look at the menu as Hades bar and Grill served your typical burger joint staples. A variety of burgers, chicken fingers, chicken salad, fries, onion rings and the like. When people came here they wanted a burger and fries. If they wanted something else they would've gone someplace else.

"I reckon it's okay. This just isn't really your scene. You got more money than all the people in this place combined. So, I gather the real reason you're here is to watch everyone." Jeff Meyers picked up his iced tea and took a long drink.

"It doesn't matter where I go Jeffrey," Neal said. "I'm always watching wherever I go. You know how it works. We were tasked long ago to keep a chronicle of the covens. And I take the job seriously."

"So, as you know everything going on, maybe you could tell us what happened up at the Blackwood mansion earlier. Chris here heard Sheriff Steve going out there on the police scanners this morning." Jeff motioned to Chris Bain, the owner of the local mechanic shop.

Neal was about to speak, but Aaron jumped in first. "I'll tell you if you trade us one piece of information you don't think we know."

A wide grin appeared on Neal's face and Aaron knew that this was certainly the reason he and Neal were so good together.

Jeff narrowed his eyes. The look on his face was somewhere between contemplation and amusement. "All right. You first."

"Apparently, there was a break-in at the Blackwood mansion," Aaron offered, not giving up any details.

"What kind of break in? Was anything stolen?" Chris asked.

Neal shook his head. "Don't know."

Aaron chimed in, "Yeah, we don't always get those kinds of details. Just the basics. So, your turn."

"Is it true that The Watch is trying to start up the full moon rituals again?" Danette asked. It was a nice attempt at a diversion.

But her question didn't faze Aaron or Neal. They both kept their eyes fixed on Jeff.

"Yeah," Aaron offered, not looking at her.

Finally, Jeff spilled. "There's something a little weird going on with Lucifer's Haven. That kid, Brian Blake, the orphan. He disappeared a while back, heard he was dead. But then he shows up alive."

"Kid probably went off on a bender. I don't see how that's anything useful. Not for the ledger anyway," Neal said.

Chris leaned and then practically whispering across the small aisle between the tables. "Yeah but I listen to the police scanners, and I have a friend in the Black Rose Coven. The coroner was called out to the park. Dead kid by the name of Brian Blake. Guess who showed up at the morgue within seven hours?" When no one offered up an answer, Chris continued. "Jason, along with that new girl in Lucifer's Haven, I think her name is Connie, along with Belinda Applegate and Warren Leonard from Temple Apophis. They walked out of the morgue with Brian Blake in tow. Alive."

Aaron felt his eyes widen and noticed that Neal's had done the same. "You think Temple Apophis and Lucifer's Haven used necromancy to bring Brian Blake back from the dead?"

"We don't think it. Where pretty sure it happened," Jeff said. "Put *that* in your ledger."

If it were true, that wasn't just a simple ledger entry, it was another incident file. Aaron pulled out his pocket notebook to jot a few notes so he could type it up later.

"Now I know you both know more details about the Blackwood incident. We gave you something juicy. Tell us a little more," Jeff said.

Neal chuckled. "Very well. The story as I got it was that Thaddeus Blackwood left for New York early this morning before six-thirty AM. And sometime between then and nine this morning, Marla Blackwood woke up to find the back door open and the Temple supply room broken into. But I don't know if anything was missing. Maybe someone really needed some candles?"

Aaron breathed an inner sigh of relief that Neal hadn't revealed too much. Not that he had expected him to. But sometimes, in the course of regular conversation, things would slip. Neal gave just enough detail that members of the Temple Dagon seemed satisfied.

"I wish we knew more, too," Aaron offered. "Whoever had the gall to break into the Blackwood mansion knowing there were guns and dogs waiting for them if they were caught, had a lot of balls. Your story was far more interesting than ours."

"Ain't that the truth- all the way around," Jeff Meyers said just as the waitress approached to take Neal and Aaron's order.

By the time their order arrived, Jeff and the rest of his Temple Dagon posse had left. Aaron and Neal ate in silence, listening.

You could learn a lot by listening. By the time they'd finished lunch they'd learned that a notable Senator had been seen leaving the estate of the Ba'al Collective's Grand Magus. They learned that Ellie Ayers and Jacob of the Shadow Marbas were having ritual sex in front of her husband, who liked to watch. They found out that Tiamat-Leviathan had deemed themselves protectorates over all the solitaries, and that Carla Devlin and her girlfriend were getting married. The ladies of

Ashtaroth Briarwood had been caught dancing naked in the forest off county road twenty-three by one of the sheriff's deputies during a fertility rite for one of their members. The woman and her husband had, apparently, been trying to conceive for two years without any luck. There was also a new solitary theistic Satanist in town who only went by Leon, who liked to preach on the corner in the city park, a thing that Carl Devlin, the city manager and head of Lucifer's Haven, had little patience for.

When they left, Aaron had over ten pages of notes. He and Neal would decide later which tidbits would go into the ledger.

The air had gotten warmer, and the day more perfect. The streets of the small town were filled with voices and laughter. The scent of popcorn and coffee wafted out at them. Aaron eased into a comfortable stride next to Neal as they made their way toward the temple of Tiamat-Leviathan. Their Saturday public ritual began at two-thirty.

"We need to get out more often, even if it is only to stop by Eve's," Neal said, nodding toward Black Raven as they passed it. They'd already decided to stop there after afternoon mass.

"Yeah," Aaron agreed, feeling contented and happy. Terrified thoughts of a rogue *Sorath-in-a-bottle* were pushed to the back of his mind, for now at least.

The Temple of Tiamat-Leviathan stood next to the Temple Dagon. Both had once been Christian churches, but once the last non-coven members moved from the area in the early eighties, the churches had been abandoned and the covens had taken them over. Tiamat-Leviathan was a smaller church. It looked to have been Pentecostal pre-takeover. Whereas Temple Dagon was an older, grand Catholic affair, now boasting stained glass windows with images of serpents among the semi-opaque mosaics.

Both had black, cast iron fencing with spiked pickets encircling them, with gates that were locked at night. Today the gates were wide open, as were the doors to the temple, revealing the small crowd already in attendance. They followed a young, slender woman wearing a flowered dress and a wide brimmed sun hat, an outfit more befitting summer than a warm autumn day, through the gates and into a line. The steady stream of people moved up the flagstone pathway to the stairs and into the anti-chamber of the temple. Neal and Aaron paused only to take the programs handed them by the surprised attendant, who obviously never expected members of The Watch to step through the doors.

Aaron looked at the program. *Call of Tiamat-Leviathan and Abyssal Communion* was printed on the front of it, along with the date and time. *Presented by Tiamat-Leviathan* it said in a smaller font at the bottom. Inside, the program listed every part of the ritual, who would preside over each part, and instructions for participation in the communion for those who had never been to one before. A lot of practitioners from other parts of the country vacationed here, especially in the spring and autumn months, hoping to get a glimpse of a world where everyone practiced some flavor of pagan magick. Aaron hoped none of them left disappointed. A ritual like this one only meant something if you were dedicated. So many practitioners outside the small world in which the covens lived, were weekend occultists who would never know the deep devotion it took to live and breathe magick twenty-four-seven. Dedication was a way of life.

They sat in the left row of pews, halfway up the far-left aisle, all the way at the end, near the wall. Aaron guessed Neal had chosen these seats just in case they wanted to leave early. Neal didn't like feeling trapped, so a side aisle seat was perfect for him. This temple also had pews and kneelers, aisles, altars and pulpits. But instead of a main altar front and center like many temples had, here the main altar was in the far back, near a door likely leading into a vestry or an additional temple used for magick. This temple, however, was for worship and presentation only, and this was made evident by the lack of a magick circle on the ample wooden floor space in front of the altar.

Aaron leaned over to Neal. "Vestry or additional temple?" He nodded toward the door near the altar.

Neal shrugged, then seemed to consider it for a moment. "Both."

Settling in, both men watched as new people came in and found their seats. A man and woman who looked to be in their forties, sat next to them. The woman wore a pentagram.

"I hope we're dressed okay for this," she said to her husband, shooting Aaron a kind smile. Then she began going through the program, commenting on everything she read.

"Gods-damned tourists," Neal whispered. Someone closed the doors in back signaling the rite was about to begin.

Everyone in the nave quieted, eyes forward, several people stretching their necks, gawking as if they were waiting for the bearded lady to step into the spotlight, center-stage. Dark, brooding organ music flooded the temple and a hymn to Leviathan began. Aaron and Neal, and those who knew, stood, causing the remainder of the participants to follow suit.

Aaron had always liked this hymn, and he joined in, singing with those few among the onlookers who knew it. Glancing over he was surprised to see Neal's lips moving. Neal wasn't known to sing. But Aaron understood why. Singing wasn't dignified, and The Watch – they were dignified. The entire temple of Tiamat-Leviathan exuded warmth and belonging, and being there made Aaron feel happy. They did live their lives surrounded by practitioners of magick and mysticism, and there was a special warmth that went along with that. A sense of belonging. Of community.

The priest motioned for them to sit, then stood aside, allowing a young priest call the elements from the four quarters of the ritual space. Once he had finished, he went back to his place at a bench off to the side, and the elder priest stepped up to the pulpit.

He read the oration in a strong, deep voice, into the microphone. "We call upon you, Leviathan of the Deep. Tiamat of the Void. Come forth from the great abyss. Hear us! There are many here who seek your wisdom this day, in presence of your avatars and dedicants, here in your temple. Let us pray."

Aaron and Neal joined hands, and by habit, Aaron took the hand of the woman next to him. Both he and Neal recited the prayer along with the priest. "Masters of the watery temples of the abyss. Bring good judgement and balance to all things. Lead us to the altars of peace and joy. Let us carry in our hearts our devotion to you. Hail Tiamat. Hail Leviathan. Amen."

Aaron released his hand from the woman next to him. She was giddy with excitement. He knew that she felt it, too. That sense of belonging. Something the outside world couldn't offer her. She shined with this newfound knowledge and passed Aaron a grateful look as if it was kind of him to include her by taking her hand during prayer. For him, it was just something you did. Both he and Neal had been raised here, and The Watch's temple training had consisted of rigorous homeschool that included memorizing prayer and ritual, and reading all of the classic magickal texts and codices. He could recite a hundred more prayers from memory just like the one they'd just said.

The priest looked directly at Neal and Aaron. "It is good to see our regulars, of course. But it's also good to see so many new faces here today, and some we haven't seen in some time. Today, I am inspired to share a story about that which is hidden from us. As witches and magi, we tend to dislike the hidden, which is why we dedicate our lives to exploring the dark mysteries of nature and everything beyond this physical plane. When I was a boy, I overheard one of my friends tell another friend that something had been taken from his parents' private home temple…."

Aaron and Neal exchanged a look. There was no doubt High Priest Roberts, or Michael outside the temple, was talking about what everyone knew about the Blackwood robbery. Jeff Meyers had probably stopped here on his way to his temple next door, and told Roberts everything Aaron and Neal had told him. There were no closer covens than Tiamat Leviathan and Temple Dagon when it came to working together for the public good. Which was likely the reason Danette Lyons had asked about The Watch's push for the town of Haileyville to reinstate the Full Moon Rituals. That would have been the type of thing their temple would have done. Not The Watch.

Roberts adjusted his stole and brushed a wisp of brown hair from the corner of his eye and continued on, "I went home and told my parents, who told their friends, and by the time the rumor was addressed, it had become a full-blown story of cops and robbers. In some versions of the story, my friend's parents had even been knocked unconscious."

Light laughs and murmurs of amusement ran through the room.

"Which is why," continued Roberts, "when we hear a rumor we should consider it just that, and not spread it until we know its truth. Even then, each of us should ask ourselves what we gain from spreading gossip. Is it our story to tell?"

"No, but it is *our* story to record. So, if people tell the truth to begin with, at least the truth will be in the record," Neal said, loud enough that everyone in the temple turned to look at him, and Aaron wanted to crawl under a rock.

"Magister Watts, would you like to step up here and address those in attendance?" Roberts took two steps to the left of the pulpit.

Much to Aaron's horror, and High Priest Roberts', Neal stood. "I would. Yes."

He walked briskly to the pulpit, his footfalls the only noise in the entire temple. "I'll be brief," Neal said, stepping up to the microphone. "I am Magister Neal Watts of The Watch. As you know, we are the chronical keepers of *the thirteen*. If you have news you'd like written in the official record, including births and marriages, initiations or deaths, please be sure to let us know. If you are looking into family history or research for your group, you are welcome to contact us and request records of events. If you would like to correct the record by rectifying any rumors or mistruths, we will be happy to take this down, too and correct our records accordingly. That's what we're here for. After today's ritual, my husband Aaron and I will be over in the park, at the gazebo. You may talk to us there." Then he turned to High Priest Roberts. "Thank you for allowing me the floor for a moment, sir."

Then he turned his heel and walked smugly back to the pew and sat down next to Aaron.

Roberts smiled graciously and stepped back up to his pulpit. "Thank you, Magister Watts. And now, the Hymn to Tiamat."

Everyone present stood again, and those who knew the hymn rose their voices and sang praise to Tiamat, the primordial goddess of the raging ocean, consort to Leviathan, avatar of Yam.

When the communion started, the woman sitting next to Aaron leaned over. "Would it be okay for us to participate in this if we're not initiated into this temple?"

"Yes," Aaron told her.

She blushed a little, then said cautiously. "I want to participate, but I don't know how to do it.

Aaron was happy to be helpful, and leaned in and whispered to both her and her husband, "It's rather simple. When you go up, you will take a piece of salt and a piece of bread and place them on your tongue. Then you inhale the incense, then feel the warmth of the flame of the candle. Then you drink the wine, which helps to wash down the bread and salt. Finally, the priest anoints your third eye with a balancing oleum. Then we come back to our seats and sit in silent prayer. There's usually one more oration and prayer after that, then the closing."

The tourists nodded and mouthed *thank you*.

Both Aaron and Neal took communion, and they both participated in prayer. Finally, when the ritual was over, they waited until the temple emptied.

Roberts approached them. "You were the last person I expected to crash my Saturday service, Watts."

"I hadn't come here expecting a lecture on doing what The Watch was created to do," he countered.

Aaron stood back, staying out of it. Of course, he sided with Neal, but he was not nearly as confrontational as his significant other.

"Fair enough," Roberts said. "I heard about the robbery at the Blackwood estate."

"Yes, I wish we knew more. I should have Aaron call Marla to make sure she's okay. I know Thaddeus is in the city today. Of course, I have no doubt she has her coven family to lean on. Though if there is anything the rest of us could do to help... we should check. Aaron?" Neal turned to Aaron with an expectant look.

"I'm on it." Aaron took the opportunity to leave the uncomfortable conversation behind and step outside to call Marla.

She answered on the third ring. "Aaron, hi."

Caller ID left nothing a mystery. "Neal and I wanted to check on you to make sure you were all right. Did Sheriff Watson find any clues as to who did it?"

"Hold on," she handed the phone to someone.

Thaddeus was the next to speak. "I think we have a bit of a problem," he said.

Aaron felt a sick twist in his gut.

"It doesn't look like someone broke in after all." There was silence for a moment.

"But the bottle, and the door…" Aaron started.

"Yeah. We found the bottle." Thad audibly hesitated.

"What are you not telling me, Thad." He placed a hand over his right ear so he could hear Thaddeus over the noisy group of teenagers walking on the sidewalk in front of the temple.

"Where are you?"

"Tiamat-Leviathan Saturday mass."

Thad snorted, but kept his opinion of Aaron's whereabouts to himself. "Well, if I tell you, you can put it in your record, but you keep it to yourself. I have it under control, Aaron. So, I don't need any help here."

"I will keep it to myself," he said, knowing he wouldn't. He was pretty sure Thaddeus knew that he wouldn't either. You didn't tell a member of The Watch something and expect them not to tell the other watchers. On top of that, this situation was dangerous, and keeping it to oneself amounted to irresponsibility.

"Now don't freak out," Thad said.

Aaron's stomach dropped and the burger he'd had for lunch threatened to make an appearance.

"The house wasn't broken *into*. It was broken *out of*. Sorath's death aspect got out. The alchemy lab room door was busted out from the inside, and the same with the French doors. I have a crew here now, fixing it. The bottle was smashed to bits on the floor of the lab." Thad paused, waiting for a response.

"Oh." Aaron felt stunned, numb even. "Wow."

"Don't panic, okay?" Thad paused, then added, "Thank you for all of your help and I trust you'll be keeping that ritual I gave you under wraps."

His own voice sounded distant to his ears. "Of course. I put it in the archive last night. I appreciate the update, thank you. If you need anything, you have my number." Aaron shifted uneasily and noticed Neal coming out of the temple with Roberts, in full robes, still talking his ear off.

"Goodbye, Aaron," Thad said. Then the other end of the line went dead.

Aaron hated it when people did that. It was the equivalent of having the last word, and he considered it rude. He walked back over to where Neal and Michael Roberts were talking at the bottom of the stairs.

"How is Marla? Still shaken?" Neal asked. Then he seemed to notice something was wrong. "Are you okay?

"I'm fine, and she's fine." At that point, he didn't care if Michael Roberts was standing there. "Thad is back in town. We have a huge problem."

It must have been the look on Aaron's face, because Neal and Roberts both began to look concerned.

"The Blackwood mansion wasn't broken *into* at all." He paused, not for dramatic effect, but because he was trying to find a way to say it that made it seem less dangerous. There wasn't one. "It was broken *out of.* They found the bottle, broken in the lab."

"Fuck me," Neal said.

"What does that mean?" Roberts asked, a tinge of panic rising in his voice. "That something…"

Aaron cut him off. "Sorath, a rather destructive death aspect, broke loose."

Then his stomach took a violent turn, he bent over, and vomited into the bush right next to the stairs.

They sat in the cool shade of the gazebo in the park. Michael Roberts, now changed into his street clothes, was there along with his wife Sharon, and Jeff Myers had shown up at some point to, but Aaron didn't remember when. Neal had chalked up Aaron's vomiting to the burger not agreeing with him.

"We just don't eat like that at home," Neal explained to Michael and Sharon.

A few people had stopped by to talk to Neal about historic records. They'd heard his commentary at the temple and had been waiting in the park for them to arrive. Naturally, no one offered any new information that The Watch wasn't already aware of. Whether there were any facts that altered what was in the recorded records, Aaron didn't know. He had been too busy nursing his queasy stomach to listen.

Someone brought them fresh lemonade from the stand on the far side of the park. But Aaron couldn't drink anything. His stomach was still sour.

Neal rubbed Aaron's back. "Is there anything I can get you?"

Aaron shook his head. "I'll be okay in a few minutes."

Once the stray coven members had drifted off to other things, and it was only the leaders of three covens, Michael gave them all a pensive look. "So, there's an entire part of the story that we're missing."

"I'm sure you all heard the rumor that Thaddeus Blackwood has figured out how to conjure spirits to physical manifestation and trap them inside spirit vessels, right?" Neal asked.

The three of them nodded, so Neal continued. "Well, it wasn't just a rumor. They had it in a bottle all right. Aaron and I saw it last night when we went there for dinner. We told Thaddeus that he needed to dissipate it or let it go, and that it was dangerous to have around. And then this happened."

"That would explain why Martin Six and the Shadow Marbas were so freaked out," Roberts said. "Thaddeus is probably lucky that it got out when it did. That could've been nastier business. But since no one died and the Blackwood mansion is still standing, I think we can safely say that the spirit went back to where it came from and probably won't fall for the same trick twice. I hope Thaddeus has learned his lesson."

"I think we all hope so. But what if, what if Sorath has not left this physical plane and wants revenge. What then?" Neal asked.

It was the same question that Aaron had been going over in his mind. There was something wrong with the energy in the bottle. Something so terrifying that it made him ill. He still had an uneasy feeling about it. Why, he couldn't say. Perhaps Roberts was right. Perhaps the Daemon had gone back to where it came from. After all, Daemons were often invoked during ritual in these parts, and they usually dissipated on their own.

"Well then it's not our problem. Thaddeus is the one who conjured it, and if Sorath destroys him, then he brought it on himself," Roberts said plainly. By his tone, it was clear there was no love loss there. Thaddeus wasn't well-liked.

After about ten minutes, Aaron's stomach began to settle and he was able to take a sip of the sweet, tart lemonade. He wasn't sure how well that would keep his stomach settled, but he was willing to risk it because his throat was dry and the day was warm. They still had to stop by Evelyn Winters' shop, Black Raven, because some of Neal's books were in, and they were low on frankincense and Clary Sage oil. Plus, they both enjoyed browsing Black Raven's shelves of rare volumes, special editions, and new releases.

"Well, thanks for stopping by and it was good to see you guys," Roberts said. He held out his hand and Neal shook it. "I wouldn't worry about the Sorath business. As always, we'll all keep an eye out, and hopefully if any of us see anything, we can let each other know. If action needs to be taken, we'll all get together. But until then, I don't see any cause for worry."

Jeff shook Neal's hand, too, and Sharon merely waved. Aaron waved after them and took another slow sip of the lemonade. Then he got up. "Let's go to Black Raven, and then head for home. I have a feeling this burger is going to wreak more havoc in the next few hours."

Neal nodded in agreement. "All right."

They started down the street and took a right and walked up to Black Raven. It was almost four-thirty, and despite the number of people out, the shop wasn't as busy as Aaron expected. He found some frankincense and Clary Sage first and left Neal to browse the books. When he returned with the items, he found Neal lusting over a brand-new copy of the new printing of Colin DePlancy's Dictionairre Infernale.

It was no wonder Black Raven did so well, and was such a staple in a small town like this. Five hundred dollars later, Aaron and Neal left the store with three bags of purchases. Neal with his books and Aaron with his frankincense and Clary Sage, and a new tarot deck. Aaron was sorry that he hadn't enjoyed their shopping excursion as much as he'd hoped, because by the time they reach the car he threw up in the grass on the side of the parking lot. It was definitely food poisoning. Either that or his stomach could no longer handle burgers and fries.

The drive home seemed to take forever and once they got home Aaron went straight to the bathroom only to get sick again. After that, he fell into bed thankfully and didn't wake up until the next morning.

5

Sunday morning brought no phone calls, and no distractions over breakfast. Aaron kept it to a piece of dry toast that he washed down with some decaf coffee. They spent the rest of the morning doing coven business, recording ledgers, updating incident files. The group only met once a month, and that wouldn't happen until next weekend. Aaron was happy for that. It meant that he could stay at home and lie around the house. Maybe Roberts was right. Maybe they had nothing to worry about. The queasy sensation that Aaron had been feeling had vanished with his illness, and now a strange, pervading sense of calm had washed over him.

Just as things seemed like they were getting back to normal that afternoon, the phone rang. Neal was on the back deck reading a book, so Aaron answered.

"Hi," the woman's voice said with some uncertainty. "Can I talk to Neal or Aaron please?"

"This is Aaron."

"This is Belinda Applegate from Temple Apophis." Another uncertain pause. "I have a message for you from Esther Branson."

Oh crap, Aaron thought. He'd forgotten to send flowers from The Watch. He jotted a note to do it as soon as he got off the phone. "How is Esther doing?"

"They say she'll make a full recovery." Belinda paused again. "Esther wanted me to tell you that you need to be careful. She said, and I quote, *Sorath was stolen?*"

Aaron felt like he'd been hit in the stomach with a bat. "What?"

"Yeah, I thought it was a strange message, too, but she insisted I call you. She also said that if you don't figure out what happened, someone would die." Then she went silent, as if waiting for a response.

Aaron fought to find his words. "Thank you, I'll handle it."

He didn't stop to think that his response had been short and terse, just as he didn't believe for a second that Belinda Applegate didn't know what was going on. She was Esther's protégé, which meant she had talent and she could see far more than she led on to. He bade her goodbye and then sat staring at the phone for a few moments. This was the part were being a member of The Watch, and bearing the brunt of the responsibility bestowed upon them, became stressful. After composing his thoughts, he got up and went out to the back deck.

Neal looked up from his book as Aaron approached. "How are you doing?"

Aaron gave him a weak smile. "I was fine until the phone call we just received."

Neal set down the book, giving Aaron his full attention.

"First, I forgot to send Esther Branson flowers in the hospital. I'm going to do that in a minute. However, we just got a call from Belinda Applegate who had a message for us from Esther. She said that Sorath was stolen, by magick I presume, and if we don't find out who took him, someone is going to die."

Neal bit his lip. "That's a problem."

"You think?"

"Because magick isn't supposed to work like that..." Neal's sober gaze went distant. "Magick doesn't work that way. Does it? That a captured spirit could be stolen from its prison from the inside out? Presumably imprisoned again. Which means someone in the thirteen has Thad's *Sorath of Death*. *Sorath upon Ocat*?"

"So, what to do about it?" Aaron asked, ignoring what he assumed was a long string of rhetorical questions. In his mind, he was thinking prophesies. Many prophecies had been recorded in the coven records and chronicle. Those who dealt with The Watch always suggested it would be The Watch that would have to take up the mantle and bring the covens together to fight something big. Was it possible this incident was a prophecy come to pass? But he didn't say any of this, just looked to Neal for guidance. It was Neal, after all, who led them.

"We assemble the Council and we watch. What else is there to be done?" Neal stood and picked up his book and ushered Aaron back into the house.

But Aaron knew that it was time for The Watch to pull something else from the codex. Be Vigilant. Proactive. The watchers were always watching, but this time they had to do something about it.

BA'AL COLLECTIVE

1

Senator Langley slipped down the shadowed corridor to a large oak door at the end of the hallway, He knocked lightly, clutching a large manila envelope in his left hand.

"Enter," came the low, baritone voice from the other side.

He reached down, turned the doorknob, and entered. The cavernous space was lit by a single candle at the center of the room, and standing next to the altar, holding the candle, stood a man draped in black robes, his face hidden by the over-sized hood.

Langley unclasped the envelope and pulled out the contents. Inside was a five by seven photograph of a woman by a car. He held the picture out to the dark figure.

"Belinda Applegate?" the high priest asked.

"You know her then?"

"Temple Apophis." The high priest took the picture and held it closer to the light. "Yes, that's her. She's the one who came to see you?"

With a nod, Langley lifted an eyebrow. "The message was clear, but I'm certain she wasn't the one delivering it."

"Oh?"

"I would bet my blood she was hosting a spirit."

"Apophis..." The high priest let out a deep sigh. From behind the black hood, there was a flash of light as the priest's eyes went white. "Chaos has been unleashed, a new seer rises. The Temple of the Magi have unleashed forces they don't understand, and the Daemons conjured among the covens stir. Did you vote for the bill?"

"Of course, I did. Do you think I want..." the senator's voice trailed off. There was no point going into a rant for the high priest's benefit. Langley was certain the older man already knew how he felt anyway. "Should I leave the photo?"

The priest handed it back to him. "No, take it with you. Now go. Wait for my call. We'll convene a secret council when the time is right."

The senator took the photo and slipped it back into the envelope, bowed his head in reverence toward the high priest and left, leaving the priest to his work.

**

Once the senator was gone, the high priest turned back to the operation. With a wave of his right hand, he did a spell to reveal that which he'd hidden from the senator. The tenebrous ritual chamber loomed before him in its grandeur. The high ceilings and intricate moldings were lost to the darkness. Upon the altar, incense billowed from the thurible in wide tendrils of gray smoke, twisting and twining upward into a hazy plume that hung thick in the air. The gates had been open now for well over forty-eight hours and he could feel *them* congregating there – the *others*, the *devils*. Their essence culminating into a malevolence that filled the room with a palpable energy that made all of his instincts scream run. But he didn't. He forced himself to approach the triangle that bound them. *If the barrier was broken, even for a second...*

Fear overwhelmed him. He didn't want to think about the *what if.* Plunging the world into a black abyss was the last thing he wanted. No, he merely wanted power and was willing to do anything to get it. He was too powerful a magus for them to escape anyway. They were his minions now, bound to him and willing to work for their ultimate release back to the astral plane. In the meantime, they would do his bidding, here, now. The fact that Thaddeus Blackwood had also figured out how to conjure to physical manifestation angered him. This wasn't the only thing that angered him though. The outsider, Belinda Applegate, was communing with Apophis, and Lucifer's Haven was hiding something, too. When it came to Lucifer's Haven, though, his vision grew hazy. All of this meant there were powerful magi in the other covens, and he found that annoying. Clearly, *they* were all playing with things they didn't understand.

Before him, the swirling mass of entities bulged outward in a brilliant bluish glow of energetic fervor. All that power, his.

He couldn't help but smile. It had taken him years to figure out how to open the gates. He'd spent months summoning and charging the entities with menial tasks, just to see if they would perform them. His work with the infernal spirits had gotten him the six-figure job. He had the big house and fleet of new cars. He even had beautiful girls willing to do his every bidding and satiate his every carnal desire.

Despite this, he knew that power, real power, didn't come from making a paltry five hundred thousand a year. It didn't come from having scores of women. No, it came from having millions, even billions, and a prestigious leadership position. It could take a few years, but he had faith the entities had gotten him this far and they could certainly get him further. Perhaps he could secure a senate seat, and later, the presidency. It was all within his grasp. He could feel his own power. This led him to the only logical conclusion: he was *The One* all the prophecies spoke of. That alone could be enough for him to usher in a new world order - a single world government – and *he* would be the one standing at the helm.

A sharp pain pierced his jaw, jarring him from his fantasy. That's when he realized he'd been grinding his teeth. He stopped and regarded the mass of writhing etheric creatures hovering inside the triangle before him, then without further thought turned his heel and left the ritual chamber, closing and locking the heavy oak door behind him.

2

Mary Rose put the flowered centerpiece that she'd labored over for hours, onto the dining room table. After adjusting a few daisies and roses, she leaned back and admired her handiwork. These were the things a dedicated housewife did to amuse herself. John would be home soon, and with him, he'd bring Garrett, the coven's grand Magus and lawyer, and Dean, the coven coordinator. They often had their meetings here, though she didn't understand why they hadn't started holding them at Garrett's. Garret was a lawyer and his job afforded him a much larger home and likely more privacy. Though she had no idea what a single man, scarcely thirty-eight, was doing up in that huge house alone, back in the forest like that. He had no one to take care of him. It was a shame.

The Ba'al Collective was one of the up and coming covens whose members may not have been as wealthy as the members of The Watch or Temple of the Magi, but they could be, and it seemed many members were working toward that, John included. All with the help of Garrett's magick.

She regarded her centerpiece again, then lifted it from the dining room table and set it on the sideboard to the left of the table. John wouldn't want it on the table once he and the others arrived anyway. With a heavy sigh, she went back into the kitchen to finish putting together a quick meal for the men. They likely wouldn't eat all of what she'd fixed either. *Too much talk, not enough eating*, she thought bitterly. In the early days, after John took over for her father, Mary would cook big meals, and it always resulted in a fridge full of leftovers. She'd finally figured out that small sandwiches, dips, and chips were all the men ever wanted.

She looked at the clock. It was almost five thirty. They'd arrive any…

"Mary, we're here," came John's voice through the front door. She heard him drop his keys on the side table and walk through the living room, toward the dining room. Then she heard the front door open again, and several more sets of footsteps.

She picked up the first platter of food and took it into the dining room, setting it at the center of the table.

John leaned down to kiss her cheek.

"Hello, Mary. How was your day, honey?" John gave her a kind smile and his gentle gray eyes gave her attire the once over. He nodded in approval.

"A woman's work is never done." She beamed a bright smile to John, then at Garrett and Dean. "Now, what drinks may I serve you?"

They always asked for the same thing, but she asked anyway. One never knew when a man would change his mind. But like usual, all three asked for the same thing. Beer.

She smiled, hoping her lipstick was still perfect, then bowed her head and went to retrieve the beer.

"Your wife is such a delight, John," she heard Dean say. "I honestly don't know why more young women don't submit to their role in the natural order of things."

Garret let out a hearty chuckle. "Hopefully she's a delight in the bedroom, too, eh?"

Mary shook her head. They had to know the walls were thin and their voices carried. But it was no matter. She was exactly what John liked in the bedroom, however he liked it. And if that made her a *delight in the bedroom*, and it pleased John, then she was pleased, too. She removed the caps from the beers and took the cold, perspiring bottles to the dining room. "Here you are. Is there anything else I can get for any of you?"

John looked at Garrett and Dean who both shook their heads, and then he smiled up at her. "I think we're fine in here. But stay close in case we need anything, okay pet?"

225

"Of course, John," she said with a girlish smile. Once she'd been dismissed, she slipped back into the kitchen to make sure everything there was cleaned and ready for John's inspection if he wished it, and then retreated to the family room to work on her knitting.

3

There was no way John could have run the coven on his own. Garrett and Dean provided great support and he was happy to allow them a hand in keeping the coven on track. Especially since both were agreeable and dedicated to the success of the coven. With Garrett's legal advice and magick, Dean and John had increased their income ten-fold in scarcely three years. Some of that was due to sound financial decisions, certainly, but Garret was the most proficient magus of all of them, and spells he'd done, in honor to Ba'al, had brought them more wealth than they could imagine. Garrett promised more, too, and John was willing to do whatever Garrett said. If he and Mary benefitted, then it was worth it. Now, he wanted a massage before bed.

"Mary?" he called to her and snapped his fingers. This brought Mary obediently into the bedroom, hair perfectly done, and makeup still intact. She wore the plain white house dress she'd been wearing all day.

"I could really use a massage before bed tonight," he said.

Her soft, smooth voice washed over him, "Would you like me to undress?"

"Yes. I wouldn't want you to ruin that beautiful dress with the massage oil." His wife had been trained to be obedient by her step-mother, and her father, and was the pinnacle of feminine beauty and grace. John felt lucky to have her. It was unfortunate she couldn't be bred. A rare anomaly from birth had made her barren and worthless in that regard. Unfortunately, it hadn't been discovered until after they'd been married. He still hadn't had the heart to tell her that he had another woman, a woman born into the coven just as obedient and submissive, living in an apartment off of main street in

Haileyville, carrying his child. The coven needed an heir, and adoption from outside the coven was not a viable solution. Mary wouldn't be able to raise the child either. It seemed cruel to take it from its mother. Once he made more money, he would set up the woman he intended to breed, and his children, in another house, and keep both his wife, and his mistress. Mary would submit to his wisdom in this, she always did. Even if his mistress, Myrna, was her half-sister.

He watched her slip out of her dress and hang it neatly in the closet. Once clad in nothing more than a black bra, matching panties, garters and stockings, she retrieved the massage oil and brought it over to the bed. Rolling onto his stomach, he lifted his right shoulder. "Get that side, right there."

Her oil slicked hands worked deftly across his back, loosening the tension in his muscles along his spine. As she worked on his shoulders, he wondered how disappointed she'd be that he'd offered her cleaning services to Garret for the weekend. They were planning on moving coven meetings to Garrett's since he had more space and the coven was growing. So, when Garrett had asked if Mary could help out, John saw it as an opportunity and offered her up willingly. Not only was it beneficial to John, Mary, Myrna and baby, to keep Garrett happy, but it would also give John time to spend with Myrna who, at four months pregnant, was beginning to feel neglected.

John decided then that he would wait to tell Mary about Garrett needing her help until tomorrow night – a Friday. She wouldn't have time to protest, if that were even possible. He'd explain that she could stay at Garrett's for the weekend. The exercise would do her good. Not that Mary was heavy by any means, but their own house offered her little in the way of exertion. She was slightly underweight as it was, but that suited John just fine. He liked that she looked frail and petite, and good on his arm. She was far more attractive than

Myrna. That's why he had to keep them both. Myrna wasn't suitable as the wife of the coven leader, and Mary couldn't produce an heir to inherit the coven leadership. There were also those in the coven who saw Mary, and whoever she married, as the rightful leaders of The Collective. She was, after all, the only blood daughter of the coven's founder, Richard Sanderson. He couldn't risk that she would marry again if he divorced her. Together, both women served a purpose – to keep John, and his own eventual bloodline, in power.

Content with his decision, he fell asleep half-way through the massage.

4

Mary tidied the living room, then ran the duster over all of the furniture. There was no dust, but one could never be too sure. It was almost five-thirty and John was due home any minute. The smell of the roast in the crockpot was heaven to her nose, and hopefully to John's, too. She double checked to make sure everything was in order, that her clothing was clean and smooth, her blond curls were perfect and her makeup unscathed. She heard him pull up in the driveway, and rushed to the door to greet him.

He greeted her with a kiss on the cheek and set his keys on the side table like he did every night, then moved past her wordlessly to the dining room while loosening his tie. "I'm starving. What's for dinner?"

"I made your favorite, pot roast, just like you wanted," she told him, following him several paces behind.

"I wanted to talk to you about something. But first, serve dinner and then we'll talk." He sat down and waited patiently for her to go into the kitchen and plate up his meal. She brought nothing back for herself, just his plate, now filled high with steaming pot roast with potatoes, onions, and carrots – just how he liked it.

She sat in the chair to the left of him and politely folded her hands in her lap.

"I was talking to Garrett the other night and he could really use a hand up at his place this weekend. His cleaning woman hasn't been able to get to him for a few weeks and we'd like to start holding coven meetings there," John started.

Her eyes sparked and she visibly perked up and smiled, holding back jumping at the opportunity to help. If it pleased John, then she was glad to do it.

"I'd really like you to go to Garrett's for the weekend and help him out. It would be a great favor to the coven, and I would appreciate it immensely," he finished. Then he dug into his meal.

Husband first, her mind cautioned. It was a precept that had been instilled in her at a young age. "I would be happy to, but who would cook and clean for you while I'm there? Or would you come, too?"

He shook his head and swallowed the mouth of food before saying, "I can manage a few days without you. I imagine there's plenty of pot roast to get me through the weekend, and if not, there's always carry out. I have some work to do at the office this weekend, so don't worry your pretty little head about that. I will certainly miss you, pet, but it's for the greater good," he said, reaching out and caressing her cheek.

"Will you drive me up in the morning?" She kept her hands obediently folded in her lap.

"Garrett is coming in from Albany tonight and thought he would pick you up on his way home. He said he should be working in his home office all weekend. A big case. So, you likely won't see much of him, but it would be helpful if you would make sure he eats while you're there. Garrett is our chance at a bigger house, among other things. You deserve a big house," he said. "And I intend to provide you with one."

John had been promising her the bigger house for two years now and had assured her it was coming soon. That sent her insides jumping with excitement. With a bigger home, perhaps John would entertain the coven more, and she could shine where she excelled – cooking and playing hostess. It wasn't that she was ungrateful for this home. John was a good provider, and he had never once complained about her diligence in her wifely duties or the fact that she could never bear him children. She couldn't have married a better man.

Keeping her composure, like a good wife did, she smiled sweetly. "You really are my knight in shining armor, John."

He gave her an appreciative smile. "No one has a wife more attentive than mine," he said. "Now go pack a weekend bag, and by the time you're done you can clean the kitchen. Once that's settled, Garrett should be here. Run along."

She rose from the chair and obediently went to the bedroom to pack a bag. She carefully included three house dresses, in case one got dirty, two aprons as one could be in the laundry while she wore the other, and of course her underthings, bathing supplies, and makeup. Just because she was away from John, didn't mean she shouldn't look presentable while cleaning the home of a well-known attorney. One never knew who would stop by. She packed her sensible shoes as she figured she would be on her feet far more than she normally was at home. Once satisfied she had everything, she closed the small case and carried it to the living room and gingerly set it near the front door.

John was sitting on the couch with the remote in his hand. She approached him and asked, "Is it all right for me to clean the kitchen now?"

He nodded. "Of course, pet."

Without rushing, she cleared the dining room table and wiped it down, then moved into the kitchen to clean up and put the pot roast in containers. One for each meal to make it easier for John. Sure, she'd come home to a dirtier kitchen with more dishes to clean, but she didn't want him to have to portion food out for himself if he didn't have to. Especially if he was tired from a hard day's work. Once satisfied the kitchen was clean enough for inspection, John did love his impromptu inspections, she returned to the living room and waited for John to give her his attention.

"Should I wait in here or in the kitchen for Garrett?"

"Is the kitchen completely clean?" His voice bore a stern edge. Some days she never knew how he would react to a single item out of place.

"Yes, Sir."

"If I inspect it, it will be completely clean?"

Her mind raced back to the kitchen. No, she knew it was all in place. She checked it multiple times a day now, ever since the time he'd spanked her for not cleaning it properly. He'd also pulled the dishes from all of the cupboards and drawers, and made her wash them by hand, naked. That was a humiliation she never wished to relive. But it had been several years since that incident, and she'd kept the kitchen spotless since. Finally, she said, "Yes. Would you like to check it now?"

"No. I'll take your word for it. But I will be in there this weekend." His attention turned toward the front window. A car had pulled into the driveway. "That's Garrett. Now you be polite, no backtalk, and make sure he eats. Can you do that for me?"

She smiled and looked at her feet. "Yes, John."

"Good." He stood, pulled her to him, and kissed her forehead. Then he picked up her bag and walked her out to Garrett's car and made sure she and the bag were securely inside before saying, "Be a good girl."

5

Garrett didn't like John Rose, or the Rose family. His father, despite having been loyal to the coven, had resented the Roses and their sexist, opportunistic ways. That bias had been passed on to Garrett. Garrett did, however, like John's wife, Mary. He hated seeing how she'd been raised to be a subservient wife, and how John treated her. To Garrett, it was unconscionable that John was cheating on Mary with Myrna of all people. Now, the docile creature sitting in the passenger seat of his silver BMW kept her head down and didn't speak. There had to be a strong woman in there somewhere, and he hoped to find her. Eliza Sanderson had been an opinionated woman, or so Garrett had heard from some of the elder coven members over the years. But Eliza passed on when Mary was scarcely two, from cancer, and Mary had been raised by her repressed and submissive stepmother, Myrtle. Mary's family, the Sanderson's, were the rightful heirs to the Collective's priesthood. But since Mary's father had passed and had no sons, that leadership fell to the next able male in line, Mary's husband, John Rose. Unlike many of the covens, leadership in The Ba'al Collective could only be passed on to a man – a rule that Garrett, and many other coven members, found misogynistic and antiquated. *They weren't The Watch, for fuck's sake.* Garrett was pretty sure the only reason John Rose married Mary was for the title. When Mary was unable to produce an heir, John naturally went to Myrna, even though Myrna was an adopted Sanderson. Not a Sanderson by blood. Surely, he had to know that a child by Myrna couldn't produce a blood heir to the coven leadership. John, of course, didn't think things through, and this is where Garrett had the advantage.

Just like his father before him, John was an opportunist, and had handed Mary over willingly when Garrett dared ask to borrow her. It made him sick to do it, asking to borrow an adult woman from her husband, but he did it anyway. It was important he got her away from John for as long as possible. She needed to be safe.

He let out an audible sigh and kept his eyes on the increasingly winding road ahead. Everything he was doing – he was doing for his loyalty to his god Ba'al and The Collective. The Ba'al Collective would not have been in the rising financial state it was in had it not been for Garrett. Consequently, all the high-level members were beholden to Garrett's magick. He had them right where he wanted them – kissing his ass, while simultaneously thinking he was a faithful servant to the coven. It all fed right into his plan.

The silence was beginning to make him uncomfortable. "So, Mary, how have you been?" It was a lame start, but he didn't want to rush into telling her that her husband was an asshole. She was an abused woman, after all, and it was likely she suffered Stockholm Syndrome, or something like it.

"I've been well, Garrett. How have you been?" She sounded relieved that they'd started a conversation.

"I've been busy. I'm working with the State Senate on a case. I really appreciate you agreeing to help me out. I just need to get the house in order before we start holding meetings there. I hope it's not too much problem switching locations since I know you enjoy entertaining…"

There was a pause as if Mary was considering this. Then she said, "I don't mind at all. John wants to have meetings at your home and that is what matters."

"Well, I was kind of hoping you'd still manage the coven parties and meetings, and supply the refreshments even though we're moving to my place." He smiled when he saw the surprised look on her face.

"I, I'd have to ask John…" Her eyes quickly went back down to her hands in her lap.

Garrett bit his inner lip. What he wanted to tell her was that she wouldn't have to worry about John for much longer. Garrett had gone through great pains to get hold of the death essence of Sorath. The black sun would burn anyone who misused it, and that was the beauty of his plan. He didn't have to do anything. He could stand back and watch the inner circle of the Ba'al Collective, sans himself and his own inner circle, get greedy and destroy themselves. Securing Mary's support meant securing the support of the entire coven.

Of course, there was one part of the plan that upset Garrett. The High Magus, the one who had secured Sorath from Temple of the Magi, insisted that Myrna and the baby had to die, too. Even though Garrett had told the elder that he would have no part of it, the elder said it would have to happen anyway, whether sanctioned by Garrett or not. The death of the child, he'd said, would be used to restore Mary's fertility, so that a proper, blood-born Sanderson heir could rise from the coven tragedy that was about to unfold.

The deafening silence was almost too much. He tried again. "I don't think John will mind. Besides, every member of the inner council loves how well you take care of us. I was thinking you might just help me get two rooms and the temple together this weekend."

"I can take care of more of the house. I doubt three rooms will take me long at all." She almost sounded offended.

"All right," he agreed immediately. He didn't want to scare her off and decided to pick and choose his words carefully. He needed Mary to either agree to stay longer than the weekend, or risk being destroyed by John's greed. He was starting to have second thoughts. His voice took on an unintentional sterner tone. "I think that will be fine."

Mary just nodded and turned her soft blue eyes back to her hands.

The High Magus had given him a magickal elixir prepared by the alchemists of Ashtaroth Briarwood to give to her. The Gatorade bottle of green liquid currently sitting in his fridge, to preserve the ingredients, would allegedly give her the power of her own free will again, but Garrett wanted her to tap her own strength, to find that free will without the help of magick. If that failed, he'd have no choice but to use it, for Mary had to be safe at all costs.

"We'll start with the main living room then, since that is likely where the council will be meeting," he said, wanting to keep the conversation going. This wasn't nearly as easy as it had been in his head.

"That will be fine," Mary said in a most amiable way.

The drive would take at least another ten minutes, and the thought of strained silence between them was off-putting. Garrett needed more. "So, read any good books lately?"

He inwardly cringed at how inept the question was.

To his surprise, she laughed. "What I read wouldn't interest you, I'm sure."

"How do you know I don't read trashy romance novels?" he asked.

A giggle escaped her and he smiled.

"I've flipped through a knitting magazine once or twice, too," he said, hoping to make her feel more at ease – to get her to open up a little. "My grandmother was a fierce knitter in her day. I have a sweater collection to prove it."

In the almost black of the car, he was certain he saw her smile. Still, she said nothing.

"So, are you knitting sweaters for John?" Though the topic of knitting was boring as hell, he wasn't sure what else to talk about. He certainly didn't know anything about romance novels.

"John doesn't care for sweaters," she said simply, then surprised him by adding, "He's very particular about his clothing."

"John's always been a bit picky about things. My father might have been that way had my mother allowed it, but I think she kept him grounded. That's what some men need," he said, thinking he'd finally hit the right topic.

"Is that what you need?" she asked. She sounded genuinely curious.

"Yeah. I think I might need a woman to keep me in line. Make me clean up after myself. Make sure I eat a healthy meal now and again, and maybe even keep me from working so hard." He shrugged, then slowed the car as they came up on the turn to the winding road that led up to his house.

"You certainly live in a remote part of the county." Her remark suggested she'd thought about this before.

"I like the peace and quiet, and, for the most part, it keeps the gossip of Haileyville out of my business. After my parents moved to Florida, it seemed a good idea to get out of that town." None of it was an outright lie.

"Why did your parents leave the coven?"

"They technically didn't leave. You notice they come up for three months out of the year, during the Ba'al Rites. With my mom's arthritis though, the warmer weather does her good. They still keep an altar to Ba'al up in their condo down there, and one to Lucifuge, of course. And apparently, they participate in the local pagan and witch community down there, though it's nothing like here. They have more privacy. On the upside, they think the next generation of coven leadership is doing a fantastic job." Now *that* last part was a lie. For three months out of every year, Garrett endured the complaining and ranting of his parents about John Rose. It was no wonder a lot of the coven elders had retreated and let the next generation take over. Many of them were disgusted at the way things were going. John Rose wasn't dedicated to Ba'al. Not like Garrett was. John was a heathen who didn't seem to care about the coven Patron at all. To Garrett – that was sacrilege. The Rose house didn't even house a temple.

From here, they could see the lights from Garrett's house. It was more like a small estate surrounded by miles of tall trees and nature paths. With his salary and a little help from Ba'al, he'd been able to buy the estate, and the forty acres around it, outright. When he looked over at Mary, he noticed she was frowning.

"John won't allow me to keep an altar in the house. Just in case non-coven come by." She sounded bitter.

Garrett held back a nasty remark and instead said, "I'm sorry to hear that. I imagine your parents would have found that…"

"My father is likely rolling over in his grave. I've considered going to the Temple of Eurynome to see if one of the necromancers would." She stopped mid-sentence. "Never mind. It's silly. Childish really."

He pulled into the six-car garage, parked, and turned off the ignition. "It must be hard for you. No longer having your parents for guidance. It's not stupid or childish at all, and if you ever wanted to go see the necromancers so you could speak with your parents, I could take you and John would never have to know."

She turned to him with wet eyes. "That's very kind of you, Garrett. Thank you. I might take you up on that someday."

"Nonsense. It's what friends do for each other. I want you to think of me like that. As a friend, I mean. I'm not just John's friend, I'm yours, too. I hope you know that." He reached out and gently squeezed her arm and gave her a reassuring smile. "Should we go inside? You know, I'm really enjoying talking to you. Maybe I should make us some hot cocoa and we could play a hand of gin rummy before bed."

He almost grimaced at his own suggestion. Every time he talked to her, whatever slipped out of his mouth felt like something out of *Leave it to Beaver*. That was because anytime he dealt with John and Mary, it felt like stepping back into nineteen fifty-one, and quite frankly, he found it maddening. He wasn't the only one, of course. Plenty of other coven members felt the same.

Mary seemed guarded again.

Garrett got out of the car, retrieved her suitcase, then opened the passenger side door to let her out of the vehicle. "Sorry if I got that in the wrong order. The ladies who usually get into my car don't mind letting themselves out, so I don't often get to open car doors for them."

"Thank you, Garrett," she said politely.

He led the way into the house, up the stairs, and showed her the guest room only two doors down from his. The entire time, he noticed how she appraised the cleanliness of his house and saw her smile at the small altars all around the house. Garrett's mother had helped him set them up when she came out to help him decorate after he moved in. Since then, they were the only thing he made sure to clean every weekend himself.

Setting her suitcase at the foot of the bed in the large, spacious guest room, he gave her an apologetic smile. "I'm sorry there's no altar in here for you, but you're welcome to any of them for prayer or offerings while you're here. And I really apologize for the state of the place."

Much to his surprise though, Mary seemed happy. "No, this is beautiful, and I'm happy to make use of whatever altars you allow. Perhaps I could clean them all?" A spark of light he had never seen in her before, glinted in her eyes.

"How about you get settled in here, and I'll go down and make us the cocoa. You can come down when you're ready."

A look of horror washed over her face and she went pale, her pretty painted lips struggling to form words. "No, I should do that."

"Nonsense. You're a guest in my home, a friend, and you've been so kind to come help me out, it's the least I could do. You'd think no man had ever shown you the proper respect you deserve," he said carefully. Then he left the room, hoping the seed he'd just planted would cause her to start questioning the way John treated her.

It took her over fifteen minutes to come down, and by then, the milk and cocoa were gently simmering on the stove.

Mary, still wearing a proper frock, hair perfect, and face still made up, gave him a surprised look. "You know how to make real cocoa?"

"My mother didn't raise an invalid. I haven't survived bachelorhood this long without knowing how to cook, and clean sometimes. I just don't often have company or time to do it. But I enjoy cooking." He concentrated on pouring the now done mixture into the two waiting mugs on the counter.

"It's a shame. A man of your importance shouldn't be doing these things… you should have a woman taking care of you." She had picked up a towel and began wiping the counter of imaginary crumbs.

"But I like doing things. You know, you're a dying breed, Mary Rose." He took the cups to the living room and set them on coasters on the table. "Ignore the counters and come have some cocoa before it gets cold."

Obediently she set the towel down and joined him, poised, on the couch, and picked up her cocoa.

"I think it's admirable that of all the things you could have been, that you chose to become a housewife."

"I don't think." She stopped mid-sentence again. "It is my duty to care for my husband."

"What do you do when John isn't home or is out of town?" He asked.

She shrugged. "I make sure I keep the house clean."

"There's only the two of you. How do you spend the rest of your days? You can't tell me you knit all that time."

Her pale cheeks flushed pink, pinker than the blush she wore. "I sometimes watch television. But please don't tell John, he would hate that if he knew."

"Because you watch TV? I have to admit, Mary, I … you two have a unique relationship." Garrett wanted to shake her and tell her to snap out of it, but he refrained.

"How so?"

"Normal, modern day couples, don't work like this. The woman has an equal say in the relationship. Hell, lots of women have jobs. And you know, there are a lot of covens ran by women, too." He bit the inside of his lip, afraid he'd gone too far.

"Nonsense. Name one." She shook her head as if to say, *silly man.*

"Belinda Applegate took over Temple Apophis and her fiancé and the rest of the coven just stepped aside and let her. Ellie Ayers – everyone says it's Marcus running that coven, but it's Ellie. Lucifer's Haven – you have Karla Devlin. She's slated to take over when Carl and his sisters decide to retire, and she's a lesbian. She and her girlfriend will eventually be running things. Then there's Ashtaroth Briarwood. They're ran by women. The Seeress is a woman. The biggest occult store in the tri-county area is ran by a woman. We live in a hotbed of powerful women who run the show." He took a sip of cocoa and waited for her response. When she said nothing, he just blurted out the next thought that crossed his mind. "Before your mother got sick, I heard she kept the entire coven in line and in order, too."

Mary just looked at him, wide-eyed for a moment, then set her half drank cocoa back on the table. "You think I should take a more active role in the coven?"

That wasn't exactly what he'd been getting at, but it was close enough. "Yes. I do."

She blushed again. "Well, I always hoped John would entertain the entire coven more. We just don't have meetings like we did when I was a child..." She paused as if remembering, then continued. "I have often thought I'd like to be hostess to more events, but John would never allow it..."

The exasperation Garrett felt was too much for him to bear. "The coven does have more events, but John never attends them. We have been holding them at Blake's for the past five years."

Mary looked truly shocked. "Does John know?"

"Of course, he knows. He's more interested in the financial stakes of the coven, and himself. You do realize John is practically agnostic, right? Not that there's anything wrong with that, but there are some of us who are true believers and who want to practice the rites. John certainly has no problem benefiting from my magick, but he can't even be bothered erecting a single altar to Ba'al in his own home." Now it was out, and if Mary went home and told John everything he'd just said, it could ruin everything. But it was a chance he'd have to take. "He keeps you a prisoner, miserable in your own home. The entire coven misses you, Mary. We all pray for your safety and your return to us."

"My safety?" It came out a mere whisper from her soft, pink lips.

"Does he hurt you?" Garret had always feared that Mary could be in danger by the way John treated her - like an indentured servant.

Mary shook her head. "John wouldn't like that we are having this conversation."

"Of course, he wouldn't. I like John, I do," he lied. "But I like you, too, and I hate to see you isolated from your coven family. It isn't right. When I suggested you should take a more active role in the coven, I didn't mean just coordinating events or baking cookies. You're so much more than that. You have your own ideas, and your input on the direction The Collective should be heading is just as valuable as John's or anyone else's. Perhaps even more so considering you're the last living Sanderson."

"My sister Myrna..."

He cut her off. "She's not blood," he said. "Perhaps before bed tonight you should seek guidance from Ba'al. A lot of us want to see you more active in the coven leadership. You don't have to take control over from John."

"I don't know. I really don't know anything about all of that, and it's a man's place..."

"That's your stepmother talking. It's a shame your mother passed over when you were so young. Perhaps then you would have had the good sense to tell your step mother to knock it off, and your father to snap out of his fifties housewife fantasy." He couldn't hide the disgust in his voice. Right now, it felt like tough love was the only way to get through to her. "Your stepmother crippled you. Your mother would have been sorely disappointed in how you turned out. I'm not saying that to be mean, because it's not your fault how you were brought up, but I know this isn't what your mother wanted for you."

He saw her eyes go moist and a pang of guilt ran through his chest. Standing, he took his cup to the kitchen and put it in the sink, then turned and left wordlessly, retreating to his bedroom.

Saving Mary from John was one thing, but how was he supposed to save her from herself?

6

Mary got up long before Garrett, and had been cleaning for three hours, before she finally heard him stir upstairs. A good cry before bed the night before had done her good, and she'd slept well. So why didn't she feel better? Garrett had said so many hurtful things. She'd already decided to be formal with him and to hurry and complete the job so that he would take her home. She didn't want to be in this house anymore. His words had ruined the house for her. Had he not been so cruel, she would have relished in the fantasy that this was her home and that she and John lived here.

Of course, Garrett had promised John that they would have a house like this, too. Now, she didn't know if she trusted Garrett. Big coven meetings without her and John? John would have told her if there had been coven meetings. Saying all those lies about her mother? True, she had never known her mother, but she couldn't imagine her father, who had allowed his step-wife to wait on him hand and foot, would have tolerated a woman who backtalked or wanted to run the coven. Then suggesting that John had hurt her. Her frowned deepened because there - he was right. John did sometimes hurt her, but it was for her own good. Sometimes she was disobedient and she deserved punishment.

Worst of all – he'd pointed out John's lack of religious observance… the nerve. Though that part only made her mad because Garrett was again right. Mary hated that John wouldn't allow her to put up an altar. She hated living a life lacking in religious observance. It made her sad. Worse yet – Garrett was also right in that Mary was miserable. She couldn't remember the last time she'd been happy. Even if she did decide to start doing more and getting more involved with the coven, would John let her? Finally, after hours of wrestling with all of it, she realized that she was angry with Garrett for pointing out truths that she'd been ignoring. Then she thought of how miserable she must look outwardly, and how obvious it all was, to Garrett anyway. Did others see the same things he saw? She did want more for her life, but she still had to care for John. She had given up her choice to say otherwise when she said, I do.

She rummaged around the kitchen and scoured the fridge to see what she had to work with. A bottle of green colored Gatorade sat on the top shelf. She grabbed it, unscrewed the bottle, and gave it a quick sniff. It smelled like melons. Curious, she took a mouthful and scrunched her nose in disgust. It tasted like cold cotton candy with a bitter aftertaste. She put the cap back on and put the bottle back on the shelf. The eggs looked fresh, and a slab of bacon sat in the meat drawer at the ready. By the time Garrett was out of the shower and down the stairs, she had his eggs, bacon, and coffee ready, along with the morning paper.

Garrett's eyes traveled around the large airy kitchen and breakfast nook. He gave her an appreciative nod. "You started early. You've gotten a lot done."

"It was best I get an early start. I would hate to inconvenience you longer than necessary." With her back to him, she winced at her own insolence then corrected herself. "Sorry, that came out wrong."

"Don't apologize," he said, sitting down to the table. "Mary, I'm really sorry for a lot of what I said last night. I hope you know everything I said, I said out of love and friendship. I just want you to be happy. I hope you can forgive me for being so bold. It was ungallant of me."

She sat down across from him, afraid to meet his gaze. "It's all right. You're right. I owe it to my family, to my mother, to be more assertive. I've decided that when I get home I am going to ask John if I can put up an altar in the bedroom and start attending coven meetings and taking a more active role in The Collective as a whole. You're right, it's not like I have a big house like this to keep."

"Well, you'll have a house like this to call your own soon enough," he said as if he knew something she didn't. "You've already eaten?"

"I had toast," she said. "The house isn't nearly as bad as I thought it would be. It just needs a good dusting and vacuuming. I should get back to work. I may be able to finish tonight and be out of your hair. I know you have work to do."

"No, stay. Keep me company while I eat." He pushed the newspaper away from him in a show that he was giving her his undivided attention.

She stayed obediently even though she wanted to get up and go back to her work. "As you wish."

He gave her a sly look. "As a friend can I make a suggestion?"

This made her look him straight in the eye, fearing what he would say next.

"Instead of asking John for his permission, why not just tell him that you're doing it whether he likes it or not? What's he going to do? Throw a tantrum? Tell you no? You're a grown woman. Do what makes you happy. You deserve at least that much. Now, I'll drop it because I know I hurt your feelings last night. I promise that if you stay the weekend, we don't have to talk about this anymore. We can talk about other things."

She was torn. On one hand, she wanted to talk it over more because she didn't have friends or family to confide in. She'd been isolated for so long. On the other hand, letting the matter go sounded more pleasant. "Such as?"

"Well, we could swap tales of trashy romance novels, or we could take a break and go for a walk to the lake this afternoon. It's a beautiful day, the leaves are turning, and the air is crisp. It would do us both good. You don't get out much. You're as pale as a ghost." He gave her a warm smile. "And I don't mean that as an insult because you're as beautiful as ever."

She felt heat rush into her cheeks and she blushed. "Thank you, Garrett. I would like that."

All her anger melted and it was with a lighter heart that she went back to cleaning after he retreated to his office study. She managed the downstairs bathroom, the dining room, and the formal living room by the time three o'clock came around. She'd even had time to dust and replenish the offerings on all of the altars, leaving apples and oranges in the offering baskets. The only room on this floor she hadn't touched was his study. She imagined his private ritual space was in the basement. Most mages liked being connected with the earth and made use of outdoor temples or rooms lowest to the ground. And since she hadn't found a temple in the open layout of the main floor, it was her best guess. Unless it was accessed by the study, in which case she'd likely not get to see it before she left. She longed to be in a real temple again. It had been more than twelve years since she was last in her father's house, just weeks before he died. He always burned incense cones of cypress, sandalwood, and frankincense that reminded her of magick. She closed her eyes, remembering the scent, and inhaled deeply. With a sigh, she opened her eyes and got back to her dusting.

He emerged from his study just as she'd finished using the pole duster to remove a light layer of dust from the crystal chandelier that hung in the grand entry way. It was her intention to dust and vacuum the banisters on the staircase next, and move to the second floor to refresh all of the altars and dust all the rooms up there. She even considered changing all of the bedding.

"Should we have that walk now?" He looked exhausted, but calm.

"You look much too tired," she said sympathetically. "Perhaps I should make you an early dinner so you can take it easy the rest of the evening."

"No, I still think a walk would do us both good. I need to get out of this house and so do you. You need some recreation. Perhaps tonight, after we get back from our walk, we should go out to dinner and see a movie."

A sick pang ran through her stomach. Not because she was upset at Garrett for speaking the truth and hurting her feelings the night before, or because she disliked him, but because she wanted to go to dinner and a movie. Wanting that made her feel like she was doing something unfaithful behind John's back.

"It's the least I could do for you since you've been so good to come here and help me out. I doubt any of my other friends would ever agree to come over and help me clean. Though I feel bad for not helping today. Maybe tomorrow we can do the upstairs together. It's just this case with Senator Langley's office. It's all consuming." His voice sounded resigned, but genuine. "Let me grab our jackets."

He started toward the coat closet inset into a niche along the hallway leading to the kitchen.

It made her a bit nervous. Usually she was the one to get the jackets. It was so rare for a man to do anything for her. Though John did open doors for her, but that was only when they were out in public. At home, he didn't lift a finger.

Garrett put on his own jacket then brought hers to her and took the duster from her hand. She'd been so focused on his words and actions that she'd forgotten to set it down. He leaned it against the wall, and then held her jacket up for her to put her arms into. Once he was done helping her with the jacket, he picked up the duster and returned it to the cleaning closet in the mud room. She followed behind quietly and watched him. He knew where everything in his own house was, including the cleaning supplies. She found it fascinating.

Then he held the back door open for her. "After you?"

She moved past him onto the large back porch and waited while he closed the door behind him and led the way down the steps to the path leading back to the woods.

They'd been walking for about five minutes in the silence and splendor of nature before she finally said, "Do you ever get lonely up here?"

They were surrounded by dense trees and underbrush, and if it weren't for the well-worn path, she would have felt lost.

He shrugged. "I'm an introvert. I like the peace and quiet most of the time. Let me show you something." He pressed on along the path until they came to a stream, then took a right into the forest.

She paused, afraid to follow. He was far ahead of her now, but he paused and turned.

"Come on, it's okay. You won't lose your footing. The ground is dry." He beckoned her forward with one hand.

"I don't think we should go off the path..."

He started back toward her, and when he reached her, he took her hand into his and led her behind him. His grip was gentle, warm, and firm. "Come on. I promise, it's safe. You'll love it."

Not feeling she had much choice in the matter, she followed along becoming more and more aware of how strong and comforting his hand was, grasping hers. They emerged into a wide clearing in the trees, circular in shape. In the center was a stone fire pit, and at each of the four quadrants sat a stone bench, each flanked by torches. To the Northern point stood a statue of Ba'al and beneath it, the stone circle in which blood was offered to Ba'al during the sacred rites. She felt her jaw drop slightly. It was an outdoor ritual space, perfect in every imperfection and detail. Dropping his hand, she wandered into the middle of the circle and looked up at the high trees towering over them, fully encircling them. The stream ran behind the statue. She could hear the water moving through it. All around them, birds sang high in the branches. A slow smile spread over her lips. Closing her eyes, she remembered back to when she was just a girl and the camping trip the entire coven took. They'd found a space similar to this and performed the Ba'al Rites out in nature. She'd been happy and carefree then.

Garrett broke into her serene fantasy. "What do you think?"

"This is beautiful. The coven uses this every year?" Melancholy overwhelmed her. "What if John never allows me to come?"

"Then Dean and I, and the others – we'll insist. We've missed you." It was the second time he'd said that in two days. The coven missed her.

"I'd like that because I can't imagine not being here…" Her voice trailed off into a surreal silence.

Garret came up behind her and put his hands on her shoulders, squeezing gently. "You belong with the coven. With me."

This statement took her by surprise and she whirled around and faced him. "I…"

He caught her by the shoulders again and leaned down, looking into her eyes. "If things ever get bad, you always have a home here, with me. You always have friends and family in the coven. We will protect you."

His face was only inches from her and for the first time, she really saw Garrett. Not as some random male she served at the whim of her husband, but as a man. A ruggedly handsome man with dark hair and dark eyes. The razor stubble on his jaw only increased the appeal. In that moment, she wanted nothing more than to forget about John and stay here, in this temple of Ba'al, and worship at the altar nude, with Garrett. She felt lust beginning to burn between her thighs. She could forget everything of the outside world and let him have her, here on the cool autumn ground. Animalistic-like in a ritual orgy of the flesh.

"Garrett?" came a man's voice from the direction of the house.

Mary jumped away from him like a frightened rabbit, and regained her composure, following after him as Garrett started back toward the path. They emerged onto the path where it met the stream and came face-to-face with Alex and Georgia Friesner, two coven members that Mary hadn't seen in years.

When Georgia saw her, she raced forward and threw her arms around Mary. "By Ba'al if it isn't Mary Sanderson! How have you been? It's been forever."

"I've been well, Georgia." She smiled and pulled away from the hug. Then she noticed both Garrett and Alex looking on, smiling. "It's been at least seven years."

"Oh no, love, it's been closer to nine. Last time we saw you was two years after you were married. John stopped bringing you around and said you'd been ill. Allergies and asthma were acting up. How are you feeling?" Georgia wore a concerned look on her face.

Mary blinked back the shock. She'd never had allergies or asthma. Her eyes looked to Garrett for help answering this, because she didn't understand.

Georgia turned to Garrett and Alex, both were frowning.

"Georgia," Alex said. "We shouldn't..."

"Nonsense. I want to know how she's been. The way John's always talking, Mary's been on her deathbed for years, and here she is, a bit pale, but alive and well." Georgia, who wasn't a small woman by any means, pulled Mary in for another hug.

"Georgia," Alex said. "John's been lying. Mary's been fine, he just…"

Georgia eased up on her embrace and stepped to Mary's side with a protective arm around her.

Garrett cut Alex off. "We should go back to the house. Mary and I were just checking on the temple to make sure it was all in order. We were planning to go to dinner tonight."

This time, Mary cut in. She had to know what the hell was going on. "What has John been saying?"

"It doesn't matter," Garrett said.

"It does matter, but no one will let me speak," Alex said, rubbing his balding head and looking up. "Even the weather wants me to shut up."

A few drops of rain splattered on her cheek, but she didn't move, even when Georgia tried to urge her forward on the path back toward the house. A cold feeling of anger and fear washed over her. Jealousy. "Stop. All of you."

They did. Garrett looked down at his feet and let out a heavy sigh. "Mary, after last night I didn't want to tell you and there's no easy way to bring it up."

"Someone should tell her," Alex said. He took off his glasses and wiped them with the lower half of his flannel shirt and put them back on. "He hasn't been bringing her to coven gatherings for years because he's an asshole, and he's been sleeping with other women."

Alex's words hit her like an arrow in the chest.

Garret gave Alex a sharp glare, but didn't say anything.

Georgia said quietly, "He told Jesse that he and Mary had an open relationship and with how sick Mary always was, she never wanted to come to coven meetings."

Garrett moved alongside her and put his hands on her shoulders and started pushing her gently back toward the house.

Her legs followed almost instinctively even though her entire body felt numb. She scarcely remembered the walk back to the house, or Garrett sitting her on the couch, or Georgia bringing her a steaming mug of tea.

Uncomfortable silence hung thick in the air. Finally, Garrett said, "I was going to tell you, I just didn't know how."

Her voice came out in barely a whisper. "That's why you said what you did. That I could stay here if I needed to."

"That's not the half of it," Alex said in barely a murmur.

"You've said enough," Georgia told him with a warning look.

"No." Mary looked up from the deep brown depths of the tea in her cup. "No. I want you to tell me. No matter how painful it is, I have to know."

"John's been with Myrna for the past year." This time, Alex looked truly sorry.

Georgia's jaw dropped. "But Myrna's pregnant…"

Mary's eyes went wide and then the tears came. Big, wet tears. Outside, the sky gave way to rain, and thunder sounded somewhere close by. She began sobbing.

7

It took an anxiety pill and twenty minutes to get her to calm down and finally fall asleep. Georgia sat with her and occasionally glanced at Alex and Garrett on the other side of the room.

"I told you to stop by and make Mary feel welcome and to let her know she was missed. Not to tell her that John is a lying, cheating bastard who is fucking her sister, and having a baby with her," Garrett hissed. "Gods damn it Alex. You should have probably filled Georgia in, too."

"Sorry. I didn't think."

Garrett gave him an exaggerated nod. "Obviously."

"Someone had to tell the poor woman the truth. He keeps her locked up and isolated in that house." Alex wasn't usually one to frown, but today he did and it made him look somewhat like an angry Al Roker.

"Now we're going to have to pick up the pieces." Garrett was looking forward to this least of all. Alex and Georgia were coven members he could trust with many things, including being on Mary's side, but they couldn't be trusted to keep secrets, clearly, or to know what Garrett and some of the others were planning to do, and he had no intention of telling them. "I suppose the idea of going into Saratoga for dinner and movie is out now. I was hoping to give her a good night out. A happy night. Something she could remember fondly and want for, so when I took her home tomorrow she'd stand up to him and tell him to either get his shit together or he'd end up divorced."

"We can still make that happen," Alex said, narrowing his eyes.

Then Garrett said something that he hoped would make its way through the entire coven, as he knew it would if

Alex had anything to do with it. "You didn't hear this from me, and you know John's my friend, but I think he abuses her. And if I find out he has ever put a hand on her…"

Alex's eyes went wide. "He wouldn't." An uncertain pause. "Did she say something?"

"She didn't have to. Come on, man, you know as well as I do that all the signs are there. He treats her like a servant. Like you said – he locks her up. Isolates her from her friends. Those are all things abusers do to their victims to keep them under their control." Garrett looked at the sleeping form of Mary on his couch. Even in her disheveled state she was beautiful. John didn't deserve her. He thought back to that moment in the outdoor temple. She'd been happy and that look she gave him – he saw it. The woman she could be. The woman he *wanted* her to be. The woman she *was* deep down. He smiled then because he knew he had touched something primal inside her. Desire.

"So, what are we going to do?" Alex asked.

"I don't know yet. I just need her to know that she has friends in the coven. People who care about her. People who want her around. To be an active part of her father's legacy." He looked at Alex then. "She's the last blood Sanderson."

Alex nodded, completely missing the point. "You're right. She deserves to be part of her father's legacy, and John shouldn't be able to keep her from it. Or her friends. I know Georgia and a lot of the other women adore her. What can we do?"

"I know what to do," Georgia said, coming over to them. "I'm going to get together with the girls and we're going to invite her out for lunch, and if John Rose objects, then we'll go to her house and take her, and kick his skinny little ass if he fights us. The nerve of that man."

"We don't need to start an internal coven war, Georgia," Alex warned.

"Well, it would have been one thing if she consented to an open relationship and knew her sister was pregnant with his child. But since he's such a coward and he's been lying to her, and about her to all of us, I sincerely doubt he's going to get much sympathy among the women of The Collective. You don't cross a Sanderson without crossing the entire coven," Georgia told them, matter-of-fact, crossing her arms over her chest. Her dark eyes threatened retribution to anyone who opposed her.

"Myrna is also a Sanderson, and she's now pregnant with John's child," Garrett reminded them in a quiet voice.

Georgia groaned. "Myrna is a spoiled child and we'll continue to treat her as such. She's not blood and she knows it. And the Roses have always been underhanded. I had a bad feeling about Mary marrying John Rose the moment I heard about their engagement."

"I don't think Mary will be going anywhere tonight. I think I'll have to rely on you and the ladies to show her that she still has friends and is still wanted in the coven. Can I count on you to do that?" Garrett gave Georgia a hopeful look.

With a forced smile, Georgia nodded. "You bet. Alex and I should get going. There's nothing we can do here now, but do tell her I'll be calling on her sometime next week with some of the girls. I don't have John Rose's phone number and I doubt she has a cell phone."

"I'll let her know. Thank you for coming, even if it didn't go exactly as planned." Garrett gave them a resigned grin, shook Alex's hand, gave Georgia a hug, and showed them to the door. Then he returned and sat in the chair across from the couch and watched Mary sleep.

8

She woke to the heady scent of garlic laden marinara. Her hands went to her hair so she could straighten it. An immediate swell of panic washed over her and she sat up on the couch, swinging her legs over the side. She must have looked a mess.

"You look fine. Don't worry, we won't go out. I've already started dinner. It should be ready in about twenty minutes. In the meantime, wine?" Garrett stood at the ready with two half-filled wine glasses. "You've had quite a shock. I hope getting a few hours of sleep has helped."

"You should clean out your fridge more regularly," she said, trying to change the subject. "I mean, how long has that half empty bottle of Gatorade been in there?"

A look of panic washed over him and he set the wine glasses down on the counter. "Oh, yeah, I've been meaning to throw that out."

He hurried to the fridge, pulled the bottle out, and emptied it into the sink. She refrained from giggling. She hadn't intended to embarrass him.

"Anything else I should get rid of?" he asked.

"The orange juice is getting ready to turn, and that half gallon of milk will likely go before the week is out." Being able to tell when food was about to turn was one of her fine-tuned super-powers.

With a nervous laugh, he emptied both the milk and the orange juice. "It's easier this way," he said.

She forced a smile. The events of late that afternoon flooded back to her.

"Georgia wanted me to tell you that she would be visiting you this coming week, even if John tries to prevent it." Garret grabbed the wine glasses again and then moved into the living room and set her wine on the end table and sat in the chair diagonal to her. "I think you'll be seeing more of the coven from here on out."

She nodded and lifted the wine glass absently, took a drink and cringed at how dry the aftertaste was. "I am not going back to John."

Garrett said nothing.

"I can't go back to him now, can I?" Internally she chastised herself, because she was already second guessing her choices. When Garrett still didn't respond she looked at him directly with pleading eyes. "Can I?"

"You don't have to do anything you don't want to do. It's your decision. My offer for you to stay here still stands." He immediately took a drink.

"But I don't want John to be mad at you… or punish you because of me. Maybe I should find the courage to go home and confront him." That thought, said aloud, caused her to shudder involuntarily. Her defiance was sure to enrage John either way, and Garrett would be blamed no matter what. If she stayed here, at least she was safe. If she went home, he might physically hurt her.

"Don't worry about me." Garrett sounded very calm. "I will endure whatever comes of this. It was my choice to invite Georgia and Alex over to say hello. So, finding out what you did, that was my fault, too. I am willing to accept responsibility. Even if that means John kicks me from his inner circle and tries to throw me out of The Collective."

"He can't revoke your initiation or membership," Mary said with a frown, knowing that's exactly what John would try to do. Or he would tell lies saying that Garrett and Mary were having an affair. Then she thought of Myrna and John, and who knows how many other women he'd slept with. If that's what he told people, she decided, so be it. He'd already told everyone they were in an open relationship, so they would be perplexed at his anger at her for having taken on a lover. She almost laughed at this thought. Almost.

"No," Garrett said with confidence. "The only person who has the authority to excommunicate initiated coven members is you. You're the one with all the power here, Mary. I know your stepmother conditioned you to think otherwise and John took advantage of that. It's time you realize your power and use it to help yourself, in the very least."

Swallowing the lump in her throat she nodded. She knew he meant to help her out of a bad relationship, but Garrett was too much a gentleman to say it outright. Just like he had a hard time telling her about John's extracurricular activities. This was uncertain territory and she was terrified. She'd never been independent of someone to take care of her. Had never had a job beyond keeping her husband's house. She noticed Garrett watching her. "I don't know. What should I do?"

"I can't imagine how hard this is for you, but I do know that I can't tell you what to do. All I can say is that, if it was me, and I had a girlfriend who treated me like John has treated you, I wouldn't stand for it. Whatever you decide, I will support you." Garrett stood. "I should go check the pasta."

She watched him as he went to the kitchen and dealt with dinner. It smelled heavenly and her stomach growled in an undignified way. She hadn't had anything substantial to eat since the toast she had for breakfast. Standing, she took her wine glass into the kitchen. "I've never had a job."

"I imagine a court would grant you the house and alimony," he said.

"That would still be John having power over me, wouldn't it? I'd still be reliant on him for my survival. Would I remove him from the coven? What about his supporters?" The fear in her own voice startled her.

"You have enough of us that I wouldn't worry about the handful of John's supporters. If they really support him. The true test is to see which ones help him out of loyalty to the coven, and which ones truly like him." Garrett's eyes went distant for a moment, as if he was contemplating some great puzzle.

"Then I would be dependent on the coven." She looked down, feeling defeated. No matter how things turned out, she was beholden to someone else for her fate.

"Only until you figured things out. Maybe went back to college, got a career. Got your own place," Garrett said. His soothing tone gave her hope.

She perked up a little, then looked past him to the stove. "It smells divine."

"I make a mean marinara with spinach pasta and meatballs." He laughed. "Have a seat. I'll serve."

A man serving her dinner. Other than waiters or chefs in restaurants, having a man cook for her and serve her was a new experience. When he set the plate of steaming pasta and sauce, with two oversized meatballs in front of her, her mouth began to water. Suddenly she felt ravenous, but she held back and waited until he had replenished their wine and joined her at the table with his own plate before lifting her fork and saying a silent prayer of thanks to Ba'al for the food she was about to eat. She added in, *thank you also for the truths that have been revealed to me.* Praying in silence was something she'd grown accustomed to over the years.

"Should we take some of this out to the temple as an offering after dinner?" he asked, sounding hopeful. "How long has it been since you've placed an offering?"

With her fork poised over one of the meatballs, she shrugged. "It's been years, like so many things." Then the anger returned. So many things she felt deeply about had been cast aside in service of John. In that brief moment, she almost hated Garrett for using the weekend to make her see the cold truth of her entire life. She knew it wasn't Garrett's fault and knew she should be grateful that, for the first time in years, she was seeing things as they truly were – no matter how painful. In her turbulent emotional state, her empathy returned and just as quickly as she hated him, she was grateful to him.

They ate the rest of the meal in silence, only pausing to talk about cooking. She was surprised to learn that he loved to cook on the weekends, especially if he had someone over. When dinner was done, they put together a bowl with plain pasta and a sliced apple, donned their shoes and jackets, and by flashlight, made their way to the outdoor temple. It had stopped raining, but the ground was still damp, and an almost full moon in a clear sky helped to further light their path.

By moonlight, the outdoor ritual space felt comfortable and inviting. While the air had that cool nip of autumn to it, she didn't feel it. When she was here, in presence of Ba'al, her heart felt light and her problems seemed distant and unimportant. She hadn't felt this alive in years. She took the bowl to the stone altar and set it on the cool, damp, even surface.

She felt Garrett next to her, so close that she could almost feel the heat radiating from his shoulder and arm, to hers. "Do you want to do the honors and say a prayer?"

In the darkness, she smiled. "Yes." She reached down and took his hand into hers. Garrett squeezed her hand gently and bowed his head. She recited an offering prayer from memory. "Lord Ba'al, please accept this offering as our devotion to you. Bestow upon us abundance and guidance and know that our dedication is true. We are blessed in the light of Ba'al. So be it."

Not letting go of Garrett's hand, she breathed in deeply the scent of damp earth, trying to reclaim that feeling she first had when he'd brought her here earlier. It didn't take long.

Tilting her head back she looked up and saw the trees surrounding the clearing, and the light of the moon casting its glow upon them.

Garrett let out a deep cleansing breath, let go of her hand, and stepped up behind her, gently placing his hands on her shoulders. His mouth next to her ear. "There's no one to interrupt this time."

Then she felt his tongue and lips on her neck as he kissed her with fervent passion, his hands moving around her to gently cup her breasts. His erect penis pressed into the small of her back.

In a moment of panic, she put her hands on his to stop them from exploring further beneath the fabric of the bodice of her dress. "We can't."

"No one has to know," he whispered. "It's between us and Ba'al."

He pulled his hands from her grasp and took off her jacket, then his own, and then, he unzipped her dress, gently guiding the straps off her shoulders and down over her arms, leaving her breasts bare to the cool night air. Her nipples hardened and her breath caught in her throat. She could have stopped him. Should have. But she didn't want to. For the first time in years, a vaguely familiar sensation flooded her loins. Lust. She hadn't felt lust for so long. Hadn't been allowed to. But here it was okay. Here – she could lose herself in Garrett's embrace. His hands glided down her body, pushing her dress with it until the frock passed over her narrow hips and fell into a soft heap around her ankles. Garrett's eager hand slipped between her thighs, through her wanting sex, two fingers probing her deeply and his other hand caressing her swollen clitoris. She threw her head back onto his shoulder and pushed her hips forward, wanting more.

His kisses became more urgent, more beast-like, and he growled with his hunger for her. Gently, he guided her to all fours and positioned himself behind her. When he entered her, she pushed back on him, taking him deeply. A moan so loud and desperate escaped her lips and she didn't care if the dark forest heard her cries. Their lovemaking quickened and became more desperate and primal. Even when he pulled out and rolled her over onto her back, both of them covered in the damp forest floor, and re-entered her, she didn't care. She wrapped her legs around his hips, pulling him down on her, wanting him to ravage her. And so he did. He tasted and smelled of the sweet wine they'd had with dinner. His hard body melded with hers with each thrust. She met her release first, exploding and screaming out, rocking against him. Then he moved against her faster taking long, deep strokes until finally, he buried himself deep inside her and let out a deep, primal growl, finally collapsing against her. Panting.

They lay there for a few moments, in the center of the clearing, the large stone altar and statue of Ba'al looking down on them. Garrett brushed some dirt from her cheek and kissed her hard on the lips then pulled back and whispered, "I want you again."

She wanted him, too. Her body burned for him. Her only response was to kiss him back. But this time he made love to her gently, slowly, prolonging her orgasm until she couldn't control herself. His own release was not far behind, and when they had finished, they both lay nude, covered in dirt, on their backs, staring up at the clear night sky.

Neither of them said anything, but Mary presumed it was because that one final question hung between them. *What now?* She didn't want to think about it, not now. Instead, she wanted to lay here with him, and leave the rest of the world outside the temple.

"We're going to have to go in at some point," he whispered.

"I don't want to leave here," she said dreamily. "Nothing exists outside this temple…"

"Except those rain clouds moving in," he said, pointing. Sure enough, a bank of clouds were rolling in, bringing with them the promise of more rain. Then he propped himself up on one arm and put his hand on her stomach. "But, that doesn't mean we can't just move into the temple in the house. We can leave everything outside that temple, too."

An unbidden smile made its way across her lips and she turned to him. "I must look a mess."

"You are gorgeous with mud on your face," he said, leaning down and kissing her deeply.

She wanted him again. Screw the consequences. "All right, up to the house and straight to the temple."

He laughed. "Let's just grab our clothes and carry them, drop them in the laundry room, and go straight down. No sense wasting time dressing and undressing again."

She laughed, too. She felt like a teenager again. They scooped up their clothing and carefully made their way back to the house, then spent a few hours consecrating Garrett's basement temple. When they were finished satiating their lust, they made their way up to the shower in Garrett's bedroom, and once clean and assured they were both free of ticks, they collapsed gratefully into his bed and slept soundly until the following morning.

9

Garrett woke to the blinding brilliance of the sunlight streaming into the bedroom window, and his cell phone blaring on the bedside table. He grabbed it, swiped to answer and put it up to his ear. He put on his best *awake* voice. "Garrett Hammon."

"Garrett, buddy!" It was John.

Garrett sat up and looked over at Mary's nude body in the bed next to him. "Hey, what's up?" She stirred and rolled onto her back, looking at him. He put a finger up to his lips. Mary immediately sat wide-eyed and pulled the sheets up around her, as if John were standing there in the room with them.

"I hate to ask this man, but do you think you could let Mary hang out there for a few more days?"

Garrett shook his head in disbelief. First because John was so confident he had Mary wrapped around his finger that he believed he could keep screwing around on her. Second, because he was putting so much trust in Garrett, assuming him to be a loyal servant. John got what he had coming. "Of course, but…"

John cut him off. "Myrna is feeling a little neglected and Mary could use a vacation from the house, so… did you do that ritual yet? The one that's supposed to make us a lot of money? I'm counting on you, man! I've got a couple of women to provide for, and a baby to feed here soon…"

Garrett set his jaw. "Yeah. I had planned on it for later tonight."

He added silently, *So the sun and Sorath can burn your ass, you piece of shit.*

"Just do it after she goes to bed. I hope she hasn't been a bother and is taking care of you and the house?" John said it with all of the affection of a business man asking if the weekly reports were done.

"Yes. She's been taking care of me just fine. Last night she made me a buffet and I ate until I was full." A sly grin slipped onto his lips. "I'm sure Mary won't mind staying. There are entire rooms I haven't let her explore yet."

"Wonderful! Thank you, Garrett, I owe you one!"

"No problem, brother," Garrett said.

"Later."

"Yeah, later." He tapped off the phone then looked at Mary. "It seems John was wondering if you could stay with me for a few more days."

Much to Garrett's surprise, Mary nodded. "So he can screw Myrna? Whatever."

"I don't expect you to clean, you know. As far as I'm concerned, you can hang out, watch television, or do whatever you want. I actually have a housekeeper who comes in twice a week." He stopped himself. He'd said too much, and he still wasn't sure she was stable from all the shocking news she'd received. That, and he suddenly felt like he'd taken advantage of her…. "Mary, I hope you know that it wasn't my intention to take advantage of you last night. You should know that I've been admiring you from afar since we were younger."

She let the sheet drop into her lap. "I was so blinded by John's charm that I didn't even notice."

"Pretty much. I hope you won't think less of me."

She reached out and pulled his head to hers and kissed him. "Maybe I am vulnerable, and maybe we have allowed lust to win out, but why not? I'm soon to be single and my husband is sleeping around. If anything, I feel like I'm using you."

"I just don't want you to get hurt…" He stopped. While this was true, he found his heartbeat quickening, and not just because he was into her. But because everything was going as planned. Did the high magus do a spell to influence the situation? *Of course he did*, Garrett thought.

Mary considered his comment for a moment and said thoughtfully, "We could always go see Esther and find out how it will turn out."

He laughed. "I suppose. Or Belinda Applegate."

"Who?"

"Esther's new protégé. The new head of Temple Apophis." Pulling the blanket and sheets back, he swung his legs over the side of the bed. "Let's get up and have some breakfast."

10

"Basically, a lot of the covens are wary that the new seer will be part of the thirteen, and not neutral. I mean, Temple Apophis doesn't have the greatest reputation, but that's when Brady was running everything," Garrett told her. He dug into the omelet she made him. "This is good."

Mary smiled appreciatively and took a bite. She'd probably eaten more in this single weekend than she did two or three days normally. Starving herself so she would be thin and beautiful for John, who'd kept her in the dark about everything. She imagined what she was feeling must be something akin to a coma patient waking up after fifteen years to discover the entire world had gone on without her. Now, she could only catch up and decide what to do next, because there was no going back. Not now.

"You look pensive." Garrett paused from eating and gave her a curious smile. He seemed content and happy. Happier than she'd ever noticed him being.

She wondered then what she would have done had she discovered Myrna and John on her own, without the support of the coven. The coven was on her side, Garrett said so. "What am I going to do?"

It was an honest question. She'd never lived on her own before. Never had a job. It wouldn't be fair to expect the coven, or Garrett, to take care of her.

"Well, if you want, I can have a friend of mine, who's a hot shot divorce lawyer, draw up the paperwork tomorrow and have John served as soon as Tuesday. Then, you can stay here with me as long as you like." He seemed to have it all figured out. As if he could tell she was contemplating her entire existence he said, "You could check out the community college. Take some classes. See if there's a career or trade you'd like to learn?"

"I just can't imagine… will this fracture the coven?"

He set down his fork and reached across the table taking her hand into his. "The fact that you are considering the consequences of your… no, of John's actions on the coven puts you ahead of John. The coven will support you. Even if you wanted to stick around this house and manage the coven from now until your death – the coven will make sure you are cared for. I would make sure you were cared for. The coven is family and you're our matriarch."

Garrett opened his mouth like he wanted to add more, but thought better of it because he closed his mouth, shook his head once and pulled his hand back to take up his coffee cup for a drink.

"What?"

Garrett's look had gone dark and he bit his inner lip, then said, "We should do a formal excommunication of both John and Myrna. What they've done to you is not only disrespectful to you, but also to your father and the coven itself. The coven suffers for it. They have no right…"

She stopped him. "I know. But we can cross that bridge when we come to it. If the coven really is behind me, John and Myrna would be shunned anyway. And isn't that worse? Being shunned by your family?"

He nodded. "You're right."

"It seems so overwhelming." She looked down at her own plate, realizing she'd eaten everything on it. The vigorous love making had obviously made her hungry. How long had it been since she and John had made love like that? Far too long. As a matter-of-fact, in the past four years they'd only had sex once every four to six months, and she hadn't even enjoyed it, let alone looked forward to more. With Garrett, she couldn't wait until the next time. *It's only because it's new*, her mind cautioned. Thoughts of her own dependency crushed the lustful ones as Garrett finished his breakfast.

"Maybe we should do lunch in Saratoga and go see that movie this afternoon," he suggested.

Fear and anxiety gripped her. "What if we run into Myrna and John?"

"We could take the drive to Albany instead," he said with a shrug. "I seriously doubt we'd run into anyone there. Besides, it feels dangerous and exciting to sneak around during your final days as a married woman."

She laughed and narrowed her eyes. "You have always said such wicked things to me."

"Now you know why." He smiled and got up. "Let's get ready. It's going to be a fun afternoon."

Smiling back at him she recalled all the times he'd made sexual comments, or smiled at her, or winked at her when John wasn't paying attention. Garrett really had liked her all along, and she was just now seeing it. With that she saw what she had missed. Years spent with a man who wasn't enamored with her. Unlike Garrett, who treated her like a queen. She rather liked the change of pace. When she did something for John, he praised her, but in a practiced, pacifying way. When she did something for Garrett, he sincerely thanked her and was deeply moved by it. She could see the difference in his eyes. Garrett and John where night and day. This made her feel more confident, more resolute, that Garrett was right. She needed to get an attorney to send the divorce papers right away.

Their afternoon together started with a movie, then an early dinner. When they returned home, it was her home now, after all, Garrett called his friend and made her an appointment for early Monday morning. She also discovered a channel on cable all about cooking and fell asleep on the couch watching it. In her slumbering state, she didn't notice Garrett, and another cloaked figure, slip through the living room and down to the basement dressed in full ritual robes.

11

"**H**ow is Mary doing?" The elder magus asked.

Garrett shrugged. "Not good. She just had a terrible emotional shock."

"Did you use the elixir?" The older man, nearly seventy, raised his bushy gray eyebrows.

"I didn't have to. I just told her the truth. It was enough. Besides, I threw the Elixir out." Garrett gave his mentor, his uncle, a brief grin. "Thank you for agreeing to do this with me here. I don't want to leave her alone just yet."

"Will she sleep through it?" He glanced toward the stairs as if he expected Mary to appear any second.

"I think so. She isn't used to so much human interaction as she got today." He handed his uncle the black handled athame with a bull-headed pommel.

"Your father will be proud to hear it, though I'm sure he still would have preferred you initiated into Lucifuge instead of The Collective." His uncle set the blade on the altar and took up the incense charcoal, lighting it with a lighter he produced from a pocket in his robes. "Perhaps, with your father and sister in Lucifuge, you can at least bring the covens together as they formerly were. My father, your grandfather, almost succeeded in bringing them into a single coven."

"For what purpose though? Lucifuge is Lucifuge and The Collective is The Collective. The Patron spirits are different." He lit the candles. For him, choosing a coven had been difficult. Ultimately, it was his admiration for Mary, as well as his relationship with Ba'al, and his love for the raw, animalistic energy of a solid Ba'al Rite that made him initiate into The Collective instead of Lucifuge. Part of his family, to this day, remained in charge of Lucifuge, while he and others in his family had chosen The Ba'al Collective. Family reunions often resembled a double coven get-together. It was fine though, as Lucifuge and The Collective didn't war with one another. There had been talk for years about trying to combine both covens, and ultimately, if his relationship with Mary worked out, the covens would be bound by the union of both familial bloodlines.

His uncle didn't respond. Instead, he opened the grimoire and held it aloft in one hand. When he was sure he had Garrett's attention he said, "By Sorath may The Collective be cleansed."

Garrett didn't push his uncle for an answer. He turned out the lights, but the room was still bright due to the many candles around the temple. His uncle raised an eyebrow as if to ask if it was all right to begin. With a quick nod Garrett signaled him to start.

The elder began by intoning the ancient invocation. Within the triangle in the southern quadrant of the temple a spark of light appeared, shimmering, and growing brighter until it began to pulsate and writhe like a million tiny ethereal creatures culminating into an electric mass.

Garrett held his hands in front of him, somber, knowing that sacrifices would be made. There was no going back now. In the triangle, he could see two bright burning eyes staring back at him from the swirling mass. Sorath. Born of necromancy and captured in a bottle, and then kidnapped by a lineage of Magi stronger than most of the witches and wizards in the thirteen covens combined. Garrett was proud to be part of this lineage and knew that eventually, once the elders had passed, he and three others would be called upon to take up the mantle of this covert, independent order.

His uncle finished the first of three orations. Garrett's only job was to assist as his uncle needed him to, but in this particular ritual there was little to be done other than provide the blood necessary at the end to solidify the pact. He listened, trying to focus on the orations and the intent of the operation. If he lost focus the consequences could be dire. Spirits, left to their own devices, would improvise. There was no room for improvisation here. John, and potentially Dean, needed to be removed. More importantly, Myrna and her unborn child would also need to be dealt with. He didn't want anyone in the coven or outside it contesting Mary's blood-borne right to the coven leadership. A bastard child born of an adopted daughter was an obstacle they could not afford. His stomach did a sickening somersault.

Now, his uncle charged Sorath with the fateful deed. "Destroy by greed John Rose, and those who would harbor him. Destroy his seed within the imposter who seeks only to reinforce the Rose bloodline. Bring a fertile womb to the last blood-borne Sanderson that she may usher in a new generation of leadership. With this pact, sealed with our blood, so be it."

His uncle took the ritual blade from the altar and carefully drove the tip into his left ring finger, allowing a single drop to fall upon the written parchment pact. He handed the knife over to Garrett and Garrett did the same, watching as two drops of his blood fell onto the dry, crisp surface of the pact. Then the elder Magus lifted the pact from the altar, held it mere inches from the beast within the triangle and let it go. There the parchment hung in mid-air as if gravity did not affect it at all. The thing within the triangle pulsated a few more times and then, as if it were a black hole, it sucked the air from the room, dimming the candles in the process. In doing this the hovering parchment was also pulled into the triangle and burst into flame, disappearing into Sorath.

Then was read the license to depart. "I bid you go Sorath to do our task. When you're finished you shall return to us, in the name of the quintessence, be it Atem. El. Ba'al."

The energy ball began to collapse in on itself until it grew smaller and smaller into a tiny pin point of light that blinked out into nothing. The entire ritual chamber felt hollow and Garrett felt his heart slamming in his chest. Even after a few breaths his heartbeat wouldn't slow. He didn't know how long he stood there, staring at the now empty triangle, before he felt his uncle's hand on his shoulder. "We did what had to be done."

"I think you misunderstand," Garrett said. "I have no problem sacrificing John Rose. It is sacrificing a baby that I have a problem with."

His uncle let out a sigh. "Sadly, this cannot be helped. The seers have all confirmed that the child would be an obstacle later on if allowed to survive. It's easiest to deal with it now."

Something about his uncle's words seemed final, so Garrett said nothing more of it and swallowed the acrid taste in his mouth, pretending to be immersed in the task of cleaning up the temple. When he was done he showed his uncle to the door where they wordlessly acknowledged one another, and his uncle slipped into the night without so much as a goodbye.

Mary was still blissfully unaware and sleeping on the couch. Garrett took the chair across from her and watched her sleep, all the while thinking about what he'd just done and how it would affect Mary. One never knew the ways in which spirits would work. There was any number of ways this could go down. Now was just a matter of waiting and watching to see if the spirit of Sorath was beholden to do their bidding. He rose and went to the kitchen to get himself a drink. After a glass of Scotch and a cigarette on the back porch, Garrett went back inside and gently woke Mary, guiding her up the stairs to his bedroom where they slept side-by-side until the next morning

12

Mary signed the paper and pushed it back across the table to the attorney. "How long then?"

"We'll get it filed today and the divorce papers will be served on him tomorrow," the rigid man in the black suit told her. He had graying hair and stern steely gray eyes framed by square glasses, and looked exactly what she expected a high-priced divorce lawyer to look like. Garrett sat next to her and squeezed her hand.

"Depending on his reaction, the divorce could be quick and painless, or he could draw it out for a year," the man continued.

She knew John and knew he wouldn't just sheepishly sign the papers, in which she was asking for the house and alimony for the years she spent out of work. If anything, she could sell the house and use the money to pay for college. Meanwhile, she'd live with Garrett and get more involved with the coven. While the entire situation was more frightening than she ever imagined, somehow, she knew she could trust Garrett. Intuition told her she could.

Garrett put his arm around her and helped her to her feet. "Thank you for doing this first thing this morning," he said, extending his hand to the man across from them. They shook hands briefly and Mary followed suit, shaking the man's hand quickly and wanting nothing more than to get back to Garrett's so she could hide from the world and regain her bearings.

"Don't worry Mrs. Rose. You have a solid case here and this should go smoothly with no children in the picture." Then the man led them from the office and back to the elevator.

Mary and Garrett made their way to the car without words. Though it was a beautiful, cool day outside, it somehow felt dreary. She couldn't help but feel loss and grief, and anger that John had done this to her. Garrett opened the car door for her and helped her in, then closed the door and made his way around to the driver side.

Maybe she'd relearn how to drive and get her license. She looked at the steering wheel as Garrett got in, and a pang of fear gripped her. Who was she to think she could drive herself anywhere? She was a scared rabbit, out of place in the big, cold world.

"So, lunch somewhere?"

"Don't you have to work?" She felt bad that Garrett was taking so much time and effort to help her even though he didn't seem to mind it at all.

"No. I called the firm and told them I'd be working from home this afternoon. I took the morning off. At my rates, I can afford a morning off." He chuckled. "You worry too much."

With her hands in her lap she sat quietly, submissively.

"Hey." He reached out a strong hand and took her chin into it, turning her head to face him. "I can't imagine how terrifying this is for you, but it's going to be okay."

"Promise?" she asked in a small voice.

He nodded. "I promise."

Then his phone rang and he let out a heavy sigh as he pulled the phone out. His look changed from reassurance to annoyance then, but he answered anyway. "Hammon."

She couldn't make out the words through the tiny speaker he held up to his ear, but she could tell it wasn't good because Garrett's annoyance turned to concern and shock.

"When?" he asked. Then he said, "Good gods."

He listened for a few more minutes with a few well-placed acknowledgements and finally said. "I'll let her know."

Thank you, Sheriff. I don't know when we can come down, but we will try to before the end of the day."

Then he said goodbye and hung up, staring out the windshield into the wall of the parking garage before finally turning to her and saying slowly, "Apparently John got some good news about an investment this morning from his broker. He was with Myrna and they decided to hurry over to the brokerage to sign some paperwork."

The way he said it sent a chill through her and she knew it was something bad.

"About forty-five minutes ago John ran a red light and the car was broadsided by a semi. Both John and Myrna were killed on impact." He bit his lower lip and looked at her as if trying to gage her reaction.

Mary swallowed the hard lump in her throat and nodded. Her entire body felt numb. Drawing in a breath, it caught in her throat. She wasn't sure how to feel and she looked a Garrett, knowing her eyes pleaded with him for guidance.

"It's going to be okay. Sheriff Steve will need you to come and identify the bodies later." His voice seemed distant.

Nodding absently, she drew in another shuddering breath. "The divorce…."

"At this point, everything relies on his will. Let me call the divorce lawyer and tell him to cancel those papers. There's no need for them now." Garrett took his phone and dialed the number.

She didn't remember the call, or lunch, or the drive home. Everything seemed so surreal. At the same time, she'd never felt freer in her entire life. She was finally free.

13

THE WATCH – REPORT 0752
THE ROSE INCIDENT
Compiled by Aaron Steele and Neal Watts [Date Redacted]

It has been alleged by Dean Charleston, formerly of The Ba'al Collective (now Solitary) that Mary Rose (now Sanderson) discovered her husband John's affair with her stepsister, Myrna Sanderson (by adoption) and Myrna's subsequent pregnancy with John's child, and cursed her husband with the help of High Mage Garrett Hammon. Sheriff Steve Watson's testimony states Mrs. Mary Sanderson (then Rose) and Garrett Hammon seemed "shaken up" when identifying the remains of John Rose and Myrna Sanderson, casting doubt that either of them were involved in the alleged accident.

Two months after this incident, Mary Rose retook her maiden name Sanderson, reclaimed her authority over The Ba'al Collective and married Garrett Hammon, who took on her last name. Two months after this, Mary Sanderson, who was diagnosed with primary infertility by OBGYN Alan Maise years earlier, became pregnant. Dean Charleston claims this was the deal with the spirits made during the curse. The lives of John Rose and Myrna Sanderson (and unborn child), for a life with Garrett Hammon and the ability to produce Sanderson offspring bearing the bloodline.

We are investigating to see if this is what caused the fatal car accident that killed both John Rose and Myrna Sanderson on [Date Redacted – see File TS0752]. We have reason to believe the SORATH INCIDENT [Case Report 0651, Temple of the Magi] and this case are related due to vague testimony by Seer

Esther Branson, who foretold that someone within The Thirteen would die due to the SORATH INCIDENT. Both cases are open and still under investigation by The Watch.

ORDER OF EURYNOME

1

"I want this put in the permanent record so that people know exactly what happened," Dean told them. He rubbed a thin, pale finger over the rim of the mug of tea in front of him.

Aaron Steel and Neal Watts of The Watch, sat across from Dean Charleston formerly of The Ba'al Collective, waiting. Aaron held a pen in his left hand, poised over a pad of paper. On the oak dining room table between them sat a small digital recorder to catch anything Aaron might miss with his shorthand.

Dean looked awful. His face had sunken in and his skin had a pale gray tinge to it. The formerly robust man was now frail and thin. He'd lost every strand of hair on his head. Radiation and chemotherapy hadn't worked.

"I was cursed. Now I have terminal pancreatic cancer and I'm lucky if I'll last to the end of the month." His eyes turned to the patio doors, framing the picturesque backyard forest of Aaron and Neal's pristine estate. New snow fell from the sky, lightly dusting the balcony and the trees and lawn below.

"Do you have proof of a curse?" Neal crossed his arms over his chest.

Dean turned his attention to the two men across from him and frowned. It was just like The Watch to be so damn stuck up about everything. "Do you mind if I smoke?"

"Do you think that's wise?" Neal frowned.

"I think at this point it doesn't matter. I'm a… dead man walking?" Dean let out a bitter laugh and pulled out a pack of Marlboros and a gray lighter.

Wordlessly, Aaron got up, went to the kitchen, and returned with a glass ashtray, setting it between them. Then he took up his pen again. "So when did you realize you were cursed?"

"When John, Myrna, and the baby died." He pulled a cigarette from the pack, shoved it between his lips and lit it, taking a long, deep drag. "Mary didn't seem too broken up at the funeral. You saw her."

Members from all the covens had been at the funeral. Oftentimes, heads of covens would attend out of politeness, especially if the deceased was someone high up in one of the covens.

Neal and Aaron's expressions didn't change, so he flicked the cigarette in the ashtray, took another long inhale, and said on the exhale, "The rumor is that she and Garrett Hammond are an item now. She's taken the coven over, and I've been shunned. What does that sound like to you?"

Neal narrowed his eyes. "That does sound odd that your entire coven would abandon you considering your current state."

"You mean the fact that I'm dying. You don't have to downplay it to me. I can feel my body dying. I think Garrett convinced Mary to curse us, John and me. Myrna was just an unfortunate casualty caught in the crossfire." He took another drag, exhaling tendrils of smoke that rose upward. In the large great room to his left, a fire burned in the black iron fireplace, faced with gray marble. "Of course Myrna was carrying John's kid, so maybe she was a target, too."

Aaron and Neal exchanged a symbiotic look, then both looked back at him, not offering any commentary.

"I want it in the record that The Ba'al Collective killed us," he told them, tamping out the now finished cigarette into the ashtray. His eyes went to the empty pad of paper still poised beneath Aaron's pen. "Aren't you going to write something down?"

"I'm not sure what to write. I think I can remember the accusation without making notes, I just don't know what you want me to say..." Aaron set the pen down, and leaned onto the table on his elbows. "I need something more. Do you know how? Have you seen anything? For all we know, John just wasn't paying attention when they got into that accident, and your cancer could be an unfortunate coincidence. As for Mary, everyone grieves differently, and I know from experience that you can only cry so much after a loved one dies before you go numb. You could be mistaking Garrett's support for Mary as a relationship, and it's also possible your coven-mates are just jerks for not being there for you during your illness. Unless you found a poppet, or saw something that points directly to a curse, we can only enter it into the official record as an alleged curse."

"Alleged," Dean repeated, and then chuckled.

"It's an unfounded accusation," Neal said, as if to clarify Aaron's points.

Dean gave the handsome couple a nod and stood. Both Aaron and Neal were lean and tall, clean shaven and wearing khakis and knit sweaters in earth tones. "Well then I guess I have nothing else for you since gut feelings don't count."

"Don't get us wrong," Neal said, standing. "We'll put this in the official record as you were sure your coven cursed both you and John."

"And Myrna," Aaron added.

"But we can only enter it into the record as an allegation and not a certainty. Have you told Steve Watson? Made an official police report?" Neal glanced over at Aaron, then gave Dean a questioning look.

Dean nodded. "The Sheriff said he'd check it out. He went to Mary and Garrett and asked, but obviously they played innocent."

Aaron bit his lower lip. "Do you think that having the sheriff go to see them is why your coven isn't currently keen on talking to you?"

Dean snorted. "I'm sorry to have wasted your time. Mark my words – don't piss off Ba'al Collective if you want to live. Nor Cult of Lucifuge. You know those two are tight, right? Part of Garrett's family are Lucifuge. Part are Ba'al Collective."

"Yes, we know," Neal said.

Dean started toward the front door.

Aaron rushed ahead to get his coat from the hook near the front door. He held it out to Dean as if he were going to help him into it.

Dean grabbed the coat.

"So are you saying Lucifuge and Ba'al are going to combine?" Neal stepped in front of the front door as if to bar his way.

"It might. Or maybe they'll just keep the two separate to retain twice the power." Dean shrugged and pulled on his coat. "It's none of my affair. Not anymore."

Neal opened the door and produced a business card. "Well thank you for coming and if you think of anything else, anything at all, just call us."

Dean took the card and slipped it into his coat pocket. He had one more stop. Order of Eurynome headquarters. He still had to plan his funeral.

2

Jason Ray, Jay Ray to his friends, gave the thin, gaunt man before him, a wary look. Did he appear shocked? Dismayed? Julie and Brian, fellow funeral coordinators, and heads of Order of Eurynome, appeared to share his feelings, except he could see the surprise and distaste on their faces. Did his features hide or highlight his feelings?

"I see that perhaps I was wrong to come here…"

Julie cleared her throat and shoved a long blond curl over her shoulder. "I, we… we don't do that, Mr. Charleston."

"For an order of funerary priests you certainly don't do much, do you?" The frail man before them looked almost disgusted. "Perhaps I'll seek out someone from Temple of the Magi, or that young man over at Temple Apophis. Rumor has it both of those covens have no qualms about doing the sort of thing I'm asking you to do."

Brian Price, the head director, wasn't nearly as diplomatic as Julie on the matter. He put their stance directly on the table. "We're funerary priests, Mr. Charleston. We do not wait for someone to die and then resurrect them. Especially in the name of a personal vendetta. It goes against nature. Death is the natural conclusion to life. Now, we can help you pass over. We can make sure your soul travels beyond the veil into the afterlife with no tethers holding you to this world. We can plan the reception for your loved ones afterward, and we can commit your flesh to the ground or the flame as you so choose. But we do not do that."

Jay Ray said nothing. Admittedly, he found the idea of raising the dead intriguing. He, too, had heard the stories of Warren Leonard and Temple of the Magi raising the dead, and he wanted to see it at least once in his lifetime, but Brian and Julie were right. That type of necromancy was forbidden by the codes of conduct of Order of Eurynome. As an order, a coven, of funerary priests, they held one another to rigorous standards to help people pass from this world to the next, and to send them off peacefully. Nothing more.

It wasn't long before Dean turned to Jay and asked, "And what about you? Do you agree with your brethren on the matter?"

Jay Ray felt his face tighten and his mind scramble. "Uh, yeah. Yeah we don't do that sort of thing."

His words sounded hollow in his own ears.

Dean stood and took up the folder of paperwork they gave him. "I will get back to you with your packet filled out."

"Be sure to consult with your coven to see if there are any special observances we need to deal with," Julie said, her voice even and smooth. Something about her voice always put the dying and the bereaved at ease.

"Yes, I will," Dean said. He let out an exasperated sigh and left the room.

Brian shook his head. "What the hell will they come up with next? Why can't people just accept their deaths and move on. We're all going to die."

"Not everyone is pragmatic about death as we are, Brian," Julie said. "This is the first time I've ever had anyone ask me to resurrect them from the dead."

Brian laughed. "Remember the one guy who wanted us to put a stele in the coffin with him so his wife could conjure him from the grave?"

"Oh yeah. I forgot about that one," Julie said with a smile at the memory. "I actually did that for them. I don't know if she ever summoned him or not."

This was the opening Jay needed. He'd never dared to ask the question before, but the door seemed open. "Have either of you ever tried that kind of necromancy?"

Brian shook his head, but Julie paused thoughtfully.

Then she said, "I've considered it, though I've never run across a practical use for that kind of magick." She looked down at the paperwork in front of her and frowned. "Damn it, I forgot to give him the music selection form."

Jay Ray jumped up and reached his hand across the table. "I'll go catch him in the parking lot if I can."

She handed it over and Jay hurried from the room, down the richly decorated halls of Eurynome Mortuary, and out into the blinding brightness of the parking lot. He shielded his eyes, searching for Mr. Charleston.

"Sir?!" He started forward upon finding the man struggling to open his car door.

Dean turned with a quizzical look. "Yes?"

"Ms. Grier forgot to give you a form." He thrust it at the man. "By the way, I'm sorry we're unable to help you. However..." he paused, because he wasn't sure he should offer it up. "Death isn't as bad as people think. I've talked to the dead and many of them find the other side rather peaceful..."

"Unless they're tethered to this world with an axe to grind. Then they become tortured spirits. I'm only asking that someone help me find peace so I can go to my death vindicated. Thank you for the form." The man placed the errant sheet into the folder and tossed it into the passenger seat.

"What if..." He couldn't believe he was going to say this. He wanted to help this man. Whether for his own curiosity, or out of a genuine want to help, he wasn't sure. Either way his mouth opened and he said it. "What if I could talk to Warren Leonard and we could arrange to give you forty-eight hours after death?"

The man turned to him, his eyes brimming with tears of gratitude. "That's all I want."

"Let me talk to him and I'll get back to you," he said.

The man smiled and nodded. "Very good. I appreciate your open-mindedness."

Jay returned the smile and turned to go back into the funeral home.

The remainder of his workday seemed to float by muddled with doubt. Why had he said that to Mr. Charleston? Wasn't it unethical? After all, he was helping a man exact revenge for real, or imagined, slights against him. What if that revenge resulted in more death? By the time he'd reached his last consultation of the day, he had to admit that he had offered because true necromancy fascinated him. There was no other reason.

"Isn't Order of Eurynome kind of a misnomer?" The older gray-haired gentleman across from him had come in to schedule a graveside offering to Bune in honor of his wife, who'd been gone for ten years now.

"What?" These types of rites were Jay's specialty, and so he was the only one in the room.

"Order of Eurynome. I thought Eurynome was a Greek Titan Goddess of water or something. One of Zeus' wives. Eurynomous is a god of the underworld. Did someone get confused?" The man looked at him with amused blue-gray eyes.

It wasn't the first time Jay had been asked this question. It was a common one. Usually, members of his order would sigh heavily before answering, including Jay. This time he didn't. He gave the man a kind smile. "Actually, Eurynome, or Eury, is a common pet name for Eurynomous or Euronymous, depending on your preference. Kind of like how instead of Anubis, a lot of dedicants will call him Anpu."

"Ah. I see. So you don't see Eurynomous as a devourer of flesh?" Still amused, the man toyed with the edge of the elegant black folder with silver sigil and lettering that was filled with the paperwork he would need to fill out.

"No. We view him as a peaceful overseer of the dead." Obviously, he added silently.

"But you'll have a priest or priestess of Bune oversee the offering?"

Jay nodded. "Of course. We have dedicants to many of the Death Daemonic in The Order. Including Bune." He opened the scheduling software on his laptop and with a few clicks found what he was looking for. "On January fifth we have two priests, dedicants of Bune, who have openings in their schedules. HP Frater Scott MacVoy, and HP Soror Michelle Anders. Did you have a preference?"

"Which one has the better sense of humor?" The man leaned forward, looking at the back of the laptop as if he could somehow see through the back to the screen.

Jay scrunched his forehead. MacVoy and Anders were both quiet ones. He didn't know MacVoy well at all, but he'd had many encounters with Anders, and he couldn't recall whether he'd ever seen her laugh. Then he noticed that Anders had blocked herself as unavailable after three that day, which likely meant she had somewhere she needed to be. Being conscientious of the priests' schedules, he nodded and said, "MacVoy is your man then. So, January fifth at one in the afternoon, graveside. Just fill out the information in there and drop it off, email, or fax it to us, and he'll contact you to go over your preferences. Our billing department will get with you for payment."

"That sounds fine. Thank you, my boy. Jason Ray, was it?" He reached out his hand.

"Yes, Sir," Jay said, taking the man's hand firmly and giving it a strong, professional shake. "We appreciate you entrusting this ritual to us here at Eurynome."

The man shrugged. "Well, it's only natural. You're the only decent funeral home in the tri-county area, and you're the only religious order that deals with the dead and offering rituals. Who else would I contact?"

Jason laughed. The man had a point. Of course everyone would choose Order of Eurynome. Not only would they perform any pagan or magickal funerary rite, but they were the only order comprised of all priests or priests in training. Even the few atheists and even fewer Christians in the area called on their coven ran funeral home for viewings and graveside services. There were several priests among them who had no issue with performing a Rite to Thanatos in the morning, and Christian graveside service in the afternoon. They even switched their priestly garb and titles as necessary to match the religion the family requested. As funerary priests went, they were a versatile group. As Brian Price, co-leader of their order always said, death is the same journey regardless your religion. Since Jay could see and hear the dead, he knew this to be true. All divine death spirits, while they differed in backstory and attribution, were each parts of the Death Divine, the Death Daemonic as they called it. Each of those spirits was a part of the whole of death.

Once he saw the man out, he breathed a sigh of relief. Now he could focus on contacting Warren Leonard. Warren was no stranger to Order of Eurynome. The Apophis acolyte even considered, albeit briefly, leaving Temple Apophis, the coven he'd been born into, to become a funerary priest. However, when his fiancé had taken over Apophis due to her rather intimate relationship with the coven's patron, Warren had opted to only seek Eurynome for training so that Temple Apophis would have their own funerary priest. Not surprisingly, Warren's personal patron was Anubis.

As Jay passed Julie's office he heard the beginning of Blue Oyster Cult's *Don't Fear the Reaper* coming from the boom box she kept on the bookshelf. He paused and knocked on the door.

"Come!" Julie said.

He stepped into her office. She sat behind her desk bopping her head of long blond curls and sorting through paperwork. She glanced up at him as he entered.

"Another offering rite for Mr. Gavin?"

"Yeah, every five years."

"Bune?"

"Yep."

"Who did you schedule for that?"

"MacVoy."

She nodded approval. "What are you up to tonight?"

"Dinner next to a fire and some sleep," he told her, stifling a yawn and glancing out her office window to see if it had begun snowing again.

"With Carolyn?" she asked. Julie wasn't a busy body, just to-the point. Her version of small talk was to ask terse, pointed questions without any fluff or formality. It helped in her position as a funeral director, but socially, it came off cold and indifferent. You had to know Julie to know it was just how she was.

"Carolyn is staying with her sister tonight and they'll be driving down to Massachusetts early in the morning." He sat down in one of the plush leather chairs facing her.

"Ah. A baptism is it?" Julie paused from her paperwork and looked up at him with a smile.

"Yeah." He didn't mind not elaborating because he knew it would only annoy her. His live-in girlfriend, Carolyn, who also worked at the funeral home, had taken two weeks off so she could spend time with her sister and brother, and be present for her nephew's baptism.

"I was going to see if you wanted to go out with Brian, Jack, and I. We're going to swing by Hades and grab a few beers." She'd gone back to studying something on her desk. Lifting the paper, she shoved it back into a folder.

He stifled another yawn. At least his body was cooperating. "I don't know. I'm kind of tired. I thought I'd go home, heat up a TV dinner and pass out on the couch."

"Enjoying some alone time while Carolyn is out of town?"

"Yeah." A pang of guilt ran through his gut. On one hand, having beers with the temple heads was always a good career move, but on the other hand, his desire to talk to Warren Leonard about Dean Charleston was greater.

Julie's phone rang. She held up a finger to him. "Hold on a moment."

She answered, "Hey Jack. Yeah, Brian and I are coming. We're also bringing Jason Ray." A long pause. "Well we need to deal with it because if those kinds of rumors start, it could ruin us. Maybe we should try to capture that death spirit of Sorath the Magi conjured. If it was even stolen." She laughed as if she were kidding, but then her tone turned grave. "Regardless, we need to do some divination to find out what they're doing exactly. We need to see what they're up to."

Jay felt awkward and out of place, feeling like he was eavesdropping on a conversation not meant for him. It was obviously coven drama. Then he began wondering why Julie would want to involve him at all.

"Okay, see you in about ten minutes." She smiled. "Okay, bye then."

"What's going on? Is everything okay?" Jay couldn't help but be concerned, especially if someone was trying to tarnish The Order.

"There's a situation involving Tiamat-Leviathan and potentially Cult of Lucifuge. We're not sure yet, but we're hoping you can help us." She stood. "We'll talk about it more at Hades. Only half an hour, then I promise you can get back to your frozen dinner."

"Okay," he finally said. It was only five o'clock. He could still catch Warren before it got too late.

"Good, head on over to Hades and Brian and I will be right behind you. Jack will probably already be there." She stood and gathered her coat and purse from the coat rack behind her desk, then went over to the boom box and turned it off.

3

Hades Bar and Grill was the most popular hang-out in all of Haileyville. All of the covens were there. Jay didn't understand why they were at such a public place to discuss something so secret until after they were seated in the far back corner.

He almost laughed when a man called Six, who hailed from the coven Shadow Marbas, asked the server, "Could we sit at this booth over here? I don't want to be too close to the death squad. It's creepy." Then he called out to them, "No offense."

It seemed many people from other covens felt the same way, as if crossing the path with a funerary priest was somehow a bad omen. This left their table with a barrier of empty tables, free from prying ears.

They ordered their beers. Jay still felt uncomfortable, wedged next to the wall in the booth with Jack at his right, and Julie and Brian across from him. Julie Grier and Brian Price were officially leaders of the group. Unofficially, they'd been dating and living together as domestic partners for years. It almost seemed the habit of this generation of funerary priests not to be legally hand fasted. Even Jay hadn't made his romantic relationship with Carolyn official. It was just assumed everyone knew who was coupled with who and that seemed to be enough.

"You look troubled, Jay." Julie paused a took a drink of her beer, scrunched her nose, and set it down. "This isn't that good."

"I'll get you another one," Brian offered, raising his hand to attract the serving girl. Once he'd changed the order, he took the offending beer and set it next to his own. "I'll just drink both."

Jay was starting to feel nervous. He looked at his watch.

"You got a hot date?" Brian asked.

Jack, who never said much, laughed.

"With a frozen dinner and prime time television, right Jay?" Julie laughed and leaned across the table, gently squeezing his arm. Just like she always did though, she went from happy to serious. "We need to deal with this quickly. Probably in the next seventy-two hours."

The server returned with another beer, and left. It seemed she didn't want to stay at their table any longer than necessary either.

Jay took a drink of his beer, set it down in front of him, and scanned them with his eyes. "So what's going on and how can I help?"

"See? I told you," Julie told Brian.

"You haven't told him what you want," Brian countered.

"I want you to contact one of your *dead*, and see if they'll do some spying on Tiamat-Leviathan and Cult of Lucifuge for us. Find out what they're actually saying about Order of Eurynome so we can prepare official statements ahead of time." Julie tried the new beer, this time without making a face.

"Why?"

Jack, a sturdy, bald, short mustached man who looked more like a wrestler than a funerary priest turned to him. "Cult of Lucifuge allegedly started telling people it was Order of Eurynome who stole the Sorath spirit from Temple of the Magi. They also claim we gave the ritual to Thaddeus Blackwood and helped him resurrect the spirit through a corpse. This rumor got back to Tiamat-Leviathan, and those…"

"Be nice," Julie said.

"Those do-gooders allegedly told Lucifuge they'd look into it, and try to resolve the situation," Jack finished. He tipped his head to Julie. "I was nice."

"Why is Tiamat playing politics? Isn't that The Watch's job? Or Sheriff Steve's?" Jay hated coven politics and tried to stay out of them as much as possible. With as much as Eurynome interacted with all the covens though, rumors were bound to crop up. He usually only overheard the rumors during Carolyn's long conversations with her mother over Skype. In a way, he was glad she was out of town for the next week, because if Carolyn knew what The Order wanted him to do, she'd want to talk about nothing else.

"Tiamat seems to think they're everyone's guidance counselor," Brian said, then shrugged, as if that explained everything.

Julie gave Jay a hopeful look. "So, could you do that for us and just let us know if your *dead* hear anything? We could really use the inside information."

Jay thought about it briefly. "I could, I just don't understand why we don't go to Esther Branson, or go directly to Tiamat-Leviathan directly. Michael and Sharon Roberts are bound to tell us."

"No," Julie said, frowning. "If we go to Esther we appear to play into the rumors. If we go to Tiamat-Leviathan, we look like we're worried."

"Do we have anything to worry about?" Jay asked carefully. There was something in Julie's voice that made him wonder, like she was hiding something.

"No. Of course, not," she said, and gave him a reassuring smile. "You should finish your beer, it's almost six."

Jay looked at the time. "Yeah, I should go."

"You are taking this date with a TV dinner too seriously," Brian said, narrowing his eyes. "You sure maybe you're not getting a little on the side while Carolyn is out of town?"

Jay's jaw dropped. "Gods no. I just…" he paused. "I just sometimes miss the complete silence. But don't tell Carolyn I said that. I'm an introvert and when she's home she just…"

"Yeah, Carolyn is chatty," Julie told Brian. "You know how she is."

"That doesn't leave this table though, okay? I don't need a war at home," Jay said, pulling out a ten and leaving it on the table.

"No worries, love. Brian and Jack didn't hear that, did you guys?" Julie gave them both a stern look.

Both men laughed, and Jack stood so Jay could get out of the booth.

As he turned to leave Julie said, "See you tomorrow, bright and early. We have the organizers for next year's Samhain festival wanting to get an early start. Nine in the morning." She beamed another bright smile at him.

"You got it," he said. As he walked to the car, he made a mental note to send his ancestral spirits on a fact-finding mission for The Order.

He waited until he got into the car before dialing Warren's number. It rang three times before he answered. "Warren, Jay Ray over here at Order of Eurynome. I was wondering if you had a few minutes to chat this evening. Maybe I could swing by?"

The voice on the other end of the line sounded unsure. "Okay?"

"It's a personal matter, actually. Something I thought you could help with. I've got a client for whom the Order couldn't help, but I thought maybe you and I could help him privately?" He didn't want to give up too much information over the phone, just in case someone in the parking lot heard him through the closed car doors and windows, which he knew was unlikely, but still…

Warren seemed quiet almost too long. "Well, okay. You want to come over now?"

"Yeah, I'd like that, if you have time that is," Jay said, noticing that it had begun snowing.

"You know the address?"

"I live two blocks over, so yeah. I'll be there in a few."

They hung up and Jay started the car, backed out of the parking space, put the Subaru in drive, and headed toward Warren's.

Brian and Julie were somewhat wary of the Temple Apophis acolyte. Warren Leonard seemed like a nice guy, and was ideal for the Sem Priest training. But the rumors that Warren had risen Brian Blake, of Lucifer's Haven, from the dead made the Order of Eurynome leaders uneasy. Jay, however, wasn't nearly as put off by idle coven gossip. In fact, it seemed to make Warren's candidacy more attractive to Jay. Then again, Jay considered himself a connoisseur of archaic necromancy and his tastes led to… darker things.

A lot of necromancy seemed to be happening in or around Haileyville lately, and none of it by the Order of Eurynome. To Jay, that didn't seem fair, or right. If anyone should know the secrets of necromancy, it should have been the funerary priests. It was no wonder other covens thought Eurynome had something to do with Temple of the Magi's necromantic Sorath experiment.

His mind wandered to the ethics of what he was doing, and it was the ethics of the matter that he was still wrestling with when he brought the Subaru to a stop in front of Warren's small house. The snow wasn't sticking yet, but he knew in two hours, that wouldn't be the case. There were still frozen mounds of the stuff on people's lawns and melting in the gutters from the last snow fall a few days ago. Drawing a deep breath, he got out of the car, made his way up to the front door, and knocked.

Warren, with dark hair and eyes, was taller than Jay by about six inches and ten years his junior. He opened the door dressed in jeans and a t-shirt. He didn't look like an ex-con, but then Warren wasn't your typical criminal. He was a computer geek, only guilty of smoking some pot. That had been years ago. Now, Warren was the guy people called when they needed someone to program an app or a database, or to fix their network. He was a programmer and hardware guy all in one.

He opened the screen door and beckoned Jay in. The sizzle and scent of meat frying in the kitchen filled the house. "Come on in," Warren said.

A gray housecat leisurely draped itself over the back of the couch, licking a paw. It paused to look at Jay, then went pack to cleaning itself.

"You want something to drink? Beer?" Warren seemed like a shy guy.

Belinda Applegate, who everyone thought was sweet at some point, stepped into the living room, a pair of tongs in her right hand. "Hi…"

"Jay. Jay Ray. Order of Eurynome." He nodded at her, wondering if he should hold out his hand. Then he realized how out of place he looked in the button-down shirt and black slacks he wore. He looked exactly like an undertaker sans jacket, black gloves, and black hat.

"Did someone die?" Belinda asked the question with a great deal of cheer. From all the rumors about her, he'd expected someone more homely and quiet.

"Not yet," he said with a forced smile. He wasn't sure how he felt asking Warren to participate with Belinda present. Then again, Warren was bound to tell her and if Belinda Applegate was to be the town's next Seer, then she probably already knew anyway. She was just being polite and not being openly nosey.

"Babe, could you grab us a few beers?" Warren asked. He motioned to the couch. "Have a seat."

Jay moved over to the couch, noting the muted television was showing a rerun of *Big Bang Theory*. He sat down, not sure how he was going to sound or how Warren and Belinda would take it.

Belinda returned with two amber ales in bottles with the caps already removed and set them on the coffee table across from the men. She promptly returned to the kitchen.

"I didn't mean to interrupt your dinner," Jay started. "I just really need…"

Warren sat down next to him and leaned back, reaching over to pet the cat on the couch back between them. The gray cat gave him a derisive look and jumped down, wandering to a cat tower next to the television. It clawed at the tree, climbed up to the very top, and settled down for a nap.

"So, I have to tell you the whole story," Jay tried again. "Dean Charleston, you know, from Ba'al Collective? He showed up at the funeral home today. He's dying."

"Pancreatic cancer, I heard. So terrible," came Belinda's voice from the kitchen doorway.

Jay nodded. "He had a strange request. Apparently, he believes he was cursed and that he and John Rose, Myrna, and their unborn child were the targets."

Neither Belinda nor Warren reacted. Did they already know what he was going to say? Jay took a deep drink of the beer, hoping it would steady his nerves. "He wanted the Eurynome priests to raise him from the dead with enough energy to exact revenge on the people he thinks cast the spell."

More silence.

"He said if we wouldn't do it, he would seek out you, or Temple of the Magi to help him." He took another drink.

303

Not being a drinker, and having already had half a beer at Hades on an empty stomach, he could feel the warmth from the alcohol start to make its way to his head.

"Because he heard that I raised Brian Blake from the dead," Warren said, glancing over at Belinda. "Are you worried I would do it?"

How was he going to ask Warren to do something that he himself was morally conflicted about? Judging by Warren's reaction, he balked. "Yeah... I..."

"Maybe you both should do it," Belinda said. "Besides, when you called Warren you did say you wanted him to help you help a guy. So it seems to me, you came here with the intention of enlisting Warren's help to do it. Though I can tell you're conflicted and having second thoughts."

Both men looked at her wide-eyed.

"There are ethical considerations," Jay said, but it sounded like he was trying to convince himself more than anyone else. "I mean, if his motive is revenge, and we raise him from the dead, are we responsible if more people end up dead because of it? And what if he kills us?"

He hadn't thought about that last possibility until just then.

Belinda shook her head. "Well I suppose that's possible, but I imagine his want for revenge is greater than his desire to hurt the people who helped him."

Jay felt his stomach turn. Why had he come here? So Belinda and Warren could talk him out of it, he quickly decided. However, it didn't appear that would happen. For some reason, Belinda Applegate seemed to think it was a good idea.

Jay frowned. "I feel bad for the guy, I really do. I do think that if what is killing him is due to a curse, then those responsible should be held accountable, but shouldn't the gods deal with that themselves?"

Warren looked visibly worried. "Babe, I'm with Jay on this. I agree that whoever cast the curse should have to pay for what they did, but I don't think we're qualified to be judge or jury. Besides, if anyone finds out that we did it, Apophis gets more bad publicity and it's quite possible that Jay here loses his ordainment as a funerary priest. He could be ousted from his coven." He shook his head. "That would be terrible."

"I could try to foresee the outcome." Belinda went over to the bookshelf on the wall and pulled down a four-inch crystal ball.

"Really I shouldn't be keeping you. I've interrupted your dinner. Dean might be coming by. I should go." Jay set the beer, half full, on the coffee table and stood.

"No, wait," Belinda said. "Warren has a gift for this. For necromancy. You know, you're curious about it too, Jay." She looked into the crystal ball for a few minutes, then looked at both of the men. "You both want to do this, though for different reasons. Jay wants to know how it's done, and wants proof that it can be done. Warren is curious to know if he can do it without daemonic intervention this time."

Jay sat back down.

"Warren knows this first hand, but you, Jay, should be aware that this kind of necromancy is dangerous. There are always possibilities that things could go wrong. Though from what I'm seeing you both come from it unscathed and more experienced. I think funerary priests should be educated in raising the dead. Not just metaphorically or spiritually." The young seer sounded sure of herself.

"What kind of danger are we talking about?" Jay asked. He reached out for his beer again and took another drink. It was no use; the beer was too weak. He was going to need something stronger.

Belinda seemed to notice this. She looked at Warren. "Maybe we should get Jay a real drink. Would you like to stay for dinner Jay?"

"Oh, I shouldn't." What he wanted to do was run home and hide, forget the conversation had ever happened. But if he did that he knew he'd always wonder how it turned out. For someone who had such an interest in the dark arts, he certainly was a coward. He almost laughed at his own stupidity but caught himself.

"Nonsense. I always make a little extra because you never know who's going to stop by. Besides, I imagine Warren would be thrilled to not have to eat leftovers for lunch." Belinda stood as if the matter was settled, and motioned them toward the kitchen. "Bourbon? We also have vodka, rum, or tequila. What's your poison?"

"Bourbon, a small one, I still have to drive."

Belinda certainly did most of the talking, but Warren seemed fine with it, so Jay was, too. The men followed her into the kitchen and took their places at the table. Jay to the right of Warren and Belinda to Warren's left.

Belinda had been keeping their dinner warm in the oven. Fried pork chops, potatoes and onions, along with asparagus spears were placed before them. Then Belinda poured bourbon for all three of them, and then joined them to eat. The Apophis high priestess was certainly a fantastic cook. There was more eating than conversation, and except for some small talk about the weather and work, they mostly ate in silence.

When they were finished, more bourbon was poured, and they retreated back to the living room to find the gray cat sprawled on the sofa sleeping. Warren scooped up the cat and set it on one of the recliners much to the cat's chagrin.

"Are we really going to do this?" Jay asked. He hoped they wouldn't think of him as faint-hearted, even though he was.

"Belinda's right. I've always wanted to see if I could formulate a ritual by myself, without the help of other *magicians*." The way he put emphasis on the word magicians sounded ominous. "Not that I'm saying you're not a magician. But I had someone who was more experienced helping me last time."

"So, it is true. You really did raise Blake from the dead." Jay sipped the bourbon.

"Yes, it's true, but you have to understand that Blake's death was an accident. It wasn't supposed to happen. We weren't raising him from the dead just as an experiment. We were simply righting something that shouldn't have happened to begin with." Warren looked at his own bourbon thoughtfully. "Maybe in this case, that's also what we're doing. Righting a wrong."

"How can we know for certain that we're doing the right thing? How do we know if the man was truly cursed? It's not like the cancer is proof. For all we know, he's just a crazy paranoid man who is struggling with the fact that he's dying." Jay looked at Belinda, knowing that if she wanted to, she could look into the crystal ball and see the answer to that exact question.

Belinda knew it, too, and reached out and took the crystal into her thin delicate hand, pulling it in front of her and staring into its depths. Whatever she saw, Jay did not. To him, the crystal remained clear and transparent. It didn't cloud or sparkle, or anything like that. Belinda's eyes grew wide and she gasped, her mouth slightly agape.

"Wow. Remember the rumor about Sorath?" She narrowed her eyes and looked at them as if expecting an answer. When they offered none, she continued. "I think it was a curse, but I can't see who cast it. It had something to do with Sorath. The death energy of Sorath. I saw one of the men who cast the curse, he's older but, I've never seen him before. There was another with him but he's in the shadows. So, it wasn't Dean's coven, or anyone well known in any of the covens, who cursed him. I know most of them. I don't know this one."

Warren leaned forward, interested in this information. Most people in this town would have been interested. Coven gossip was priceless. The only people you wanted to keep that information from was The Watch. The chroniclers of the thirteen could be nosy bastards, and they took coven gossip far too seriously. Then again, this was kind of serious, and while it was treated like idle gossip, if the seer saw it, it was fact.

"Is it someone outside the thirteen then? Not someone in Temple of the Magi?" Warren appeared to have a great deal of interest in this, probably because the rumor behind Sorath was that he had been conjured through a corpse brought to life by the ritual. The rumor was that the corpse still walked the grounds of the Blackwood estate. Perhaps as a servitor, or guardian dead to protect Thaddeus and Marla Blackwood. No one knew the identity of the corpse.

So much necromancy going on, and none of it out of the Order of Eurynome, Jay thought bitterly. Not that it was a status symbol, but if someone else's dead came knocking on The Order's door, Jay wanted to be prepared. To fight necromancy with necromancy. He also didn't want the other covens thinking The Order was inept and unable to perform such a basic rite of necromancy that the other covens had already mastered. Of course, if Julie and Brian found out that he was doing this, he would most certainly be excommunicated unless he had a good explanation. Even then, a good explanation might not save him. Right now, The Order was trying to keep themselves out of rumors of necromancy. Not start them.

Belinda had been staring into the crystal ball for the better part of three minutes. Finally, she pulled her eyes away from the reflective surface. "No, not Temple of the Magi. But I am getting it's someone in the thirteen. I just don't know who. It's not like they're active members. I don't know how to describe it. They're in the thirteen, but they're not. Does that make sense?"

"Not at all," Warren said, clearly disappointed. He took another sip of his bourbon and looked at Jay. "So, he was cursed. That should settle it then. He wants revenge and we want to practice raising the dead. I'd really rather not be the only person in this town who knows how to raise the dead, just in case."

Jay laughed. His sentiments exactly. "I could call him. When would you like to meet with him? I mean, obviously the details would have to be worked out. Like how to get his corpse after he dies. We can always sit with him while he died, but maybe his family would get suspicious by that."

"You know what would be perfect? If we had a place out of the way where we could, I dunno, maybe keep him in hospice care until he passed? Something like that. Fresh bodies are easier to work with. That way we don't have to steal his corpse from the morgue, funeral home, or worse yet – his grave. I have no desire to become a gravedigger. That's rough work." Warren gave him a wry smile

"I have a small cabin up by Moore's Creek. It's kind of remote, but close enough that we can swing by there regularly without it being suspicious to anyone. It isn't much to look at, but it has electricity, water, kitchen and all that. A dying man could be comfortable there." Jay used the cabin once or twice a year when he went fishing. Few people knew about it, and no one ever asked him to borrow it.

"That sounds perfect. Let's meet with Dean tomorrow, see what he thinks about the idea." Warren finished his bourbon. "You want more?"

While Jay wasn't drunk, he did feel the effects of the bourbon settling in his muscles. His reaction time was likely severely impaired. He began questioning his ability to drive home even though it was only two blocks away. "No. Would you mind if I left my car here and picked it up in the morning?"

Belinda stood and put her crystal ball back up on the shelf where she'd gotten it from. "You do realize if the neighbors see your car here overnight, there are going to be rumors."

Warren snorted. "Everyone knows I'm interested in necromancy. They won't think anything of it. If anyone asks, we'll just throw it out there that I'm interested in funerary priest training, and Jay here was kind enough to stop by and give me the rundown."

More likely, leaving his car in front of their house overnight would fuel the rumors that Order of Eurynome was running some kind of necromancy ring, but he wasn't telling Belinda and Warren that. They'd hear it soon enough anyway. He stifled a laugh by coughing.

"I suppose that would work," Belinda said. "Maybe I should drive you home."

"I should be fine to walk. Really, it's no problem. Besides, we've all been drinking. I have a jacket in the car and I'll lock it up. I'll just walk over here in the morning and drive to work from here." He gave her a grateful smile. "I appreciate your hospitality though. Thank you for dinner, it was absolutely delicious."

They said their goodbyes and Jay left their small house behind, grabbed his jacket from the car, and made his way home. The house was dark when he arrived. Carolyn had forgotten to leave the light over the kitchen sink on. She'd be gone for a week, which gave him plenty of time to work out the specifics with Warren and Dean. He sat down on the couch and turned on the television, flipping through the stations looking for something to watch. Finally, he gave up and left it on an old *Star Trek* rerun. He fell asleep right there.

4

Dean Charleston sat in the far corner of a small diner off of I-90 just past Saratoga. When the funerary priest, Jason Ray, had called him, he'd been a bit surprised. He hadn't expected to hear from the man, let alone learn that he'd talked to Warren Leonard and they planned to help him. Finally, someone believed that he'd been cursed and didn't take him for a crazy, dying person.

A sharp pain ran through his side, into his stomach, and he reached down and hit the morphine pump – twice. He shouldn't have gone out. He was supposed to be home bound, unless he had someone drive him. It was no matter to him if he died on the highway or at home in his bed. He was going to die either way. The cancer he had was aggressive and they hadn't caught it until stage four. Even though the doctors knew he didn't have a chance in hell of surviving, they insisted he try the chemo and radiation – at least a single round of each. So, for the first month, that same month John and Myrna had died, he'd allowed the doctors to poison him to see if the cancer would die while his body held on. Neither had happened.

Dean's father had died years back – heart attack. His mother was in a nursing home up near Lake George. The dementia kept her from knowing who she was, let alone who he was. He'd had no one except John and Myrna. It was no surprise the coven hadn't really taken an interest in his illness. Sure, a few of them had stopped by and brought food, but it was clear they had nothing to talk about. Georgia Friesner had merely dropped off the casserole, and upon not being able to start a conversation with him, she'd promised to stop by again, and promptly left. Burke Tidwell came over to mow his lawn. But everything else, the groceries, and the healthcare providers, were all paid to come to him.

It was his own fault. He'd pushed them all away in favor of being John's right hand man. He looked at his watch, it was three minutes after four, they were late. His thoughts were broken when he heard someone say his name.

"Mr. Charleston." It was the funerary priest, Mr. Ray. Jason Ray. A man no older than forty, and next to him, a tall lanky kid who couldn't have been more than thirty. Both of them younger, and far healthier, than his cancer riddled body – aged fifty-two.

"Call me Dean," he told them, motioning them to sit.

"You know Warren Leonard, Temple Apophis." Jason Ray nodded toward the youngster.

Dean acknowledged him with a nod. "So, you're the kid who resurrected the Blake boy?"

All the covens seemed to be ran by young kids these days. Most of them between twenty-five and forty-five, few of them a day over fifty. Even John had been a young man, thirty-four. The elders had stepped aside for quieter lives, giving guidance when needed, but otherwise keeping to themselves. The rumors around Haileyville were rarely about the elders, just their progeny. Most of the kids were wild and reckless. Hotshot sorcerers who were willing to try anything once. He briefly marveled in his luck in landing two of them.

He noticed the Leonard kid hadn't answered his question. "Well?"

"It's a long story," the kid said, looking around as if to make sure no one could hear them.

"Don't mind the people around here. We're outside of coven territory. Most people wouldn't know what we were talking about." He took a sip of the coffee and thought better of it. His stomach was perpetually sour these days, and the coffee felt like bitter acid. "Let's talk business. You actually did bring the Blake kid back, didn't you? Because if you didn't and that was just a rumor, you need to let me know right now and we can end this meeting right here."

"It's true, I did," Warren said. "But… I had help. Someone more experienced."

"Can you get that person?" Dean gave Jay a wary look.

"I don't think so, but I am positive I can do it myself." Warren puffed out his chest a little.

Dean chuckled. These damn kids thought they knew everything. Maybe he should have just gone to Thaddeus Blackwood and asked for his help. Thaddeus was older, more experienced, and hadn't needed anyone to show him how to do it, or so he'd heard. "Well you have Jason here to help you, am I right?"

Jason Ray, who today didn't look like a ghoulish funeral director, just nodded.

"Suits don't suit you," Dean told him, this time taking the glass of water and drinking.

A waitress brought a plate of toast and set it in front of him. "Anything else I can get you?"

Dean shook his head, but then motioned to the men across from him.

"Coffee," Jason said.

Warren nodded. "Make that two, please."

The waitress forced a smile, didn't hide the eyeroll, and left. Dean turned back to them. "So, let's talk business."

Warren looked at Jason, and Jason leaned forward. It was clear who the leader was. "The plan is to do this at my cabin by Moore's Creek, off of Blue Ridge Road. But here's the thing – moving your remains would be difficult, and suspicious. We were hoping we could move you there before…"

"You want me to die up in a cabin in the woods?" Dean felt laughter tumble from the back of his throat.

314

"It's better than being pulled over with you in the back of the car, or trying to dig you up after the fact. Or confiscate your remains from the morgue or the funeral home," Jason said in barely a whisper.

"Fair enough. My intention isn't to cause either of you any harm. I just want to get that bitch and her new boyfriend back." He reached for the coffee, remembered the grief it caused him, and grabbed the water instead. He took another drink, and another pain shot through his right side. With a grimace he leaned forward slightly.

"Can I get you anything?" Jason looked concerned and leaned forward as if there was something he could do.

Dean waved him off. "A less painful death."

"It wasn't Mary or Garrett who cursed you," Warren said, out of the blue.

"What?"

"My wife is the new seer in training with Esther Branson. She did a scrying for us last night, when Jay first came over to discuss your situation with me. She said whoever did it was someone who was in the thirteen, but who wasn't. It wasn't anyone from your coven." Warren sat back as the waitress returned with two cups, which she set on the table and then filled from the carafe in her left hand. When they were brimming with the hot black liquid, she left the carafe on the table, checked their cream and sugar, and upon deciding all was adequate, left again.

Dean took a moment to digest this information. He wasn't sure he knew anyone else he and John could have pissed off. Maybe Aaron and Neal from The Watch had been right. Perhaps Myrna was an unfortunate casualty. Especially if her sister wasn't involved. "Are you sure?"

"The man was older, but Belinda didn't recognize him. Maybe one of the old timers?" Warren said with a shrug.

Dean nodded. There were some elders who didn't like the way John was running things, and being that Dean was John's right-hand man, it made sense that whoever went after John would go after him, too. So, who had John pissed off? A list of names began to form in his mind. Some of the old timers had gone solitary, giving up coven life because the constant drama and rumor mill could wear on a person. Especially as one got older, the tolerance for other people's bullshit hit rock bottom. A person started to run out of fucks to give.

"Knowing this new information, do you still want to do this?" Jason Ray asked him.

The priest must have seen something in Dean's face because the truth was, Dean was having second thoughts now. "I need to think about it."

"That's not a problem. We thought that might be the case," Jason said.

Relief washed over the youngster's face and Dean smiled. "Well then, in the meantime, indulge a dying man and drink your coffee. Either of you seen any good movies lately?"

5

Jay didn't expect Dean Charleston to call back after he learned the people he'd been blaming for his cancer these past few months weren't to blame after all. Yet he did call back, exactly two weeks after that meeting in the restaurant.

He almost didn't recognize the man's voice. It was raspy and paused with sharp wheezing. Jay took the phone outside to the park across from the funeral home, just to be sure no one heard. He was glad the man had called his cell, so Carolyn wouldn't ask questions and he was able to take the call someplace else.

"It's Dean Charleston. I want to do it." The man said. He coughed.

"Are you sure Mr. Charleston? Do you know who did it?" If anything, Jay wanted to make sure he was sure. Bringing someone back from the dead wasn't a decision to be made lightly. "I mean – you will only have forty-eight hours, and if you plan to kill someone…"

More wheezing, but this turned into cackling. Dean Charleston was laughing and it sounded pained and horrible. Worse than nails on a chalkboard. "Kill someone? You thought I was going to kill someone? No man! I have every intention of scaring the hell out of them though. Make them paranoid my corpse will be following them to the end of their days. Of course, as old as they are, maybe a few of them will see me and have a heart attack."

Jay nodded to no one. "Okay, when can we move you to the cabin then?"

The man cough then his mood turned grave. "The sooner the better. I'm not long for this world, Mr. Ray. I've got maybe a week. Two weeks tops. I told my hospice nurse today that I was thinking of spending my last days in the woods, to die in nature as Ba'al intended. It doesn't sound half bad, actually. As long as I got my morphine and oxygen, I should be fine. Don't eat much these days except pudding and apple sauce, if my stomach can take it. When can you come get me?"

"Tomorrow, we can take you up tomorrow," Jay said.

"Good, bring a bigger car. We need my oxygen and wheelchair, and a few creature comforts if you don't mind. A dying man still needs some comforts, you know?" He coughed again, his voice sounding weaker. "I need a nap now. I'll see you tomorrow."

The line went dead and Jay hurried and called Warren's cell. Luckily, he picked up on the second ring. "Warren, it's Jay. Dean wants to go through with it. Wants us to move him to the cabin tomorrow. Says he wants to die in nature, as Ba'al intended."

Jay could almost imagine that slow nod thing that Warren did when he agreed or said all right. "Okay. Does he know who cursed him?"

"Yeah, but he didn't say who. He implied it was a couple of people. Old guys." From across the street, he saw Julie step out onto the sidewalk and wave at him. "Oh damn. I have to go. Work."

"Call me after work," Warren said.

"You got it." Jay hung up and smiled at Julie, rushing over to her. "Sorry, gardener. I was going to surprise Carolyn with a new flowerbed in the front of the house this coming spring, but you have to book them early. She's in her office right now, so I didn't want her to overhear."

"Really? You have to book them by December?" Julie asked.

He wasn't completely lying to her. It was true. He was putting in a new garden in the front yard for Carolyn, but he'd already gotten with the garden guy the week before, and it was set to go in the first weekend in April. But Carolyn's office was right next to his. He couldn't have her overhearing his conversation, either. Life partner or not, Carolyn wouldn't agree.

"I'll have to remember that," she said. "Can I get you and Carolyn to go out to the Rencer residence this afternoon? They're *planners.*"

Planners was a term Julie used for those people who wanted to make their final arrangements well ahead of time so it was all paid for and settled. That way, when they died, their families had very little to deal with. Jay nodded. "Not a problem. I'm on it."

He'd been extra agreeable with Julie in the last two weeks, since he felt bad that his *dead* had so far come back with nothing on rumors about Order of Eurynome – anywhere. It was as if none of the other covens gossiped about The Order at all.

Julie, while disappointed, had accepted this and dropped it. This left Jay free to concentrate on Dean's situation. Thank goodness no one in Order of Eurynome was any the wiser.

6

Between Jay, Warren, and Belinda, it wasn't as much of a chore moving Dean Charleston to the small cabin. The roads were thankfully clear despite a heavy snow only a week before. Belinda helped them move everything into the cabin, made sure Dean was comfortable, then took her car back into town. Warren and Jay stayed behind. Jay wasn't comfortable leaving Dean there, all alone.

He kept finding reasons to keep them there. Making sure there were enough towels. Checking the water temperature and the refrigerator. Making sure the heater worked. It was the dead of winter, after all. Everything in the cabin was in working order, of course. He even spent some time sweeping a few errant spiders from their corner webs.

"You really can go," Dean said. The man had grown even thinner, if that was possible. He looked like a walking skeleton, his gray flesh hanging from him in some places, and stretched tight against the bones in others. "I have the television, my oxygen, and the morphine. I've got pillows and pudding. I'm fine."

"We'll be checking on you in shifts," Jay reminded him. "Warren will be here in the morning, Belinda in the afternoon, and I'll be here at night. Are you sure you'll be able to make it to the bathroom or kitchen alone?"

The man smiled, and it looked like a ghoulish sneer on his skeletal face. "What is the worst that could happen? You'll find me dead. You can still do the ritual even if I've been dead ten to twenty hours already, yes?"

"Yes," Warren answered. Warren had spent countless hours going over the ritual, and walking through it with Jay. It had become an obsession for both of them even before Mr.

Charleston agreed. It was a fascination both Jay and Warren shared. It made them kindred.

"Go, go," Dean prodded them, motioning them toward the door with his skeletal hands. The skin had already begun to pull back from his nails a little. The man was turning into a corpse before their very eyes.

Finally, at his insistence, they left. There was nothing left to do but to make Mr. Charleston as comfortable as possible and wait. Once he died, they'd have to move quickly. The ritual had to be performed in the first twenty-four hours after death. The old necromancy texts insisted a fresh corpse made for better results.

It took six days for Mr. Charleston to die.

As luck had it, it was Belinda who was checking on him when she found him unconscious and unresponsive. They thought for sure he'd die slowly, lingering for days, requiring Belinda to stay with him as the death watcher so she could alert them of his passing and so that Warren and Jay's absence wouldn't arise suspicion.

But it didn't take nearly that long. She found him unresponsive at one in the afternoon, and at six fourteen that night, he had taken his last breath. His eyes and mouth drooped open and he'd urinated himself. Belinda drew the line at handling the corpse, but waited until both Warren and Jay were there before heading home.

"I bet she's glad she'll never have to see this place again," Jay said, joking.

Warren responded with a hollow laugh and went about setting all the required ritual implements out on the table. They draped the wood block table with a thick plastic tarp, then carefully moved the piss soaked body there.

"Do we need to undress him?" Jay asked. He'd seen a lot of corpses. All of them already embalmed with their lips sewn shut. Real death, however, wasn't nearly as palatable. It was no wonder people paid other people to prepare their dead for viewing. In that moment, he acquired a great respect for his fellow Order members who were morticians, embalmers, and crematorium workers. They were on the front lines of death and saw this every day. He only dealt with the aftermath of their work, and the living who were left behind.

"I don't think it matters," Warren said, flipping through his hand-written grimoire where he'd carefully written every detail from what he remembered of the ritual that resurrected Blake.

Jay didn't want to screw this up. He and Warren went over the final checklist to make sure they had everything. It wasn't much. Some candles, some chants, invocations and prayers, and an offering of marigolds and wine for death itself.

This spell differed from the Blake resurrection in that they weren't giving Dean Charleston his life back. They were giving him forty-eight hours to do what he needed to do, to send a message to those who'd cursed him.

Warren had researched it and put a limit on the spell, so it wouldn't last indefinitely. He'd explained to Jay that even if he wanted to, he wouldn't have enough energy to give Dean back his full life. Dean was too old and too sick, for that to work.

Jay had no problem with that.

Finally, when the time came to start the ritual, his stomach fluttered with anticipation and a tinge of fear. *It would be stupid not to fear something this powerful,* he told himself. It helped that Warren seemed nervous, too. Not arrogant. Humility was a good thing, especially when one held in one's hands great power.

Warren took a deep breath and started. He began by burning mullein and asperging the body with melted snow mixed with frankincense oil to bless the body long enough to keep Dean's soul attached to it once they called it back from the land of the dead.

Jay began intoning the incantations that Warren had carefully printed out on notebook paper for him to read from. The candles flickered violently even though the air was still. Both men worked methodically, moving around the body and performing the rite that would bring Dean Charleston back from the dead for two nights.

A half hour into the ritual, Jay was starting to feel tired. He had his doubts it was going to work. Again, the body was asperged and incantations were read over it. The offerings were held on high to the Death Daemonic. Warren set about opening the gates, his eyes squeezed shut, his voice bellowing from deep in his chest as he repeated the incantations. A cold rush of air blasted through the room as the gates opened.

Jay then said the final invocation: "I draw thee forth, Dean Charleston - come forth from beyond the veil, back to this earthly coil, by permission of Anubis! We conjure you – rise!"

In the background, he could hear Warren furiously whispering the incantations in a barbarous tongue. Those incantations were the ones that gave Dean Charleston forty-eight hours and no more.

Jay didn't know what he expected. Perhaps a flash of bright light. Maybe a loud noise. In the very least some type of supernatural phenomena that would indicate something was happening. He could usually see and hear the dead. They often approached in deep shadows and hushed voices. Instead, nothing. No fanfare. No bright lights. No shadows or voices. Nothing. It was disappointing to say the least.

Warren, however, was unfettered. At the utterance of the last invocation, he solemnly bowed his head and prayed to Anubis, then sat back on his heels and waited patiently.

"Is it okay to speak?" Jay asked cautiously.

"It could take a few minutes," Warren said, as if oblivious to Jay's question.

"How will we know if it worked?"

"The corpse will open its eyes and blink, probably sit up," Warren said, not taking his eyes from the body on the table.

"Then what?"

"We open the door, let it out of the cabin, it goes on to do what it needs to do, and we clean up and get the hell out of here." Warren shrugged. "When the spell wears off, the corpse falls wherever it is, and that's that. His remains will either be lost to the forest or someone will find them and they'll end up cremated or buried."

"Got it." Jay sat silently then, watching with Warren - waiting for the corpse to rise.

The half open eyes of the corpse blinked once, then twice. Then the lifeless body of Dean Charleston turned its head and looked at them. Its tongue hung half out of its mouth and it pulled it in, moving it around as if trying to regain control of its speech.

"Life," it finally said in a grating, throaty voice. It sounded nothing like the man Jay had known.

"Life," it said again, its muscles twitching and contorting in unnatural ways. Rigor mortis appeared to have made moving difficult. With some strain, the thing sat up.

Warren's face had gone white – the first indication that something was wrong. He swallowed hard and turned to Jay. "This is wrong, it's not supposed to be like this…"

Panic swelled up in Jay's stomach. Somehow, he managed, "What do you mean?"

"That's not Dean Charleston. Not anymore." The fear in Warren's voice caused the hair on the back of Jay's neck to rise.

"What is it then?" Jay took a step backward, prepared to bolt. "What did we do wrong?"

"I, I don't know." Warren took two steps back.

"What do we do? Is there a way to stop it?" Jay watched in horror as the thing on the table twisted and contorted in short jerking motions and up righted itself until it was sitting on the edge of the table. The eyes were milky white and its tongue still hung out of its partly opened mouth. A thin stream of thick saliva slid from its top lip to the bottom, rolling down its chin.

The damn thing looked like a zombie, sans bloodied open wounds or calling for brains.

Warren made it for the door and opened it. "We get the fuck out of here!"

Jay didn't need to be told twice. He started toward the door, looking back into the cabin one time over his shoulder before feeling the wall of cold hit him from the frigid night air. The thing in the cabin had managed to get off the table and stand, and was making its way toward the door.

His hands fumbled to his pockets and he breathed a sigh of relief. His wallet and keys were there. He pulled out the keys and hit unlock on the fob, twice. Warren jumped into the passenger side, and Jay into the driver's seat. They locked the doors immediately. Jay shoved the key into the ignition and started the Subaru. Warren peered back over his seat, watching the still open door on the cabin.

"What about your cabin?"

"What about it?" Jay didn't give a shit about the cabin. He was more interested in saving their own lives. He put the car in drive.

"No, wait," Warren said, his voice forceful.

Jay kept his foot on the brake. "What?"

"It's going into the forest, away from us and the cabin." Warren breathed an audible sigh of relief. "Leave the car running and let's run in and put out the candles and everything, lock the cabin up and then we can go."

"What if it comes back?" Jay looked in the rearview and saw the shadow of the living corpse slipping into the darkness. Then he estimated how many strides it would take to get into the cabin, do what needed to be done, and get out again, in the shortest amount of time.

"You stay here, I'll go in." Warren looked at him, his eyes full of hope. "I don't want to leave burning candles in there. They could start a fire. Besides, my books are inside. You stay here and keep the car running, I'll chance it."

Warren was younger, and probably in better shape. Jay nodded. "Okay – but make it quick. If it comes back I'll honk the horn."

Warren nodded, and in a flash, jumped from the car and ran back to the cabin. He went inside.

Jay's eyes watched the direction the corpse had gone in, and then he looked all around the forest on either side of the car. He didn't want to take the chance that the corpse had circled back to catch them unexpectedly. It felt like it took forever for Warren to do what he wanted to do, and with each passing minute, Jay felt more and more anxious.

Finally, the cabin lights went off, shrouding the entire thing in darkness, and Warren emerged from the cabin carrying two big packs. Jay unlocked the doors and waited while Warren shoved the packs in the back seat and climbed back into the passenger side. His hands were shaking as he closed the door and slammed down the lock.

"Let's go," he said in a quiet, almost ominous voice.

Jay didn't need prompting. He put the car in drive and hit the gas, driving faster than he should have away from the cabin. When they reached the main road that would take them back to Haileyville, he breathed a sigh of relief.

"I'm never doing that again," Warren said, quietly. "It was stupid to do it."

"Me neither," Jay agreed, glad that he wasn't alone in being scared shitless. He didn't care if Warren thought he was a coward or not. Now he knew why Order of Eurynome had such strict ethics about not raising the dead. "What the hell was that?"

"I don't know."

"You researched all this stuff..." Jay quickly glanced over at Warren, noticing the young necromancer's face was no longer as pale as it had been.

Warren let out a nervous laugh. "You're the funerary priest."

"Touché," he said. "But we have strict rules about forbidden rites and that was one of them. As far as that goes – you're far more experienced than I am."

"When we brought Blake back, it was different. He seemed himself. His body warmed and his skin changed. It turned pink as the blood flow came back. He was alive. It took a few minutes and he was jerky like that, too. Raspy voice and all that at first, but his eyes were normal. You could feel his soul return from beyond the veil, but..." Warren paused and looked at Jay. "Whatever that was, it wasn't Dean. I can't explain it. It's like I can feel souls of the dead and they feel different from a Daemon or something else. It's just a gut feeling."

"Discernment. You're describing discernment," Jay said, noticing Warren was getting fidgety and looking around the car as if something was missing. That made Jay nervous. "What's wrong?"

"I need water or something."

"We can stop at the gas station just off the highway near home," he said, then tried to direct Warren's attention back to the conversation. "You have a natural ability to discern types of spirits by how they feel. I can see why Julie and Brian liked you as a candidate for funerary priest training."

"Well, I ruined that possibility with the whole Blake incident," Warren said, sounding disappointed. "But if there was another Blake-like incident, I would do it again. His death was accidental - a wrong that needed to be righted. In this case, I think we were deluding ourselves in thinking that we were helping Mr. Charleston right a wrong. Belinda was right. I wanted to do it to see if I could do it alone. You wanted to do it because you wanted the experience. Well, we both got what we wanted, but what did we do? What was that thing? And if we unleashed something awful, what did Temple of the Magi release? These are the questions we need answers to."

Jay realized then that Warren didn't have the answers. Neither of them did. They were nothing more than two inexperienced dabblers messing with things they had no business messing with. If they had been experienced, they would have known those answers and likely wouldn't have done the ritual to begin with. *Nothing like age and experience to show you how little you actually know*, he thought. "So, who does know these answers?"

"We have to talk to Connie Hudson. Lucifer's Haven." Warren set his jaw and stared straight ahead.

"Tonight? Now?" It was pushing eleven-thirty and by the time they made it back to Haileyville, it would be closer to midnight.

"I think we better. It may be the only chance we have to fix this. See, Connie is…" Warren looked at him as if he wanted to say something else, but he must have decided against it because he turned his attention back toward the road in front of them and just said, "She is an accomplished magician and necromancer and knows about this stuff."

Jay nodded in acknowledgement. He wondered then why Warren hadn't contacted Connie Hudson to begin with, and thought about asking, but figured that would be pouring salt in the wound. It was clear enough that Warren felt defeated and was beating himself up already. Jay was not one to kick a man while he was down.

7

Connie Hudson was thin and blonde and... weird.

Jay couldn't quite place his finger on it. There was something off about the young woman, who appeared to be even younger than Warren. Twenty-something he guessed. How did she know more about necromancy than either of them?

Connie was the only one home since her roommate Corrina was out of town. The young woman, who appeared wide awake, ushered them into the house, not mentioning the late hour or asking who Jay was. Maybe she didn't care.

Warren wasted no time. "We're sorry for the late hour, but we have a situation. It's kind of an emergency..."

The young woman lifted a well-manicured eyebrow and cocked her head to one side like a curious dog. "What did you do?"

His mouth dropped and Warren looked at Jay for support. "I, uh, we were helping a friend and things went bad."

"In Lucifer's name, what is it with you odd creatures?" She shook her head. "You conjured something. Tell me what it was."

Was she a seer? Jay suddenly feared for his private thoughts and imagined a wall keeping her out. Warren looked like a terrified child, afraid to get in trouble for what they'd done.

That's when Jay stepped in. "I'm Jason Ray of Order of Eurynome. We haven't met yet. I work at the funeral home. I'm a funerary priest." He extended his hand.

She looked at it as if he were trying to hand her a dead fish.

He pulled his hand back and got to the point. "We promised a dying man forty-eight hours after death to avenge his own death."

Warren's eyes widened and he stepped back, dropping his eyes to the floor.

A slow smile spread across the woman's lips and she started laughing, full body laughs until she was bent over holding her sides. When she stopped to catch her breath, she shook her head. "Did it work?"

"Well, yeah, but what came back wasn't him." He looked at Warren. "I think we did something wrong. Whatever it was kept saying the word *life* and ran off into the woods."

She sighed. "It could have been a number of things." Her eyes went to Warren. "You felt it wasn't the spirit of your dead friend."

It wasn't a question.

Warren nodded. "Yeah, it wasn't him."

"Well, one of two things will happen. Either it will die and dissipate when the spell wears off, or it will live in the woods and occasionally terrorize the corporeal beings it encounters," she said with a flippant shrug.

"How do we undo the spell?" By the look on his face, even Warren could hear the desperation in his own voice.

"You don't undo it, you wait it out." She narrowed her eyes as if thinking about it. "Yeah, I think it will wear off eventually. What did your friend die of?"

Jay answered this time. "Cancer."

She nodded as if that was a good thing. "It will wear off. A body like that won't last through a lot of activity. He was probably frail. Until then I'm afraid you have a walking dead, likely controlled by a weaker spirit class. It takes a lot of energy to animate a corpse. You only gave it an initial jolt of energy."

"Then what happened to our friend?" he asked.

"He probably changed his mind last minute and decided to move beyond the veil willingly. Otherwise he would have been there to jump into his own body. Unless the spirit shoved him out of the way. That's usually not how those spirits work though. The human spirit, if tethered to this world out of revenge, will step back into its body rather quickly. Not leaving enough time for an *other* to step in." The casual, conversational style she used suggested she knew a great deal about these sorts of things.

"So you can't help us?" Now Jay was annoyed.

"Why would I? This is a lesson you need to learn. Now, off you go," she said as if she were sending small children off to play. She opened the door. "One last thing."

Both Jay and Warren paused at the entryway. "Sometimes these things return to their makers in hopes for more life once they realize they're losing their *charge*."

"Can it hurt us?" Warren asked.

"Ward your homes. Be alert." She motioned them out the door.

Jay balked. "You didn't answer the question."

A heavy sigh emerged from the woman's lips. "It could, but I doubt it could kill you. Of course you have learned something from this I hope?"

"Don't do necromancy," Warren mumbled as both he and Jay stepped onto the porch.

"Indeed," she said, closing the door behind them.

"She's a weird broad," Jay said as they got back in the car.

"You don't know the half of it," Warren said with no other explanation.

They drove back to Warren's in silence.

8

His first stop the following morning was Esther Branson's. The Seer's storefront stood among the quaint early twentieth century shops lining Haileyville's Main Street. He found parking on the street directly in front of Esther's. In the window, a sign written in a friendly cursive font assured visitors that walk-ins were welcome. Esther opened at nine and it was ten after. He got out of the Subaru and pocketed the keys, not bothering to lock it. While he usually locked the car, Haileyville didn't have a theft problem, probably because everyone local knew better than to steal from their fellow witches and sorcerers. It was a bitter, gray day, and the three inches of snow that had fallen overnight had already been plowed or shoveled. It was now heaped at the edge of parking lots and next to buildings. He navigated the curb and parts of the sidewalk that looked iced, and made it safely to the shop's unassuming front door. Pulling open the door, he entered the dimly lit warmth of the seer's domain, causing the bell to ring as he did so.

"I'll be with you in a moment Jay Ray," came the seer's voice from the back room.

He wasn't sure what was more unsettling. That she knew it was him, or that her shop had a back room that no one, to his knowledge, had ever seen.

"Would you like a cup of coffee or tea?" The elderly woman poked her neat gray head of curls from around the corner.

"Umm, coffee, please," he said, removing his driving gloves and shoving them in the pockets of his black trench coat. Rubbing his hands together vigorously, he curiously examined the cases along the far wall. They housed decks of Lenormand cards, tarot cards, pendulums, and crystal balls. None of it for sale, but all of it old. It was Esther's prized collection of vintage divination tools and was legendary in these parts. Sometimes people would stop by her shop just to see them, and Esther enjoyed talking about each item in rich historical detail. If anyone needed information on divination, Esther was the person to talk to. Rumor had it she would even tell a person all about their deck or device if they brought it to her. She could tell who owned it, if there were spirits attached, when it was made, by who, and how it had come into a person's possession. The only thing Esther didn't do was give people winning lottery numbers. Oh, she could, she'd once told him, but she didn't think it was the proper use of *the gift*.

Spry for a woman who looked to only be in her fifties, but was rumored to be almost seventy, Esther Branson breezed out from the mysterious back room holding a steaming mug aloft in each hand. She motioned to the table where she did her readings. "Be a dear and grab the coasters from the sideboard there."

Jay's eyes darted to the inconspicuous walnut sideboard that seemed to blend into the walnut paneled wall behind it. There, sitting on the side, were a set of plain black coasters. He took two, and set them on the table; one in front of her, and one in front of himself.

She placed a mug of coffee on each one. "I know you take it black, like me."

"Yes, Ma'am," he said, waiting for her to sit before he sat, too.

"I know you're not here to sell me funeral insurance. Julie Grier sold me my own funeral," she paused and looked up as if trying to remember, "Fifteen years ago. Back when she was barely out of high school. How is Julie doing? I haven't seen her around much."

Jay forced a smile, "She's doing well, but the coven business keeps her busy. We've been found out as the funeral home to go to if you have pagan tendencies. We've got priests traveling all over New England to perform pagan funerary rites these days."

"So, if you're not here on coven business, then I guess it's personal." She took a sip of her coffee and gave him an expectant look. In this light, her eyes seemed to change colors from gray, to blue, to green depending how she tilted her head.

"Yes, I…" He fumbled through the breast pocket of his coat and pulled out his wallet.

Esther pointed to the coat rack near the door behind him. "Take off your coat. Stay awhile. I have a feeling we have much to talk about."

He stood, put his wallet in his back pocket, and commenced pulling off his coat, then carefully took it to the coat rack and hung it. He wasn't about to argue with the seer. She probably already knew why he was there. *Of course, she does,* he told himself. He returned to the table, took out his wallet, and pulled a fifty from inside. After gently setting the money on the table, he tucked the wallet into his back pocket and sat down.

"Drink your coffee." Esther watched him for a few moments, then said, "You've already talked to Belinda."

"Belinda is as young and stupid as we are." He figured he'd get that part out of the way, since what they'd done was a product of their own egos and stupidity. She knew it, he knew it, and he wasn't sure he wanted it pointed out to him.

Esther nodded and smiled. "We have all done stupid things I suppose. Though this town has seen its fair share of it lately. That's for sure. Of course, you were simply given the opportunity to be stupid and you took it."

He laughed. "Isn't that usually how it works?"

She let out a chuckle. "I suppose. As a young woman, I used to investigate hauntings with a paranormal research group at my college. This was back in the late sixties, early seventies. A few decade before you were born at least. I was in my early twenties. I knew I could feel spirits. I can't see them, mind you, but I can feel them. Especially when they're attached to things. I thought I could also chase them off. Well, we got a real hot spot this one time. Right next to an open portal and that place was filled with spirits. I puffed up my chest and told them all - be gone! Get out. I was knocked down a flight of stairs and had to be taken to the hospital for a concussion."

He opened his mouth to say something, but realized he had nothing to say.

"I stopped doing paranormal investigations after that. It scared me back to divination and I've been here ever since." She took another drink from her cup, set it down and put her hands on the table, palms up. "Give me your hands."

Setting down his own cup, he gave her his hands, feeling the thin smoothness of her skin on his. He held his breath, as if breathing would somehow ruin the divination session.

"Ah, I see." Then, from under the table, Esther produced a deck of tarot cards and drew three. The first card was the five of cups. The second, death. The third, the magician. She looked up at him.

He lowered his eyes in shame. He was in his thirties, well respected, with a job as a funerary priest. He had a life-partner, owned his own home, and even had investments and retirement accounts. What he'd done felt like something his younger self, late teens maybe, would have done.

"What do those cards say to you?" The look on her face said she truly wanted to know.

He drew in a breath and shrugged. "Judging by the pictures, I helped a dying man cheat death through magick."

"That's rather direct, but you're simply seeing what has already passed. What I see is that there is nothing you can do but move on. What's done is done. It's time to take responsibility for your magick and use it for good.

Necromancers often get a bad rapport. Use your talents to help the living. Use it release the dead from this earthly plane - not bring them back to it. Besides – what you brought back wasn't Dean Charleston. But then you knew that…"

"I need to undo what I did. Get rid of it." He looked her square in the eye, pleading.

"That kind of magick is hard to undo. It has to run its course." She shook her head.

"Connie Hudson told us the same thing," he mumbled, thinking back to the night before and their conversation with the young woman. There had been something not right about her. Something about her eyes. Though he couldn't quite put his finger on it.

"Yes, well *Miss Hudson would* know," Esther said in a somewhat mocking tone. Then her voice softened. "You fear it coming back."

"I don't need Carolyn knowing what I've done. I don't want anyone to know." His phone beeped in his coat pocket and he turned toward it, fighting the urge to get up and grab it. It was likely Julie or Carolyn wondering where he was, or wanting him to pick up something on his way in. He'd told them both he was taking the morning off to run errands.

"Yes, well I imagine Warren feels the same way. I'll tell you what, perhaps you should go see Evelyn Winters. See if she has any books about ridding yourself of a devil." Esther picked up the cards and slipped them back into the deck.

"A devil?" He laughed. "Like a malevolent spirit."

"Yes."

His blood ran cold for a second. Just a second.

"Eve knows a great deal about devils." Esther smiled at him in a way that told him she knew a lot she wasn't saying. "Now finish your coffee and let's talk about you and Carolyn."

"Carolyn?"

"You sound like a parrot, Jason. Of course – Carolyn. She wants children and you're wary."

"Did she talk to you?" For a brief moment, all worry about Dean Charleston's devil infested, animated corpse receded, and a new fear surfaced. Carolyn had been talking about babies for six months now, and Dean wasn't sure he liked the idea. He'd never been good with kids, even back when he was a kid.

"No, she's said nothing to me," Esther said. She shuffled the cards and drew one. "You'll have two children with Carolyn. You probably ought to get used to the idea."

He gulped and involuntarily made a strangled noise in his throat. "When?"

"Next spring. Congratulations, daddy." A broad smile covered the seer's lips.

His heart thumped in his chest and he felt all the color drain from his face.

She nodded. "*This* is why you needed to know ahead of time. Carolyn, poor dear, doesn't need this kind of reaction from you when she tells you she's pregnant. Now, I have nothing more to tell you, but once you and Carolyn have had a talk and you've dealt with this Charleston business, you and Carolyn come see me and we can talk about the children. Off you go." She waved a hand at him and he got up, still shocked.

Shaking it off he drew in an unsteady breath. "You know, Esther, you really have a way of messing with a person's head."

A light, lyrical laugh escaped her lips. "Well I wouldn't be much of a seer if I couldn't see beyond the problems my clients can't see beyond, would I?"

Once bundled up in his coat and gloves, he decided to walk down, instead of drive, to Black Raven. It was the local occult shop ran by a solitary named Evelyn Winters. Eve, everyone called her. He wondered then if Esther habitually told her clients to visit Eve's shop for something or other. The women were friends, after all. Shoving thoughts of Carolyn and children from his mind, he focused on what he needed to deal with more immediately. Dean Charleston and the devil. Or was it *a* devil? It was a pretty common belief, in these parts anyway, that *the* devils other religions spoke of were actually pagan gods and goddesses, or Daemons, divine intelligences. A devil was only a devil if it was mischievous and meant to cause harm. Malevolent spirits were devils, and since there wasn't only one malevolent spirit, there was no such thing as *the* devil. *A* devil was the more proper usage.

By the time he emerged from his own thoughts, he found himself at the door of the Black Raven, face to face with Sheriff Steve.

"Mr. Ray. Good morning to you. They let you out of the funeral home once in awhile on a weekday I see." Sheriff Steve Watson was a tall man with broad shoulders and sturdy build. His brown, buzzcut hair was starting to show some gray. But the gray was more evident in his goatee.

He immediately slipped into his professional demeanor. "Indeed, they do, Sheriff. How are things with you and Allison?"

"We're both healthy and well, thank the gods. I trust you an Carolyn are also well?"

Jay fought the urge to just smile and nod. "Yes. Everything has been good. Decorating for solstice around the homestead this coming weekend. Anything new going on in Haileyville?"

The sheriff laughed. "Now you sound like someone from The Watch. But I will say, this cold weather must be making kids bored because we've gotten three calls in the last two nights about zombies in the forests just outside town. Zombies."

The sheriff shook his head and laughed again.

Inwardly, Jay panicked and felt like he would hurl the coffee he'd just had, right at the sheriff's feet, but that cool detachment he'd learned working at the funeral home for so many years must have kicked in because the sheriff didn't seem to notice and Jay said, "That's kids for you."

"Have a nice rest of your morning, Mr. Ray. I'm hoping we don't get any more snow." The sheriff ambled toward his waiting SUV, and waved to Chelsea Delint at the café across the street.

Jay let out a short breath and entered the inviting warmth of Eve's shop. It smelled like cinnamon and pine, probably her new Winter Solstice blend. Being that it was a weekday and only ten in the morning, there were only two other people in the shop aside from Eve. One tall, thin lanky lad, had his head buried in a used copy of *Falxifer*. The other was Connie Hudson, who was sniffing incenses and wrinkling her nose in disgust at most of them.

He wandered into the section about spirit evocation and began examining the spines of the books.

"Looking for something specific?" Eve asked, cradling a stack of books in one arm. Evelyn Winters wasn't nearly as old as Esther, but she was still at least in her fifties. There was something youthful about her, though. Something in her kind, steel blue eyes.

His eyes went from Connie to the young man reading and back to Eve. "It's delicate. I'm looking on information about devils, and banishing them."

Connie Hudson glanced over her shoulder at him. The young man reading on the other side of the shop didn't even flinch. He was too engrossed in the book.

"Let's see." Eve leaned over and pulled a thick volume from the shelf behind him and handed it to him. "That has a lot of good information on malevolent spirits and banishing them, however, devils can be tricky."

He raised an eyebrow.

"She means they're not easily dispatched," Connie Hudson clarified, moving over toward them and taking the book from Jay's hands. "Bayou Witchcraft?"

The odd young woman began flipping through the pages.

"See," Eve started, giving Connie a strange look, "Devils have to be conjured and they're usually conjured to hurt people."

"So…" He remembered back to the invocation that was supposed to draw Dean's spirit back into his body after death. There had been no curse. No instruction to the thing. "What if, for example, one was conjured accidentally and placed in a vessel and not given any orders?"

Connie Hudson looked up from the book. "By vessel he means corpse."

Jay shot her a look that hopefully said, *shut up*.

The surprised look on Evelyn Winter's face would have been comical had the situation not been so grave. "Well, I can't imagine why someone would do that, but if that's the case… eventually devils have to return to where they came from. They're conjured by a sorcerer to destroy an enemy and oftentimes they're led by smell. The sorcerer usually has an item of the person to be cursed at hand to let the thing sniff it. They can follow that stink, as my grandmother used to call it, wherever it goes. Anything in its path can end up dead."

"Oh." His mind began racing. Was it possible this devil thought he was the target? What if it came back to the house, to Carolyn – who was pregnant with his child? "Okay, so there has to be a way to stop it."

Eve's look turned stern and she whispered. "Are you in some kind of trouble, Frater Ray?"

"I'm helping out a friend."

Connie Hudson snorted and handed the book back to him. "There's nothing in here except basic protections. You can stand inside a circle of salt until it returns to the netherworld. But then you have a corpse to dispose of."

"A circle of salt?" Jay rolled his eyes. How many television shows had he seen where people were protected from certain types of spirits by salt? Quite a few, he imagined.

"Believe it or not, against devils, salt actually works." Connie Hudson shrugged. "Ask Evelyn. It was the one thing her grandmother taught her that saved her ass."

Eve's mouth contorted into half shock, half offense.

"You people are so... predictable sometimes. If I were hu... you, I would use warding symbols and protection oleum. All doors and windows. Keep everything locked and if it calls you out, don't go. Now, how much for the lavender incense? My employer says it calms his patients who fear his dental procedures." There was something strange and mechanical in the way Connie spoke, as if common things were somehow foreign.

"Those are on special. Twelve dollars for the one hundred twenty sticks," Eve said. She wasn't smiling. If looks were daggers, Connie Hudson would have been dead.

Jay put the book back on the shelf and followed as Eve took Connie to the register to ring up her incense. She gave Connie a dark look. "I don't know what stories you've heard about me, but you shouldn't come in here repeating them. It's bad manners."

"Oh, I didn't realize that. I apologize. Though you have dealt with devils before." Connie seemed completely oblivious to the social rule she'd just broken.

"I have, but I'd rather not broadcast it," came Eve's curt reply.

"Then I will say nothing else of it." Connie smiled at her and handed her the twelve dollars and seventy-six cents and picked up her bag.

Eve handed her the receipt, still glaring at the young blonde. Connie turned to leave.

"Wait, what warding symbols?" he asked her. He knew what a protection oleum was, and he knew how to cleanse his house, but he'd never practiced regular warding before. He'd never felt a need to. Vaguely, he did recall the process of warding from his pre-initiate training more than fifteen years back, but he didn't recall the symbols.

"Eve knows," Connie said and without a care in the world, the strange woman left the shop without looking back.

Jay turned to Eve and she gave him an apologetic smile. "I know what you need. Come on."

When they returned to the counter he had a protection oleum, a two-pound bucket of solar sea salt, and a book of warding sigils.

Eve began to ring them up. "Now, place the salt across the threshold of each door and each window, anoint above each door and window with the protection oleum, and draw the protection sigils on every door. Have a safe space somewhere in the house for you and Carolyn, or rather your friend, where you are protected by warding sigils, the protection oleum, and salt on all sides. A closet in the interior of the house might work best."

"Thank you," he said. "You won't say anything to anyone…"

"I heard nothing, Frater Ray. Nothing at all. Hopefully you heard nothing either." She gave him a kind smile. "Oh, have you visited any friends recently? Because it might go sniffing around there, too, on its way to you. In which case, they should ward their homes, too."

"I saw Esther earlier, and… my friend." Jay thought about Warren and decided to call him once he got back to the car. "Is it possible the thing would return to where it was conjured? I mean, since it doesn't have a target?"

There was no way in hell he was going back to the cabin until he knew it was dead. Even then, he began considering selling the cabin. He wasn't sure he'd be able to return there and stay the night. Not after this.

"It usually seeks the sorcerer whose stink was strongest," she said.

"So, it may not touch my friend if, for example, it was conjured in another person's home." He was hopeful. If anything, he could save Warren and Belinda from his mistake. He was, after all, the person who dragged Warren into the mess. While Jay had read the main conjurations, Warren had done the energy work and the infusing incantations.

Eve saw through his flimsy lie. "I wouldn't count on it. Make sure your friend and his friends who helped him, ward their homes. I'll call Esther and have her ward her shop and herself, especially if you touched her. I'll ward the shop here, and you might want to ward your car and the funeral home as well."

He looked at the plain paper bag she handed him, and the bucket of salt, and wondered then if he had enough supplies. "Will do. Thank you, Eve."

"It's always a pleasure Frater Ray." She gave him a tight smile and then turned to the young man reading the book. "Leon? Are you going to buy that or just use my shop as a public library? Leon!"

The kid snapped out of whatever trance he was in and started moving toward the counter. "No, I'll buy it."

Jay made haste back out into the bitter cold and up the street to his car. After throwing the supplies in the back seat, he pulled out his phone. There was a text message from both

Carolyn and Julie. Carolyn's was requesting he do the lunch run on his way in, along with a list of items to grab from Hades. Julie's was to change her order. He responded to each with a smiling emoji and '*K*', and then called Warren on his cell phone.

"Warren Leonard," he said. In the background, Jay could hear Warren's fingers tapping a keyboard.

"Warren, it's Jay. Do you keep your house warded?" Then Jay felt stupid for bringing it up so quickly.

There was a pause. "Yeah, of course. Doesn't everyone?"

"We're dealing with a devil. Somehow, we managed to summon it instead of Dean," he started.

"Yeah, Belinda and I have it covered. We're thinking it was waiting just outside the portal we opened and slipped in because Dean wasn't there waiting to get back. Fucker probably decided it wasn't worth it in his last moments and passed beyond the veil without looking back." More typing.

"That's the impression I got, too. I just wanted to make sure you warded. The forty-eight hours doesn't end until tomorrow night." He wasn't sure what else to say.

"We could be stuck with it until the new moon, too," Warren said.

Jay didn't like the sound of that. "You put the part about the forty-eight hours into the incantations though, right?"

"Yeah, but that was only designed to work with the dead. This thing has to lose its *battery charge*."

Warren's casual tone made Jay nervous. Was he the only one who was freaked out by this? "How can you be so… calm?"

"Belinda says we'll be fine. She's always right."

Jay imagined him shrugging. "Yeah. Esther didn't seem too concerned either. Maybe I shouldn't be concerned."

"Just keep your wits about you. Stay inside the house. These things, they don't generally travel in broad daylight. They prefer the dark," he said.

Jay shuddered. "Okay, thanks man."

"Later Brah," Warren said. The line went dead.

With a resigned sigh, Jay looked back at the lunch list, put on his seatbelt, started the car, and headed toward Hades to get lunch for the Order of Eurynome crew.

9

He waited until Carolyn got on video chat with her mother before setting to work establishing wards and erecting thin lines of salt barriers on the window sills and over thresholds around the house. The call would last an hour or more and would give him plenty of time to do what needed doing without having to answer a lot of questions. He hadn't told her what he and Warren had done, and wouldn't unless he absolutely had to. The fact that it was already dark outside made him nervous. He didn't know how far the thing had traveled, or if it had yet realized it would soon lose its charge and come looking for its maker.

He took his time warding the house, and then he emptied the large linen closet in the hall. He was starting toward the guest room with the last armful of blue bath towels when he heard her office door open.

"Jay? What are you doing with the towels?"

"Uh, I thought it would be good to clean and air out the closet," he said in a tremulous voice.

She gave him a suspicious look, her green, almost cat-like eyes examining him carefully. Then she shook her head. "You know, I was going to tell you something tonight. Leave the closet. Let's go sit down."

He set the towels on top of the dresser in the spare room, then returned to the hall. A lump started to form in his throat. Then he remembered - she was pregnant. Twins. *Act surprised*, he told himself. His heart began thumping in his chest and he followed her to the living room.

She let out a light laugh. "That face, Jay. You act like I'm leading you to your death."

"No good comes of a woman telling a man they need to sit down and have a talk," he said, sitting down on the edge of the couch.

A loud crash sounded from the back of the house, then they heard a guttural voice croak, "More life."

Jay jumped up and Carolyn's eyes went wide. She took a step toward the hallway. "What the..."

Jay grabbed her by the arm, dragging her to the closet which was empty except for a flashlight, and the bucket of salt. He pushed her inside and took up the salt, shoving it into her hands. "Circle of salt - now!"

Terror and disbelief crossed her face. "Jay?"

"Salt!" He pointed at the bucket, then at the floor. "Circle! Now!"

Then he closed the closet door and took two uncertain steps toward the bedroom. That's where it was, he could feel it. He'd researched spirit banishing spells late that afternoon after the last mourners had left the funeral home. He committed the structure of the ritual to memory. *It doesn't matter what you say*, he told himself, *as long as it's said with intent.*

"More life, Jason Ray," the thing croaked from the bedroom.

The hair on Jay's arms stood on end. He pulled out his cell phone and dialed Warren. No one answered. *What if it killed Warren and Belinda?* His heart thumped hard in his chest. Even if he could give it more life, he wouldn't have the first clue how. What came next felt surreal.

It was as if he were swimming in his own thoughts and his body floated toward the door. He no longer felt the physical flesh around him, just his heart beating and his mind floating toward the thing, whatever it was, in the bedroom. Face to face he stood before it.

Dean's skin had gone gray and the eyes were sunken in. It still wore the white t-shirt and gray sweat pants Dean had died in. Its nails seemed longer, too, but that appeared to be the only sign of decay, other than the smell. That sweet, putrid smell of death. Jay was no stranger to that.

He drew a deep breath and gathered his will. "I command, in the name of the Daemon Euronymous - that you leave this vessel and this earthly plane!"

The thing's mouth contorted into a twisted grin and it took two steps toward him.

Jay looked into its now black eyes. "Rise Euronymous and drag this spawn back from whence it came!"

Then it laughed. "More life, Jason Ray," it said again.

Unbidden, Jay felt his feet start moving, carrying him into the room with the thing. He felt possessed - violated. "No - leave now! I banish you!"

It reached out to him with a hand that appeared to be nothing more than gray skin stretched tightly over bone. Jay's hand rose to meet it. The cold, breathless touch of death.

He felt a jolt, and then he fell backward, the impact with the floor knocking the wind from him.

He watched as the corpse and whatever it contained moved quickly to the window and out it. It was moving well now.

"Oh gods, Jay!" Carolyn dropped to the floor beside him. "What was that? Are you okay?"

"I don't know." His voice sounded distant to his own ears. He'd placed salt on all the window seals, and wards above them, and it had still gotten in. This meant three things. First, it wasn't a spirit of the dead. Second, it was impervious to wards. Third, salt didn't slow it down. It wasn't a devil after all.

"I'm calling Sherriff Steve," she said, and got up.

10

"**S**o, it was a zombie?" Steve Watson raised a thick graying eyebrow.

"Well I don't know. It looked like Dean Charleston's corpse," Carolyn said. "That would qualify as a zombie."

Jay sat on the edge of the couch nursing a glass of water. Somehow Carolyn had managed to get him upright and into the living room again. It all happened so fast.

Outside, the flashing red and blues from the sheriff's vehicles lit up the night, and he could hear the voices of deputies and dogs searching around the house and the yard.

"Mr. Ray," Sheriff Steve started, "What do you think it was? You seemed to be expecting it according to your wife."

"Domestic partner," Carolyn corrected him, waggling a ringless finger at the Sherriff. "But maybe there will be a hand-fasting in the near future."

Jay fought back a groan and set the glass of water on the coffee table then leaned back into the couch with his palms pressed against his eyes. After a deep breath, he told them the story, leaving out Warren's name altogether and replacing it with *a friend* just in case. "So, whatever came back wasn't Dean Charleston. It wasn't a spirit of the dead, and whatever it is, it's impervious to wards," he finished.

"Holy Beelzebub, this town is gonna be the death of me." Sherriff Steve shook his head. "I've got those naked wood-nymphs in Ashtaroth Briarwood causing crashes off Route Nine, ghosts and zombies in the forests around the Blackwood estate, zombies breaking into houses…"

The deputy laughed.

"You find this amusing Torres?" The sheriff appeared to be genuinely exasperated by it all.

Deputy Torres shrugged. "At least our job is interesting."

The sheriff grunted in half agreement and then said, "Well, we'll have our patrols keep a look out. In the meantime, board up the window, call the glass company in the morning and get it replaced. Get an alarm system. Call us if you see it again. You sure you don't want to tell me who your friend is so I can go check on him and talk to him?"

Jay immediately remembered that Warren hadn't answered the phone. "Can I check something first?"

"Fine." Sheriff Steve gave Jay a wary look.

Not taking it personally, Jay stood on unstable legs to pull the phone from his pocket. Then he fell back onto the couch and texted Warren. "*Sheriff Steve is here. Dean broke into my house. Need me to send Sheriff over?*"

He jumped when the phone almost immediately buzzed and a text from Warren asked, "*Did it touch U?*"

"Yeah, why?" he said aloud as he typed those words back to Warren, suddenly aware everyone in the room was staring at him expectantly. "No. No. He's okay and he doesn't want to get involved."

"Of course not," Steve said. Then he gave Carolyn a warm smile. "Then we'll be going."

She followed them to the door with a grateful smile. "Thank you so much for getting here so quickly."

"Come down and get a police report from my office in the morning and you can turn it in to your insurance company along with your repair bill. See if they'll cover it," the Sheriff added.

Then they were gone and Carolyn sat down on the couch next to him. "Why did you do that?"

His phone buzzed and he looked at it. Warren's text read: "*Call me.*"

He stood. "I have to call someone."

"No, Jay. You don't get to walk away and not talk to me about this." A pout formed on her lips and she crossed her arms over her chest.

"Carolyn, I *will* tell you about it, but I need to talk to Warren. He needs me to call him. It's important." He strode into the kitchen, half expecting to find Dean's withered face and sunken eyes staring back at him from the kitchen window. He dialed Warren's number, aware that Caroyln was right behind him and wasn't going to let it go.

"Warren?" she asked, clearly trying to figure out who Warren was. Temple Apophis members weren't their usual crowd.

Warren picked up on the first ring. "I fucked up. It touched you?"

"What do you mean you fucked up?"

Carolyn started to say something and Jay held up a hand to silence her.

"I think I mistranslated a text. I think we accidentally invoked a servitor into Dean, and if it touched you, you own it, man." Warren sounded apologetic, but there was something else in his voice. A hint of excitement.

"You mean it wasn't a devil?"

"No. Not a devil." From Warren's tone, Jay could tell he was relieved.

"I wasn't the only one who invoked it though…" Jay's stomach did a sickening flip.

"Yeah, but you're the only one who touched it. Which means it answers to you now." Then his voice went up a pitch and he began talking faster. "You can summon it and give it tasks."

"I don't want to summon it and give it tasks. What if it hurts Carolyn? What if…"

"What's he saying?" Carolyn asked.

"You don't get it, Jay," Warren said. "You have a fully functioning servitor. When it touched you, it took some of your life force. This servitor knows what life is and is probably hanging out in the forest chasing bunnies and feeling the bark on trees, enjoying all the sensations that physical beings get to experience that non-physical beings don't. Once a servitor takes on the form of physical flesh, we call it a familiar."

"How the hell did you fuck up the invocation?" Jay's mind raced with what this meant. If what Warren was saying were true, all he had to do was refuse to feed it and banish it from Dean's body, back to the astral plane.

This time, Warren's voice took on a sheepish tone. "I think I accidently skipped a page when I was writing it down. Like two pages got stuck together."

"Fuck!"

His use of an expletive caused Carolyn to recoil and her jaw to drop. Jay wasn't one to use curse words liberally.

"Relax, man," Warren said. "I think you can take this little mishap and use it for good, you know?"

Jay wasn't interested though. "How do I get rid of it, Warren? I tried banishing it with Eurynomous and it did nothing."

A long sigh erupted on the other end of the line. "You can't banish something that was never alive via the denizens of the dead. A lot of spirits in the Goetia deal with familiars, so I suspect we might be able to get rid of it by conjuring one of them."

"Goetia?" Jay had never been into Goetia in practice or theory, though a few of the spirits The Order worked with fell into that hierarchal paradigm.

"Yeah, like Solomonic magick. The high, ceremonial stuff," Warren explained.

"I know what it is," Jay snapped back. "I'm just not a ceremonial magician. I'm a funerary priest."

On the other end of the line, it sounded like Warren was flipping through books. "Well, you know anyone who works with Belial? He's a death Daemonic, isn't he?"

"Loosely, yeah." Of course he knew someone who worked with Belial often, but he wasn't going to go to her with this. Julie Grier would kick his ass and excommunicate him for sure.

"He's the perfect Daemon to handle this then. We just conjure Belial, summon the servitor, and banish it in the name of Belial," Warren said, matter-of-fact. That was the same confidence Warren had when he explained the ritual to conjure Dean's soul back into his body, too.

"Forgive me if I don't have nearly as much confidence in you at this moment," Jay said.

Carolyn excitedly gave him her *what's going on* gesture. He waved her off again.

"I get that. We can find someone well-versed in Belial to help us. We just need to find someone who won't go blabbing it all over town. Speaking of which, why did you call Sheriff Steve?"

"I didn't. Carolyn did. Told him a zombie broke into our house." He held up a finger to Carolyn whose anxiety at not knowing what was going on was starting to manifest as a series of bizarre facial expressions and hand gestures.

"Oh. So do you know anyone who has any relationship with Belial?" Warren wasted no time getting to the point.

"I do, but I'm not..." he paused, thought carefully, then said, "If I bring her into this my career is over and I either need to move from the area or find a new coven, much to the shame of my family."

Carolyn's face dropped.

Jay knew why. Some lucky souls came into Thirteen Coven territory from the outside, but Jay had been born into it, and his father and his grandfather had both been members of The Order and had served their time as funerary priests. His father still performed the death rites for old family friends, even though nowadays he spent most of his time at the Haileyville Country Club playing golf.

Despite the fact that Jay's parents were retired from active coven life, they took their family's birthright into The Order seriously. Then there was Carolyn. Where would that leave her if he were excommunicated? Where would that leave their children? Sure, she had family scattered all across the country and was proof that not all those born into the coven stuck around. Unlike a lot of the covens, Order of Eurynome encouraged members to move to other parts of the world to provide last rites and pastoral care to the dying and grieving. Even though not all their members lived in the tri-county area, they were still members of The Order and kept in close contact with the coven outreach coordinators. Order of Eurynome was, perhaps, one of the most well-organized and widespread covens out of The Thirteen.

If Jay were excommunicated, he would be a shame to three generations of funerary priests, the mother of his children, and his children. No matter where he moved, that shame would follow him.

"Tell them it was my mistake," Warren said. "Tell them I did it and came to you for help."

While the lie would most likely work, Jay knew the truth would come out eventually. He knew he had to do what he'd been taught his entire life. What Esther had reminded him of. "No. I'm not letting you take the fall for me. I have to take responsibility for the magick I've done."

Warren gulped. "All right. I'll stand with you. It's my fault this got fucked up. Had I not screwed up the invocation... I'm sorry, man."

Jay shook his head. "I have to tell Julie. She knows Belial."

"I understand." Warren said in a somber whisper. "I want to go with you. I'm not letting you tell them alone."

"Yeah. Okay." He hung up and looked into Carolyn's pleading eyes. "Warren screwed up and accidently put together an invocation to instill a servitor into Dean Charleston's corpse. It touched me and took some of my life essence. Now, it's a familiar and it's mine. We can banish it, but we need someone familiar with Belial to remove it."

Carolyn's eyes welled with tears.

"I wouldn't blame you if you wanted to leave me over this. I made a mistake and I'm going to pay for it. Probably with excommunication." He lowered his head, wondering what was going through her mind. Would she leave him? Would she ever let him see his children?

"No," Carolyn said. She swallowed and nodded, wiping tears from her eyes. "We'll go to Julie together. If they excommunicate you, then they'll have to excommunicate me, too."

"I can't let you do that."

"Jay, I love you. I'm pregnant." She stopped herself and looked at him, a sad smile forming on her perfect lips. "I don't care if we have to move and start over somewhere else."

He took her into his arms. "Oh, thank gods. I love you, too."

11

One couldn't talk to Julie alone about coven business without Brian. Jay, Carolyn, and Warren sat across from the coven leaders waiting for their reaction to the story. Carolyn's grip on his hand was firm, and she gave it a reassuring squeeze. She'd been uncharacteristically quiet since they arrived. Warren looked down at his hands.

Julie and Brian exchanged glances, then Julie leaned forward.

Brian just sat there, frowning.

"So you took it upon yourself to do for Mr. Charleston what I said Order of Eurynome would not do." Julie leaned forward on her elbows, fingertips together. "Why would you do that?"

Jay felt small, child-like, under their gazes. "I wasn't thinking. I thought it would be interesting to see if it could be done and I heard the stories about Warren and the Blake kid. I know, I fucked up. I didn't follow the first rule of any magickal operation. I didn't understand fully what I was doing. I have no excuses. I shouldn't have done it at all."

Brian hadn't said anything. He exchanged another look with Julie.

"So, it's a servitor?" She directed this question to Warren.

"Yes, ma'am. Well, more of a familiar now that it has solid form. But can I say in Jay's defense that he trusted me to know what I was doing and I was the one who screwed it up. I don't want the blame to rest solely on his shoulders." Warren looked up with those dark eyes of his. They almost begged her to show leniency. "I can help banish it and then we can just forget it ever happened. Sheriff Steve didn't even use the word zombie in the police report," he added, as if that fact would sway her.

Jay let out a nervous chuckle. "Sheriff Steve doesn't want outsiders seeing our police blotters and wondering what the hell is going on over here. He just called it a break in. Said we scared the robber. Made it look routine."

But he wasn't sure if Julie heard him because she was looking at Brian. "You know, I think the dead have been blocked or warded against and that's why we're not getting information on Lucifuge or Tiamat-Leviathan. We could really use some help in that area."

Brian lifted an eyebrow. "That's not a bad idea."

"Can you transfer the ownership of a servitor or familiar?" Julie's face contorted into a look of serious consideration.

"Umm, yeah," Warren said, reaching into his knapsack and pulling out an old book with a brown discolored cover. He began flipping through the pages. When he found what he was looking for he nodded. "Here it is. Sending a servitor or familiar to someone else. You summon the servitor or familiar, you introduce it to the new owner, and they touch it. It seems pretty straight forward, but Jay and I really have no use for it, so I think we should just banish it."

Julie shrugged and looked at Brian. "Neither of you have use for it, but Brian and I, we've always wanted a familiar. More recently, we've needed one."

Brian nodded, a sly grin playing on his lips. "I think that's a splendid idea."

Jay felt his jaw drop. "But, wait. What?"

Even Carolyn looked shocked.

Julie stood and straightened her suit jacket. Brian stood, too. "The temple is empty. How long does this ritual take?"

"Uh, maybe twenty minutes." Warren fumbled, shoving his book back into his knapsack. "If the familiar can get here quickly."

With a flip of her blonde curls, Julie said, "Let's summon it, transfer ownership and be done with it. Then we'll never speak of it again, directly at least." She gave Jay, Carolyn, and Warren a smile. "And by that, I mean this is between the five of us and no one else."

The three exchanged glances. The sick feeling in Jay's stomach hadn't gone away yet. "So you're not going to excommunicate me? Or refuse Warren the funerary priest training?"

Julie looked square at Warren. "You're reckless and stupid. Brian and I haven't decided if we're letting you into the funerary priest training." Then her eyes went to Jay. "And I'm surprised you had it in you to do something so crazy and stupid. We're not going to cast you out, but if you pull another stupid ass stunt again..." She paused and looked at Brian, who gave her a single nod, "If you do anything this stupid again, then there will be a meeting to decide your fate. In the meantime, at least this mistake was actually in our favor. In these uncertain times with talk of Warren raising the dead and Temple of the Magi with their own walking dead, and with everyone warding against the dead, it's probably best we have a secret weapon of our own, too. Not to mention if they're going to start rumors about Eurynome and necromancy anyway, maybe we should just jump on the necromancy train and go with it. Right?"

"I guess," Jay said with uncertainty.

She motioned them toward the door and they all filed from the room and started toward the temple. "Good. For the good of The Order, Hail Eurynomous."

Reflexively, Brian, Jay and Carolyn responded, "Hail Eurynomous."

Warren smiled. Maybe he had The Order right where he wanted them.

FINIS

INCIDENT REPORT DIRECTORY
THE WATCH

The following is an index to the archive listing incidents involving members of each of the Thirteen Covens dated 2016-2018, compiled by The Watch High Priest **Neal Watts** and **Aaron Steele**.

Solitary Practitioners

The following individuals have allegiance to no covens, but **Tiamat-Leviathan** has been resolute in making it clear to everyone in the tri-county area that these individuals are under their protection.

Evelyn Winters (Eve) — Owns Black Raven, a local landmark. Evelyn Winters, to our knowledge, comes from a traditional witchcraft background out of one of the southern states. From what The Watch has learned, her grandmother was a witch and disappeared years ago under mysterious circumstances. Evelyn, was staying with her when it happened. We do not see Evelyn as a threat, just as a central figure for all of the covens. It's unfortunate she's a woman, otherwise The

Watch would recruit her, as we imagine her eyes and ears have picked up a great deal. Brother Ken Franklin (Watch member) has befriended the shop owner and has been able to occasionally get information from her.

Esther Branson - Our local seer who works with all of the covens. While she knows a great deal about most of the covens, she remains discreet and is not considered a threat. Again, were she not a woman, The Watch would have attempted recruitment. Unfortunately none of The Watch members have been able to get Esther to give them information unless it's widely known already. This is probably why all of the covens are willing to trust her with their secrets.

Leon (?) - A "theistic" Satanist named Leon moved into Haileyville in 2016. We initially thought he was homeless, then found he was renting an apartment at Lakeview, off of 5th Street in Haileyville. He often preaches on Main Street. Sheriff Steve has arrested him twice for disturbing the peace. He is not a member of the Thirteen Covens and is a potential threat.

Temple Apophis

The Temple Apophis coven has no direct familial associations when it comes to leadership. They often bring in outsiders and outsiders have just as much of a chance at coven leadership as those born into the fold.

Brady Loren - Former leader of Temple Apophis. The coven ousted him as leader in favor of Belinda Applegate.

Lawrence - Brady's right hand man.

Belinda Applegate - New leader of Temple Apophis. A powerful seeress. She is currently training under the Solitary, Esther Branson. Rumor has it she will replace Esther at some point, but many of the covens are against this and it has created quite a stir among the thirteen. Is implicated in the Lucifer's Haven necromancy incident as a witness.

Warren Leonard - Ex-con convicted of marijuana possession. While harmless, he is the significant other of Belinda Applegate. Implicated in the Lucifer's Haven incident as having performed a successful necromantic operation.

Other Apophis members who may have information regarding the Lucifer's Haven Incident: Tara Stanly, Gayle Dugan

Lucifer's Haven

This coven has a great deal going on internally, though we have still been unable to resolve several matters. The leadership is still familial belonging to the Devlin family. This coven does occasionally bring in outsiders as members.

Carl Devlin - City Manager (Haileyville) still manages the coven alongside his sisters:
Lacy Devlin
Linda Devlin

The next in line for leadership is **Karla Devlin** and her girlfriend, **Jennifer Reese**.

The Lucifer's Haven Necromancy Incident: (See File) Brief summary: Member Brian Blake was found dead. It is rumored members of Temple Apophis assisted in bringing Blake back from death.

Brian Blake: The only known person in the tri-county area known to have been brought back from the dead after a twenty-four hour period.

Other involved members in the incident include: **Jason Tate** and outside member **Connie Hudson,** who most people agree is odd.

Members who may have information on the incident: **Karla Devlin, Jennifer Reese, Corrina Morse, Victor Penzak, Shawn Dunn, Gary Movell,** and **Scott Drescher**

Shadow Marbas

This coven is largely generational only, but they have, on rare occasion, brought outsiders into their membership. Shadow Marbas is usually of little concern except for the Temple of the Magi Incident. It was members of this coven who are rumored to have built the temple Thaddeus Blackwood used to summon and capture a spirit, allegedly using necromancy.

Marcus Ayer: Temple Head and High Priest
Ellie Ayer: Marcus' wife and co-High Priestess
Martin "Six" Randall: Inner Circle
Jacob Mallory: Inner Circle despite an altercation where he temporarily left the coven.
Nicole Garda: Inner Circle

Members who allegedly helped to build the ritual construct: **Marcus Ayer, Jacob Mallory**, and **Martin "Six" Randall**. All who work in the construction trade.

There is one known Shadow Marbas witness to the Temple of the Magi incident - **Martin "Six" Randall**, a generational member.

Members who may have information about this incident: **Jacob Mallory**, an outsider brought into the coven due to his friendship with coven leaders Marcus and **Ellie Ayer**, and Ayer's right hand man, **Randall**. **Ellie Ayer**, and Randall's long-time girlfriend, **Nicole Garda**.

Ba'al Collective

Mary Sanderson (formerly Rose): High Priestess
Garrett Hammon-Sanderson: High Priest and Grand Magus
John Rose (Deceased): Former High Priest, killed in car crash.
Myrna Sanderson (Deceased): Step-sister of Mary Sanderson, killed in car crash.
Dean Charleston (Deceased): Former inner circle of this coven, before dying from cancer.
Georgia Friesner: Coven Hospitality chairwoman, well-known in the community, knows a lot of what's going on.

This coven is fiercely generational and traditional and comes from the Sanderson line. They are implicated, though we are unsure how just yet, in the Temple of the Magi Sorath Incident. Due to accusations made by **Dean Charleston**, it is alleged that the deaths of **John Rose** (former coven head), **Myrna Sanderson** (not a blood born Sanderson, adopted, who was allegedly pregnant with Rose's child at the time) and the death of **Dean Charleston** were all a direct result of a curse thrown at them by the coven's Grand Magus Hammon and Rose's former wife, Mary.

Allegedly complicit in the Sorath incident are **Mary Sanderson** (current coven head - Sanderson by birth, formerly Rose by marriage), **Garrett Hammon-Sanderson**, the coven Grand Magus (he took on the coven leadership surname when he married Mary).

Coven members who may have additional information include: **Georgia and Alex Friesner**.

We know this coven didn't act alone, and we are positive they were not the ones who initially stole the captured spirit from the Temple of the Magi's magickal experiment due to information from **Esther Branson**. It is possible this incident also includes a district representative **Senator Langly**, who was born into Circle of the Black Moon and is a cousin of the **Tidwells**.

Order of Eurynome

Julie Grier: Co-Leader of The Order.
Brian Price: Co-Leader of The Order.
Jason (Jay) Ray: Funeral Director in the inner circle of The Order leadership.

Consulted with this coven on the matter of increased necromancy in the tri-county area. The two coven heads, **Julie Grier** and **Brian Price**, acted suspiciously. As did funeral director, **Jason (Jay) Ray**. We think they may know something, but if they do, they're not talking.

END
666

Sign up for the Audrey Brice Newsletter to receive **free fiction** and updates on Thirteen Covens, the OTS Series, and other releases!

About the Author

Audrey Brice is the pseudonym of a renowned Daemonolatress and practicing magician who has been performing her artes since the mid-eighties. She lives with her husband and several cats along the front range of the beautiful Rocky Mountains.

Also by Audrey Brice

Outer Darkness

When socialite Chloe Brigid is murdered and the crime seems to have occult overtones, outed daemon worshiper Senator Steve Mitchell is arrested. It's up to magician Elizabeth Tanner, the public figurehead of the Ordo Templi Serpentis, to find out who outed the senator and who killed Chloe Brigid before the senator is falsely accused of the crime and The Order is investigated. What she finds, however, is not what she expects. The killer's attention soon turns toward her. Will she be able to help the police find the killer before she becomes the next victim?

Into Darkness

Magus Elizabeth Tanner has been gifted some cursed magickal items. While trying to break the curse, she and her boyfriend Michael become suspects in a murder they didn't commit. To clear their names they must find the real killer by delving into a dark bdsm underworld where sex magick and the Daemonic meet. Will they be able to find a killer, clear their names, and escape their descent into darkness?

Also Available
Rising Darkness, Ascending Darkness, Dead Man's Knock, When Good Angels Go Bad,
Sunny Satan Arizona, Rocky Mountain Haunt, Within Darkness (paperback of the OTS novellas), Samuel, The Danbury Ghost
Thirteen Covens: A Rising Damp, Temple Apophis, Lucifer's Haven, Shadow Marbas, The Watch, Ba'al Collective, Order of Eurynome (Compiled as Bloodlines Part One)

Forthcoming:
Illuminated Darkness
Blackrose Coven
Tiamat-Leviathan

By Audrey Brice as Anne O'Connell

Training Amy

When Amy starts her new job at a book shop she has no idea what kind of merchandise her two bosses have stored in a private back room for select customers. She's never been allowed back there. One night, when she's closing shop alone she decides to take a look. Big mistake. Brad and Eric (her bosses) catch her snooping around. They don't tolerate rule-breakers and Amy must be punished. Will her secret desires plunge her deeper into their world? Or will she run back to the safety of her normal life and the dull boyfriend who has a dark side of his own?

Publisher's Note: This book contains explicit sexual content, graphic language, and situations that some readers may find objectionable: BDSM theme and content includes: dubious consent, bondage, spanking, toys, anal play, and menage m/f/m and m/f/f.

Other Titles:
Weekend Captive, Sincerely, Megan
Nice Girls Don't, My Neighbor Enslaved
Switched, Domme X, The Rite, DOM359
Her Demon Lover, Her Demon Wedding
Black Lily, Temple of Lilith, Taming Trish

Forthcoming From Anne O'Connell:
Falling from Grace, Her Demon Master

By Audrey Brice as S. J. Reisner

Left Horse Black (Sorcerers' Twilight Book 1)

For centuries, the zealot Kersian sorcerers have abducted innocent women and children for sacrifice to their 'no name' god, and have waged war upon Danaria's sorcerers. Now, they are covertly usurping the thrones of human-ruled kingdoms to do the unthinkable; they are building a massive human army to assist them in destroying Danaria's sorcerer bloodlines in an attempt to save their own. Armed with nothing more than meager weapons, untrained sorcery, and mere instinct, a troubled human prince, an inept Danarian sorceress, and their friends, rise up and become the world's last hope to stop the Kersians, and save the sorcerers' dying race. Will they succeed?

Other Titles:
Warrior's Blood Red (Sorcerers' Twilight Book 2)
Saving Sarah May (Contemporary Romance)

Forthcoming:
Eagle's Talon Gray (Sorcerers' Twilight Book 3)

CPSIA information can be obtained
at www.ICGtesting.com
Printed in the USA
LVOW13s2357041017
551236LV00007B/174/P